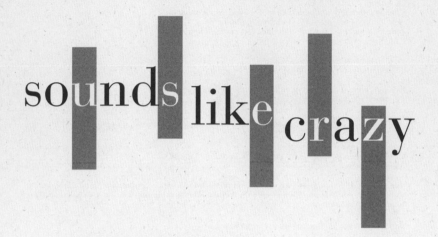

sounds like crazy

shana mahaffey

NAL
ACCENT

NAL Accent
Published by New American Library, a division of
Penguin Group (USA) Inc., 375 Hudson Street,
New York, New York 10014, USA
Penguin Group (Canada), 90 Eglinton Avenue East, Suite 700, Toronto,
Ontario M4P 2Y3, Canada (a division of Pearson Penguin Canada Inc.)
Penguin Books Ltd., 80 Strand, London WC2R 0RL, England
Penguin Ireland, 25 St. Stephen's Green, Dublin 2,
Ireland (a division of Penguin Books Ltd.)
Penguin Group (Australia), 250 Camberwell Road, Camberwell, Victoria 3124,
Australia (a division of Pearson Australia Group Pty. Ltd.)
Penguin Books India Pvt. Ltd., 11 Community Centre, Panchsheel Park,
New Delhi - 110 017, India
Penguin Group (NZ), 67 Apollo Drive, Rosedale, North Shore 0632,
New Zealand (a division of Pearson New Zealand Ltd.)
Penguin Books (South Africa) (Pty.) Ltd., 24 Sturdee Avenue,
Rosebank, Johannesburg 2196, South Africa

Penguin Books Ltd., Registered Offices:
80 Strand, London WC2R 0RL, England

First published by NAL Accent, an imprint of New American Library,
a division of Penguin Group (USA) Inc.

First Printing, October 2009
10   9   8   7   6   5   4   3   2   1

 REGISTERED TRADEMARK—MARCA REGISTRADA

LIBRARY OF CONGRESS CATALOGING-IN-PUBLICATION DATA:

Mahaffey, Shana.
   Sounds like crazy/Shana Mahaffey.
      p.   cm.
   ISBN 978-0-451-22791-1
   1. Multiple personality—Fiction.   2. Dissociative disorders—Fiction.   3. Psychological fiction.
I. Title.
   PS3613.A34924S68   2009
   813'.6—dc22   2009018140

Set in Bembo
Designed by Ginger Legato

Printed in the United States of America

For Joe McGrath, Poppa, Uncle Joe, Joey, Coach,

Old Nut, K.O.D. (Kindly Old Director)

ACKNOWLEDGMENTS

I was taught as a child to measure your wealth by the love and support of the people around you. As such, it goes without saying that I am one of the richest people on the planet. And words can never express how grateful I am for all the wonderful folks in my life who helped me go from thinking about becoming an author to actually becoming one, but I will give it a go.

Thank you, Scott James, for your unwavering friendship and support and for the San Francisco Writer's Bloc. Also, thank you, WB members—Arlene Heitner, David Gleeson, Ken Grosserode, James Warner, Melodie Bowsher, and Sean Beaudoin—for your support, feedback, and insight all along the way.

Thank you, Doug Wilkins, for providing an excellent writing retreat in the Sanchez Annex Grotto, and for your friendship, encouragement and support.

Thank you, David Henry Sterry, Mark Evenier, and David Gleeson, for giving me the inside scoop on working as a voice-over artist.

A special thanks to my early readers—everyone at the Sandra

Dijkstra Literary Agency, Anne Friedman, Annabelle Fritz, Anne Rogers, Andrea Meyer, Alice Rennhoff, Barbara Trimborn, Billy Bosworth, Christian Schmidt, Colleen Mahaffey, Dan McGrath, Dave Viney, David Gleason, Donna Kopfer, Doug Wilkins, Erin O'Connor, Fabio Zurcher, Ingo Haussermann, James Warner, Jan Vaeth, Jana Brauer, Jeff Banks, Jerry FM Walter, Joan McGrath, Kathleen Edmunds, Kathleen McGrath, Kirsten Koch, Kris Tenhunfeld, Kristen Kopfer, Lorraine Gnecco, Lynn Sutliff, Martha Alderson, Maryanne Bushnell, Meredith McAdam, Rachael McGrath, Ralf Schundelmeier, Ralph Manfredi, Richard Gentenaar, Rudd Canaday, and Scott James—for your time, commitment, feedback, insight, kindness, and unwavering support all along the way; and, especially for helping make *Sounds Like Crazy* a better book.

Another special thanks and recognition go to Martha Alderson for whispering the plot of *Sounds Like Crazy* right out of me, and to Paul McCarthy for your early editing insights!

And finally, my heartfelt thanks and deepest gratitude to Kevan Lyon for your unwavering belief in me and my book, and for being the best agent in the world! And to Ellen Edwards for your kindness, support, insight, guidance and help in bringing *Sounds Like Crazy* across the finish line.

To my families (immediate, extended, and urban) and dear friends, more heartfelt gratitude, appreciation, and thanks.

Everyone I didn't name—a simple thank-you that hopefully speaks volumes.

Ingo, for pushing me to pursue my dreams all those years ago, and so much more.

Martin McGrath, for providing the zany Pierce Street Compound; I couldn't ask for a better place to live.

My Pierce Street Compound community, especially Annabelle, Katie, Lucky, Duke, Del, Howard, and Raphael.

My fellow Spartans for helping me grow up and never leaving my side. Pass the biscuits!

My brother, Brendan; my parents, Mike and Kathleen; my aunts and uncles, Mickey, Maryanne, Marty, Joan, Dan; and especially my sister, Colleen, for your love, encouragement, and support.

The Kopfers (Goo, Donnie, Dansie, Princess, Ne, Q, Johnny, and Ricky) for making me a part of your family and always cheering me on.

My urban family, Alex, Alice, Alfredo, Andrea, Barbara, Chris, Dirky, Erik, Fabio, Georg, Jeanette, Jenny, Katrin, Kirsten, Kris, Lynn, Philippe, Ralfie, Sabine, Stefan, Svenja, Thorsten, Tom, and Turhan, for being the family I choose and always believing in me.

And once more to Kirsten Koch and Thorsten Raab, my two dearest and closest friends, for teaching me the true value of friendship.

Last but not least to Poppa, who taught me what is most important in life and who never gave up on me. Thank you for sticking around until I knew I could do this on my own.

I am truly blessed.

"For the ones who had a notion, a notion deep inside,
That it ain't no sin to be glad you're alive."

—"Badlands" BY BRUCE SPRINGSTEEN

sounds like crazy

PROLOGUE

My mother taught me that image is more important than reality. Everyone has secrets. If you belong to a family that keeps them, then you also have an unwritten contract that you will play your part in the theater of appearances. Trust me, I kept my secrets. I played my part. I did it so well, and I did it for so long, that the secrets I'd been keeping started keeping me.

I have five people living inside my head. In the order they appeared, there is the Boy in the red Converse sneakers—I can't see his face, only his shoes. Next, the ancient man who spends all his time in meditation. I call him the Silent One because he's spoken to me only once since I met him, which makes him the perfect manager of my spiritual life. Third, Sarge, who keeps me safe. Fourth, Ruffles, a whale-sized woman who sits on a purple pillow eating Ruffles potato chips all day. And, saving the best for last, fifth, Betty Jane, a modern-day Scarlett O'Hara who makes my life hell on a good day.

My condition is called dissociative identity disorder. A far more serious form was made famous by Sybil back when it was known as multiple personality disorder. Either predicament, according to my shrink, Milton, is a result of severe and repeated trauma; he's been trying to get me to talk about it for the past five years. The problem is, I don't remember any trauma, severe or repeated, before I was eighteen and Betty Jane appeared. Since that time, living with her is what any sane person would call severe and repeated trauma.

Milton has never labeled me or my condition. Instead, he subscribes to a progressive notion of psychoanalysis that disregards diagnostic classifications in favor of facts and aims at treatment specific to the patient's needs. The only label in our work is the one Milton has for the voices—he calls them the Committee to make it easier when we talk about them as a group. But don't be fooled into thinking that "Committee" means each voice has equal representation. The truth is more like an autocracy, with Betty Jane as the despot and me and the others as the servants doing her bidding.

The Committee and I can switch back and forth with an ease as natural as blinking. Okay, with Betty Jane the switch is really a coup de main that requires coercion or a show of force, usually by Sarge, to regain control. Regardless, the best way to describe the switch is to compare it to driving. As the driver, I have my hands on the proverbial wheel and the open road is right in front of me. Having one of the Committee members take over is the same as allowing them to take the wheel while I move to the passenger side or backseat. Either way, I am no longer in charge. When this happens, I experience everything taking place externally from a different perspective. Basically, I experience everything taking place outside from the inside of my head.

It goes without saying that my Committee is a lot more than the voices most people have in their heads—the ones that recount the events of the day or the last conversation with a friend. Not that I have friends. How could I? You try walking around with five fully formed, visible people in your head and see if you have the space or even the need for friends. I don't have either. Besides, no friendship, or relationship for that matter, can flourish under these circumstances. I stopped trying to have an honest relationship with anyone other than my older sister, Sarah, and Milton, who both unearthed my secret despite my best efforts. But analysts are paid to stay, and family is permanent. Friends, on the other hand, are easy to lose.

The Boy, the Silent One, Sarge, Ruffles, and Betty Jane serve as family and friends. They talk to me. They talk to one another. They have their own lives, hobbies, and interests. They even have a fully furnished house with front and back doors, a well-manicured lawn, and a rosebush complete with thorns. And I see all of it inside my head from the moment I awake until the moment I go to sleep. We share a terrible intimacy where no words are required. But, like family, they judge me, sometimes a lot; and they keep secrets from me. So does my sister. Like I said, we all have secrets. I've kept the Committee's secrets, at least the ones I know, and in return, they've kept mine—the ones I know, and the ones I don't know.

{ 1 }

I sat in my darkened room, lit a cigarette, and watched the orange tip glow as it burned.

Six hours to go. Then it would be over. Six more hours and I, Holly Miller, could mark off another milestone—twelve Christmases spent alone. Well, technically not alone if you counted the Committee. At least, that was what I told Sarah last April when she started asking how and where I planned to spend Christmas. She'd asked me the same question for the last eleven years, each year asking it earlier than the last. Each year I evaded the question until the day came and went with me still sitting in my New York City apartment counting the hours until the birth of Jesus passed and "normal" loomed once more on the horizon.

The first time I said I wouldn't make it home for the holidays nobody protested. My mother said, "Things are too complicated at the moment to add you to the mix." Sarah had just gotten married, so she was caught up in making memories and didn't ask probing questions about what I'd do for the holiday.

I remember sitting in my freshman dorm room on Christmas

day thinking this was how cracked glass must feel—not broken enough to be shattered and replaced but disfigured enough that it marred the view of the world. The following year my mother sent my Christmas gifts in October. She lives in Palo Alto, California, where I grew up. Okay, mail deliveries are notoriously slow around the holidays, but you don't need two and a half months to deliver a package to the East Coast.

When I'd interviewed at New York University, they'd asked me if the distance from home would be a problem. My answer was "New York is as far away as I can get from my mother without leaving the continental United States." Unlike with my father, whose random appearances in between business trips made it easy to ignore him regardless of proximity, I could avoid my mother's duplicitous deeds only with physical distance between us. I didn't realize my mother shared my need for distance until my Christmas gifts arrived early. After that, the tacit agreement between us went like this: as long as I remained in New York City, my family would continue to supply financial aid. In my absence, Mom could spin any tale she wanted to her bridge club. Having me show up on her doorstep would be the equivalent of perfect fiction colliding with imperfect reality. Trust me when I say that comparison would provoke from my mother far more than an end to money flowing from a bank account in Northern California.

I lit another cigarette and listened to people shouting at one another outside on the streets. In the Lower East Side, holidays are not exempt from altercations when you have a bottle of Colt 45 and an attitude to match. I didn't have either, so I sat there muting my own regret-tinged anger by chain-smoking.

I inhaled and wondered what the people hurling insults were so angry about. What was I angry about? To root out the cause meant I'd have to dig into my past. *Avoid the past* was another one of my mother's lessons. Trust me, I've mastered the ability to avoid all introspective journeys down memory lane.

When I pulled back the curtains, I didn't see anything. Never did. I'd rented my place sight unseen because I couldn't believe "a four-room apartment with a view" was offered for such a low rent with no up-front fee. The day I moved in, I understood. My new abode consisted of a hallway (so small you had to step into the bathroom to enter and exit), bathroom, main room, and a closet. That's four rooms in Manhattan. After eight years, I had yet to find the view. All I saw outside my two windows was a brick wall. But if I angled my body just right, I caught a sliver of sky. Regardless, the small space with only enough room for my bed, armchair, dresser, and tiny table with two chairs suited me just fine; and the brick vista had grown on me.

My childhood was spent in a large house where we each had our own bedroom. We also had guest bedrooms, a great room, a living room, a family room, library, dining room, kitchen, hallways, pantries, sunporches, and way too many bathrooms. Sometimes hours—and, when I got older, days—passed without my seeing another family member.

Since leaving the Miller mansion, I've preferred snug spaces. After all there's just me and the two cats I've never bothered to name. I refer to as them Cat One and Cat Two. For the Committee, whose house inside my head mirrors mine, the cramped quarters create a strain. The deal is that the Committee lives at my level of means. I live in a studio apartment. They live in a studio apartment inside my head. When we moved to New York, I gave up my car, so Sarge had to leave his '57 Chevy behind. You get the picture. All to say, the Committee's snug space has to accommodate Ruffles on her pillow and Betty Jane's California King. This doesn't leave much room for the other three. Sarge installed a triple bunk bed with the Boy on top, him in the middle, and the Silent One on the bottom so he doesn't have to climb over anyone to get into bed after nighttime prayers. At least they don't have pets. Not yet anyway.

I let the curtain drop and took another drag on my cigarette. I shouldn't be smoking, but I liked to smoke. Cat One ran into the room and let out his siren sound, a warning that the vomiting was about to begin. I looked at the cigarette. *Do I keep smoking and wait for him to barf up his Christmas surprise, or do I get up and chase him around with the newspapers?* I'd always thought Cat One was bulimic. Cat Two? He's just fat. Me? I have five people living inside my head. What do you think?

Being my mother's daughter, I do manage to appear passably normal even though I don't do cute outfits with matching shoes. I wash my pale Irish skin, brush my dark brown hair, and iron my black and blue clothing. The dark colors down to my footwear help me blend in. Even my workout clothes follow this color scheme. The only variation is the white beacon of Nike hope on my feet for the forty-five minutes a day I run, although my hope remains fixed on a smaller ass, not a brighter wardrobe. As for the rest of it, lipstick equals trauma in my world, because I have had to look at Betty Jane's ruby red lips issuing one searing indictment after another for the last twelve years. So I don't use it and rarely wear makeup of any kind. I walk through life looking like a permanent bruise on a bleached background, half the time so focused on what is going on in my head I don't hear people talking to me. I'd probably go completely unnoticed if Ruffles hadn't parked her pillow in the upper left corner of my skull. At over three hundred pounds, her bulk always causes my head to lean to the left. The first time I meet someone, they feel the need to mimic my left lean, as if to let me know my head isn't on straight.

Appearances aside, most days the Committee's chaos kept me discombobulated, but it rarely made me lonely. Holidays were an exception and required extra everything to keep the pressure from closing in. Fortunately, without my asking, the Committee found something to do that didn't involve conversation or sound of any kind.

Christmas evening, when I lit up, I was hoping I could sit, smoke, and enjoy the quiet while I waited for everything to turn normal again. The shouts on the street helped. Watching the cat puke was an unexpected bonus.

I stubbed out my cigarette and started to light another one when the phone rang.

"Hello," I said.

"Hey, it's me," said Sarah.

"Please tell me you're not calling to find out what I am doing next Christmas."

"No, I want to know what you're doing for your birthday. I thought I'd fly out."

I was born on New Year's Eve. You might think it's great that the whole world has a party every year on my birthday, but I've never been big on celebrations. I usually spend the anniversary of my birth avoiding the ghosts of the past. This year I was turning thirty. Entering a new decade would bring a multitude of ghosts and their friends. Having Sarah cross the country to see me safely over that threshold quashed any worries I had about yesteryear clamoring for attention.

Sarah was the only family member who'd ever visited me during the twelve years I'd lived on the East Coast. My parents would have come for my graduation, but getting them there together was complicated, and getting me on the stage was more complicated. I told them I'd decided to skip it. Then I made sure to charge my cap and gown on the emergency credit card my mother gave me when I started at NYU. I did so with the faint hope that someone might see the bill and show up. At least take me out to dinner.

Turned out my mother didn't bother to look at the credit card statement until a couple of months after I graduated. Sarah wouldn't fill me in on the particulars of the conversation they had. She didn't need to. The expletives Sarah uttered after I told her I had marched in the graduation ceremony said it all. After that, Sarah started reviewing my statements on her weekly visits to our mother's house. She noticed everything.

After she had her first child, Sarah no longer liked to travel. Then she had the second one and she started saying, "I have my male alphabet—Doug, Elliot, and Francis—and the Bay Area offers everything you could ever need. Why would I want to be anywhere else?" One of Sarah's goals in life was to be a better partner and parent than her role models growing up. Just thinking about doing a better job put her far ahead of my parents. But that wasn't enough for Sarah. What she accomplished as wife and mother would put most spouses and parents to shame.

The thing was, Sarah hadn't turned up on my twentieth birthday, and she only had her first letter of the alphabet—D— then. So why my thirtieth? I immediately ignored that thought, because if I asked her, Sarah would tell the truth, and I didn't want any honesty to trump the happiness I felt at that moment.

When Sarah finished giving me her flight details, I said, "I'm glad you're coming. See you next week at six p.m. Hanging up now." I never said good-bye and I hated it when people said it to me, because I always felt like good-bye meant I would never see them again.

"Hang on, Holly," Sarah interrupted. "For the short time that I am there, I'd like to set some limits around that Committee of yours." What was about to follow bit into my anticipation of her

visit. "I'd like to request that Betty Jane not be prese
birthday festivities."

Before I could react, I felt what can only be descr
invisible hook around my waist and caught a glimpse of Betty
Jane's red lips pursed in a resentful line as she executed what
Milton and I referred to as a hostile takeover.

"Who do you think you are to banish me?" shot out of my
mouth in a sugary Southern tone edged with sour.

"Betty Jane"—Sarah's voice sounded severe—"how dare
you? I will not tell you again that you are not to speak to me. You
return my sister immediately or I will take steps you will not
like."

Inside my head, the Committee and I exchanged worried
glances while we waited for Betty Jane to respond. None of us
had any idea what Sarah meant, but her voice made clear that
whatever it was, she could make good on it.

"Do you understand me?" said Sarah.

Betty Jane immediately let go, but I felt the sting of her out-
rage as we transitioned.

"Holly?" said Sarah.

"Yes," I whispered. Betty Jane had never backed down to
anyone, and I didn't know what scared me more: that she did it,
or that Sarah's threat made her do it.

"I am serious. No Betty Jane."

Sarah still didn't get that I couldn't exactly banish someone
who lived in my head, and for a moment, I considered telling her
to forget it. But as funny as it sounds coming from someone living in New York City, I was lonesome and wanted physical inter-
action that didn't include pretenses, wasn't superficial, and/or
didn't have fur and four legs. I wanted my sister, my confidante,
my friend, the one person who accepted me rips, tears, cracks,

leaks, the Committee, and all. It was a tough blow to discover Sarah accepted all but one part of me. That transformed the idea of a fun birthday into a day like any other day in my life, with me trying to muddle through while trying to manage Betty Jane. After all these years, I'd been successful on that front only when our desires matched.

I sighed. "Okay."

"Also, Holly," said Sarah, "it would be nice to meet your boyfriend."

I had learned a long time ago that separation of church and state, as it were, was the best way to maintain secrets. My relationships always ended when the sex got boring and the guy wanted to know my middle name. Suffice it to say that my boyfriend, Peter, didn't know about the Committee, that I had a sister, that New Year's Eve was my birthday, and that I didn't have a middle name.

I sighed again. "I'm sure he'd like to meet you too."

My boyfriend, Peter, was an enigma. Half of him was a tall, sexy, urbane devotee of Tim Gunn and *Project Runway*, mimicking him down to the suit, tie, and slicked-back hair. The other half was a serious graduate student in religious studies. I met him at the diner where I worked as a waitress when he came in early one morning to try to stave off his post-all-night-partying hangover with greasy food. He never would have noticed me if not for an off-the-cuff reference to Kierkegaard I made. We'd been together for only two months and, as the antithesis of all his previous girlfriends, in height, weight, intelligence, looks, and so on, I found myself wondering, hourly, if we really were in a relationship. Luckily, we hadn't yet reached the point where the stardust had worn off and/or I'd lost my ability to charm him with my witty repartee. I'd been there with previous boyfriends enough times to know no stardust meant you had to actually learn more about each other or hop off the train. You can guess which choice I always made. But I wasn't ready to let Peter go yet.

Meeting Sarah would definitely accelerate our journey to that fork in the road.

I called Peter immediately after Sarah and I hung up. His big New Year's plan included Times Square, the most populated place in the country, me, and all of his friends. He'd mentioned it a few weeks earlier and my response had been the same one I had for most things I didn't want to do—remain noncommittal and pray for a solution. When Sarah called and offered me one, I figured God was having a light day.

"So, my sister is going to be here on New Year's Eve," I said.

"Cool, she can come with us to Times Square," said Peter.

"Well, the thing is"—I hesitated—"she's arriving at six o'clock in the evening and leaving the following morning. She was kind of hoping we could do a quiet sister thing."

I heard Peter breathing on the other end of the phone and asked the obvious question: "Are you mad?" He remained silent.

"Are you?" I asked again.

He still didn't answer.

"I'll see if I can work it out," I said, "but if not, you'll be with your friends."

"Yeah, that's why I have a girlfriend."

"I'll figure it out," I said.

The day before New Year's Eve, Peter still thought Sarah and I were spending the next evening with him and half the world in Times Square, and Sarah thought Peter had other plans.

I grew up with a woman who excelled at igniting roaring blazes with one word; and I'd had the pleasure of Betty Jane, who'd lived inside my head for the past twelve years and was equally good at setting fires. I probably had other options, but when desperate, you go with what you know.

I took a seemingly innocuous comment from Peter—"The jeans you wore the other day look better on you"—and doused it with verbal gasoline: "You think I'm fat."

"Don't be difficult—"

"Fat and difficult." I raised my voice several octaves for effect. "What else?"

And with that, I ignited the roaring fight that got me out of introducing my sister and my boyfriend.

Most people would probably think I'm a horrible person for doing this; they'd probably also think one night in Times Square was not a big deal. Maybe I am a horrible person, but I live in a crowd. I didn't need to extend it by standing in the middle of a much larger one. Not to mention that I'd be with people I didn't know well enough to dislike; a boyfriend who didn't have the first clue about me; my sister, who'd probably expose me in her attempt to protect me; and Betty Jane, who was liable to pull something really awful because she'd been excluded. If you were in my shoes, even if you said you wouldn't, when the time came, you'd be willing to do anything to avoid that situation. Trust me on this.

When I opened my eyes on the morning of my birthday, Betty Jane raised her glass in a toast. I thought she'd forgiven me for her impending banishment. Then, as I buttoned my work uniform, she said, "I've told you many times that style doesn't flatter your figure, or maybe Peter was right, and you've put on weight."

"He never said that," I said. She arched one eyebrow. "I said it." Betty Jane smiled. "Never mind."

I stood five-foot-three if I held my head up straight. My waitress uniform with its tie at the waist drew attention to my long torso and short legs, making me appear squat and fat. Betty Jane had an eye for clothing that flattered. I didn't. But Betty Jane and I had been playing the game of retribution in the form of insults thinly veiled as truth for a long time. Only she played it much better than I did. She knew all my weaknesses and played on them like Beethoven on a fortepiano. The notes were soft or hard depending on her anger. Commenting on my weight meant her hands were crashing down on the keys. You couldn't find an ounce of excess fat on my body if you put me under a microscope.

In other words, I was not forgiven.

She raised her glass again at that thought and I realized that there was more than orange juice in it. I'd never seen Betty Jane drunk before, but having witnessed the combination of my father and a bottle of booze on many occasions while growing up, I recognized a mean drunk when I saw one. But I'd chosen to comply with my sister's wishes, and I left the responsibility of containing Betty Jane to Ruffles.

On my way home from the diner, I made my daily stop at the A & P grocery store. I believed that shopping weekly would force me into choices I might not like. How was I to know on Tuesday what I would want to eat on Saturday?

I stood in front of the cereal boxes debating with Ruffles and Sarge about whether Sarah would want Cheerios or toast for breakfast. Then Betty Jane slurred, "She banished me. Don't get her anything."

"I can't believe you silenced her with a bottle of gin," I said.

Inside my head, Ruffles held up her hands. *"Hey, I did the best I could under the circumstances."* Betty Jane controlled the Committee, so they couldn't banish her any more than I could. The only other option was to make her unavailable. Getting her drunk accomplished that and then some.

"Can you at least take the bottle away and hide it?" I asked.

I closed my eyes. Sarge reached for it. Betty Jane slapped him as she stumbled toward her bed, upending and draining the bottle on the way.

"Jesus, she's smashed," I said. I shook my head. "Quick, before she goes down, cereal or toast?"

Chatting in front of the Cheerios with myself went unnoticed in a big city. If I let down my guard like this back in Palo Alto, Nancy from my mother's bridge club would spot me and tell Marjorie and Kate, and the next thing you knew all the families would be sitting poolside at some neighborhood barbecue whispering about me instead of their monthly Botox treatments.

Living in New York definitely had its abject moments, but when the woman standing next to me pulling a box of Rice Krispies off the shelf didn't even glance sidelong as I discussed Betty Jane's inebriation along with the pros and cons of cereal versus toast, those moments didn't seem so bad.

We decided on cereal *and* toast, and I also bought the makings for a salad and pasta. On the way to the checkout, I grabbed a thirty-dollar bottle of wine and a coffee cake in a box. We'd need something to stick the candles on later. Then I decided I should start the new year with a new toothbrush, toothpaste, and floss and walked over to the dental hygiene section.

I picked up two packages and said, "Do you know the difference between unwaxed and waxed floss?"

"I read that dental tape is better," said Ruffles.

"Is it?"

"Is what?" I turned and saw an A & P clerk standing next to me. I shook my head and threw both packages into the cart.

By the time I arrived home, Betty Jane lay sprawled on her bed in a drunken stupor inside my head. Her incapacitation made the Committee unable to speak and participate. I knew the rest of the

Committee would give me a pass on this one, especially since the solution to the "how to keep Betty Jane out of Sarah's face" problem came from Ruffles. Hopefully, nasty remarks and a hangover would be the extent of Betty Jane's retribution.

The upside of Betty Jane's drinking was that her hangover should keep her in bed for at least a day after Sarah's departure, which would give me time to apologize to Peter, grovel if necessary, and then initiate a passionate reunion. Milton had warned me once about the consequences of using this method to restore harmony in a relationship. He said, "Do this and you become more enmeshed in the fantasy, when the reality is that the relationship wouldn't exist if you ever thought about what made you stay." This time, I ignored him.

I checked my watch, two o'clock. I had four hours to kill before Sarah arrived.

It was just past ten o'clock. Sarah and I sat under the covers in my bed. We'd had all our conversations like this while growing up—me against my pillow and Sarah with her back against the wall and legs hooked over mine. "Holly," said Sarah, "Mom asked me to ask you when are you going to get a real job and support yourself like most people your age do? She thinks you wait tables to spite her."

My working as a waitress bothered my mother almost as much as it did Betty Jane—especially when she compared me to Sarah, who went from high school, to college, to marriage, and to a career in accounting, hitting all the success milestones at just the right time. By age thirty, Sarah had embarked on motherhood, and four years and two perfectly timed children later she was now hitting all the right child-rearing achievements on schedule. From my mother's perspective, by now I should have a successful career and a husband trying fervently to impregnate me.

I said to Sarah, "Ask Mom if she'd prefer to tell the bridge club that her NYU honor student can't seem to find career success outside of the food industry because she has a little problem of five people inhabiting her head." I smirked.

My sister sat silent. A few years ago she had decided it was best to remain neutral on the topic of my employment. She could not see the causal link between the fact that my jobs required me to interact with so many people and how often I changed employers. The missing piece I never shared was that I waited tables, and subsequently, it was Betty Jane's behavior that always got me fired within six to eight months. When Sarah suggested I try to stay put, build stability in my life, I asked her to trust me that this was the best I could do.

"At least I have a boyfriend," I said, hoping to direct the conversation to accomplishments my mother did care about.

"Well, yes," said Sarah, "she was thrilled until I told her your boyfriend is a graduate student on scholarship. She figured out where the excess charges were coming from pretty quickly after that, Holly."

"Is that why you wanted to meet him?" I asked. "Did she tell you to?"

"She didn't have to. I see the credit card bill. And—"

"You're always going to protect me," I said. Sarah had told me this so many times over the years, I recognized the specific way her mouth shaped right before the words came out.

"I am always going to protect you." Sarah squeezed my hand and my chest ached. Just once I wanted to be the one who protected her. It wasn't fair that she seemed to walk through life as my bulletproof vest.

I sighed, then said, "I expected Mom to take comfort in the fact that my mind was not wasting. This seemed to be her chief complaint," I said. "I addressed it and still she's not satisfied."

"We are now on the avenue called sarcastic," said Sarah. "Maybe she is right. You do keep working as a waitress to spite her."

A few years earlier my mother had asked Sarah how someone with an expensive education could have no ambition other than to serve breakfast. It was an appropriate question for most parents, and had my mother been like most parents, we would have had a credible, albeit misleading answer prepared. My mother so rarely asked questions about me or my life that her query had caught Sarah off guard. Her answer came across as vague and neutral, and my mother immediately interpreted my behavior as a slight against her. I'd never admit it to Sarah, but I did derive a certain pleasure from imagining my mother trying to explain my career to her friends.

Betty Jane stirred inside my head. I looked at the view out my bedroom window and whispered, "Not her."

"What? And why are you whispering?" Sarah raised her voice.

I reached out my hand to cover her mouth while I pressed my forefinger to mine and shushed. "Betty Jane," I said softly. "I don't want to wake her." If Betty Jane was a mean drunk, she'd definitely be meaner the day after, with a hangover.

"I'm not going to whisper," said Sarah.

"Please, Sarah. You asked that she not appear. Please. You're leaving tomorrow but I'll still be here with her."

"Oh, all right." Sarah made a face but her voice had dropped a few decibals. "What did you just say?" she whispered.

"Nothing."

Waiting tables in a diner meant my means were meager, which was the main source of contention between me and Betty Jane. I wanted to work as a waitress until I retired to keep that one tiny corner of control. She was inclined to charm her way into earning every penny possible waiting tables. Explaining to

Sarah that my battle was with Betty Jane and not my mother would take us straight out of the valley of whispers and right up the mountain of screams.

Sarah sat silent, no doubt struggling over whether to push me or let it lie. I bit my lower lip. *Please let it lie.* I bit harder and tasted blood. Sarah's face became pained.

"I can't keep excusing your working as a waitress," she said quietly.

I mouthed the words *thank you*.

"Holly, your inability to exercise any control over your life . . ." Sarah let the rest of the comment hang suspended. This tired discussion only resulted in my feeling more inadequate, and inadequacy was not exactly a means to motivate me. It was easy to hide under the blanket of anonymity a big city offered, but that just covered my social anxiety and failure to manage many areas of daily life. It didn't get rid of them.

"I'm doing the best I can," I said sadly. "Asking me to lead your version of a normal life is like asking a quadriplegic to get up and walk. Of course he is desperate to stand up and run as fast as he can away from that chair. But he can't, and neither can I."

Sarah frowned and shook her head. "Holly, nobody is asking—"

I stopped her with the palm of my hand. "I know my inability to lead a normal life, with a normal job, a normal relationship, and normal friends after all these years seems excessive and unreasonable, but I'm not you and I never will be."

"You're spending way too much money, Holly," said Sarah. "We're having a hard time explaining the extravagant charges to the Father."

I laughed softly. I had started calling my father "the Father" when I was fourteen and his conversion from alcohol to God had failed. I'd never heard Sarah use the moniker. She usually said it was disrespectful. I wondered what the Father had done to overcome Sarah's deference, but I didn't ask.

"Your life *is* excessive and unreasonable under the circumstances," she said.

"Not true. I'm making enough now to cover my rent. Betty Jane is even helping."

"How?" said Sarah.

"Well." I paused. I realized that I'd just blurted out something I should have left safely unsaid. This was the downside of Betty Jane passed out drunk. She usually prevented me from blurting out Committee secrets.

"Are you letting her speak?" Sarah sounded ominous.

I nodded slightly and looked away. By taking over when I worked, Betty Jane managed to turn waitressing straw into gratuity gold. Ruffles helped me in my fight to maintain control by also working through me in the diner. The resulting competition between them had quadrupled the tips. I knew I was playing a dangerous game, but when you're trying to hang on, the risks seem smaller and the consequences are always too far ahead to notice.

Sarah said, "Part of the process of integration involves limiting the Committee as much as possible. You know this. Why are you giving them free rein?"

Your process, I thought. Sarah and Milton's goal was integration of the Committee, which meant one Holly and no Committee. My goal was to avoid the immobilizing anguish I felt at the thought of losing everyone. "People like it. Besides," I said indignantly, "it's only Betty Jane. Well, and Ruffles. But only those two."

"Oh, for God's sake, Holly. If you let your Committee, as you call them, do everything for you, you'll never have any control over your life."

"It's only fair that they help."

"You can't do this, Holly," said Sarah. "I forbid it." Sarah always "used her words" when she wanted to assert control over me. She should have learned that the phrase made no difference when she *forbade me* from continuing to see Peter after several charges for expensive restaurants came in on the emergency credit card. She thought he was using me, which was another reason for them not to meet.

I listened to the sound of Sarah's breathing. "Holly, I'm very concerned," she said. "Does Milton know about this?"

Yeah, right, I thought. *Betty Jane is going to let that conversation happen.* I shook my head.

"No wonder you've made absolutely no progress in the last five years." Sarah paid the bill Milton sent her every month.

"Making it through the day is progress, Sarah," I said. "It's a constant battle, one that requires all my energy to hold the line. You have no idea how exhausting it is to live with her, Sarah. No idea."

"Maybe not, but you still place me in a very awkward position, Holly. I have to explain to the Father why there's no end in sight to the therapy bills."

I sat up straighter. "He pays for my therapy?" My father and I hadn't spoken since the day I graduated from high school. I thought Sarah's contact with him was limited to a Christmas card and the annual perfunctory birthday call. I realized that for her to get him to cover these costs, the contact had to be a lot more than rare.

Sarah nodded. "Yes, he's been paying since you started."

Knowing my father covered the costs of my treatment and Sarah had had a hand in getting him to do it made me happy in a sick sort of way. I thought everyone in our family should make restitution in some form or another for what had happened.

Everyone including me. We were all guilty. Some of us more than others.

After I blew out the candles, Sarah said, "Holly, I really want you to have a good life. I want you to have everything you deserve." When she said it, a heavy wash of sadness pressed in on my chest. "You have to forgive yourself, Holly. You have to forgive yourself. It's the only way through it."

"Have you forgiven yourself, Sarah?" I said.

"A long time ago." She sighed and squeezed my hand.

I couldn't tell her that even when you decide you've paid in full, if what you've paid for has become part of the framework of your life, you can't let it go that easily. But if Sarah had forgiven herself, maybe it was time for me to try.

{ 2 }

I awoke New Year's Day with a commitment to make changes in my life. When Sarah told me commitments mean more when they're written down, I said, "Hey, I left California to get away from crunchy granola crap."

"You left California to get away from yourself," said Sarah. I set my mouth in a straight line. "And how's that working for you?" I pressed my lips together, creating dimples on either side in response to her obviously rhetorical question.

Sarah handed me a pad and a pen. "'Forgive yourself' goes on top."

I thought about what she'd said the night before and for one heartbeat, I allowed myself a glimpse of a different life. In it, I walked down a beautiful country road with green poplar trees on either side. The kind of road we used to drive down in the summers when we met our extended family for picnics. Then I remembered I hadn't been on a picnic since I was six and a half, and my body became hollow and two-dimensional. I sighed and still wrote down *forgiveness*, but I knew it was just a word, a word that had nothing to offer me.

"Here's my list." I handed it to Sarah. *1. Forgiveness 2. Punctuality 3. Staying within my budget.*

"Smoking?"

"I give that up every day."

All I can say is, the minute Sarah's taxi disappeared around the corner, I bolstered my flagging spirit by telling myself I needed to learn the meaning of forgiveness before I could even consider the act. Then I asked myself, *Who keeps resolutions anyway?* I'd read that the resolve behind New Year's resolutions usually falters after twenty-four hours. The fact that I couldn't keep this particular resolution for twenty-four minutes didn't mean anything. I still had punctuality and budget. Keeping two out of three resolutions was something I could hang my hat on.

Two weeks later, I had managed to arrive late to work every day, charge more than five hundred dollars for unnecessary items, and smoke a carton of cigarettes. On the morning of January 15, when I realized I had ten minutes to get to work, and the diner was four subway stops away and another five minutes on foot if I ran, I threw in the towel on resolutions. Then I wondered if I could use this as an excuse for my tardiness.

I pushed through the turnstile at the Broadway and Houston subway station, hoping I didn't have to wait long for the F train.

"Back by popular demand," said Ruffles inside my head, "the 'sorry, I don't wear a watch' excuse."

"Do you have to be so cheerful in the morning?" I said loudly. Nobody even glanced at me. I was just another woman in New York City talking to herself.

I rode the subway with a keen awareness of the hard plastic seat, even though my coat, uniform, tights, and underwear were between it and me. My chest ached with that feeling you get when you've been defeated by your own fear and failed to push past something really difficult because the effort requires you to cross over something you've spent your life avoiding: something you've avoided for so long you can no longer name it. But you can't escape it either, because it floats just outside your awareness like a frightening ghost from a bad dream you had as a child. The kind of dream where the images fade but the feeling becomes more vivid as the years pass. The kind of dream you know is shielding you from the real nightmare, the true nightmare. The stuff you couldn't change. The words you couldn't take back. The choice you couldn't unmake. The resolutions you couldn't keep.

I hated empty early-morning subway rides because they invited all kinds of unwanted thoughts, feelings, ghosts. I wondered if I'd be sitting here next year fighting the same battle. The idea felt as cold as the plastic I sat on.

I closed my eyes. Inside my head, Ruffles sat quietly on her pillow. Her sad countenance told me she'd taken everything in. I wanted to ask her if we could have a better life. If change was possible. If hope was a friend that owed us a big favor and today was payday. Instead, I said, "Does my hair look okay?"

Ruffles sighed. Most people never have to admit when they've been beaten by their own fears. I, on the other hand, suffered my defeats in front of the Committee, which would have been all right if not for Betty Jane. She didn't just bear witness to my defeats; she made sure to repeatedly remind me of them afterward. Nobody can make progress under those circumstances.

"Why did you try to curl it?" said Ruffles.

I had dark brown, perfectly straight hair. I held a thick hank of it before my eyes, relieved that Ruffles was willing to focus on a more banal topic. "I don't know," I said. Then I noticed the woman sitting opposite, gaping at me. I dropped the hair.

As the train sped along, I stared at the ads, domestic violence to the left, AIDS to the right, poetry project underneath. I liked poetry on the subway. Maybe I should buy a watch. I willed the subway to go faster. It didn't.

Ruffles's corpulent cheeks jiggled as she crunched her potato chips, adding staccato notes to the whirring sound of the subway moving along the tracks. The devil slept on her California King, her satin sheets pulled just up to her sunflower pin. I shuddered and shifted my inner gaze to the other three, also sleeping, and wished I were as well. The train pulled into West Fourth Street. Two more stops. With any luck, we'd be less than fifteen minutes late.

When the doors opened at Forty-second Street/Bryant Park, I darted through the crowd, sprinted up the stairs, exited, and ran toward the diner. As I neared it, I noticed the girls who attended the Catholic middle school across the street marching toward a school bus. Slowing to a jog, I thought, Early field trip. Really early. Because I had the morning shift, I usually only saw them after work, when they were beyond the fence on the playground.

I drifted by the lineup and glanced into their sleepy eyes. I was seven, about their age, when I heard that right before he died, Jesus cried out, "My God, my God, why have you forsaken me?" I'd already experienced the bitterness of denied prayers and had an inkling about how he felt. Knowing God had ignored his only son with his hands and feet nailed to a cross, while he screamed his bloody, crowned-with-thorns head off for some help, strengthened my resolve to keep my back turned on him and everything that smacked of religion. He was one man. What about all the people who were left living with the fact that someone sacrificed himself on their behalf? I'm sure if given the choice, they'd prefer to make the sacrifice rather than to be the one who has to live on the charity of someone else's act of surrender. I know I would.

A smile from the girl at the end of the line interrupted my reverie. *Maybe she's already caught on.* "Run for your life," I whispered to her. "Get away while you still can."

She tipped her head to one side, her eyes clouded with confusion. With this gesture, she managed to make me instantly feel the lifetime of self-loathing that had started before kids her age teased me because my head tilted to the left.

"Never mind," I said, already looking past her to the diner.

With not one empty seat in the diner, I found myself wondering if everyone in Manhattan had run out of food for breakfast. I mumbled, "Sorry," to no one, put on my apron, and grabbed a couple of plates without asking, "What table?" I'd just look for empty tabletops and hungry faces and ask until I found the right match.

By seven fifteen, the sounds of people talking, forks colliding with plates, and sausage and bacon frying had reached a dull roar. I was about to drop a stack of potato pancakes in front of a couple when a man walked in. He stood more than a foot taller than me and wore a blue pin-striped suit accompanied by a red silk tie and a shirt as stiff as his shellacked hair. His stature, raven-colored hair, and emerald green eyes set him apart from the morning diner clientele, who mostly looked like they had just rolled out of something, and it wasn't bed. We did get the occasional fancy-dressed man (usually the guy looking out for his "lady" around the corner), but this one was different. His clothes reeked of expensiveness, and I knew expensive, because Betty Jane was a connoisseur of fine clothing and footwear, and I generated monthly credit card charges equaling the debt of a small nation to prove it.

"Well, now," said Betty Jane inside my head. She usually didn't bother to get up until midway through the morning shift. More surprising than seeing her awake this early was finding her attired in a freshly starched uniform with her sunflower pin affixed to her apron like an evil lapel pet. Even though nobody but me and the other Committee members ever saw Betty Jane, she liked to dress for the occasion, be it an afternoon in the public library or a trip to the supermarket.

"Sit wherever you can find a spot," I said to the man. He walked quickly toward me instead. I stepped back and slid sideways. He stopped at the counter and leaned in. Even though the purple Formica separated us, I pressed against the metal shelves holding the coffee cups and silverware. He probably stole the clothes, I thought.

"That's a real Rolex," said Betty Jane inside my head.

"I'm looking for Holly," said the man. "Holly with the Southern voice." Then he did what people always did when they looked at me for the first time: He tipped his head to the left. I pressed my palm against my jaw to force my head into a vertical line. Ruffles tumbled off her pillow. I felt as if someone had flipped a big rock against my skull.

"Tell him you're Holly," said Betty Jane. I shook my head slightly.

"Holly isn't here?" said the man. He straightened his head and dropped his gaze from my face to my name tag. I covered it with my hand. "You're Holly." He extended his hand. "Walter Torrent." His deep voice echoed off the morning din. "I heard about you from my PA, Robbie."

Robbie was a regular customer. A real climber. Exactly the kind of guy who appealed to Betty Jane. She always took over to wait on him, and I didn't mind, because I'd never liked him. "Why would he talk to you about me?" I said. "And what's a PA?"

"I came in to hear your Southern voice myself," he said.

Before I could respond, Betty Jane seized control. I fell back into the Committee's room as she extended my hand to meet Walter Torrent's.

"Why, hello." Betty Jane's breathy Southern drawl tumbled out of my mouth.

Ignoring their conversation, I said, "Did you see what she did?" to the other Committee members.

"What's she doing up this early?" asked Sarge.

"Holly, pay attention," said Ruffles.

She heaved herself up off her pillow. The Committee's house swayed. We all gripped any available furniture to keep from toppling over. Betty Jane stood stock-still. Her uncanny ability to manage my body perfectly no matter what we were doing inside reminded me of my mother, who could be in the middle of a raging battle and still answer the door with a smile.

"Holly!" snapped Ruffles. My eyes alternated between Sarge and Ruffles. I saw blotches of anger and concern on her face. The scar that ran from the corner of Sarge's jawline, diving down the collar of his T-shirt, pulsed white against his red neck.

I refocused on Betty Jane and Walter.

"Not bad." Walter pointed at my mouth.

"You mean perfect," said Betty Jane as she raised a hand to fluff my hair.

Walter waited. Betty Jane giggled. "Oh, my, are you going to eat, or are you here just to stare at li'l ol' me?" she said.

"Is she flirting with that guy?" I asked. My confusion combined with the awareness that I was the only one who seemed to be missing something here rushed at me.

Ruffles narrowed her eyes. "No. But she's up to something. I may need to intervene."

"Hush," said Betty Jane. She pressed my hand against my lips. "We will have none of that." Walter smiled as if the comment were addressed to him, and not me and the Committee that he couldn't see. "How about you sit down right here?" My hand waved at a just vacated table.

Walter sat down. Betty Jane stood with poised pen and order pad at the ready. "I need a menu," he said.

"Of course you do." She sashayed my body to the counter, retrieved the menu, and sauntered back. With my short legs and wide hips, I never had the confidence to blatantly do the catwalk like that for any man. Somehow, when Betty Jane was in control, I had a model's body—thin and very tall. We all watched, mesmerized.

Betty Jane held out the menu for him to take. "Why, here you go."

Walter's gaze burned so intently it seared me where I sat on the Committee's couch inside my head.

Betty Jane smiled coquettishly.

"That's enough!" said Ruffles. Sarge stood up. "You step back, or I'll have Sarge make you."

Betty Jane could read Sarge's scar thermometer. She didn't hesitate to cede control.

Walter ordered eggs, toast, and coffee from me. A few minutes later, I felt his eyes on my back as I ceded control to Ruffles, whose favorite customer had just walked in the door. Just as with Betty Jane, my body felt different. Uncomfortably different, like a severe bloat that accompanies a late period. And I knew from the way Walter was watching me, because I was grew up with a man just like him, that he was a man who hated an ounce of fat on a woman. Good thing Ruffles didn't care about her bulk. In fact, she celebrated it.

I turned my attention to the other hungry patrons in my area and forgot about Walter. After about twenty minutes, Robbie entered with another tall, casually dressed man. They sat down at Walter's table. I saw them speaking; then Walter pointed at me. Robbie nodded in agreement.

"Miss?" a voice behind me said. I turned around. The woman speaking pointed at the food in front of her. "I didn't want these as an appetizer. He doesn't have his meal." Her finger now aimed at her thin companion sitting across from her. "We wanted our food together."

I split my gaze between her table and the table one over from it, where Walter and Robbie conferred while the companion listened. If I read their faces right, Robbie was selling something Walter wasn't too keen on buying. I couldn't read the other guy.

Robbie noticed me surveilling them. He made a gesture I didn't know how to interpret.

"Well?" barked the woman. I shook off my confusion. "Are you going to stand there staring into space or are you going to do something?"

"Oh—"

Betty Jane pulled. As I landed on the Committee's floor, she fixed my eyes on Walter and his companion and fluttered my fingers at Robbie, and then she turned to the unhappy woman. "Miss," Betty Jane purred, "I am terribly sorry for the mix-up. I can take these and bring out a new batch with your order." My hand reached for the plate. The woman grabbed my wrist. "I am going to take these right back to the kitchen and have them make three orders. No charge."

"Could be Violet," said Walter. "I don't know. What do you think?" he asked the guy sitting between him and Robbie.

"Or, if y'all like," said Betty Jane, "I can leave these as a li'l ol' snack for you to share. I'll bring the other two orders with his meal. Sound nice?" The woman nodded and let go of my wrist.

The guy sitting between Walter and Robbie nodded and said, "I've heard enough."

Enough what? I didn't know what this was about, but whatever it was, Betty Jane wanted it. Badly. She was never this nice to any customer.

Robbie, Walter, and the third guy sat quietly at their table. Betty Jane stood watching, still holding the plate of potato pancakes. I sat frozen on the Committee's floor as anxiety and indecision did the tango in my stomach while confusion watched from the side.

"Well," said the woman, obviously dismissing me.

Shit. No indecision now. "Betty Jane," I said, "what are you doing?"

"Nothing." She ceded control. My knees buckled. I dove forward to catch my body just before it went down. When I felt the ground under my feet, I bolted through the kitchen toward the back exit.

"Yur stackin' up orders here. Where da hell ya goin'?" yelled the exasperated cook.

"I need a cigarette."

"Fuggedaboutit." He handed me food for another table.

Luna, the only other waitress working that morning, walked in and said, "Holly, your friend and that other guy want to order."

Betty Jane blindsided me again. My head smacked on the Committee's coffee table. I rubbed the swelling bump and watched as the plates of food dropped from my hands and crashed to the floor.

"Watch it!" screamed the cook.

"Oh, my," exclaimed Betty Jane from my mouth. Then she turned my body, leaving the dishes where they'd fallen.

"The dishes?" I cried.

"Do you mind?" Betty Jane said sweetly to a busboy. "I have so many tables."

"What the hell is wrong with her?" I asked Ruffles. She waved me off and turned her attention back to Betty Jane and the trio of men.

"And this is Mike Davey, the director for Walter's new animated television show called *The Neighborhood*," said Robbie.

Betty Jane smiled as Robbie handed her some sheets of paper that looked like a script from a play. He nodded and she read a few lines. He read the response and then it went back to Betty Jane.

"Oh," I said with more relief than I felt. "They've been doing this for weeks. Nothing to be alarmed over."

Ruffles shook her head. Instinct told me she was right, something was up, but I didn't have it in me to fight Betty Jane. I decided ignoring her might carry more impact, so I picked up her discarded copy of *Vogue* and started paging through it.

"Holly," said Luna. I looked up from my reading. Betty Jane didn't even recognize her presence. "You'd better take care of your other tables and orders, or you're going to be fired."

I stood up and tried to move forward to take control. Betty Jane held on tighter than a barnacle to a ship's hull. Guilt over not trusting Ruffles when she said Betty Jane was up to no good spread from my abdomen up into my throat. I remained standing, waiting for any opening.

"I get the part as Violet and Robbie gets his money?"

Part? Money? "What is she talking about?" I asked Ruffles.

"In a minute," said Ruffles. "Now shush."

"Not so fast," said Walter. "You might have a great voice—might—but the question can you use it behind a microphone? Can you act?"

I paused. I didn't know what he meant about a microphone, but this guy had no idea how well I could act.

"Why don't we get her some training and see how she does?" said Mike Davey.

"That sounds like a plan. Set it up. And, Little Waitress . . ." He looked at me. Betty Jane flashed a twenty-four-tooth smile at the insult. I'd have returned a face shot through with repugnance. "Just remember, Walt's World only has stars." He dropped a twenty-dollar bill on the table and stood up.

"Give Robbie your contact details and someone will get back to you about classes and so forth," said Mike.

Walt tapped his watch and said, "Let's go." He nodded at me and Mike waved. Robbie high-fived Betty Jane and followed them out the door.

I turned to Ruffles. "What did I miss?" I said with apprehension.

"That guy Walter Torrent offered ten thousand dollars to anyone who found him the exact voice for the lead character, Violet, on his new show, *The Neighborhood,* or something," she said. "Guess who wants to be that voice."

I couldn't do anything other than sigh as Betty Jane waited for me to transition with her.

"Holly," said the cook, "nobody drops plates and walks away in my diner."

"But the busboy—"

"I warned ya already about that Southern diva crap," said the cook. "And ya drop a plate, ya pick it up." Luna and the busboy looked away, and I knew I was about to lose another job because of Betty Jane.

I opened my mouth to argue.

"Forget it, Holly," said Ruffles inside my head. She was right. Goddamn Betty Jane. We'd had this job for only three months. This was a record, even for her.

"Here's your pay for today." The cook handed me some bills in exchange for my apron.

I grabbed my bag, and went out back for the cigarette I'd wanted earlier.

I leaned against the wall and lit my next cigarette with the remains of the last. "Do you realize what you've done?" I fumed.

"You should be thanking me for what I've done," said Betty Jane inside my head.

"Thanking you?" I yelled.

Betty Jane sat demurely filing her nails. She paused midscrape. "Well, no thanks required, really. I know that deep down you are pleased."

See what I mean about a terrible intimacy? But we had an unspoken rule, the Committee and I. Even though they could read my mind, the Committee still had to treat my private thoughts as if they were the family laundry—and we didn't air the family laundry. Betty Jane had carried me unscathed through the patch of secrets, delivering me safely on the other side and on the path to a new life. She knew it, and she knew I knew it, and that was why she sat there arching her left eyebrow, daring me to chastise her for this latest violation.

"Just remember, Holly, next time you want to change, don't rely on hope. Rely on me. I deliver."

"What have you delivered? Unemployment? We're running out of diners in Manhattan."

"I have delivered the possibility of a new life," said Betty Jane.

"A new life I didn't ask for and don't want. Besides, I didn't hear anything other than maybes and training. I didn't hear paycheck. You're smoking crack if you think we can become a voice-whatever for a cartoon."

"Well, you have a choice, Holly Miller. Get Sarge to transform our stultifying routine into one that will actually result in something, or give up and try to find a diner in Queens that will hire you. Without me."

I scanned the inside of my head. "Betty Jane, what did you do with Sarge?"

"Why, he and that frankincense-smelling man took the Boy on an excursion."

"Like I believe that," I fumed. "*What did you*— Oh!"

Mike stood in the doorway to the diner.

"How long have you, uh, been . . . ?" The puzzled look on his face told me he'd heard some if not all of my side of the conversation with Betty Jane. I froze.

"Did you lose your job?" said Mike.

"Of course I lost my job," I snapped. *Maybe he didn't hear anything.*

He smiled warmly and I felt oddly at ease and awkward at the same time. I took a drag on my cigarette and looked him over. Not bad. He and Walter were about the same height, but Mike looked British with his straight, tight black jeans, leather jacket, and pale skin. And I liked the dark, wavy hair that was just long enough, but not so long it would get restrained in a ponytail. Betty Jane smirked. I flashed guiltily on Peter even though he was still punishing me for New Year's Eve.

"You up for this?" said Mike.

I waited for Betty Jane to seize control. She merely yawned and moved on to the next finger with her nail file. "Up for what? All I heard was training. I need to earn money. Pay rent."

Mike's face appeared confused. Then he smiled warmly again and I felt that rush of recognition that said your frequency had just been aligned with the other's. The kind that fans a flame of things to come. The kind that you know is more reality than hope.

I exhaled the tension from my body while he watched me.

"We talked about that earlier, remember?" He tapped his lips with his forefinger and pointed at me. I felt naked. "Well, if you can manage the training, your next job could be as the lead voice on *The Neighborhood.*"

"What is that anyway?" I asked.

"You don't remember?" He paused and I gestured for him to continue instead of acknowledging the unspoken words.

"*The Neighborhood* is an animated comedy centered around Violet Dupree, a scheming Southern belle who spends her days stirring up trouble, forcing her neighbors to constantly question their own values." I pulled a face. Sounded like Betty Jane to me. Misreading my thoughts, Mike held up his hand. "Make no mistake, the character of Violet has a good heart that always triumphs in the end."

No wonder Robbie had pegged Betty Jane for this part. It was almost as if someone had crawled into my head, studied her, and created this character of Violet. Sans the good heart, Betty Jane was Violet. Doing this would be no stretch for her.

"Even though we'll maintain humor throughout," Mike continued, "the show is not going to be a sitcom that features unusual or improbable events. We're going to take on themes ranging from the everyday, such as friendship, to more serious issues, including gender roles, women's liberation, and drug abuse, and deal with them in a humorous way."

"Sounds like you've repeated that part of your spiel more than once," I said.

"Yeah." He laughed. "Anyway, it's my show. I handle the creative aspects. Actually, I call all the shots—script, direction, you name it. The buck stops with me." He smiled. "And your Southern voice is exactly what we're looking for."

I felt Mike watching me and realized he was probably waiting for me to say something. So I pointed at his feet. "Nice shoes." He had on red Converse high-tops, just like the Boy always wore.

"Thanks," he said.

"So what would I have to do?" I ignored Ruffles's surprise, because the question surprised me too. But there it was, hanging between me and Mike Davey, director with the red Converse shoes like the Boy always wore.

"You need to take a lot of classes and prove to us that you can do that voice when it counts."

Classes sounded easy. I was a good student, after all.

"Do I get paid?"

"Not until you get the part. Anyway, I already spoke to a friend of mine who's an agent and told her to expect your call." He handed me a card. "She'll set you up with all the training required. Her contact details are on the back, and that's my number if you have any questions."

Betty Jane remained nonchalant inside my head. I accepted the card and said, "So, what's a PA?"

"Ah, you mean Robbie? He is Walter's personal assistant. PA. He's going to make ten thousand dollars if you deliver. Nicely done, by the way. Robbie deserves it. Even I'll admit PA's get paid shit."

Well, that was the first time Betty Jane had actually done anything nice for anyone. On second thought, he got the money only if I could manage this. What a bitch. Even if I had no interest in it, she knew I wouldn't say no if doing so meant disappointing someone else.

"This voice-over thing isn't for us," said Ruffles inside my head. Betty Jane rolled her eyes. I lit another cigarette and inhaled. I wanted Mike to leave and I wanted him to stay.

"You're going to have to give that up." He pointed at my cigarette. "My voice-over artists don't smoke. It's a strict rule."

"This?" I held up the cigarette. "Not even an issue. I barely smoke." Betty Jane smiled triumphantly as Ruffles's visage changed from cherubic pink to hospital gray.

After Mike left, I waited a few minutes and lit another cigarette.

"There has to be a catch," said Ruffles. "This kind of thing doesn't happen in real life."

"There is a catch," I said, "and her name is Betty Jane."

{ 3 }

I heard about dissociative identity disorder during my last term at New York University when I attended a guest lecture by Dr. Milton Lawler. These talks offered me the opportunity to fill my time and earn extra credit for attending. I always showed up to get the credit, but I stayed only if the topic held my interest.

I glanced at the flyer on the lap of the person sitting next to me. "*DID and MPD* by Dr. Milton Lawler." A lecture of acronyms. I expected to depart in less than ten minutes.

After he was introduced, Dr. Lawler surveyed the crowd through his rimless spectacles; then he said, "What is dissociation?" *Separate from a group*, I thought to myself. Like anyone familiar with Latin, I could dissect the word and get a basic answer. Maybe I'd go in five minutes.

A hand in the front shot up. I'd read somewhere that people who sat in the front always got high marks. I never sat in the front and I had a four-point GPA. Go figure.

"Yes," said Dr. Lawler, pointing at the questioner.

"Dissociation is a mental process that produces a lack of con-

nection in a person's thoughts, memories, feelings, actions, or
sense of identity."

Know-it-all.

"A textbook answer," said Dr. Lawler.

"He agrees," said Ruffles inside my head.

"And dissociative identity disorder, DID?" said Dr. Lawler.

"Multiple personality disorder, MPD," said the know-it-all.
"That's what it used to be called."

I caught my breath. I knew what multiple personality disorder was. Sarah had given me a copy of *Sybil* when she discovered
my secret. I'd read the book and was relieved to report to Sarah
that I wasn't Sybil. There were parts of the book that resonated,
though, and because of that, I decided to stay.

I watched Dr. Lawler speak. He certainly looked like the
textbook picture of a psychoanalyst, with his burgundy corduroy
pants, brown tweed jacket with a sweater vest underneath, and
oxblood leather walking shoes.

As I assessed his attire, Dr. Lawler's discussion of DID and
MPD nipped at my thoughts like a stalker horse. The proverbial
critical-stage attack came when he said something about co-
consciousness and a level of shared awareness, of existence and
behavior, among the personalities. I began to listen to what he
was saying.

"In DID, levels of co-consciousness vary from person to
person. Some people are completely unaware of what the
other personalities are doing and/or thinking, while others are
completely aware. Regardless of the level of consciousness,
the system of dissociation is in place to cover up specific trauma
and nothing more," said Dr. Lawler.

I felt like I did as a small child when I sat in the middle of a
conversation between my mother and one of her sisters. I knew
they were talking about something of interest; and I knew if I

made one peep or moved one inch, I'd be unceremoniously tossed from the room. But if I remained statuelike, they'd forget about me and talk in hushed tones about things I didn't understand while I strained to hear every word.

The person sitting next to me raised his hand. This surprised me. People in the back rows didn't ask questions. "Are you saying that people can dissociate, or switch personalities, without losing their sense of time and place?" said my neighbor.

"If they are co-conscious, the dissociation serves to shield the person from painful events in the past without compromising awareness of what is occurring in the present. Therefore, the understanding of time and place remains coherent, but the trauma remains hidden."

"In a co-conscious setup, where do the personalities go when they are not in control?"

"It all depends on the complexity of the co-conscious system," said Dr. Lawler. "For example, in some cases, the personalities remain in the host body awareness, ready to step in at any time. In other cases, the personalities can be independent and leave for periods of time. However, even in these cases, they hover somewhere around the awareness and can return if the situation requires."

"Sounds crowded."

"It certainly can be if the number of personalities is large. In fact, the larger the number, the more difficult the condition is to manage and the more it impacts daily life for a variety of reasons. One being the anxiety and stress this condition places on the individual, and the other, more critical one being that the personalities represent a specific aspect of the self and do not necessarily have the same moral compass as an integrated person. These are some of the many reasons why the treatment goal is always integration."

Inside my head, the Committee sat together on the couch, listening with interest. Usually only Ruffles attended lectures with me.

"Can someone with DID lead a normal life?" asked my neighbor.

"Absolutely. In fact, there are many people with dissociative disorders holding highly responsible jobs, contributing to society in a variety of professions—the arts, and public service, and so forth—appearing to function normally to coworkers, neighbors, and others with whom they interact daily."

I felt like I did when a random memory of one of those conversations between my mother and my aunts happened across my adult mind. The confusion finally disappeared and I understood everything.

"Human beings are very complicated. The person next to you is weirder than you can possibly imagine," Dr. Lawler said with a mischievous smile. The person sitting next to me laughed along with the rest of the class. I laughed too, but not for the same reason. The guy who asked the question had no idea whom he was sitting next to.

While things were wrapping up, I read Dr. Lawler's bio on the handout. He was a doctor of psychology with postdoc analytic training instead of the formal medical training most psychoanalysts had. He said one of the keys to his work was that he did not categorize his patients; rather, he treated the uniqueness of the individual.

A few days later, I told Sarah about the lecture, and then I forgot about Dr. Lawler. After I finished university and had been working as a waitress for three years, Sarah offered me a choice: Enter into treatment with Dr. Lawler, or find a way to finance my life in New York City without help from her, my mother, or the emergency credit card. I didn't really want to see a shrink, but

Betty Jane refused to give up the financial aid, so I agreed. That was five years ago. Since that time, I've often wondered if Sarah would have held fast to her terms if she'd known it was Betty Jane who made the choice to enter treatment. Betty Jane reasoned that dealing with a quack was much easier than going without.

For five years, Dr. Lawler—or Milton, as I called him—had met with me every Tuesday and Thursday afternoon at four o'clock for fifty minutes. I'd found that Thursdays were usually the better day to spring the tricky stuff on Milton. Lucky for me, I'd lost my job on a Wednesday.

I shifted in my chair as I strained to hear the soft shutting of the other door. Milton's office was set up so that the just-treated were ushered out a different exit, through a hallway, and released a couple of doors down from the office entrance. This maintained anonymity.

I had arrived earlier than usual because somehow I thought waiting in Milton's waiting room would quell the anxiety I felt over how he would respond to the news that I'd lost my job and was considering voice-over training. Waiting only made it worse.

I heard the departure door whine through the wall and said a silent thanks to the maintenance people in this old building who never got around to fixing the squeak. Milton probably told them not to because that creaking complaint meant you were next.

"Holly. Come in," said Milton.

I jumped up and brushed past him, in a rush to get into his office. Then I froze in the middle of the room. My throat opened but no air seemed to get past. "I'm in big trouble," I said.

I heard the door close. I shifted my eyes from the pink armchair to the green sofa. I couldn't decide which I wanted today. New Agers say that pink is love and green is healing. I wondered what color is lobotomy. Milton settled into his chair. It faced both choices. I remained fixed in front of him. I pressed my hand against my chest in an effort to slow my breathing.

"Try the couch," said Milton. How can he always be so calm in a crisis?

I sat down and said, "I got fired and I have a chance to audition as a voice-over talent for an animated show on television."

"Interesting," said Milton, seemingly unfazed. "How did this happen?"

I wanted to throw a pillow at him.

"Betty Jane made friends with someone who works for a producer and the friend taped her talking; then the producer came in and wanted to hear this great Southern voice I do. I didn't know he wanted to hear it, but Betty Jane knew, and he heard it." My tone climbed several octaves, but Milton's face remained unchanged. "Betty Jane did a hostile takeover even though you've told her over and over not to. She started speaking and the producer said they'd pay for classes and give me an audition in a month or two. I don't know when, but soon." My voice trailed there at the end. The changes in Milton's face told me that he'd connected all the dots and knew there were plenty missing.

Milton made a steeple with his fingers. I hated it when he did this because it reminded me of a church, and he knew how I felt about church and anything religious; and he knew I thought this pointed gesture was meant to mock me. But now wasn't the time to bring that up. Milton continued to stare at me.

"I guess you want to know how the first guy heard Betty Jane's voice."

Milton raised his eyebrows and nodded.

Inside my head, Betty Jane sat ramrod straight on the couch, fiddling with her sunflower pin. She never took that damn thing off. She even pinned it to her nighttime negligee so I'd see it when she slept. I expected the nail file to be out at any moment. When Betty Jane wanted to pretend she wasn't paying attention, she attended to her manicure. We all knew she was listening, and she knew we knew, but the game went on anyway. As soon as this conversation got interesting, she'd start filing her nails while that sunflower jeered at me.

"Well, I let her speak from time to time in the diner," I lied sheepishly. Milton's eyebrows shot up a bit farther. *Nice arch,* I thought.

"Pay attention!" snapped Ruffles inside my head.

Oh. I closed my eyes. Ruffles sat on her pillow shoveling in chips at an accelerated pace, which meant she was still mad. Last night I had told her not to blame me for this mess with Walter, Mike, and their TV show. She was just as culpable, because she had spoken in the diner too.

I opened my eyes again. Milton's face remained unchanged. "Okay, well, Betty Jane and sometimes Ruffles . . ." I saw Ruffles narrow her eyes because I'd just thrown her under the bus. Although, if that were truly the case, given her massiveness, the bus would fold up like an accordion on impact if she were lying in front of it. So, technically, I didn't throw her under the bus.

"Goddamn it, Holly," said Ruffles.

See what I mean? Never allowed a private thought.

"Betty Jane started taking over to get better tips. We did get better tips, and, well, I tried to fight it, but I couldn't. Then Ruffles offered to pitch in and it kind of became a competition of who could get the most tips. It helped when I was really behind and I needed to make people laugh or smooth things over. They're both really good at that. And then this guy came in and Betty Jane flirted with him. . . ." My voice trailed off. Betty Jane might be good at making people think what she wanted them to, but I wasn't.

"You were too lazy to work and I saw an opportunity," said Betty Jane. She smiled at me and I swear I saw that sunflower shake and cackle. But she was half-right.

"Holly, how can I trust you when you've been keeping things from me?" said Milton.

"A few minor things," I said. His face remained impassive. "She wouldn't let me tell you." I left out the part where I never tried.

"Holly—"

"Okay, but now I'm in a real mess," I said.

"Let me think a moment," Milton snapped.

For a normal person, snapping conveyed irritation. For Milton, it meant the whistle on the kettle was about to blow. I'd seen him this angry only once, when I brought coffee to a session and then accidentally kicked it over on his pink Oriental rug. Apparently, it was a family heirloom. I thought it was just old. Since then no liquid of any form made it out of the waiting room.

I sat on the couch breathing hard. I wanted Milton to be on my side and help me. I hated it when he was mad at me. It made me feel stretched across a middle that was more like a chasm.

"You have a real dilemma here," said Milton. That brought me back.

"Never one to miss the obvious, are you?" I said. Tears threatened.

"So, what do you propose to do?"

"Well, if I knew, would I be here?" I crossed my arms and sat back.

"Holly, you have placed yourself in a serious predicament," said Milton. His voice at least sounded kind.

"I didn't. Betty Jane did. Now you have to fix it." The tears broke through. I pulled a tissue from the box on the end table and blew my nose.

"Let's start with the most important question," said Milton. "Do you want to do this?"

"*No!*" I said.

"No?" said Milton.

See what I mean? Never one to miss the obvious.

"Well, I did think about it, but only because I got a call from an agent yesterday. Turns out the director made an appointment for me. We're supposed to meet tomorrow."

"Holly!" said Ruffles. For the first time I felt a spark of anger toward her. So what if I lied about the call? So what if there was no meeting? I was tired of being so incapacitated. I wanted a better life. Why didn't she? "Not like this, Holly," said Ruffles. And with that, the spark went out and I felt deflated again.

"Well, it sounds like you're committed," said Milton.

"Not really. I can cancel. I mean, to even try to do this, I'd have to give Betty Jane control." I didn't have to tell Milton how frightening that thought was. I shrugged my shoulders. "It's not really something I can do. Right?" I whispered.

"Well, if it is something you want to do, then let's talk about how you can."

My jaw dropped and hung in an astonished gape. The entire Committee froze inside my head as if put on pause. Milton had just taken an unexpected turn off the road of *no way*, crossed *maybe*, and veered onto the road of *let's see if we can make this happen.*

I inhaled and the Committee sat down. "Uh, okay. But, I mean, how? It is not like the Committee speaks on demand. You know that. They won't even talk to you. Well, all right, some of them will, but *she* doesn't talk to you unless *she* wants to. I've never been able to make her do anything I want. And neither have you." I was referring to the time when Milton, through me, had subtly suggested that Betty Jane ease off just a bit. In response, she eased off and out completely. At first we were all relieved. Her departure felt like having the bullying boss go on vacation. After a couple of days, though, everything went wrong. It reminded me of the summer I graduated from high school—a time of my life I didn't want to relive. Ever. When Betty Jane returned declaring she'd been on a shopping trip, we welcomed her back with open arms. Admittedly, the hugs, kisses, and presents she brought for us made the open-arms part a lot easier. She had something for everyone but Milton. Obviously, the delivery of any gift to Milton would have been a challenge, but that didn't make Betty Jane's slight any less calculated or intentional. They hadn't spoken since that time, though. So, technically, Milton never had to deal with her return.

"Holly, one hurdle at a time," said Milton. Inside my head I saw Ruffles's chip-filled hand hanging midway to her mouth, and I knew she and I had the same thought—Milton actually meant it when he said, "Let's talk about how you can do this."

Milton and I both stared at his finger church. Finally he said, "I have an idea."

"Uh . . ." Unable to speak, I finished my thought with a nod.

"To be a voice-over artist, you need to be able to speak in the Committee's voices on demand, correct?" said Milton.

"Yes."

"Betty Jane controls the Committee, correct?"

"Yes," I said, "she's the chairman. Or chairwoman, as she likes to call herself."

"Then I want to speak with her," said Milton.

"I do not speak to him," said Betty Jane inside my head.

"She won't talk to you," I said.

"Then there is nothing more to discuss." Milton sat back in his chair. "I recommend you cancel the meeting."

"Okay," I said, relieved and awash with guilt over my earlier anger at Ruffles.

"Now, wait just a moment. We are all being too hasty here," drawled Betty Jane inside my head. "'Forgive and forget' is my motto. I have always been happy to speak to Milton. The need just has not arisen until now."

"You're telling me there's been no need to talk to Milton for the past three years?"

"Holly, dear," said Betty Jane sweetly, "you misunderstand and misjudge. I simply did not want to interfere. Besides, Milton never asks for me." She sniffed. Talk about rewriting history.

"Well, he did now," I said. I steeled my body for her takeover. Milton sat observing me. Even though he heard only my side of the conversation, we'd been together long enough for him to understand when a Committee discussion was taking place. He knew I'd convey the particulars to him upon its conclusion.

"Holly," said Betty Jane, "do I have your permission?"

"Milton," I said, "she's changed her mind and she'll talk to you if she has my permission to take over." Milton nodded his head. *He's going Switzerland on this one*, I thought. *He must still feel burned that I let Betty Jane and Ruffles speak without telling him.* My chest ached a bit. I needed Milton on my side and not neutral. This new stance scared me. "Before I do this, though," I said, "what's the deal?"

"I want to discuss a new set of rules with Betty Jane. If she and I can agree on these, then we can consider your taking the job."

"I thought we said cancel? I'm not sure I like this idea."

"Holly," said Milton, "I am going to ask you to trust me." His eyes locked with mine. Milton had not steered me wrong in five years, but I wasn't sure that counted, because based on our lack of progress, technically he hadn't steered me anywhere. "A leap of faith, Holly, that's all I'm asking for."

Well, I was no worse off than when I started with Milton. "Okay," I whispered.

"I want her to speak directly. Please allow her to come forward."

You may, I thought. Then I closed my eyes and let myself drift backward so that Betty Jane could take over. My body straightened and my legs crossed demurely at the ankle.

"Why, Milton," came out of my mouth in a breathy Southern drawl.

"Ah, Betty Jane."

My chin did a dainty drop.

I sat on the Committee's couch inside my head and fingered the nail file Betty Jane had left while the kind of dread you feel when you realize you've just made a bad decision but you're powerless to take it back spread throughout my body.

"Let's get straight to the point, shall we?" said Milton.

I heard Ruffles say, "Why did you do that?" through an angry mouthful of chips.

My eyes narrowed. Betty Jane giggled and from my mouth she said, "Because she wanted to." From my vantage point on the Committee's couch, I saw Milton's brow crease. A snicker escaped my lips. "That was for my fat friend in here." My hand tapped my head. "Certainly not for you, Milton."

"I understand you want Holly to be a voice-over artist?" said Milton sternly.

"Now, Milton," came out of my mouth in a silky Southern tone, "I recall a very dull lecture at NYU in which you said that people with dissociative disorders can work and function, hold down jobs, and attend to their daily lives like normal people. Why,

I only remember it because my neighbor left the house without a shower." My hand smoothed my hair. "The smell overpowered me so that I could not sleep like I normally would during a tedious lecture." My mouth smiled. I didn't remember any body odor and wondered why Betty Jane needed an excuse other than the truth for the reason she had listened to that lecture. "Now, if you tell me that I—or, I mean, Holly—is not ready for a real job, then it might be time to start questioning the job you are doing." *Here we go.* I had to hand it to her, though, because I'd never have the guts to say something like that to Milton, even though the thought had crossed my mind. More than once.

"Betty Jane," said Milton, "if we are even going to discuss the possibility of Holly pursuing this opportunity, then the first thing we have to agree upon is a new set of rules."

Inside my head, we all waited for Betty Jane to tell Milton what he could do with his rules. "And what would those be?" she said.

Milton was not surprised by her response. He didn't miss a beat. "For starters, you and the rest of the Committee will have to limit yourselves to taking over and speaking through Holly only to train as a voice-over artist and in therapy," said Milton. "Only in these two places. Under no other circumstances may you take over. Do you understand?"

"I do," Betty Jane said with satisfaction.

"And if she gets the job, this agreement extends to include work. So, you would initially be limited to training and therapy and, if all goes well, ultimately training, work, and therapy."

The corners of my mouth dropped to an irritated line.

"What about the other voices?" I asked Betty Jane from inside my head.

"A beached whale, a broken-down Vietnam vet with a drug

problem, and a faceless boy?" she said out of my mouth. Milton's head tilted askance. "Nobody wants to hear from them. And how can a mute be a voice-over artist?" She laughed.

"Holly, if you need my voice, you can have it," said Ruffles inside my head. "I think that goes for the rest of us."

"Well, well, look at you, my fat little saint," said Betty Jane. "You forget that I decide who speaks. Me. Not you. Not them. Me. Nobody will speak unless I deem it so. I am in charge."

"I can surmise from the words coming out of Holly's mouth that there is a discussion about the other voices?" said Milton. My head nodded. "Let me be very clear with you, Betty Jane." My body went taut with anger. "This agreement covers all the voices. Under the new terms, you will not decide if they may speak for training, work, or in therapy—or under any circumstances, for that matter—any longer. If any voice, including the Silent One, is needed, Holly may have it. If she or I request anyone, they may speak. You may continue to rule the Committee, but you will no longer decide who speaks." Milton's face was implacable, the tension in the room thick and the silence like fog. "Do you understand me, Betty Jane?" said Milton.

"Yes." My voice sounded bored. "May I communicate my terms?"

Terms? Ruffles and I cast worried glances at each other. I should have known. I wished I could smoke in the Committee's house, but that "dirty habit" was absolutely verboten since Betty Jane had moved in twelve years ago.

Milton waved his hand for her to go ahead, as if he'd anticipated this too. Betty Jane rattled off a list of demands that rivaled Santa's entire Christmas catalog. Top on it was no more donating to charity the clothes and shoes we bought. I had one closet. At the rate at which Betty Jane made me buy stuff, I had to clear it out on a regular basis. And Goodwill picked up. Along with clothes and shoes, Betty Jane wanted a maid, a car service, me to stop smoking, respect, lipstick, regular facials, hand cream, face cream, trips to the Bahamas, a better mattress. Then she said I deserved nothing in exchange for my largesse because having her was more gift than anyone could ever have or expect. I sat stupefied.

Milton held up his hand. My mouth paused midstipulation. "If Holly gives you what you want, then in addition to limiting your speaking, I have two more binding terms that you must agree to." My head nodded for Milton to proceed.

"First, you must agree to never allow yourself more power than Holly has."

Betty Jane considered this for a moment. "I would be equal, though? And I still control the Committee?"

"You may have control of the Committee, but you may never have more power than Holly," said Milton.

Betty Jane considered this for a moment and then said, "I will agree to that." I wished I could read her thoughts with the same facility that she read mine. But it didn't work that way. "And in exchange, I need the entire Committee to pitch in and get us this job so I can finally live in the style I have dictated—and deserve, I might add."

Deserve, my ass. And does she really just want a few facials and some nice clothes?

"We have not discussed the final term," said Milton.

"Oh?"

"You and the rest of the Committee must agree to always resolve any conflicts in therapy whenever Holly makes the request. I will not support your endeavor if this particular condition is not accepted."

"Is that all?" said Betty Jane. My voice sounded bored again.

"Then to be crystal clear, in exchange for the frippery you've requested, you and the others agree to my terms?" said Milton.

"Yes." Betty Jane sniffed.

"Okay, then let Holly come back."

I resumed control, suddenly aware of the scary side effect that accompanied this new direction—the demanding social aspect this line of work would certainly require. "Milton, how am I going to handle the social part if the Committee is so restricted?"

Milton's eyes became compassionate. The fear cracking my voice would have been hard for an untrained seal to miss.

"Holly, one step at a time. You've always said you excel at learning. Well, then you can apply yourself to learning how to handle the social aspects—"

"I didn't mean this kind of learning," I said.

"Remember, a leap of faith is all I am asking for," said Milton.

Milton's requested leap of faith felt more like a jump out of an airplane wearing a parachute packed by Betty Jane.

{ 4 }

The following Monday, I stood on Avenue A wrestling with the buttons on my blouse as my hair whipped across my face. I had allotted plenty of time to make my appointment with Brenda Barry, the agent Mike recommended. Then I lingered too long over coffee and cigarettes. Now, half-dressed and late, I'd lost the cushion I needed to get Betty Jane on public transportation, our only option under my current financial circumstances.

I popped the last button through the hole and clipped my hair back. Times Square, the location of Brenda's office, wasn't getting any closer. May as well face the music.

The street was dotted with enough people to make it a giant slalom run to the subway station. But what did I expect? New York City never offered deserted streets. I glanced at my watch, drew in a deep breath.

"Ready. Set. Go!" said Sarge inside my head. He waved the green starter flag.

On cue, Ruffles took over the live inner-cranium commentary.

"And she's off, rounding the corner of First and First." Her steady and even voice helped me find my race rhythm. "Old lady laden with shopping bags to the left," said Ruffles.

Sarge waved a yellow caution flag. I swooped down and veered right. The familiar refrain of crunching chips kept perfect time with each footfall.

"Yes." Sarge raised a victory fist. I pressed forward. Betty Jane stayed silent, like a crocodile waiting for the exact right moment to strike.

"Two bogeys, eleven o'clock and three o'clock," said Ruffles inside my head. A flash of yellow skittered across my mind as I feinted left and then right. I turned the corner of Houston and Second. The street appeared empty. My lucky day. I moved faster. The Broadway subway stop stretched before me like a terminus beacon. *I'm going to make it.* Sarge reached for the red checked flag. My thigh muscles pulled. Shins screamed. Taking short breaths in through my nose and out through my mouth, I crossed the finish line and entered the station, skidding. I got the caution flag as I teetered on the stair. I heard the collective intake of breath inside my head as I stuck out my leg for balance and leaned back, followed by a collective exhale as my right foot and then my left hit the stairs.

I grabbed the handrail to steady myself. "Oh, my stars," screamed Betty Jane inside my head. "Do you realize how many unwashed, germ-ridden hands have been on that railing?" I snatched my hand back, hoping to get to and through the ticket line without incident. "Disgusting," she snarled. "I refuse to ride the subway. I will not." Her Southern drawl felt like a bad hangover pounding against my temples.

"Until we are making money, we have to ride the subway," I said. The man in front of me turned around. *Must be a tourist*, I thought. Betty Jane opened her mouth and I wished for a mental umbrella to protect me from the litany about to rain down. I waited for my turn while she started at the top. Experience told me that Betty Jane's monologue would end with a bad job, no money, and the indecent and inhumane conditions she was forced to live in. Our first vacation should be to a third-world country.

"Christ, I have no time for this!" I yelled. The man in front of me whipped his head around again. The normally bored station attendant craned his head from behind the Plexiglas to get a glimpse of standard New York City crazy while he completed the transaction with my obstacle to the subway station booth, who made his purchase and walked off. My turn. The station attendant glared at me. My stomach did a fifteen-floor elevator drop and I floated weightless.

"She's going down," said Sarge inside my head. Different emotions blinked across his face as he ran forward. "Holly, you know the rules. I can't take over." I hovered somewhere between in control and in the Committee's living room. "Stand up, soldier!" The force of Sarge's voice put me back in control.

"We'll take a taxi home. Okay?"

"Whatever, lady," said the attendant.

"Oh, agony," shrieked Betty Jane inside my head. Then she stalked out of the Committee's room. At least she's gone, I thought.

"Four dollars on my MetroCard, please." I passed the money and the card through. Although it felt like walking through quicksand in cement boots, I made it to the turnstile, swiped my card, and crossed.

I exited at Times Square and scanned for a street sign to get my bearings. The gold front of 1516 Broadway was to my left. I walked through Brenda's door ten minutes late and sweating even though it was January.

"Holly Miller?" said the receptionist. I nodded. "I'll let Brenda know you're here."

At our first meeting, Brenda and Betty Jane came together like soul mates reuniting after several lifetimes apart. To this day, I can't put my finger on the source of the attraction. Was it Brenda's expensive clothes? Her dismissive attitude? Her unbridled greed? Probably all three.

"Do you have any idea what a lucky break you got?" Brenda said. Her legs were crossed, with one foot drawn back while the other waved like a cat's tail. I expected Betty Jane to make a cutting remark from the privacy of my head. She sat listening, and her lack of reaction unnerved me. "I understand Walter's PA found you in a restaurant?" Brenda laughed, but the sound was more like a harrumph.

"She's good," said Ruffles inside my head. I nodded.

Brenda arched an eyebrow at me. I felt like she knew I wasn't nodding at her. "Imagine that. A virtual unknown." Brenda turned the page of whatever she was reading.

Betty Jane wrenched me backward. I landed stunned on the Committee's living room floor as she made the seamless transition to control. "A virtual unknown?" The words slid out of my mouth in Betty Jane's silky Southern drawl. My eyebrow arched. "Not for long."

"Holly," said Brenda, "you don't have to do your voices here."

"Just practicing," said Betty Jane while I fumed inside my head.

"She can't take over whenever she feels like it," said Ruffles.

"I know." I stood up in the Committee's living room. "She's not supposed to do this. Milton made a deal. There are rules." As we vented inside my head about Betty Jane's peremptory manner, we missed half the conversation she was having with Brenda.

"Pay attention," interrupted Sarge. I noticed my body stood upright with my right arm raised in the air.

All those years the patrons thought I was funny, but it was Betty Jane's performances that went from their lips to the ears of God in the form of Walter. Now we were in this fancy Times Square office sitting across from a woman who made me feel like a puppet dangling on fate's strings while Betty Jane moved my body around with confidence. She wasn't dangling on anyone's strings.

Even though Brenda appeared far away and slightly out of focus, I felt her studying me as Betty Jane sat my body down, composed and in control, without losing eye contact. Inside my head, I pinched the palm of my hand to see if this was a dream. I half expected to wake up carrying two eggs over medium with a side of bacon to some sleepy patron waiting with coffee.

Brenda uncrossed her legs and pressed her hands on her desk. Those handprints would show immediately. I felt Betty Jane suppress her germ phobia with a shudder.

"Okay, here it is." Brenda's voice was now brusque and businesslike. "According to the studio, you have two months to get yourself prepared. You will immediately begin private training for acting, speech, using the microphone, and everything else that goes along with voice-over." Brenda waved her hand, blotting out part of the Times Square news ticker running across its midair track outside her office window. "The training will take about eight hours a day. On your free days, you will do auditions for the practice."

"How are we going to pay for that?" Ruffles said to me. I knew Betty Jane wouldn't ask, because it was vulgar to talk about money, which was ironic when you saw how not vulgar it was for her to spend it. I steeled myself to fight her for control. Sarge stopped me with a hand on my arm.

Betty Jane cleared my throat and tilted my head farther to the left.

"The studio pays, of course," said Brenda. Talk about your telepathic communication. These two were soul mates. "For the training only. Here's your schedule." Brenda stood and handed me a typed list of courses. "You start tomorrow."

As Betty Jane scanned it, I sat on the Committee's couch taking in the full weight of what this meant. I'd have to convince Sarah to get my parents to cover my living expenses for a few months—and I wasn't even sure I would actually succeed in the end.

"Auditioning for plays is good practice as well. It's free and will help you get the hang of speaking out loud as different characters. You can do that in your spare time."

"What spare time?" said Ruffles inside my head.

"You be quiet," snapped Betty Jane. She was in control, so the words came out of my mouth.

"Excuse me?" said Brenda.

"Nothing, nothing," said Betty Jane. She pressed my hand shyly to my mouth.

"Okay." Brenda shook her head. "In a month the studio will do a preliminary audition. If all goes well, they'll fund your second month of training."

"She said two months. Betty Jane, give me back control."

"And what if I exceed their expectations in that preliminary audition?" said Betty Jane.

What have I done? This thought started looping in continuous motion inside my head.

"You have confidence," said Brenda. "I'll definitely give you that." Betty Jane nodded demurely. "All right, say you do—and as much as I'd love that, because I'd start getting paid, you probably won't—but if you do, then in a month's time we'll get a standard SAG contract. This will cover the particulars: rates, how many roles, and so forth. Usually for the basic session fee, an actor can do two roles, plus a third for a small increase. If you do four roles, the 'count' starts over and you get paid the basic session fee again." Brenda rattled this off like she said it twenty times a day.

"Does anyone do only cartoon work?" asked Betty Jane.

What is she up to? Ruffles read my thought and shook her head.

"Holly," said Brenda. Her hands were on the glass again. I would come to recognize this as her pay-attention stance. "No one limits themselves exclusively to animated voice work. This must come as a shock to someone who idolizes Nancy Cartwright."

"Who?"

"*The Simpsons*?"

My head shook slightly.

"Famous animated show? I understand you promised Walter you'd make sure *The Neighborhood* was more popular."

Oh, my God, she didn't.

My head shook slightly again. "I do not fill my time with TV," said Betty Jane, brushing invisible lint off my pants. Well, the rest of us did. How could she make a declaration like, "My TV show will be more famous than *The Simpsons*"?

"I thought Mike said . . ." muttered Brenda. She inhaled. "At any rate, anyone who dreams of making it big in the field has to do other things. Besides, it's the other work that's more plentiful and often more lucrative."

"What other work?" said Betty Jane.

"Announcing, film dubbing, radio commercials, voice-overs for TV commercials, et cetera. One show, one cannot a living make." *Okay, Yoda.* Ruffles and I giggled and Brenda yammered on, ". . . you need to have a cell phone, pager, voice mail—every possible form of communication available—so I can reach you."

"I don't want to be that busy," I said to Ruffles inside my head.

"We can start as soon as you have the work," said Betty Jane. We let out a collective groan. None of us had expected that we would do more than this one job. Obviously, Betty Jane had other ideas.

Brenda's face appeared perplexed for a moment. She shook it off and a perfunctory smile crossed her lips. "Let's not get ahead of ourselves here, Holly. I need to see if you can even do the work, and after that what your range is."

"Oh, my," said Betty Jane breathlessly. "Range?"

"For most actors the range is about fifteen voices," Brenda said with the resignation one feels when they realize the virtual unknown in front of them knows virtually nothing.

"Oh, is that all? I can do four. Only four. But I do them well. That is a promise," said Betty Jane.

"Okay, then. We'll talk." And with that, I was dismissed.

Betty Jane ceded control as I shut the door to Brenda's office and headed down the hall. "How dare you take over like that," I said.

"You broke the rules," said Sarge sternly inside my head.

"I am guiding our destiny and you two have the nerve to complain?" said Betty Jane. "Who do you think you are?" She dimissed us with her hand.

"We are going straight to Milton," I said. Betty Jane answered my threat by disappearing through the Committee's front door.

"No need," said Sarge. "The agreement was that I enforce the rules."

"Well, let me applaud you on a job well-done." I clapped my hands.

Sarge was unmoved. "Just like in combat, Holly, you discover your enemy's intentions before acting."

"Next time," I said, gesturing dramatically with open palms, "just ask. Any one of us could have told you what Betty Jane's intentions were. Even him." I tapped my head where I thought the Silent One was sitting inside. "Of course, he'd answer by clasping his hands in prayer—"

"Holly, two o'clock. Look sharp!" said Sarge. I stopped short. A bike messenger stood slightly to my right. His startled face told me he'd taken in the whole exchange. Well, one side of it.

"Let me," said Ruffles. Sarge nodded. *I guess today's a rules holiday.* I relaxed. She took over. "I'm an actress," Ruffles said. Then she flirted with the freedom of a fat woman who knows that the object of her attention will never view her as an object of desire. The elevator arrived. Ruffles stepped in. The messenger smiled and waved at her as the elevator door closed.

When we got home, Sarge called a meeting. I lay back on my bed and entered the Committee's house.

"Sit," barked Sarge at all of us. We all looked over at Betty Jane stretched out on her bed, nail file in hand. Hers was the only space with enough room to accommodate all five of us.

"I told you, sit!" thundered Sarge. Betty Jane slid over and we all scrambled onto her bed.

"People. We have a mission. Sixty days to complete it. And I am the *only* combat-ready soldier in this unit." Sarge articulated each word, his voice a gruff tone I'd never heard before. "For the next eight weeks, you shit birds will follow the routine."

Betty Jane gasped. "Do not use that kind of language in front of the Boy." Ironically, the Boy was the only one unfazed by this Sarge with chest muscles straining against his white T-shirt.

Sarge pointed his finger right at Betty Jane. "If you want to succeed, you will not interrupt me. You will not question me. I am First Shirt here, and my orders will be followed to the letter." Betty Jane opened her mouth. Sarge waved her off. "To the letter! Do you hear me?"

We all nodded.

"When I ask a question, you answer, 'HUA.' Heard, understood, and acknowledged. Do you hear me?"

A feeble, "HUA," sounded in the room.

"Say it like you mean it," said Sarge.

"HUA," we said louder.

"We'll work on that. Now, SOP will be a weekly plan with nightly sit rep to make sure we are on target. We get up daily at zero-dark-thirty. We will not be late for classes or meetings. We will take public transportation without any backtalk. We will pull together and we will conquer this mountain. Together. I want to see assholes and elbows every day until D-day."

I got so lost in the lingo, I didn't hear the rest of the details. Later I listened while the Boy explained to Ruffles that swearing didn't bother him, *shit birds* were slobs, *first shirt* meant sergeant, *zero-dark-thirty* was really early in the morning, and *assholes and elbows* meant we'd better be working really hard.

We used my World Wildlife Fund calendar to count down to D-day. The panda hanging on the tree watched every night when the Boy crossed off the day gone by with a red pen. After a week, we were running like a well-oiled machine, down to the hospital corners on our beds.

The task Sarge couldn't prepare me for was how to convince Sarah to get me the funds I needed to cover my new line of work. I had enough money to get me halfway through the second week of private training. By the end of the first week, the fantasy of being a voice-over artist was starting to merge with reality. It was too late for her to tell me I couldn't do this, because I knew I could.

I left Sarah a message asking her to call me at seven o'clock in the evening my time. The phone rang just as I turned the key in the dead bolt. The lock snapped easily and I opened the door.

I pirouetted over Cat One crouching in the bathroom, stepped into the hallway, and reached for the phone. "Hello?"

"Hey, it's me," said Sarah.

"Hey, thanks for calling me," I said.

"Why have you been avoiding me?"

"I lost my job—"

"Oh, Holly—"

"No, it's actually a good thing. I'm in training now to become a voice-over artist."

"A what?"

"A voice-over artist. You know. They do voices for cartoons and stuff." I waited for her to respond. "I started private training a week ago and the part is the lead voice. Well, I don't have it yet. I have to audition. But I think I can get it."

"Hang on," said Sarah. "You're in private training? To be a cartoon? How?"

"Well, I speak into a microphone, they record it, and drop it over animation."

"Holly, I know what a voice-over artist does. I asked how you got the job."

"Well, like I said, I don't have the job yet. I have to audition for it. But one of my customers put me in touch with a TV producer, and he liked my voice and offered to pay for my training."

"Your voice? Are you getting paid? I don't understand."

"I don't get paid, so I need financial help until I get this job," I said.

"Wait a minute. Voice-over work requires several different voices," said Sarah.

I didn't respond.

"You heard me, Holly. Several voices. To do this, you have to speak in several voices. You are going to use that Committee"— she spit out the word—"to do this job, aren't you?"

"Uh . . ." I opened my window one inch and then, lying back on the bed, I felt around the night table for my cigarettes. I waited like an indignant child put in the corner for a time-out because he dared to assert himself. I tried to blow the smoke out the small crack in the window. My building was nonsmoking. I swore to the landlord that I didn't smoke. I said, "I never touch cigarettes. They're evil, bad." The few times he dropped by I'd told him I'd had a party the night before and my now former friends smoked in my apartment even though I asked them not to.

"You need to talk to Milton about this. He'll put a stop to it," Sarah said.

I got up and paced the cold hardwood floors, waving my cigarette, hoping the smoke would dissipate, or at least fly backward to the bedroom and out the window. Finally I said, "I did. He set up a new contract with Betty Jane."

"He *what*?" said Sarah. "How is this facilitating integration?" I'd always let Sarah and Milton believe I was on board with the whole idea of integration. But I still hadn't decided what I wanted. I only knew that the thought of life without the Committee made my world go dark. "Well, I don't care what Milton says; I forbid this, Holly, I forbid it."

Sorry, Queen Elizabeth.

"In fact, I think it's time you moved home, Holly."

"Why? Because I want to do something with my life?"

"I want you to do something with your life too, Holly, but be realistic. Doing the job you are proposing is impossible as far as I am concerned."

"Well, then you'll be happy to know that I am doing it, Sarah. I am doing it." Sarah remained silent. "And, besides, Milton said this is the only way to integrate the Committee." Sarge did tell me to treat this like a covert op and use any means necessary to secure the funds.

"How?" she snapped. "I can't believe I'm paying for this."

"The Father. You said the Father pays."

"Well, if you want to do this, then you call him and ask for the money. I won't do it."

"Give me his number then." I prayed she was bluffing. She'd told me they were in regular contact since she got married. Sarah had believed his paltry, overcome-with-grief, felt-trapped, want-to-make-up-everything, please-forgive-me excuse. I believed leopards never changed their spots. I didn't want to risk seeing those spots for this opportunity.

The door buzzer sounded. I stood up, reached around the doorjamb, and found the intercom. "Babe, it's me." It was Peter. Perfect timing.

"Sarah, Peter's here." I pushed down on the buttons until the door buzzer sounded.

"I heard," she said. "We're not through with this conversation. I want you to explain to me how you are going to do this." That explanation would definitely take longer than the three flights of stairs the banned boyfriend was now climbing.

"Are you going to make me call the Father?" I held my breath.

"Call me tomorrow and we'll see. I can't believe Milton is going along with this," said Sarah. Then I heard a dial tone.

If Sarah was going to abandon my fate to my father because I'd made a decision she didn't like, she would have said good-bye.

I heard a knock. I stepped into the bathroom, kicked the gravel from the cat box under the claw-foot tub, stepped out of the bathroom, and opened the door. Peter tilted his head to the left and smiled at me.

You might wonder how a woman with five voices in her head can manage a relationship. I found out several years ago in therapy, when I started using my boyfriends as fodder for discussion as well as diversion from the things I wanted to avoid, like the Committee and whatever they kept hidden in the corner closet: the closet I didn't go into ever, under any circumstances. Everyone should know their relationship patterns. Mine was an uncanny ability to attract men who wanted a relationship based on projection instead of intimacy. Then I sabotaged the relationship when the blinders came off. Operation Destroy My Relationship had been well under way before my thirtieth birthday. Now the voice-over training was giving me and Peter a last-minute stay of execution.

Turned out training to be one of Walter Torrent's voice-over artists included a number of social engagements. Peter had immediately volunteered to escort me to the first one. It was no surprise that he did a great job. When Peter and I first met, he was at the peak of his transformation from an ascetic lifestyle and two years in seminary to his own version of nihilism, which included beautiful clothes, beautiful girls, and many late nights in clubs. Even though his studies forced him to limit the partying, he hadn't lost his touch. With Peter as my date, I was able to hang back, mute, while he charmed everyone at the event, and then deftly got us out when he noticed my fake, flat smile in response to being called "our Little Waitress" one too many times. Given that I couldn't rely on any Committee members to help me through the social engagements, I didn't question Peter's motivation, or mine.

"Holly?" he asked. I gazed deeply into his eyes, hoping to find a glimpse of that rush I used to feel at the sight of him. All I noticed was the different blues of his irises. "Holly?" My thoughts receded as I smiled at Peter. He put his hands on my cheeks and straightened my head. Then he kissed me on the nose and said, "You ready?"

I still felt nothing. "Yeah," I said, stepping onto the landing and pulling the front door toward me.

"Do you need a jacket? Your keys?"

"Oh, right." I stepped backward and glanced furtively around.

"On the bed," said Ruffles inside my head.

I leaned over to grab my bag. I felt Peter's eyes on my double-wide ass sticking up in the air. No amount of starving made my butt any smaller. My only hope was large-pocket jeans, for all the good they did. I snatched the shoulder strap of my bag and turned, expecting to find a look of disgust on Peter's face, but instead it was blank and unreadable.

"What?" I snapped.

He shook his head and muttered, "Great, it's going to be one of those nights." And then I hoped we could get to the end of the block without having a big fight.

Sarah drove a much harder bargain than the studio that might hire me. Her terms were funds for one month. If I didn't secure the training funding for month two, I had to move back to California for treatment under her watchful eye. When I agreed to this, Ruffles said, "Holly, for God's sake, call the Father."

I buckled down instead. No distractions. We were all in training for our lives, Betty Jane most of all. She had to put her money where her mouth was, literally, while the rest of us did everything we could to make sure this endeavor didn't become a fool's errand.

After a month of private training, I met Brenda again. She came around her desk and hugged me when I walked through her office door. "Holly, sit down." She pointed at the chair and then sat back on the edge of her desk. *Get the Windex.* "All your teachers are raving about your work."

Inside my head, Sarge raised his arms, signaling a touchdown. Ruffles clapped and the Boy jumped up and down. Betty Jane remained calm, but a tiny smirk danced at the corner of her mouth.

"The studio decided to forgo the preliminary audition and wants you in tomorrow for the real deal. They'll send a car at eight o'clock."

I was dressed and waiting in the lobby of my building at seven forty-five. At exactly eight o'clock a shining black Town Car pulled up, ready to take me to the proverbial dance. Inside my head, I had a woman who was determined to be the Southern belle of the ball. As the front door to my apartment building shut behind me, I heard Betty Jane whisper, "I have arrived."

I watched the city pass as the car cruised along to Chelsea Piers, where we were taping the show. I had learned from Brenda that it was unusual to do an animated show in New York, but Mike's stature as a director made it possible. He wanted to be in New York; we were in New York. Lucky me. I wasn't thin enough to move to Los Angeles. Anyway, constant sunshine depressed me.

When we pulled into the piers, the driver rolled down his window and said, "Audition for *The Neighborhood*." I rolled down my window.

"Which part?" said the guard.

"The star," I said with a smile. I alternated between feeling embarrassed about my comment and the warm glow from Betty Jane's nod of approval.

The receptionist told me to have a seat. Mike Davey would be out in a moment. I dropped my bag on the chair next to me and opened it. I wanted to make sure I had all my highlighters, water, perfume, and, of course, two rolls of Charmin toilet paper.

I had to carry Charmin with me wherever I went. This was one of Betty Jane's rules. Only Charmin. Nothing else. My options were to bring the toilet paper or never be able to use a bathroom that didn't stock Charmin. This narrowed my choices to my apartment or my mother's house.

I felt a hand lightly touch my shoulder. "Hello, Holly."

I turned to see Mike's smiling face. My eyes lit up and I smiled back at him. Walter appeared behind Mike. I extended my smile to him. He didn't return it. The corners of my mouth dropped as fear nipped at the outer corners of my eyes.

"Make sure our Little Waitress is ready for the suits," Walter said to Mike. He walked away, tapping his watch.

The suits?

"How've you been? Did you enjoy the training?"

"Yeah," I said shyly.

"I, for one, am not a fan of any formal acting lessons. Training on the job is enough for someone who has a natural talent," said Mike.

"Oh—"

"Voice-over classes are good because you can learn technique, how to work on a mic, how to use your voice. But as soon as some teacher starts messing with your acting instincts, the next thing, you're worrying about doing something wrong. I say the best and easiest way is to go strictly by instinct. Ad-lib a little bit if the spirit moves you. Don't be tied totally to the script."

I nodded.

Mike led me by the elbow to a door down the hall. Before he opened it, he said, "We've auditioned a good pool of talent, so the competition is stiff."

The room was stuffed with at least thirty people. Mike told me these were other actors, writers, plus a few interns and hangers-on. Walter and a couple of guys stood over by the wall talking. Judging by their attire, I guessed that these guys were the unexplained "suits."

All was quiet in my head. Though she wouldn't admit it, I think even Betty Jane was a bit unnerved.

"Those are the network guys," whispered Mike, pointing over at Walter. "They wanted to see what they've been paying for, for the last thirty days; one of them has his heart set on a woman we auditioned yesterday." His honesty made me understand why my mother spent her life avoiding the truth and taught me to do the same. I smiled but I wanted to scream, *This is not helping me.*

"It's always a little stressful when they're here," said Mike.

"Uh?"

"They have approval rights over who we choose for the lead."

"I thought Walter—"

"Let's get started, shall we?" said Walter.

Mike led me into the sound booth and pointed at an empty music stand with an individual microphone in front of it. Then he introduced me and I waved at everyone. The console on the other side of the glass was crowded with Walter, the suits, Mike, the writers, and a whole bunch of other people with already forgotten names.

"Are there always this many people at a recording?" I whispered to the guy next to me.

"Not usually. But Walter has a lot riding on you, and everyone is here to see if his 'Little Waitress' . . . " He paused, and I suppressed a facial expression. "Everyone wants to see if Walter's 'Little Waitress' passes muster."

I nodded.

"No pressure," he said. I didn't hear anything comforting in his voice. I scanned the other faces behind the mics and music stands and found nothing warm on any of them.

"Let's pick up at the beginning," said Mike through the talkback.

I closed my eyes and thought, *Please don't let me be humiliated,* as I floated backward and Betty Jane took over.

We read past line fourteen and it was finally time for Violet. I read the script through Betty Jane's eyes. Violet had a good two pages' worth of bantering with a couple of other characters. After the first few lines, it was clear Betty Jane was in the zone. Mike hadn't indicated a stopping point, so the dialogue continued. My wandering thoughts wondered if he had done that to help me. Then I had a guilty thought about Peter. Betty Jane faltered a bit. *Focus, Holly.* Betty Jane found her rhythm again in time to do her last couple of lines.

"Oh, agony!" exclaimed Betty Jane as she threw out my arms. *What's she doing? That's not in the script.*

"Cut!"

Walter, Mike, the writers, and the suits huddled outside the booth. One of the writers pointed at the paper in front of him. *Oh, shit. Do we wait? Should we go out?* I couldn't ask any of these questions because Betty Jane was still in control. Mike motioned through the glass. I stood in the Committee's living room and then felt the transition between me and Betty Jane. Once back in control, I blinked my eyes and squeezed my toes in my shoes. I had read somewhere that this brings an errant spirit back into the body. I didn't feel any different.

I pushed the door in front of me. It felt impossibly heavy, but I knew that under other circumstances it would probably be featherlight.

"You changed the script," accused one of the writers. Mike shushed him.

"Oh," I said pensively, "it just felt like how Violet would end a conversation. Was it okay that I did that?"

"It was inspired," said the suit who had his heart set on some-one else. I'll say it was inspired. Betty Jane ended every conversation she didn't like with this phrase. As if she were Jesus on the cross. "Love it. Go with it. Write it in. Hire the waitress. Walter, lunch?"

Walter nodded. "Get her a pop shield," he said, and ushered the two suits out the door.

{ 5 }

We have the contract. You start in a month," said Brenda.

I hung up the phone, switched on music, and danced around my apartment while everyone, including Betty Jane, did the same inside my head. I stopped when I noticed Cats One and Two crouching warily against the wall.

Sarge granted a week's liberty, and I called Sarah to tell her the news. Brenda called me the next day with a booking for the following day. So much for liberty, but I tell you it felt good to earn enough money to pay my bills while I waited to start work on *The Neighborhood*.

The first Monday in March that same Town Car picked me up. This time, when we pulled into the Chelsea Piers, the guard said, "Well, all right, you got the part."

"Holly Miller for *The Neighborhood*," I said to the receptionist.

"Everyone's in the conference room." I didn't move. Mike had called me the night before to tell me how the day would go.

But his instructions didn't include the location of the conference room.

The receptionist looked up. "Are you the waitress?" I nodded. "They'll never let you forget it," she said.

"Looks like you won't either." I froze. I couldn't believe that had come out of my mouth.

The receptionist's face changed. Her new look wasn't one of compassion. "Down the hall, make a right."

"Thanks," I said.

"Yeah, good luck," she said in a bored tone.

Mike said it was customary to do a table reading to review the script before taping. This got everyone on the same page and saved time later.

The table reading took place in a wood-paneled room with a window that looked out over the Hudson. The table itself was big enough to seat at least thirty people. Crowded around it were the same people who'd been at my audition. I scanned the room and saw Walter and the suits standing in the same spot they'd held four weeks ago. Did they sell tickets?

Mike waved me to a chair. "No need for introductions. You all met Holly last month."

I sat down and pulled out my script and a packet of high-lighters. I'd read that highlighting the script as the director read through it was a good way to give yourself visual cues. One of the writers smiled at me. Highlighter brownie points helped me relax. A little.

Mike read through the lines that were planned for that day. He described the action, how the characters moved, where they were (sneaking around a corner . . . shouting from the third floor to someone below), so that in session, when we taped the action, we'd have a good idea of the characters' environment.

After we read through the script, we moved into the sound booth. Betty Jane and I transitioned and she took her place in front of the music stand in the center. I watched the other voice actors spread out their scripts while Betty Jane neatly stacked hers so that the paper fell together in a tidy rectangle. The voice-over tutor had told me over and over again to spread out the script, because many good recordings were ruined by rustling paper. Betty Jane knew this.

I stood up, ready to take over and fix the script.

She didn't cede control. Then I remembered what she had said to me in the car earlier. "Why, Holly, my place on the pedestal is a right. Not a privilege." I sat back down on the Committee's couch.

We waited for the engineer to roll tape and slate. I'd learned that this helped him locate the proper takes when it came time to edit. Betty Jane didn't have any lines on the take, but everyone still followed the other actors' lines in the script.

My hand turned the page at line eighteen.

"Cut!" yelled Mike through the talkback.

Everyone waited in the booth for me to adjust my script. They didn't know that inside my head we were all praying that Betty Jane would do it. She smiled and adjusted her hair instead.

"Someone get Holly's script set up. I don't want her turning pages during the recording."

Finally, the voice actor next to me reached over and spread out the papers while Betty Jane stood and watched. This was not how I wanted to start out my new life. Sarge brought a barf bucket over. Sometimes having your thoughts immediately known wasn't so bad.

"*The Neighborhood*, scene one, take two," said the engineer through the talkback.

"Action," said Mike.

We did twelve takes of that scene before Mike was happy.

When Betty Jane finally got her turn, she nailed her lines on the first try. We still had to do four more takes to get exactly what Mike wanted from the other actors.

"This is the last take for the day; make it a good one," said Mike. I looked at my watch. Four hours had passed.

When I first saw the schedule, I thought, *Four hours, a breeze.* I was used to being on my feet for a lot longer than that. At the end of the four hours, we'd done at least a hundred takes. My back hurt and my legs ached, and I wondered if this was all I'd ever remember about working as a voice-over artist, since I'd always be on the Committee's couch while Betty Jane stood in front of the microphone.

As I packed my stuff, one actor said begrudgingly, "Good work today." The others just whispered to one another, and one actually pointed at me when I exited the booth.

"Let's use one through ten from the second take and thirty through fifty from take six, but I want to edit in the pickup of line thirty from take four," said Mike.

"Got it," said the engineer.

Mike turned and walked me out the door.

"Not bad for your first day. We got through about six hours of work in four hours, thanks to you."

"How much did we actually do?" I said.

"Fifteen minutes' worth of dialogue, I'd say."

"That's all?"

Mike laughed. "You'll get used to the pace."

What pace? After my first day, it felt like an exhausting crawl.

"Hey, sorry about the script. I mean, uh, I knew, but, uh—"

"Rookie mistake." Mike held up his hand to stop my rambling apology.

My cell phone rang. I opened my bag, exposing my rolls of Charmin. We both looked down and then at each other. Mike knitted his brow. The ringing stopped. Then it started again.

"Someone wants to talk to you," he said.

"Probably Brenda."

I smiled. Mike winked at me. The chemistry between us buzzed. He pointed at my bag. I fished out my phone. Peter. It stopped ringing.

"I have to go."

His smile dropped. "Okay, see you tomorrow."

I watched Mike return to the control room. My phone started ringing again. I felt a tap on my shoulder. I turned. Walter stood in front of me. "Listen, Little Waitress, you'd better learn how to fix your script yourself or you won't last long."

He turned and walked away. When he was halfway down the hall, he yelled, "And answer your goddamn phone."

Later, when I was safely behind the rolled-up glass in the Town Car, I said, "What the hell were you doing today?"

Betty Jane's answer? "Why, Holly." She paused. "I was just exercising my rights."

One episode of *The Neighborhood* took six to eight months from start to finish. This included writing, rewriting, voice recording, storyboards, animatics, coloring, music scoring, and postproduction. Since the show was on the fall calendar, we juggled several episodes at the same time to meet the schedule. This meant we would be doing voice recording for one show, while one or two were in storyboards, another one or two in black-and-white animation, and others already in the coloring, scoring, or postproduction phase.

The schedule for the taping was intense. Betty Jane added fuel to the fire by finding numerous little ways to remind everyone in the studio, daily, about the ever rising height of her pedestal. At the end of June, Mike asked me to come in a little earlier than the rest of the cast and crew to discuss my unsportsmanlike behavior, as he called it.

We sat in the large conference room sipping coffee.

"Holly, what is going on with you?" said Mike. "You're a different person when we're taping. And not a very nice one."

I closed my eyes and sighed.

"Listen, we are under a lot of pressure to get the fall episodes in the can. Your, uh, how shall I say it . . . sense of entitlement"— he paused and I smiled weakly—"will get less notice once we secure ratings. I believe in you and this show. We're going to get those ratings. We just need to get there."

I looked down at my fingernails.

"How can I help you?" Mike leaned forward. The concern in his eyes was so genuine, I wanted to spill all the beans right there on the spot. "How, Holly?"

How indeed? Even if I told him about Betty Jane, it wouldn't do anything to adjust her attitude. I sat arms akimbo and looked out the window at the thick humidity pulsating over the Hudson.

"Okay, I have an idea," said Mike. I turned and looked him in the eye. "Are you up for more work? I can tell Walter you might be a pain, but you're doing your part to become more recognizable." Inside my head, Betty Jane smiled.

"Sure," I said. "We can do that."

"I'll talk to Brenda." Even though Mike let the *we* pass, I knew he hadn't missed it.

Brenda used all her contacts to find me off-hours work using Betty Jane's voice. But Betty Jane did not go willingly into that good night, as it were. When we were on our way to the first commercial booking, she said, "I will do this work on only one condition."

"Condition?" I said. "We are booked for this job, and negotiations have to take place with Milton." I didn't bother to hide the panic in my voice. The Committee had their hands on my pulse anyway.

"Holly, dear, when will you ever learn?"

I wanted to strangle her. I wanted to scream at her, *Stop pushing the envelope.* I wanted to remind her that we were racing to this booking and then the next because she couldn't play well with others.

"Holly?" Betty Jane smoothed her hair.

"Yes, Betty Jane," I said, "what is your condition?" I sat back and waited.

"I would like a domicile improvement."

Oh.

The Boy gasped. Sarge and Ruffles looked at each other, while the Silent One dropped to his knees to pray.

The Committee had been living in cramped quarters ever since I'd moved from my parents' home in Palo Alto. I'd have to move for them to get a bigger house.

"Is that easy enough?" she said spitefully. The driver's glance in the rearview mirror stalled my intended retort.

Betty Jane, of course, wanted a change of neighborhood along with a new apartment. I wouldn't leave the East Village, and the other four supported me.

Two weeks after she made the request, we moved to a compromise large top-floor flat on Second Street and Avenue A with a view, more than enough space to allow the Committee's matching apartment to include a separate room for Betty Jane, and, best of all, four closets and a storage locker in the basement for all the stuff Betty Jane made me buy.

The next three months passed in a blur of taping *The Neighbor-hood* in the mornings, running from one recording studio to an-other on most afternoons, reviewing scripts at night, and, on the weekends in between, the occasional social obligation. By the time *The Neighborhood* aired in the fall, Betty Jane's Southern lilt was recognizable to millions.

At the studio Christmas party, Walter raised his glass in a toast and said, "Everyone, we've had the highest Nielsen rating each week since *The Neighborhood* aired. To the hottest new show on television and our Little Waitress as the voice of Violet Dupree."

"I told you that your antics would become annoying eccen-tricities if you did your part," whispered Mike. I elbowed him lightly in response. He and I were sandwiched together next to our respective partners—Peter and what's her name. Flirting was not an option.

The best part of my new life was the crazy amounts of money I earned for letting Betty Jane speak. In addition to the regular pay for *The Neighborhood*, every time a commercial we did aired, we got paid. Flush with cash for the first time ever, Betty Jane helped me spend large sums of money on a lot of stupid things, like seventy-five-dollar lipstick, a five-hundred-dollar robot vacuum, and an eight-hundred-and-fifty-dollar Gucci yoga mat with a matching three-hundred-and-fifty-dollar leather carrying case. FYI, I've never set foot in a yoga class.

At one point in the spending frenzy I bought a car and rented a garage space so Sarge could have his Chevy back. Right after that purchase, I walked into a Buddhist specialty store. When I saw the four-hundred-dollar fleece meditation cushion I said, "Shall I buy this?"

The Silent One indicated no with a shake of his head.

I was surprised. If the pope had closets full of fancy robes and miters, the Silent One didn't have to sit on his threadbare old thing. But a few weeks later, when Betty Jane was working and I was waiting in the Committee's living room, I noticed that the Silent One had upgraded his prayer altar. Even ascetics secretly desired something comfy for their bony knees.

By the time we started taping the second season of *The Neighborhood* in March, the servant-master dynamic between Betty Jane and the rest of us had become that of benevolent chairwoman and complacent helpers. By June, I found myself believing people really could change. I'd started to trust and appreciate Betty Jane.

On the first Thursday in July, all the actors from *The Neighborhood* were gathered in a large room with chairs and couches around three walls and a large movie screen on the fourth. We were adding lines to the animation, which really meant recording dialogue for places called lip flaps. These were spots marked by the animators where there was no actual dialogue taking place or where a line was garbled or unclear sound-wise and needed to be rerecorded for clarity. We took turns standing in front of a copy stand and recording new lines to drop over the animation. Mike sat at a console with a small microphone and a TV monitor in the back of the room and the engineers sat in a studio above and behind us.

We'd been at it for three hours when Mike's PA came in and tapped him on the shoulder. "Okay, let's take fifteen," said Mike.

At that moment Sarge and the Boy entered the Committee's house. The Boy removed his baseball glove as Sarge shut the front door. They usually played catch while Betty Jane recorded Violet. She had referred to child labor laws and suggested the Boy not have to work at such a young age. At first I worried, because playtime for the Boy absented Sarge as well. But Betty Jane had behaved like a well-trained pet, and after a few months, I had replaced my concern with the belief that she had the Boy's best interests in mind. Ruffles and the Silent One were still not convinced, and always stayed in the room during taping. I wondered if they'd go if I excused them, but I never thought to actually do it.

"Holly?"

"Oh," I said, shaking my head. I hated being caught "somewhere" else. Drifting between the present and what was going on in the Committee's living room was something I did without noticing. I'd heard snatches of enough whispers to know that everyone else had noticed, though.

"What?" I felt a hand on my left shoulder. I opened my eyes. Walter's. I jerked my head straight. Ruffles tumbled off her pillow. The muscle on the right side of my head cramped from the strain.

The benefit of recording in New York City was that Walter lived in Los Angeles and dropped in only about once a month. I still hadn't gotten used to his visits, because he liked to vary the days and times so nobody ever knew when to expect him. Some of the cast and crew flourished when Walter visited. Others battened down the hatches and held on until he departed. The rest, including me, cowered and flailed. Discomposure only energized him and caused people to whisper, "Walter Torment," when he left a room.

"What did you say?" said Walter. He lingered close enough for me to smell his breath.

I recoiled. "Nothing." I slid out of my chair away from him.

"I want you to come to the front of the room with me," He held out his hand.

"Wh-what did—" I stammered.

"I didn't know I was that frightening." Walter laughed. He knew he was that frightening, and he liked it.

I sighed and followed him. No use resisting or the public put-down would be that much worse.

"Everyone." Walter clapped his hands. "Can I have your attention?"

May I please, I thought. *Everyone, may I please.* But when would he ever say *may* or *please* to anyone? In Walt's World, there were no such words.

"Our Little Waitress has been nominated for the Outstanding Voice-over Performance Emmy award for the first season."

I wish he'd stop calling me that.

Betty Jane stood up in the middle of the Committee's living room and waved to a cheering crowd that had appeared out of nowhere. She commanded Sarge to open champagne. Confetti fell to the floor. I heard whoops and celebration around me.

"An Emmy," said the Boy, jumping up and down. *Does he even know what an Emmy is? I don't even know.*

"I guess she's overcome," said Walter.

"Oh." I smiled with embarrassment. Everyone waited. I kept smiling. It was hard to hear over all the noise inside and out.

"Okay, then. Since Holly wants to keep her thoughts to herself, let's get back to work," said Walter. Then to me, "Plan to be there, Holly."

How could I tell Walter that I might not know what an Emmy was, but I did know that awards ceremonies equaled crowds and large parties, and those filled me with blood-pressure-dropping fear? Especially when he chastised me repeatedly for being such a party dud. Walter had gone so far as to say that he preferred the diva Violet in the sound booth to the shrinking violet who clung to her social-climbing boyfriend.

"Award show's late August in Los Angeles," said Walter.

I hated the month of August, the end of it in particular. Not just because of its sunny dog days of last picnics or other activities before the frenzied preparation for fall, but for other reasons. Reasons that lay hidden behind the door of the closet in the Committee's living room. And I would do anything necessary to keep those reasons behind that door.

"Let's go, people," said Mike.

I tried to walk unnoticed back to my seat. It was an ordeal of insincere backslapping. "Ingrates." Betty Jane sniffed inside my head.

At three forty-five, Sarge reminded me we had an appointment with Milton. At four fifteen he reminded me again. I managed to get out of there by four twenty. I asked the driver to step on it. When the car reached Ninth Street and Fourth Avenue, I said, "Just drop me here, please." The driver stopped the car. I waited on the curb until the taillights disappeared to walk down the block to Milton's office. My "treatment" remained a secret I was absolutely going to keep, because there was no halfway on this one. Treatment begged the question why, and *why* always became the proverbial snowball rolling down a mountain—it got bigger with each turn and left a path of destruction in its wake.

I noticed that the door to Milton's office was ajar when I entered the waiting area. *Shit, I'm really late.*

"Holly, if you paid attention when I indicated the proper departure time, you would have understood that we were late," said Sarge inside my head.

I ignored his admonishment and pushed the door all the way open. "Hello?"

Milton sat at his desk writing. The scratch of his pen filled the silence in the air. He punctuated loudly, put down his pen, and turned. "Ah, Holly," he said. "Please sit." He gestured to the couch. He sported a vexed countenance. I had left the studio early for this less than pleased look on Milton's face?

I sat in the pink chair opposite him. It always reminded me of a comfy commode. Maybe because of the shape of the seat. I lifted the corners of my mouth in one of those I-really-don't-want-to-smile-at-you gestures. Fake and flat.

"What a waste of time," exclaimed Betty Jane inside my head. I agreed.

"I'd like to talk to you about your missed appointments," said Milton.

"I paid for them." I felt indignant, but the words sounded defensive when they left my mouth.

"That is not the point. Holly, I am concerned that you are choosing a critical time in our work to stop coming."

"Tell him about the Emmy nomination," said Betty Jane inside my head.

I smiled and said out loud, "I will." Betty Jane winked at me. Milton shot me a questioning glance. "I am doing great, though," I said. "I'm the successful daughter my parents always wanted. Just like Sarah. Who thought I would fail. But I defied her and have managed to manage it all very nicely." As if on cue, Milton leaned back and made a steeple with his fingers. I wasn't going to let his finger church derail me. "Nobody has to supplement my income anymore, and my emergency credit card is gathering dust in the desk drawer."

"Holly," said Betty Jane inside my head, "Milton doesn't know about the credit card." *Shit, that's right.* A long time ago, Betty Jane had said that if we told him, he'd make me stop using it.

"I told you I moved," I said hurriedly. "To a nice top-floor flat on Second Street and Avenue A. The double-door entrance takes you into a large foyer. No stepping into the bathroom to open the door anymore. The foyer has one of the four closets in the whole apartment. Four closets! Unheard-of in Manhattan." Milton remained silent behind his finger church. "The foyer takes you into a rectangular living room, large enough for a dining room table. It's flanked by both bedrooms and the kitchen. All the rooms except the kitchen and foyer have huge windows and constant sun." Still no response. "Betty Jane has her own room now because I have a two-bedroom place."

"And she is satisfied with this arrangement, I take it?" said Milton nonchalantly.

"Well, we compromised, me and Betty Jane, on the location," I said. "But she's thrilled with the view and her private bedroom." I settled into the pink commode. This wasn't so bad. I'd thought Milton was really going to go after me.

"Holly, do you think we need to come here anymore?" said Betty Jane inside my head.

I stared at my fingernails.

Ruffles cried, "Holly, don't."

Betty Jane smiled and nodded. I kept staring at my fingernails and said quietly, as if I didn't believe what was coming out of my mouth, "I don't think I need to come here anymore."

I tried not to look inside my head or at Milton. I couldn't face his or Ruffles's reactions. Ruffles wasn't letting me off easy, though. Her anger pressed against my temples until I finally said, "Well, maybe I should come now and then for a tune-up. But definitely not twice a week. With my schedule, I don't have the time. Besides, aren't you due to leave on your very extended vacation in a few weeks?"

"You sound like Betty Jane, not Holly," said Milton.

"No, she isn't even paying attention. In fact, I don't see her in the room." I tapped the side of my head.

"Holly," said Ruffles, aghast inside my head. Betty Jane's eyes burned at her. Ruffles shrank back on her pillow. I blinked to make sure I only imagined the flames shooting out of Betty Jane's eye sockets.

"And what do the other Committee members think?" said Milton.

I shook my head to reorient myself. Milton waited for my response. I tapped my foot on the carpet. Inside my head, the Boy buried his blurred face in the couch cushion. The Silent One had paused midprayer, and Sarge paced the room. I tilted my head and looked out the window, trying to ignore all of them.

"Ah, so this is something only you and Betty Jane are advocating?" said Milton.

I glared at Milton. "She's fine with coming. I just think we're too busy."

"Holly, many patients experience a false sense of success when they cross a major hurdle in their work. We spoke about this, remember? It takes some time for behavior to catch up." He leaned forward with his hands on his thighs. I leaned back into the chair. "And as we've seen before, Betty Jane does not have any boundaries when it comes to her sense of entitlement. Your increasing popularity as a voice-over artist makes this the time to become more focused in your work here, not less."

Milton and I went back and forth like this for the whole session as if caught in a feedback loop. Talk about your road to nowhere.

"We are nearing the end of the hour." I pointed at the clock. Milton nodded. And we are right where we started, I thought.

"I cannot force you to come to therapy," said Milton, "but you know my stance on this. For the time being, I will hold your regular hours for you, without charge. You may come or not. I will be here."

"Seems kind of silly, but okay, it's your time."

"No, it's yours. I want to be sure you have it when you need it."

It pissed me off that he was so sure I would need it, and for the first time in six and a half years with Milton I didn't say thank you when I left.

I'll show him, I thought, as the departure door clicked shut behind me.

{ 6 }

The passage of time also transformed my relationship with Peter from code blue to never better. Sarah said that was because we essentially had a long-distance relationship, with a grueling work schedule instead of an ocean or continent separating us, but her bigger concern was how I'd packed my schedule to the point where nothing but work had room. It was true that I barely had time to think, breathe, read a book, or pet the cats, and maybe that was why my relationship with Peter hadn't failed. But, trust me, choosing skyrocketing success that only gets better the harder you work, compared to reflecting on why Peter stayed with me, why I stayed with him, why I had a Committee living in a house inside my head, who they were, and what was behind the closet door in their living room, was a no-brainer. Besides, now more than ever, I needed Peter for the social aspect of my job. At least, that was what I told myself.

According to Sarah and Betty Jane, Peter didn't mind, because with only a minimum investment of time he got free dinners in nice restaurants and an occasional mention in the gossip blogs, like *Perez Hilton*'s. When you're the voice of a cartoon, people don't recognize your face. Because the show was so popular, though, people were starting to recognize my name. When I saw it online and once in print, I hoped it had been a slow week in gossip and vowed never to be named in either place again. Peter didn't get my reaction. He was as thrilled as Betty Jane. I had to listen so often to the two of them crow separately about my burgeoning popularity, it went from annoying to boring.

At the end of July we had some computer glitches and production crews were running behind schedule. Mike decided to give us an unprecedented recording break.

I immediately called Brenda and told her to cancel my jobs for the following week and not to schedule anything so I could catch up on my life and finally spend some time with Peter.

When Peter told me he had to focus on his studies, but he'd do his best to fit me in, I still insisted that Betty Jane and Sarah were wrong and decided to be the supportive girlfriend and find something else to do with my days off.

I made it to noon the first day by keeping busy with all the girlie primping I hated and Peter liked, hoping he'd find some free time. Ruffles and Sarge suggested I use the extra moments to catch up with Milton, but I ignored them. Who scheduled extra sessions with their shrink on a holiday?

I sat on my bed smoking a cigarette, wishing Peter would call.

"Don't count on it," said Betty Jane inside my head. "He's getting bored with sex. That much was obvious the other night—"

"How do you . . ." I let the question dangle in the air. The Committee and I had had an agreement to maintain a zone of privacy ever since my disastrous first attempt at sex. That night there had been so much talking going on in- and outside my head, I had started to get confused about whom I was answering. Finally, I had yelled out, "Privacy." Then the Silent One rounded them all up and they disappeared. It felt the same as when you live with people and they're in another room in the house. You know they're there, but you're separated by walls.

"I have ears," said Betty Jane.

"Yeah, and you also have a lot of nerve," I shot back.

"Did you ever doubt it?" she said.

Before I could respond, the phone rang. Peter. "See?" I said.

When he arrived that evening, Peter said apologetically from the doorway, "Sorry. I know. I'm late. And don't hate me—"

"Hold that thought and I'll just get my coat. You can tell me why I am going to hate you on the way out the door," I said. "Our reservation." I tapped my wrist to indicate the time.

"That's what the 'don't hate me' is about. Can't make it for dinner."

I did hate him. I had spent the entire day arguing with Betty Jane over this exact outcome. Just once, I wanted to be the one who won an argument. Peter watched me, no doubt wondering what thoughts were running through my mind. Then he kissed me, waved, and said, "Hi," as he brushed past me into the apartment. I gripped the knob and stared into the empty hallway.

I heard Peter's backpack drop on the floor behind me. I closed the door and watched him walk into the kitchen. He opened the refrigerator and removed a beer. I stood in the entryway and stared. My freshly waxed legs burned against the fabric of my jeans. "Long day at the library?" I said.

"There's something different about you," Peter said as he twisted the cap off the beer bottle and dropped it into the sink.

"Someone give him a medal for perception," said Betty Jane inside my head.

"Give him a break. She did get a haircut," said Sarge to Betty Jane.

"How about a medal for deftly avoiding the question then? Avoiding questions is about the only thing he can do right," said Betty Jane. "But the haircut is minuscule and does not include a style change, even though I recommended—"

"Quiet," I hissed.

"What?" said Peter. He walked into the living room and I followed him.

"Oh, more quiet, I meant. I'm more quiet now. Don't you think?" I felt the grimace in my stomach dance across my face.

"Well, that part hasn't changed," said Peter. "You still blurt out weird stuff. But it's something else."

"Hmm." *A year and a half together, and this? He really is a dolt.*

Before the Committee could react—well, before Betty Jane could react—I followed up that thought with, *But I can't live without him.* I stopped there, though, because even I knew the next question was, *Why not?* And that question led to reality. I wasn't willing to face reality. Especially when I knew I wasn't the only one going to great lengths to avoid leaving.

Betty Jane shook her head and went back to reading her book. That was when I noticed that the chaise she reclined on was purple. And new. My mind's eye flashed around the Committee's room and I saw that there was a lot of new purple stuff. Ruffles had always worn purple and her lounging pillow was purple. But now the living room walls and the carpeting were an almost imperceptible lavender, and scattered about their living room were accent pillows a deep Japanese eggplant purple. Sheer lilac curtains billowed from the floor-to-ceiling windows. The Silent One knelt in prayer on a new midnight blue cushion that exactly matched his robe. Sarge still wore his standard faded jeans and white tee, but these now blended with the surroundings. The only two sharply contrasting colors were Betty Jane's sunflower pin and the Boy's red Converse sneakers. The Committee's digs had definitely improved since I'd started doing voice-overs. That was how it worked. When things got better on the outside, it showed on the inside. It startled me that I was just noticing. I guessed now I was the unaware dolt.

"Holly?" I heard my name being called from what seemed like far away. "Holly?" My body was being shaken. "Holly?"

"What?" I snapped. "Don't touch me." I pushed Peter away.

"Jesus," he said, "you don't have to be such a bitch. I was talking and you were gone. I take it back. You haven't changed."

I stared at him. If there were a mirror behind his head, I'd expect to be overcome by the reflection of the nasty look on my face. We'd had this fight so many times. So many times. And I was so tired of it. But not tired enough to do anything about it.

Peter sipped his beer and stayed silent.

After a while, I said in a neutral tone, "I thought we were going to go out."

"I didn't say we were going out. I said we might go out. But turns out I can't tonight."

"He most certainly said we were going out," said Betty Jane inside my head. She was right. "We have new Manolos and a pedicure to show off." Her voice matched the anger I felt.

"Oh—"

"But I came by to see you anyway."

Oh, well. "I am glad you came by. I've missed you," I said, taking off my shoes and kicking them over in front of the closet.

"What?" screamed Betty Jane, so loud my head shimmied on my neck.

Peter mimicked me with a wobble and said, "Me too. And I know how we can kill that couple of hours." His hands toyed playfully with the waistband of my jeans.

I heard a loud snort of disgust inside my head before the Committee left the room.

"Convince me," I teased. Peter pulled me close and started kissing me very slowly, applying what we called the lesbian kiss. Peter once told me he had met a lesbian at a party who swore to him that only a woman knew how to kiss a woman. Peter convinced her to teach him how. He liked to think he could charm the pants off even lesbians. She did teach him, though. And he was good at it. So, maybe her pants were hiding somewhere in his closet at home. Either way, this kiss was the trump card he pulled out when he wanted to avoid conflict of any kind.

Later, Peter, me, and the cats were lying in bed watching the sliver of moon as it peeked through the two buildings I could see from my window. Peter made a move to get up. I snuggled in closer and whispered, "Stay the night. We can sleep in, go for breakfast, and then wander the streets talking, like we used to."

"Can't. Gotta go."

"Of course he has to go," snapped Betty Jane inside my head. "He didn't have time to go out but he certainly had time to stay in."

Private time was over.

"Come on," I said, trying to flirt, but the tone bordered on pleading. "I have a week off."

Inside my head, I heard what sounded like a strangled expletive. Even under extreme duress, Betty Jane never swore like us mere mortals. "He got what he came for; why on earth should he stay?"

I reached out my hands to Peter.

"Tomorrow we're going to march to the bookstore looking stylish, and not in sweatpants, and buy some books on how to handle a man." Betty Jane always threatened me like this when I pushed past her limits.

"You never stay anymore." Despite having avoided buying, much less reading, any books on manhandling, even I knew I shouldn't say this. I heard a high-pitched wail at the same time Peter nudged me, not gently, aside. I sat up with the sheet wrapped around me. He was off the bed and picking up his discarded clothes.

"I'm not having this conversation," he said, pulling up his Calvins. "I told you I've been busy."

Busy doing what? I wondered.

"I came by tonight because I know we haven't seen each other much lately." He fastened his jeans and started looking around. "Where's my shirt?"

"Over there," I said, pointing to the foot of the bed. A pain that always started before a crying jag radiated behind my eyes.

"Grab that shirt and tell him you want to know what he is doing that keeps him so busy!" hissed Betty Jane inside my head.

Maybe she needed a brushup on manhandling as well. Too late, though. Even though her harangues were surely meant to motivate me back onto the market for a new man, they always had the opposite effect—fomenting a desperation I was unwilling to examine, accompanied by deep shame because the whole Committee witnessed it and even felt it. Let's face it. Even the most heedless woman intuitively knows what her lover is up to. But there are women who throw a lover out for betrayal and there are women who cling. I don't have to tell you which one I was.

Peter sat back on the bed and tied his shoes. He turned around to say good night but stopped. "Are you . . ."

I opened my mouth, but no words came out.

"It's the voices." Peter pointed at me.

My stomach dropped.

"Fire in the hole!" yelled Sarge inside my head. I started trembling. All the Committee members scrambled for the exits in their house. They'd left me to handle this grenade. How had he figured it out? After one and a half years.

"You don't change your voice anymore when you're mad or whatever."

I exhaled and anger seeped in through my pores. "Mad" meant Betty Jane, and the rest of the Committee was "whatever."

"I never liked it when you changed your voice like that," Peter said, getting up.

My resentment shifted as soon as I knew he was really going. As if my fluctuating emotions and lack of changing voices were the cause of his early departure. As if my new job, my new outlook, my success all came at the price of my relationship. Oh, God, I thought. What if Peter leaves me? What if I'm wrong and he walks out the door and never comes back? Never calls again? No explanation as to why not. Just disappears. Doesn't respond when I call. What would I do? I couldn't stand the thought. I couldn't stand it. The jagged teeth of my tears tore at my eyelids.

I quickly wiped my eyes and said, "No kiss?" I tried to mimic Betty Jane's voice, but it came out like a squeaky plea. Peter picked up the change that had fallen out of his pocket and took his wallet off the nightstand. He leaned over, pecked me on the head, turned around so I could see his wallet sliding into his back pocket as he disappeared into the living room.

When he shut the door, I curled up in a fetal position with the sheet pulled up to my chin. All was quiet except for the ringing in my ears and the noise from the street below. I felt too empty to shed any more tears.

After a while, I sat up and lit a cigarette. My phone indicated new voice mail. Maybe Peter had called me to apologize. That shred of hope turned woebegone when I heard Brenda's voice.

"Holly, I know you're catching up on, uh, life, but I have an easy two-hour job for you if you want it. It's for a movie. Really quick. Good money. I told them you'd do it tomorrow." I loved how she went from "if you want it" to "you'll do it tomorrow." At least she gave me twenty-four hours' notice. I called Brenda and told her I'd be there and to go ahead and book me for the rest of the week.

Betty Jane was in a bad mood when we got into the car. "I do not see why we have to go to that squalid little recording studio for this job," she said inside my head.

For the first time Betty Jane wore a tracksuit. Granted, it was a five-hundred-dollar designer suit, but it was casual nevertheless. The inky black velour made her sunflower pin look especially malevolent. Maybe that's because I'm tired, I thought.

Brenda had told me that the job would be a quick in and out. I just had to pop down to a recording studio of my choice and record, "Yes, Your Highness," a few times and collect a fat check. I'd asked the production assistant to book Al Basi's studio over on Fiftieth Street. I'd met Al before I started on *The Neighborhood* and I'd needed a place to practice using the microphone. He was a decent guy and he gave me a really good deal.

"Al was nice to us, so I want to help him out." I noticed the driver glance in the rearview mirror. He always did this to make sure I wasn't talking to him. I pressed the button to close the barrier between us. People whispered about me talking to myself. Ruffles and Sarge always argued that it was because I'd become careless. Betty Jane and I were sure only one person could be the source of that rumor—the driver—and he was now safely on the other side of the glass.

"I have to suffer in a three-by-three box so you can help out that lecherous, unwashed creature?" snapped Betty Jane inside my head to the Committee.

The booth wasn't that small.

"Holly," said Sarge inside my head, "you will recall that to assuage Betty Jane's claustrophobia, I took over and walked the booth for precise measurements. It was, in fact, ten-by-ten."

"It felt smaller," said Betty Jane.

"I'm sure it did." I sighed. "We're still going there."

"The sculpted foam lining had a bad odor." Betty Jane sniffed. "I had to spray half a bottle of Chanel No. 5 to manage."

How could I ever forget that one? Betty Jane had refused to speak until the booth smelled nice. Unfortunately, her version of *nice* was Chanel No. 5—not the half-price eau de toilette, mind you, but the genuine article. The stuff cost two hundred and sixty dollars a bottle. I had to use the emergency credit card to buy it. In the week we practiced at Al's, Betty Jane used a bottle a day. My mother was so angry she called me herself. I didn't even like the way it smelled, but it didn't stop me from asking my mother what pissed her off more, that I bought five bottles of two-hundred-and-sixty-dollar perfume or that I didn't buy them for her. We hadn't spoken since.

"The foam was moldy," said Ruffles inside my head.

"Thanks for the support." I sat back against the leather seat with arms crossed and ignored all of them for the remainder of the drive.

I arrived to mayhem in the studio. The director, casting director, a writer, and a couple of suits were all crammed into Al's recording room. This cast of characters was supposed to be safely far away in Los Angeles. Worst case, according to Brenda, was that they might want to be on the phone while we recorded. Why hadn't I asked them to book a better studio?

"Holly, there you are," said Al. He pulled me aside to fill me in. Turned out the studio people were in town and had decided to stop in for the recording. Also turned out one of the suits shared Betty Jane's impression of Al's. And with that, I saw my afternoon disappearing and the brief session extending into what surely would be oblivion.

Fifteen minutes and one bottle of Chanel No. 5 later, Betty Jane decided to expand, "Yes, Your Highness," into a monologue.

"No changes in the script," said the director through the talkback.

I fought to regain control. Betty Jane held on. "The script is stupid." I sank onto the Committee's couch. Because she was in control, those words came out of my mouth.

"Read it anyway," he said.

"Do you know who I am?" said Betty Jane in response. *Here we go.* And it proceeded downhill from there in a childish, "I know you are but what am I" fashion between Betty Jane and the director. Then Betty Jane appeared in the Committee's living room.

"Who's . . . ?"

Before I could finish the thought, my body fell off the stool in the booth. *Nobody's running the show right now.* I panicked. Ruffles lifted her bulk and moved to the center of the room. My head would have straightened if my body hadn't been passed out on the floor. When the smelling salts were waved under my nose, I found that Ruffles was in control.

Everyone left the booth.

"Let's try this again, shall we?" said the director icily through the talkback.

"Yes, Your Highness," said Ruffles though my mouth.

"Okay, different voice, but I like it," said the director. "Say it again, but this time draw out the *yes* and keep the whole phrase under one second."

"It appears that the fat saint has things under control," said Betty Jane to me inside my head. "I am taking a moment."

Ruffles saved the day. The big surprise came when the Boy took control to do the dog barks in the script. I could count on one hand the number of times I'd heard the Boy speak, and I had no memory of him ever being in control. But Sarge assured me that the Boy had taken over before, so it would be fine. When I asked for more details, everyone glanced at the locked closet in the Committee's living room. Then I realized that the Boy hadn't spoken since Betty Jane had arrived more than a decade ago, and I felt like a rebellious teenager with friends encouraging dangerous behavior.

When he took control I couldn't breathe. The Committee's living room started to shift and rush. Sarge moved in front of the closet while Ruffles tried to walk toward me. I shook her off.

"Action," echoed through the Committee's living room. The Boy said, "Ruff, ruff," out of my mouth. I pulled him hard. I heard the third "Ruff" fading in the sound booth as I took control.

"You nailed it," said the director. "That was the exact level of anxiety I wanted."

I wiped my clammy forehead with the back of my hand in relief. I wasn't about to let the Boy have control again.

When we left, Betty Jane hadn't returned. Two days later she was still AWOL and Peter was not returning my calls.

{ 7 }

Betty Jane returned after five days, proffering an olive branch and a pledge of friendship. I felt like I did in sixth grade, when one of the popular girls befriended me, and I welcomed Betty Jane's warmhearted attention with open arms, ignoring the fact that she had timed her return with the start of our workweek. Ruffles reminded me that fifty pounds was the only difference between me and my twelve-year-old self, and Betty Jane's leash didn't look any different from that of that popular girl whose motive turned out to be access to my homework. When I told her she was wrong, Ruffles said, "Just don't choke on your new collar."

Peter didn't forgive or forget, but when you've been repeatedly punished by people like my parents and Betty Jane, Peter's form of retaliation wasn't sharp enough to cut a wet napkin. He and I were back to our usual state of affairs after a couple of weeks. The kicker was that by mid-August, Betty Jane and I had sort of become friends.

By the third week in August, Mike said he wanted the cast

and crew at a conference room table to review the story lines.
When we left for the studio, Betty Jane declared she was taking a
day. Most likely to shop, sleep, get a facial, or whatever it was she
did when she was not in my head torturing me and the rest of
the Committee members. She had no use for these meetings
because she was the character of Violet personified. She didn't
care what anyone thought or wanted. Betty Jane did Violet the
way she considered best. Late last fall, when the network guy,
who insisted on testing me himself after our first four episodes
had aired on TV, asked her to make a certain word sound more
"violet"—the color, not the character—she flashed my eyes at
him and made the word sound exactly the way she wanted it to,
which was not, according to him, "violet." Mike told him that he
couldn't argue with the ratings, but it was this type of behavior
from Betty Jane that earned me my diva reputation and then
some.

Around midday, Walter and one of the suits showed up and
Mike called a break. Looking for a way to pass the time, I stumbled into a conference room, where two writers were discussing
a new story line. I stood by the door listening.

"That character sounds pretty interesting; let me see the
sketches," I said.

They stopped talking and looked over at me with annoyance.
I didn't need Betty Jane when I wanted something. I held out my
hand. One stared at me while the other began scribbling furi-
ously on his notepad. No surprise, since he was the one Betty
Jane tore apart the most. She ignored his cues, embellished in
places he asked her not to, and basically did what she did best:
exactly what she wanted. Once, during a reading, after making
several cutting remarks about the dialogue, Betty Jane had sweetly
said, "Well, what else can I expect from a lowbrow hack of a
writer like you?" Since nobody knew about Betty Jane, or any of

the other Committee members, of course they all thought it was me saying these things, even when I said them in her voice. No amount of ingratiating on my part could fix the situation. Halfway through taping the first season, I stopped trying and instead turned my focus to Betty Jane. She agreed to lighten up if I didn't balk when she did things her way. The result was a Mexican standoff between Betty Jane and the writers, with me caught in the middle.

I signaled impatiently to the writer with my outstretched hand.

"Sure." He handed me a sheet of paper. "We just have a general outline of what Harriet—that's her name—looks like."

I read the character synopsis: family member, overweight, sharp wit, who turns up to collect her inheritance and threatens to expose Violet and undermine the hold she has on her neighbors. Ruffles's hand froze in her bag of potato chips.

"I want to add her to escalate the comedic tension," said one of the writers. "As a nonrecurring character in an upcoming episode."

Looking up, I said, "Do you have any lines?"

He handed me another sheet of paper. "Just a few."

I scanned the lines. There was definitely an electric dynamic between Harriet and Violet in the bits I read.

"That sounds perfect for me," Ruffles said inside my head. She was right. This would be just another day for Ruffles and Betty Jane. After last month at Al Basi's, Betty Jane had rewritten history and decided getting Ruffles to share her burden was her idea, and she had declared that she'd permit her to work. I thought for sure she'd be happy to have Ruffles on *The Neighborhood*. It might even temper the tension between them.

"Do you have any more lines?" I said.

"We don't really know her yet."

I did.

Ruffles straightened her shoulders. My head bobbed a bit, a mannerism I saw people around the studio mimicking from time to time, and not in a nice way. The writer made a not-well-concealed tilt to the left. I ignored it, because the only way to show them Harriet was to let Ruffles do it. I closed my eyes and drifted backward so that Ruffles could take over.

She read the first few lines for them, and then paused. They both motioned for me to continue. Ruffles read the remaining lines. Then she introduced the writers to Harriet with a magnificent monologue. When she finished, she immediately surrendered control back to me.

I glanced at the two writers. One said, "That was inspired, Holly. Almost like you were Harriet." He turned to the other writer. "She does these voices as if they live in her head."

If they only knew. Nevertheless, it was an undisputed fact that I stayed employed because I did voices in just this way. And even though there was tension between us, the respect was genuine.

When Betty Jane heard Ruffles was doing an episode of *The Neighborhood*, she smiled warmly and said, "Well." Betty Jane sounded genuinely happy.

I relaxed. We all really were becoming friends.

"I knew that collar would eventually cut off the air to your brain," said Ruffles.

Betty Jane's smile dropped. Her eyes became cloudy.

"How dare you," I whispered. I didn't know which felt worse—Ruffles commenting on my private thoughts or her trying to sabotage this newfound amity among the three of us.

"You are so blind, Holly."

"And you are such a bitch," I said.

Ruffles straightened on her pillow. "I'm just—"

"Leave me alone," I snapped. I didn't speak to her for two days.

At the end of the week, I left work looking forward to a quiet evening when Peter called and suggested we meet for dinner. I had not completed my requisite acts of contrition for Peter, so I agreed to meet him. When I got home, I closed my eyes for a catnap. I awoke to Ruffles and Sarge arguing about whether or not to wake me. I checked the clock. *Shit. It's already eight. I'm supposed to be there now.* I grabbed my bag and called Peter from the cab.

I saw Peter waiting outside as we turned the corner. As I paid the driver, I heard Ruffles say, "He's annoyed."

I sighed. This relapse would probably require another act of penance.

"Sorry." I went to kiss him and he gave me his cheek.

"You never used to be late," he said.

"I never used to be a lot of things. Shall we go in?"

We were looking over the menu when Peter said, "Hey, Pam asked if you could speak to her evening theater group about voice-over work."

I put down my menu and glared at the back of Peter's. Pam, one of those Hallmark Card happy people, was one of his childhood friends. She was the kind of person I wished I could be, and because of this, I hated her. When Pam laughed off my consistently uncivilized reaction to her, I hated her more. She told me once that she and Peter were a package deal. After that I focused all my efforts on avoiding the delivery of the Pam package. Besides, if she really knew me, all that unconditional crap would go out the window. At least, that was the excuse with which I comforted myself.

Peter continued to hide behind his menu. Finally I said, "You've got to be kidding."

"Nope," said Peter. "So will you do it?"

"My schedule." I paused. "How could you even ask?"

"It's one evening out of your life. Can't you for once be nice to her?" said Peter.

"It's not her. It's her and a group of kids," I said. "Kids freak me out. And Pam." I paused. "I'd need a lobotomy to get through it. I mean—"

"Jesus," said Peter, "forget it." He closed his menu with a snap. The sound made my shoulders tense. I wanted to say I'd do it, but I couldn't.

"I'm sorry. I know she's your 'sister.'" Pam liked to talk in quotes, so I smiled and winked my index fingers when I said *sister*. "But I can't."

Peter shook his head in disgust and I tried to push my guilt to the side as I studied the menu.

Ten minutes later the waitress appeared. Peter still hadn't said a word to me, and my guilt had festered and expanded.

"Are you ready to order?" asked the waitress.

"I'd like a bottle of cabernet please. Whatever is good," I said.

"You're drinking?" said Peter. He knew alcohol was forbidden in my contract. It, like cigarettes, ruined the voice. He never complained about the cigarettes, though.

"A bottle of wine, please," I said to the waitress. Peter shook his head and I felt worse.

When the waitress arrived with the wine, I said, "Just pour.

"Bottoms up," I said to Peter, and I downed half the glass.

"Cheers," he replied.

Peter launched into a monologue about his dissertation on Nietzsche and nihilism. This discussion topic always ignited a lively debate between us, because Peter agreed with Nietzsche's view that God is dead, while I subscribed to the Kierkegaardian view that God exists even though I'd turned my back on the Father, the Son, and that stupid ghost years ago. But I didn't know if this was a diversion to settle tension, or Peter was needling me into a philosophical argument so he could try to crush me as punishment for refusing to help Pam. To be safe, I sipped my wine, listened, and picked at my dinner. When Peter took the last bite of his meal, he said, "So, next week I thought it would be great to stay in L.A. for a couple of days, either before or after the Emmy awards show."

"Yeah, fine," I said. We'd just avoided one skirmish; why invite another? Besides, it was easier to say this than reveal to him that I hadn't decided whether I was going to the awards show. Especially when the truth was that I had decided not to go, only I hadn't told myself that truth yet.

"Do you want to order dessert?" Ah, distraction. Peter looked at me. I smiled at the waitress. It was a grin of gratitude that Peter could easily mistake as dessert delight.

"I need to go to the bathroom," I said. "Bring us the menu."

Sitting on the toilet, I reached for my bag. No bag.

Shit. I never forget the Charmin.

I never forget.

I sighed and looked over at the perfectly acceptable toilet paper roll on the wall. Maybe she wouldn't notice.

"Do not even think about it," Betty Jane warned inside my head.

"I am almost dry anyway," I replied.

"That is disgusting."

I heard the bathroom door open. I leaned over and saw a pair of heels on the other side of the door.

"Hey," I said to the wearer of the heels, "can I ask you a big favor?"

"Sure," came the reply.

"Could I possibly ask you to go out to the table where the really cute guy with dark blond hair that looks like it needs to be cut is sitting and ask him for my bag? He's wearing a gray sweater."

I heard some rustling and then a tampon came under the door like a peace emissary. "Don't worry. I always carry extras."

"Oh. Thanks. Actually, though, I really need my bag." I passed the tampon back under the door. It made a quick retreat followed by footsteps and a closing door. I waited. My rear was starting to ache. I looked down at my knees and counted the nicks from shaving. Then I looked over my thighs. I needed a wax. I sighed.

"This is ridiculous!" I said, reaching for the dangling squares of paper.

"No!" screamed Betty Jane inside my head.

The bathroom door opened again. I spied a pair of sensible shoes, the type worn by a server, under the door.

"Miss?" asked the anonymous shoes.

"Yes?"

"Your boyfriend said you need this?" My bag slid across the tiles and under the door. I tried to put out of my mind the article I'd read about the bacteria on bathroom floors.

I retrieved the Charmin and wiped even though it was now unnecessary. "Satisfied?"

"Yes." Betty Jane sniffed.

When I walked back into the dining room, I saw our table was empty.

"Smoking," said Ruffles matter-of-factly.

I looked out the window in time to see Peter handing a cigarette to a tall, underdressed blonde. She leaned in and put her hand over his. I watched. That was how it was between us the first time we shared a cigarette. Every second her hand lingered my stomach plunged another floor, increasing my sense of deprivation.

"Smokin'!" said Sarge inside my head. His comment brought me back. I rolled my eyes. Just like Peter, Sarge had a thing for long blondes. I'd always wondered what Peter saw in me; I was the antithesis of his type.

"You're a pig just like him," snapped Betty Jane at Sarge.

Peter turned and saw me standing there. He smiled. I smiled back, even though I felt like picking up a plate from the nearest table and throwing it through the window. He turned and said something to the woman. She opened her dainty jeweled purse, pulled out a card, and handed it to him. I looked down at my bag. It was so large, the blonde would probably fit in it. At least she'd get sick from the bathroom bacteria.

"He doesn't even try to hide it anymore," said Betty Jane inside my head, "and that is your fault."

"They're just having a cigarette," I snapped. A few heads turned.

I sat down and studied the dessert menu while I waited for Peter to come back in. Chocolate Composition. It sounded heavenly.

"Hey," said Peter.

"Hey, yourself," I replied.

"Are we getting dessert?" he asked, taking a sip of wine.

"Only if we're inviting your friend," I said, trying to be playful.

"Don't even start. She came over asking for your bag. What was with that, anyway?" he demanded.

"So you took her out for a smoke to thank her for asking you for my bag?"

"She seemed pissed. I wanted to make it up to her. Did they bring the menu?"

"Here," I said, handing it to him.

The waitress appeared and said, "Have you decided?"

"That chocolate thing looks right up your alley," said Peter.

"We're not having dessert." I handed her my credit card.

The next morning, I ran down the stairs. The studio car waited in front of my building. I motioned to the driver to roll down the window.

"I'm going to run across the street and grab a paper." I pointed to the Korean market on the corner.

"I'll meet you in front," he said.

I grabbed the *New York Post* off the stand and got in the car. Okay, I live in New York, and the *New York Times* is the paper of record, but who has time to read all that? Besides, I loved the *Post*. It contained all the news I needed to get me through the day, and I could read it cover to cover in the short ride to the studio.

"Shit!" I exclaimed. "They must have gotten my name from my credit card." The driver looked in the rearview mirror.

"Oh, nothing," I said. "Sorry."

He went back to driving, and I muttered *shit* over and over under my breath as I read the celebrity gossip on Page Six. Under "Sightings" it said:

Holly Miller, minor voice talent—

"Minor voice talent. How dare they!" exclaimed Betty Jane inside my head.

"Shut up!" I muttered in between saying *shit*.

—was sighted in the popular Soho restaurant Barolo on Friday night talking to herself in the ladies' room. Our sources also say she

refused help from a fellow female patron whilst in there. Someone needs to tell her that only real celebrities can pull off that kind of attitude.

The receptionist glanced up when I pushed open the glass door. Then she looked down quickly. I tucked a stray hair behind my ear and walked past the desk, ready to smile if she looked up again. She didn't. My heart started to pound. She only did this when Walter was in the studio.

Inside my head, Sarge sat alert on the Committee's couch. Ruffles ate chips double-time. The Boy whimpered while the Silent One did calming breaths. I tried to mimic him. Inhale, two-three-four. Hold. Exhale, two-three-four. Hold. Inhale . . .

"Holly!" It hit me like an unexpected slap. I held my breath.

I turned and there stood Walter, looming over me with the *Post* rolled up like a policeman's baton. I flinched.

"I am heading out to L.A. today," he said.

I nodded my head. He tapped the rolled-up *Post* against his palm.

"I'll see you next week at the awards ceremony."

I dealt with the Emmy awards ceremony the same way I coped with everything that required something I didn't want to give, talk about, participate in, and so forth. I ignored it and hoped that, by my doing so, it would go away. When Walter mentioned the ceremony, I realized the light at the end of the proverbial tunnel had just announced itself as a speeding train.

"Next week, then," said Walter over his receding shoulder. I exhaled.

When I left the studio, I called Milton.

{ 8 }

The day before I was supposed to leave for L.A. and the Emmy awards, Milton said if I'd agree to resume our regular, twice-weekly meetings when he returned from his vacation in France, he'd have a physician friend write a note saying I had an inner-ear infection and couldn't fly. I wanted to report him for blackmailing me to come back to therapy, but I wanted to escape L.A. and the Emmy awards ceremony more, so I agreed.

We all watched the awards ceremony on TV. Having the presenter accept the award on my behalf reminded me that Walter liked to trot out his cash cows at these events, and by not going, I'd made him look bad. I hoped that a trophy and an uptick in ratings would transcend my notable absence in L.A.

Miffed barely did justice to Walter's reaction over my absence. At least, that was what I thought until I found myself suffering Betty Jane's reaction as well for the next two months. Suffice it to say that Ruffles's warning had come to pass and I choked on Betty Jane's collar. As if that weren't enough, Brenda started booking me on endless stupid projects and then I finally understood that this was a form of punishment from Walter. I swear I lapped the island of Manhattan several times a day, the entire time with Betty Jane's whip constantly striking my bloody back.

At the beginning of November, we were recording the last of the dialogue for the animation that had come back from production when Walter walked through the door. The energy in the room shifted from congenial to trepid. We'd just had the pleasure of his company a week ago. Before I skipped the Emmy awards show, we'd always had about three weeks, twenty-one days, or five hundred–plus hours in between visits. Not that I was counting. For the last two months, Walter had taken to showing up at random at least once or twice a week. He spent a lot of time in the air just to torment me. If he met Betty Jane, she'd have congratulated him for keeping me as off balance as she could by the mere showing of his face.

"Take five, everyone," said Mike. Then he said to Walter, "The focus group responses are back. They loved Harriet." Walter nodded and sat down at the console next to Mike.

Mike turned to the writers and said, "I want you guys to rewrite the scripts for the second half of the season to include her."

Inside my head, Betty picked up a book the size of the Oxford English Dictionary and threw it across the Committee's living room. My head jerked as the book dented the wall before falling spine-up on the floor.

"Who knew she could read?" said Ruffles smugly. She had responded to Betty Jane's recent tyranny with a show of solidarity. I knew she meant well with the gesture, but over the last several months I had found myself increasingly caught in the middle.

The crew watched me with exasperated faces, and I realized that if I didn't move pronto, a Walt's World lecture, or worse, would certainly ensue.

As if on cue, Mike got up and walked over to me. "Holly? Are you okay?" he said, putting a steadying hand on my shoulder.

I felt like snapping, *I have a voice throwing a tantrum in my head; of course I'm not okay.* Instead I said, "I need an aspirin." My face felt clammy and hot. Walter narrowed his eyes. After that night at Barolo, Walter's PA had mentioned to me that he'd noticed I regularly came to work hungover. I knew Walter had spies everywhere, but this remark had left me incredulous, because apart from that one night, I rarely drank. Any perceived hangover was not from alcohol. *Yeah,* I had thought when I heard this, I'd love to give Betty Jane to Walter for a day and see how he looks the morning after.

Betty Jane and Ruffles recorded the voices of Violet and Harriet through the end of December, and during that time, Betty Jane's behavior mirrored a terminal illness, growing progressively worse with each passing week. At first she said, "From now on, I want all Committee members present when Ruffles records." A few weeks later she said, "We are neglecting the Boy's education. He shall have French lessons when Ruffles records." Who knew she spoke French? But she ruled the Committee, so we had to comply.

While Ruffles's recordings improved weekly in direct proportion to Betty Jane's bad behavior, the mounting mistreatment started to fray her edges until the strain became apparent. I probably could have managed better if my pride hadn't forced me to treat my sessions with Milton as "tune-ups only." Even though he did help me out with the Emmy awards excuse, the fact that Milton thought I could not make it without him rankled. So I never talked about Betty Jane or any of the Committee members when we met.

The only bright spot during that time was the absence of Walter, who hadn't visited since November. Then I found out from Mike that Walter's spies were talking overtime, and I'd better shape up quickly or things were going to get really rough at the studio. In other words, our current state of affairs, which emulated class IV whitewater rapids, was about to transform to Niagara Falls if I didn't find a solution in the two months we had before we started recording season three.

My solution was more work.

I called Brenda and said, "I need to be so busy I can't see straight."

"Boyfriend troubles?" she asked.

I wish. "No, just troubles. Oh, and can you book jobs only for my Violet voice?"

Brenda didn't ask any additional questions. More work for me meant more money for her. She complied and then some. In a short time, Betty Jane was on top again and life became peaceful once more. So much so that I managed to convince myself the worst had passed.

We returned to work on *The Neighborhood* in March, and that meant Ruffles was back in the sound booth with Betty Jane. It took about two weeks before bad took a sharp turn to worse. Starting with me walking into the studio twenty minutes late.

The crew lounged at the mixing board sipping coffee, and the cast stood behind the glass, headphones around their necks, chatting. I didn't bother with a good morning or an apology. As I reached for the sound booth doorknob, Walter entered the studio.

"The Little Waitress arrives," he said, "without coffee." I paused, alternating between waiting for the Walt's World tirade and hoping Mike would intervene on behalf of the production costs and we'd get started. "You've heard the news?"

The banana I had eaten in the car turned to vinegar in my stomach. The Committee sat alert in my head. The crew in the room and the cast on the other side of the glass stood frozen, as if someone had paused time and movement. I searched for the words that would hopefully get me out of this public sharing unscathed, while Walter waited for me to answer. Stumped, I finally shook my head.

"Still under the influence of your celebrating, I see," said Walter.

Celebrating? I shook my head again.

"For your work this season, you've been nominated for a Juried 2 Emmy—Outstanding Voice-over Performance. Based on your current conduct, though, I can't say that you deserve it."

After I'd received my first nomination, I'd discovered that the award for Outstanding Voice-over Performance is juried, meaning each entrant is screened by a panel, as opposed to voted on, and then passed on to a second panel, which must vote unanimously in order for the nominee to win. Also, you are not competing with other nominees for the award. Rather, the second panel could give the award to multiple candidates.

Inside my head, Betty Jane fluffed her hair and looked around at the Committee members. This would be Emmy number two under her belt.

"Great," I whispered.

"We sent them an edited version of an episode from the second half of the season," Walter went on.

I froze. These were the episodes with Harriet as a permanent character.

"What?" screamed Betty Jane inside my head. "One of her episodes?" She stabbed a pointed red nail in Ruffles's direction.

"Her?" She marched over to Ruffles's pillow, grabbed her bag of Ruffles, and flung it in the air. Chips rained down in the Committee's living room. "How could they choose you?"

Ruffles shrank against the wall. My head leaned over like a flower left too long in a vase. Walter, Mike, and the crew watched me, nonplussed.

I didn't know whether to laugh or cry.

"I will not have it," she said. Betty Jane savagely kicked Ruffles's pillow until the fabric broke. Sarge and the Silent One moved to intercept her. Pillow stuffing mixed with the crushed chips on the floor.

"I will not let you win that award," said Betty Jane. Sarge reached out to pull her away from Ruffles.

"Do not touch me," she snarled. Betty Jane's and Ruffles's eyes were locked in visual combat. Without blinking, Betty Jane said, "Boy, clean up this mess." Then with force, "Now!"

The Boy pulled out the vacuum.

"Holly?" said Mike. I shook my head. My hand clutched the doorknob, now slippery with perspiration.

"Sorry. I'm a bit overwhelmed by the news." I pulled my sleeve over my hand and opened the door. I set up my script, put on my headphones, and nodded for them to start.

"I forgot to tell you," said Mike through the talkback, "we're going to start with Harriet this morning."

I closed my eyes. Betty Jane remained fixed in front of Ruffles's pillow. "Vacuum up the mess," said Betty Jane inside my head.

"We can't," whimpered the Boy. "Ruffles has to record and that means I have French."

"You," Betty Jane snarled, and pointed a finger at Sarge, "take the vacuum." She turned back to the cowering Boy and said, "Anyone worthy of an Emmy award can certainly record over vacuuming and French." Without taking her eyes off the Boy, she pointed her finger at the vacuum and screamed, "Do it now!"

Sarge plugged in the vacuum and switched it on right when Mike cued us to begin. I can safely say that the morning recordings were a catastrophe. I stopped counting the number of times I heard, "We can fix it in post; move on," after the first hour. Finally, Mike called a break. I had fifteen minutes to get this situation under control.

I checked my watch and inhaled. Even though the temperature hovered just above freezing, I went outside for an emergency cigarette. I had sweated off my three nicotine patches and I needed to calm down.

I hid behind the studio in the back alley where they probably carried out the bodies of failed voice-over artists, dragged them down to the Hudson River, and tossed them in with the rest of the sinking garbage. The guard assured me nobody ever came out here. He'd better be right, because if I got caught smoking, the old adage "it could be worse" would come true.

I replayed the day I had let Ruffles audition, over and over again in my head. I knew this obsession fed Betty Jane's fire, but I couldn't stop. "Why did I open my mouth?" I asked myself again for the millionth time.

"Why indeed," said Betty Jane inside my head.

She sat on the Committee's couch, her red lips pursed in a mean line. Her sunflower pin popped against her perfect black suit. We were halfway through the day and I didn't see one wrinkle. If I was wearing it, the suit would look like an old lady's face.

I exhaled and backed away, at the same time trying to avoid the smoky backwash. Inhaling again, I said, "Are we ready then?"

Inside my head, Ruffles brushed the potato chip salt from her hands. "I'm ready." She chuckled, and when she did, her eyes looked like little blueberries dotting the flesh of her face. Even though her hair hung limply and her face looked pale, she still had the energy to lob a salvo at Betty Jane. Relief rushed over me. At that moment, I didn't care about her excess bulk or that she filled my days with crunching. I could always count on Ruffles.

"Of course she is ready." *Course* sounded like *cause* when Betty Jane said it in her sugary, matter-of-fact way. I relaxed. Maybe the afternoon would go easier. "Unfortunately . . ." Betty Jane paused to inspect her manicure. Or maybe it wouldn't.

I waited. Betty Jane smoothed her hair. The malevolent glint in her hazel eyes deepened and her body language belied the sweetness in her voice.

"Unfortunately," continued Betty Jane, "we did all of the Emmy nominee's lines this morning. Violet has the afternoon." She was the only one I knew who veiled threats in the same voice she would use to offer you pie.

I sighed out a cloud of smoke. My shoulders sagged. I felt like a speck of dust on the coffee table of the universe. If the afternoon went like the morning, I'd be back in some diner by the end of the week. "Can you please . . ." My voice trailed off.

"Can I what?" Betty Jane had a cruel smile just at the edges of her mouth. Her python voice strangled my insides.

I dropped my intended plea on the ground with my cigarette and stubbed it out with the toe of my shoe. Then I rubbed my fingers with the slices of lemon I had in my purse. This morning when I was packing my bag of water, juice, and apples, and all the things I carried to keep my voice sharp, I had grabbed some lemon slices as an afterthought. It must have been a premonition. I took a swish of water, sprayed perfume into the air, and walked into the sprinkling scent. I'd read somewhere that this was the best way to wear perfume without seeming like you were trying to. I just wanted it to waft over the incriminating smell of Marlboro Reds.

On the way back I stopped the guard, held up my hands, and said, "Can you smell any smoke on me?"

He leaned in, sniffed, then shook his head. The lemons and perfume had worked.

I slipped back into the booth before the rest of the cast. Inside my head, Betty Jane stood in front of her music stand, wearing her expensive headset with extra padding so as not to mess up her hair. She had added this particular affectation when Ruffles became part of *The Neighborhood* cast. This unnecessary grandstanding had annoyed me in the past. Her only audience was the other Committee members, and they certainly didn't care. At that moment, I was relieved to see her in place. I hoped this meant she was willing to cooperate.

Things were fine for about five minutes. Then Betty Jane had lines. When she opened my mouth to speak for the first time, she caught the dialogue in her throat. Almost like a muscle spasm. An evil chuckle escaped from my mouth, followed by a perfect delivery. Screwing up the lines was one thing. We all did it from time to time. But it seemed as if I had been doing it all day. The laughing made it appear as if I were playing games.

I noticed through the glass Walter and Mike arguing with each other. Every few seconds they both looked up at me. Walter's face turned a darker shade of red with each subsequent giggle. *How can Betty Jane be so stupid as to do this on a day that Walter is visiting? I need to stop this.*

Ruffles stood up inside my head and my body swayed. I steadied myself against the wall. "Knock it off," she said.

"Fine," said Betty Jane. And she disappeared. I rushed forward and managed to take over before my body fell to the ground.

"That's not in the script, Holly," said Mike, his voice sharp with frustration, through the talkback.

Oh, crap. I looked frantically around the sound booth. The other voice actors glanced knowingly at one another while avoiding me altogether. Inside my head, Ruffles looked stricken.

"Holly?" said Mike through the talkback.

Crap, crap, crap.

"Call for Sarge," said Ruffles. Betty Jane had excused him and the Boy for following her earlier orders.

"Uh, I need a break," I said. Without waiting for permission, I grabbed my bag and quickly left the booth, speed-walking toward the exit.

"Holly, time is money." Walter tapped his watch with his forefinger. Studio time was a valuable commodity. Sweat formed like little pinpricks on the back of my neck.

"I need a quick trip to the bathroom."

"Make it really quick."

When I got to the bathroom, I locked the door behind me.

"Sarge!" I said in a harsh, hushed voice.

The front door to the Committee's house opened into my skull. Sarge held it ajar and the Boy trotted through. His red Converse sneakers were dusty. His face was a blur, as always. Sarge stepped into the living room and closed the door. His baseball glove was still on his hand with the ball clutched in the middle. They both stood ready to respond to whatever I needed.

"Betty Jane. She's gone. Please go find her," I said.

Sarge motioned to the Boy and then they went out the front door without putting down their gloves. I counted the blue tiles as I paced, hoping this would calm me down. It didn't. Ruffles sat on her pillows munching chips in time to my pacing. The Silent

One knelt in prayer, which never provided any help in a crisis. I thought about putting on another nicotine patch, but I knew that would just make my heart race more. Sarge and the Boy came back through the front door. They were alone.

"Shit," I said, exasperated.

I pulled my cell phone out and called Milton. I knew he wouldn't answer. What was the use of having a shrink if you always got voice mail during an emergency? But I was desperate and I hoped that the threat of him would bring Betty Jane back.

I heard a knock on the door.

"Holly?" It was Rhonda, Mike's PA. "Are you okay?"

"I'm fine. Sorry. I'll just be a minute." I looked at myself in the mirror. The dark circles under my blue eyes were so pronounced it looked like I was peering out of two fresh shiners. My hair looked like a long brown haystack. Maybe I should put on a little makeup. I never bothered with makeup at work. It was hard enough to get there on time. I picked a cat hair off my black sweater and looked at it. Cat Two, I thought.

"A makeover would be more appropriate." Betty Jane sniffed inside my head. She and her vanity, which had more makeup than the cosmetic counter at Barneys, appeared out of nowhere.

"Thank God!"

"The good Lord had nothing to do with it." Betty Jane casually applied red lipstick. "But I have told you a thousand times a hairbrush and makeup are essential accoutrements for a lady."

"More like a million. We need to go back," I snapped, trying to head off the makeup monologue.

"Only if you put on some lipstick," said Betty Jane inside my head.

"I'm not—"

She arched her eyebrow. "I tell you truly that that is the reason why you and your Northern sisters do not have husbands. We Southern women—"

"Yes." I cut her off. I knew Walter would make me feel that I had cost him personally at least a hundred dollars a minute in production time. We had to get back fast. I dug my hand in my bag and pulled out what felt like lipstick and quickly dragged it across my lips.

"All right?"

"Hairbrush." Betty Jane smiled and patted her sunflower pin. I fished in my bag again, located the brush, and raked it across my hair, pulling out more than I smoothed down. "Very nice," she said, satisfied.

I walked through the studio door with a straight back, trying to project confidence.

"Now that Holly has her lipstick on." Walter ushered me in and then stood over me, glowering. I felt like a flea in front of a burning redwood tree.

"Head up," hissed Betty Jane inside my head. I ignored her and let my head droop lower.

"Sorry," I said, taking my place in front of my music stand and putting on my headset. "Female problems." This was not exactly a lie.

Even though Betty Jane nailed her lines, she gave a few well-timed glances that unnerved some of the more junior performers and caused them to flub their turns. She emitted a couple of impossible-to-hold-back sneezes; and, for her final act, she claimed light-headedness right before swooning in the sound booth, causing three music stands to topple to the ground.

Nobody said a word to me a few hours later when Mike called it a day. I scanned the booth for any exit other than the only one, as if a wish could make trapdoor magically open under me. Neither Mike nor Walter had moved from the other side of the glass. No surprise that Betty Jane ceded control and left me to face the music.

As I walked out of the booth, the sound engineer said, "We got through the recording, but there's a lot of cleanup work to do. We might want to retake the whole day." His words bit me like fangs. I continued forward, my finish line the door out of the studio.

"Holly!" I stopped so fast my body jerked forward. Inside my head, Sarge stood up. The Boy crawled under the couch. Walter towered over me like the Empire State Building. The tip of his nose flashed a red warning. "What the hell is wrong with you?" he said. Flecks of his angry spit landed on my cheek. I focused on his clenched teeth.

Sarge held his arms out straight so that his body made a T. Everyone except Betty Jane cowered behind him. "Disgusting," she said, wiping her face with a tissue.

Stepping back, I said, "I'm just . . ." I could feel myself floating backward as I willed Sarge to take over. I knew he wouldn't. He never broke a rule.

"You're just . . ." Walter said, moving his head back and forth like a metronome. "In Walt's World everyone listens. Are you listening to me now?"

I squeezed my toes. "Now I'm listening. I'm sorry. I was just surprised that my work as Harriet got nominated so fast. It kind of left me off balance today."

"Who said the award is for Harriet?" snapped Walter.

"Oh," I said, "I thought since you said—"

"I didn't say anything," said Walter, "and in Walt's World, nobody should assume."

"Sorry."

"You just don't know what you just don't know, Holly."

"So it could be—"

"But in Walt's World, this diva shit doesn't fly."

"Diva shit!" exclaimed Betty Jane inside my head.

"He is talking about you, of course," snapped Ruffles.

"You're not that hard to replace," Walter said, already walking away.

{ 9 }

By late May, the second televised season of *The Neighborhood* ended and I couldn't tell who was the most popular character on the show—Betty Jane's Violet or Ruffles's Harriet. And that was the problem. The only solution I had remaining up my sleeve was to start arriving to work early. My show of punctuality seemed to alleviate some of the acrimony between me and the crew, and even though internal stress was at an all-time high, we had what I considered to be an almost peaceful week. The next Monday I arrived at eight forty-five feeling confident. I opened the front door to the studio and found a standing-room-only waiting area. When I entered, all talking abruptly ceased. I looked down to make sure I'd remembered my pants. I had.

I slowly passed the sitting and standing women. Their furious mutterings sounded like rustling leaves on a late-fall day. "Morning," I said brightly to the receptionist. She looked away. I glanced back at the whispering women. Suddenly, every one of them found something interesting on the floor or in her lap.

In the hallway, I ran into Rhonda walking with two women.

"Have you seen Mike?" I said.

"He's in the conference room," said one of the women.

Rhonda's face paled.

"Thanks," I said, brushing past them.

"Holly, I wouldn't—"

Too late, I thought, as I turned the knob and opened the door.

Mike, Walter, one of the suits, and the casting director for *The Neighborhood* were all seated at one end of the conference table. They didn't notice me standing in the doorway.

"Oh, my stars," said a very Southern voice.

"Violet is breathier than that," said Mike.

What does he mean, Violet is breathier than that? I felt like I'd been rear-ended hard by a car I hadn't seen coming. *Those bastards are auditioning people for my part. My part!*

"Play the recording of Holly for her again," said Mike.

I heard Betty Jane's voice exclaim, "Oh, my stars."

"You need to make your voice sound like that," said Mike. Now I felt as if the car had backed up, then careened forward and flattened me.

Betty Jane heard Walter's audition message loud and clear and diverted us from our collision course with the unemployment office of New York State by putting her studio behavior into spontaneous remission. She became the picture of professionalism. Away from the studio, I paid the price by trying to meet Betty Jane's constant demands. By July I felt close to collapse. Then Walter dropped in to let me know that I would be at this year's Emmy awards show if they had to wheel me in on a gurney. Betty Jane told me she was going to be there even if she had to break all the rules and invent some new ones to break. I ignored the whole thing, hoping it would somehow resolve itself.

———

By the third week in August, Milton had gone on vacation, so I did the only thing I could do. I called Sarah.

She wasn't home.

I sat in bed staring at my phone, willing my sister to call me back. After two hours, the phone finally rang.

"Holly, is everything okay?" said Sarah. "Your message sounded panicked."

"She's really messing with me. I don't know from one minute to the next if I can do my job—"

"Who?" interrupted Sarah.

"Betty Jane. Ever since they auditioned my replacements, she's fine at the studio, but every second we're not taping, she's constantly running me down or demanding that I get facials, or manicures, or buy a goddamn fur coat, and I believe in animal rights. Nobody can stop her, not Ruffles, not Sarge." I wiped my running nose with my sleeve.

"Deep breath," said Sarah. "What is that therapist of yours doing about this?"

"Analyst."

"Whatever. What is he doing?" Sarah demanded.

"Betty Jane didn't show up for the past couple of weeks. She knew Milton was going on his annual vacation to some remote village in the South of France. He just left. He's not back for four weeks. But there's not much he could do anyway if she won't show up," I said in a defeated tone.

"How can she just not show?" Sarah sounded angry now. "And how can he take a four-week vacation? Therapists in California only take two weeks. It's irresponsible. He allows that Committee of yours to run rampant and then he takes off? It's malpractice." Sarah was always hard on Milton when I called her in this state.

Even though Milton had assured me four weeks was normal, I admit that I felt he was the only shrink on the planet who took four weeks off every year. Each August, I'd convey my indignation at being left through variations of bad behavior. Milton had grown inured to the annual acting out before his holiday, so Betty Jane's recent disappearance didn't deter him. I don't think she meant it to, which made me feel caught in the middle once again. And even though I agreed with Sarah, and a part of me wanted her to throw Milton in jail for leaving, I knew I had to shift the conversation from Milton's ill-timed, lengthy sojourns, because he'd already left for France and she was the only one who could help me.

"She'll show up for the Emmy award ceremony," I said.

"I thought you didn't want to go."

"I told Walter I would," I said.

"Why, if you don't want to?" said Sarah.

Taking the phone with me, I walked from the kitchen into my bedroom. Even though my living room was large and comfortably furnished, with a nice view of the Manhattan rooftops, I missed the smallness of my old studio. I sat on my bed, pulled the strap of my bag over my head, and felt around in it with my left hand, searching for my pack of cigarettes. While removing one, I leaned over and opened the window, then clicked the lighter and inhaled. "I need to keep my job, Sarah. I'm still living paycheck-to-paycheck, and my credit cards are not showing zero balance. Betty Jane and Milton are expensive."

"I don't understand this, Holly," said Sarah. "Explain to me why Betty Jane and Milton are expensive," said Sarah.

"In answer to part of your question," I said, "Betty Jane holds me hostage. If I don't give in to her demands, she doesn't work. If she doesn't work, I don't get paid. Her demands are cheaper than no paycheck, so I give in."

"I'm not even going to mention integration and the fact that Betty Jane should have no control—"

Before she could go from not mentioning to a tirade, I cut Sarah off with a, "Thank you."

Sarah sighed. "Tell me why therapy is so expensive. You have health insurance."

"I don't claim it on my insurance. The studio would find out. They'd know."

"Holly, I've told you a thousand times, they expect you to be in therapy. All TV and movie actors are." Sarah said this with complete assurance. "Do you really care if they know you have a therapist?" said Sarah. "Especially if you can get reimbursed for it?"

"With Walter's spies it could go like this: Holly is in therapy. Why is Holly in therapy? Holly's a fraud. She doesn't do voices. She has voices in her head that do them for her."

"Don't get mad. I'm just trying to help."

"We are talking about how to save my job, not putting me on the fast track to unemployment."

"Hey, before I forget, we watched your show the other night. What a great episode. I love Harriet."

"Oh agony!" screamed Betty Jane inside my head. Then she stormed out of the room. *Where'd she come from?*

"Yeah, well, that is the problem."

"That I love her voice?" Sarah sounded confused. "Her humor reminds me of the sense of humor you had as a child. Remember that essay you wrote?"

"No, I don't remember any essay. No essay. I don't remember any essay."

"Okay," said Sarah. Neither of us spoke for a moment. "Anyway," she finally said, "I like the voice."

"Yeah, well, the more everyone loves it, the more out of control Betty Jane becomes. If I don't do something, I could lose my job."

"From the start, Holly, I said this was dangerous. That whole Committee, as you call them, has always had way too much power over your life. And this job has given them more." I could hear the frustration in her voice. "I don't know what that therapist—"

"Analyst—"

"Oh, all right, analyst," snapped Sarah, "was thinking. Maybe you should consider just letting it all go."

I lit a cigarette and inhaled. "This from the person who just said she loved the new voice I am doing."

"Right, the Ruffles eater or whatever—"

"Yes, Harriet is Ruffles, the Ruffles eater."

"My point is," she continued, "my point is that I have told you for years to get rid of that freaking Committee. The last thing you need is to get more lost." She was working herself up now. "I don't know what else to say. I'm at my limit here."

"Listen, will you go with me to the Emmy awards on Sunday?"

"I thought Peter was going with you."

"Sarah, the way Betty Jane is acting, I need you there, not him."

"Holly—"

"Sarah, don't—"

"Peter uses you for parties, Holly. He walks on you with cleats and you let him. You shouldn't have to work that hard for any man."

"How would you know? You've never had to work hard for anything, Sarah." It was a nasty comment and we both knew it. But, no matter what I did, no matter what I said, Sarah stuck by me, and that gave me a freedom I didn't have with anyone else. It hadn't always been that way, but we didn't talk about the time in our lives when things were different. "Peter does love me, Sarah," I said defensively.

"I have no doubt that he loves something, Holly."

"Will you go with me?"

"Of course I will."

{ 10 }

It was a hot August afternoon. Sarah, the Committee, and I rode in the limousine. As the limo rolled along, I left yet another mollifying message for Peter. He hadn't spoken to me since I'd told him Sarah was going to be my plus-one instead of him.

"Why do we have to arrive so early?" Betty Jane sniffed inside my head.

"I thought you weren't talking to me," I said. Betty Jane had threatened not to speak to me the rest of the night if I called Peter one more time. It was the only reason I'd dialed the phone.

"I said I might not speak to you."

"Whatever," I said. "I told you I want to get through the red carpet gauntlet unnoticed and as quickly as possible."

"I know, Holly," said Sarah. "We will. Just relax."

"And if I don't want to go unnoticed?" said Betty Jane in a shrill voice.

"You have no choice," said Ruffles inside my head. When

Ruffles spoke, I felt that mixture of compassion and shame that one feels for a loved one who has chosen the most awful outfit but you don't want to say. Especially if that loved one weighs more than three hundred pounds. It's hard to make that much bulk look nice. Unless it's a ship. Ruffles had tried, though, and the resulting outfit was a shiny purple thing with sequins. It looked more like a circus tent decorated to resemble a starry sky.

I fished in my bag for a cigarette. I clenched it between my teeth and pressed the button on my lighter. Everyone including Sarah screamed at once, *"Holly!"*

"Come on," I pleaded.

Sarah snatched the lit cigarette from my lips and tossed it out the open window. "We agreed that you'd use a patch," she said.

"I'm wearing three already."

"Children are not appropriate at an event like this." Inside my head, Betty Jane pointed one of her bloodred nails at the Boy. Sarge insisted he be allowed to attend. I suspected that Betty Jane capitulated because she was determined to be at the awards show this year. The Boy pressed up against Sarge, who looked uncomfortable in his new Armani suit. "Especially in those shoes," she said disdainfully. Even though he'd dressed in a little boy's tuxedo, the Boy refused to remove his red Converse sneakers. At least they were clean.

The limo stopped. I heard the driver disembark. "We're here," I said, smoothing the skirt of my dress.

I planned to run for cover the minute I exited the car. If Sarah couldn't keep up, she'd have to meet me there. "The drink tent, Sarah," I whispered as I half skipped, half ran toward the white canvas structure about a hundred feet ahead. When we walked in, I pointed to a table in the corner and said, "Over there."

———

I had gulped down my first glass of wine when I saw Walter come through the entrance with what appeared to be a nineteen-year-old female on his arm.

"Holly!" Walter spotted us.

"Here he comes," I said to Sarah. She sat calmly, not the least in awe of him.

Walter appeared before our table sans teenager, looking dapper in his expensive tuxedo. The first time I saw Walter, I thought he was a handsome man. Then I met him.

"Walter." I stood up. "This is my—"

"What kind of fucking entrance was that?" he snapped. "In Walt's World, actors have class. Do you think that was a classy entrance?" I'd worked for him long enough to know that was not a question. Then he looked me up and down without any pretense. "What the hell are you wearing? That getup makes you look fat. And boots? This is Los Angeles, not a rodeo."

I wore a flowing, violet (sans sequins), three-quarter-length dress with matching cowgirl-style designer boots. I thought I'd made a good outfit choice. Apparently not.

I flashed a warm smile at him. I had the family teeth—horsey and big. But, as my mother always said, big teeth made the best smiles. And I did have one that could light up a room. I watched Walter disappear into the crowd and then I remembered that he was the one person impervious to my smile. I sat down in a slump.

"How rude!" said Sarah. She was nice enough not to mention that she'd suggested I rethink the boots. But I didn't wear sandals—anytime, under any circumstances.

"I told you that outfit was atrocious," said Betty Jane. She wore a very expensive Chanel dress. Off the rack, as she had reminded me multiple times this week. Since her budget was the same as mine, it was all she could afford. The strappy sandals on her well-manicured feet were from a previous outfit. Worn once, but worn nevertheless. I noticed that she'd somehow upgraded her trademark sunflower pin to a jeweled version. The tiny glass stones caught the lights and sparkled, making the flower petals look like they were covered with raindrops. For once it looked lovely.

"Is this dress really ugly?" I said to Sarah.

"Well . . ." She paused, no doubt awash in the same conflict I'd been in earlier. "It makes your eyes green." I had eyes that alternated between blue and green depending on who I was. Maybe that was a sign that the award was for my work as Violet.

I sighed and gulped down my second glass of wine. I caught Walter watching me from across the room. He made a cutting sign across his throat. Godzilla had now crushed my outfit, my teeth, and my wine intake, making it a humiliation trifecta found only in Walt's World.

"Should you be drinking like that, Holly?" Sarah covered my hand with hers. I knew she wasn't chastising me, but her question still made me mad.

"Let's go into the auditorium," I said.

The Emmy awards ceremony was held at the over-six-decades-old Shrine Auditorium. According to Ruffles, the Shrine comprised the single largest theater in North America, with some six thousand, three hundred seats and a huge adjoining Expo Hall.

When we walked in, I wondered what they did at the Shrine to accommodate the obese. Not that I expected to see any of those in attendance. They'd probably get a last-minute liposuction or something.

A handful of people were already seated. We made our way to the orchestra section and found our seats about halfway to the stage. Admittedly, hiding in the balcony appealed to me far more than sitting front and center. Good luck getting Walter to agree to move anywhere out of the spotlight, though.

"Did you know that the Shrine's design is an engineering marvel?" I said.

"The cantilevered balcony is built without pillars. It seats more patrons than the floor," said Ruffles inside my head. "And if you look up, you'll see that no seat in the house has an obstructed view." No point in wishing we were seated in the balcony if it didn't come with anonymity.

"Did you know that chandelier up there is crystal? Weighs four tons and has over five hundred lightbulbs that use forty-eight thousand watts of power," I said.

"Good thing we're not sitting under it. What if it fell?" said Ruffles.

"Now, that would hurt," I said.

"Would you both stop your incessant blathering," snapped Betty Jane inside my head. Ruffles hissed at her. They'd already had a big fight back at the hotel room. Ruffles hadn't seen why she should change her outfit for the occasion. But I confess that I secretly appreciated Betty Jane's insistence that we all dress up, because elegant attire portrayed an image of élan and sophistication, which was what I wanted for the awards ceremony.

"Take a deep breath, Holly. You're being careless," said Sarah.

"It's nerves. Nerves and no cigarettes." I pressed my forefinger, middle finger, and ring finger on the three patches that were stuck to my rib cage. "I wish it would start."

"Just a little while longer. People are already coming in. Let's be quiet for a bit," said Sarah.

"How rude!" exclaimed Betty Jane.

"Always have to have the last word," said Ruffles.

Betty Jane pursed her lips so they looked like she had just

eaten a lemon, and then dramatically covered them with her fore-finger to indicate silence. Sarge unbuttoned his jacket. Even though he didn't put up a fuss, it was the first time I'd seen Sarge out of his regular blue jeans and white T-shirt. The familiar scar that always looked like it was diving off his ear down the neck band of his T-shirt glowed an eerie white against the red of his neck. He'd complained earlier that the shirt collar was too tight.

After a while, the lights dimmed and the announcer came onstage. As the awards were presented, I did my best to ignore the sensation that I needed to go to the bathroom. The bath-rooms at the Shrine were not exempt from Betty Jane's toilet paper rule, and my dollar-sized purse could fit only a few squares of Charmin.

"Now the juried awards," said the Emmy announcer.

Someone told me to pay attention.

The orchestra played a few notes.

The applause was deafening.

". . . as Harriet."

Ruffles's eyes widened.

Sarah elbowed me. I didn't move. Sarah elbowed me again.

Betty Jane's jaw dropped.

"Oh." I opened my eyes with alarm.

"Holly, get up," said Sarah. "Go," she whispered urgently.

The music rose in decibels. My head wobbled. I gripped the seat back in front of me. Inside my head, Ruffles waddled after Betty Jane, who was already sailing down the aisle while she waved at the cheering crowd. "What?"

I swayed. Sarah put her hands on my hips. I turned and, hang-ing on to the seat backs in front of me, I sidestepped as if between two panes of glass past everyone seated between me and the aisle. I didn't want to be remembered as the voice-over artist who bumped her big butt across patrons' necks and laps. At least, not more than once.

A whispered *ouch* told me that my heel dug into a foot as I exited the row. A backward glance showed me it was one of those shiny tuxedo shoes and not a bare, sandaled foot. Luckily.

Sarah shooed me onward like a fly. Once on the runway, I attempted to walk gracefully to the stage. The orchestra mixed with applause jumbled into an earsplitting cacophony.

My vision was divided between the events happening inside my head and the events happening in reality. In the head frame, Betty Jane advanced, waving like a homecoming queen—fingers together and hand tilting back and forth—with Ruffles closing in.

Horns bellowed and cymbals crashed.

I felt as if I were peering through a kaleidoscope. To my left and right, the auditorium of people looked like a giant box full of tiny puzzle pieces. Even with my fractured vision, I was pretty sure the stage lay dead ahead. I continued forward.

I saw Betty Jane seductively lift the sides of her dress and float up the stairs. My shin smacked a sharp angle. I fell to my knees. Ruffles toppled inside my head. The weight of her landing sent my cheek hard against the stage floor. I tasted blood in my mouth. I sat back on my heels, stunned. Then a pair of hands reached under my armpits and pulled me to my feet.

I have on a sleeveless dress, I thought, mortified. *I've just sweated all over someone's fingers.* I whispered, "Thank you," and stepped forward onto the Shrine stage as the music hit another crescendo. By now I couldn't distinguish between the band in my head and the band at the foot of the stage.

Hank Azaria handed me an Emmy statuette. The applause rattled against my skull like a seven-point earthquake. Mesmerized, I watched the scene inside my head. Betty Jane turned like

a supermodel, fanning arms down to her sides like a giant sunflower opening in perfect time with the dwindling music. Her
smile radiated. Ruffles rushed her and took her down with a
tackle. The last thing I remember was Sarge grabbing Betty Jane
by the shoulders.

I opened my eyes. My room glowed with gray darkness from
the fluorescent streetlights outside. *I'm in a hospital?* I searched the
sides of the bed for a call button and found something that resembled the remote usually sitting on the airplane armrest. I
pressed what appeared to be a green button. It turned on the TV.

I scanned the buttons again and was about to press when I
heard, "Quite a scene at the Emmy awards tonight, Chuck."

"I'll say."

On a news program, Chuck and a blond woman with snow-
white teeth, whose facial expressions had been all but erased by
too much Botox, both turned to the monitor behind them.
The screen filled with my big purple ass sticking straight up in
the air.

The camera retreated and I watched myself, Emmy in hand,
manage to sit back on my knees, and then stand all the way up. I
swayed slightly, reaching out my free hand for something to sta-
bilize me. Then my other hand started waving the Emmy statuette
around like a proud citizen with a flag would as I took off, zigzag-
ging across the stage in a sharp outfighting style that would have
made Ali proud. Hank Azaria was right behind me, like a swarmer
or "pressure fighter," attempting to stay close but not so close as
to get hit by the statue in my hand.

"What exactly is going on here, Chuck?" The screen zoomed
out to the two of them at the news desk.

"Well, according to the studio publicist, this was a skit put
together between Holly and Hank."

If Botox Blonde had an expression, it would have conveyed *unconvinced*.

"Watch," said Chuck.

They both turned back to the screen as it zoomed in again.

Hank reached.

I feinted left.

An animallike snarl issued from my wide-open mouth.

I raised my right arm, bent my elbow, and brought the Emmy smack down on the top of my head.

Hank immediately put a hand to the side of his mouth and yelled, "Timber," as I landed face-first and out cold on the stage.

"Oh!" exclaimed the Botox Blonde.

"'Oh' is right!" said Chuck. "And that's all the time we have tonight. Stay tuned for more on Comedy Central's Stewart and Colbert."

The credits rolled as Hank gripped the heels of my designer cowgirl boots and dragged my body off the stage.

I sat in my hospital bed wishing I were the proverbial tree alone in the woods.

"Holly?" said Sarah, standing in the doorway.

"Tonight at the Emmys," blared from the TV.

"Turn that off," said Sarah gently. I switched my gaze back to the TV and pressed the mute button.

Sarah sat on the side of the bed, but instead of looking at her, I continued to watch the video of me knocking myself out and falling over, playing in a continuous loop in a little box above and to the left of Jon Stewart's head. Every ten seconds or so, he'd look up, cover his eyes and shake his head.

Finally, I said, "Betty Jane was fighting with Ruffles. She bit her. Sarge tried to break it up."

Suddenly, Walter towered at the foot of my bed, in a red-faced rage. "You knock yourself out with the Emmy statue? You have to be dragged off the stage by your ugly fucking boots? You're damn lucky I managed to get you out of the Shrine and into this hospital, where nobody can see you! This is a fucking disaster," he screamed.

"Betty Jane wouldn't let Ruffles have the award. They were fighting; then Sarge—"

"Shushhh." Sarah reached over and covered my mouth.

"What the hell are you babbling about? There's nobody fucking here but you, me, and your girlfriend," shouted Walter.

"I'm her sister, and you need to leave her alone," said Sarah.

"Sweetheart, I don't give a good goddamn who you are. There's nobody else in this room except you, me, and Crazy there in the bed," Walter yelled. His nostrils flared like a fire-breathing dragon's.

I pressed back against my bed. Not that it made any difference.

He pulled me to a sitting position. "You were fucking drunk." Walter spit the words at me. The tip of his red nose was purple, as if an errant ounce of blood had rushed to that spot to serve as an exclamation point. And at that moment, facing him, I wished I were blackout drunk.

"In Walt's World this kind of shit doesn't happen. Not anymore. Holly Miller, Midtown waitress, has just had her last day in Walt's World."

{ 11 }

My mother once told me that Scarlett O'Hara was right to be more concerned about her expanding waistline than her failing marriage. I thought they both had their priorities backward. But standing there facing Walter's rage-mottled visage, I had an ill-timed *aha* experience, which told me my mother was right. At least the *aha* worked like adrenaline on pain and I knew exactly what to do—act first for appearances and damage control, and then deal with that which should remain hidden.

Act one, I reached for Walter's hand with the idea that I'd make like what had just happened hadn't happened.

Act two, he stepped back. The flash of his eyes told me physical contact not initiated or invited by him also didn't happen in his world.

Act three, I realized that I didn't have my mother's sense of how to right a wrong situation when Walter said, "You're through."

"Does he always refer to his world?" said Sarah. I watched her as she watched Walter's back disappear behind the closing door. Then I shut my eyes.

Ruffles sat on her pillow nursing her head with an ice pack. Her hair was tangled and matted and her face full of scratches. Betty Jane, on the other hand, sat on the couch casually flipping through a gossip magazine, her lipstick on and her hair brushed. The angry imprint of Ruffles's teeth on her arm, which had already begun to bruise, was the only marker that remained from their stage fight inside my head. It didn't matter. The sight of those two reality-checked the last bit of hope that I'd imagined everything.

Then my own headache served as the waking pinch, and all I could think was: *I need to get out of here, get home, and find a way to fix this with Mike. Right now.*

"We have to—"

"Get out of here." I finished Sarah's sentence. She nodded at me.

"Stay here. I'll get you checked out and manage a discreet exit," she said.

I closed my eyes again. Nothing had changed, and the hush inside my head fanned the spark of apprehension smoldering in my gut.

We exited through a side door at the hospital. The cab Sarah had called idled curbside. We got in and he pulled away without a word. Sarah must have told him where we were going. By the time we reached the hotel, my apprehension had developed into a five-alarm fire of horror-soaked foreboding.

Sarah stood staring out the window at the Los Angeles skyline. "Holly?" she said without looking at me. I knew she wanted to comfort me, but I also knew she couldn't grasp what it felt like to be exposed in such a public way. I hadn't walked down the street talking to myself. I had knocked myself out on national television. This carried Monica Lewinsky–caliber shame. Sarah was too perfect even to be in the same universe with that kind of discomposure. And she knew I knew this. "I'm going to take a shower," she said.

"Uh, okay," I replied in a tiny voice. I felt way too small to handle what Sarah was leaving me to handle on my own, and at that moment, I didn't need the reminder that we were so different. But instead of saying that, I said, "You don't have to leave the door open." She didn't, and I sat on the bed wishing I too could just rinse off the whole night with a shower.

The muted sound of running water told me Sarah had begun. I planned to sit there and stare until she emerged; then Betty Jane stood up inside my head and said, "Get in here; I want to speak to you."

"But who will—"

"Don't 'who will' me. You think I don't know about your late-night trips to visit Ruffles and conspire against me?" I felt stricken. Lately, Betty Jane had taken to downing a Vicodin and a glass of wine after a hard day. I always thought the combination knocked her out, making it safe for me to come in and visit on the nights Peter wasn't over. "Nobody will be in control. But you come in here. You just have to trust me." Her smoldering rage made her face alternate between different shades of red.

"Where's Sarge?"

"Get in here," commanded Betty Jane.

I sat against the headboard and closed my eyes. My feet were not yet on the Committee's hardwood floors when Betty Jane said, "I am an award-winning voice on a successful television show. It is my efforts that bring in the money that finances our life. Do I get thanks? Do I get respect? Do I get appreciation? Do I get credit? *No!* I get grief and heartache. I get recalcitrance. I get obstinacy. I get cheap shampoo and skin-drying soap."

I exhaled. *All I am going to get is a lecture.* I nodded my head just like I did as a child when my mother went on one of her crazy rants, usually because she had done something too embarrassing to face.

"I get to stand by while that fat little saint walks right over my back, crushing me with her enormous bulk, and reaches out to accept *my award*," thundered Betty Jane.

"Uh, well." I glanced over at Ruffles. My heart beat against what felt like hollow logs in my chest. "I mean it was technically Ruffles's award too," I whispered. I didn't want to remind her that if the judges had gone by the edited version of the episode Walter had sent, it was all Harriet and no Violet, meaning the award was for Ruffles's work. And the judges who awarded my work had no idea how much Ruffles had earned it. No one else would ever be able to turn in award-winning performance after award-winning performance under the same noisy circumstances.

Across the Committee's living room, Ruffles closed her eyes and inhaled. Her face rippled with the strain of managing Betty Jane's constant haranguing over the last year and a half since she'd started doing the voice of Harriet.

"Let me tell you," said Betty Jane.

I refocused on her. The Silent One sat on the floor between her and Ruffles. *Where is Sarge? He should be here.*

"Let me tell you." Betty Jane turned toward me. "The foundation for our cushy life and *your* trim figure rests solely on my shoulders. If it weren't for me, you'd be a fat waitress eating all the cake you encounter during the week. Oh, I know you think your figure is because of Sarge. He believes in following the rules. All those years in the military made him the disciplined one. But that is a lie. All action and nonaction are because of me. Me. Not Sarge, not Ruffles, not that stupid Boy who spends all his day under furniture, only coming out if dragged by that frankincense-

smelling, meditating *thing* over there." She jabbed a red nail in the
direction of the Silent One, but her face was inches from mine.

"You," she hissed. I pressed my body against the wall behind
me and she leaned in. "You would say it is everyone's efforts, and
out of altruism, I have let you live in your little bubble of delu-
sion. And how do you thank me for all that I have done?" Her
nose almost touched mine. I wanted to push her away but I was
too scared to move. "You thank me by backing her." She pointed
at Ruffles. "Supporting her. All of you support her."

I heard the front door open. Betty Jane turned and I tried to
shift away. Her arm shot out and blocked me. Sarge paused in the
doorframe, shielding the Boy behind him.

"Well . . ." I hung my head. She backed off.

"I have managed all five of you in *addition* to putting in a full
day's work and bringing home the money. After all, I am the one
they always want." She paused to inspect her manicure while I
alternated between trying to find the best way out of this escalat-
ing rant and the mounting anger I was trying to hold back. "For
all my efforts, what thanks did I get? My fat little saint wanted to
start saving. She wanted to cut the bare necessities that I must
have to survive, like my car service, my clothing allowance, my
Charmin toilet paper. When I asked her why she was not cutting
down on the Ruffles she ingests morning, noon, and night, I received no answer other than, 'Look at the credit card balances.'
What do I care about credit card balances? I win awards."

The best way out prevailed and I said, "Yes, you win awards.
And I agreed, no cheap one-ply toilet paper. I—"

"My work won that award, Holly," said Ruffles. Her words
felt like a slap. She didn't need to be difficult at this moment.

I tried to convey alliance with my eyes while I said, "I know,
uh, but as Betty Jane said, all of this is because of her efforts." I
needed Ruffles to acquiesce here. I didn't want this fight.

"No," said Ruffles matter-of-factly, "I won that award. I won it on my own, with no thanks to her." *Oh, God. Oh, God.*

Betty Jane turned. Ruffles stood. I moved toward the door.

"Do something!" I screamed at Sarge. He stepped forward.

Betty Jane held up a hand and, without taking her eyes off Ruffles or me, she said, "No. I have had enough of all of you running roughshod over me. You all are ingrates. Especially you," she sneered at Ruffles.

Ruffles, still bloodied and battered, didn't flinch. "I won that award," she repeated. "On my own. No thanks to you."

"Oh, I see what is going on here now," said Betty Jane. "You want to test my power. You think I am unaware of the fact that all of you wish me gone?"

"No, there's no testing. No power," I said frantically. "Ruffles just wanted to set the record straight. That's all. You win too. You won too." I knew I was babbling.

"You always choose wrong, Holly. Always wrong," said Betty Jane.

Peter had said the same thing to me about my choices when I told him I was taking Sarah to the Emmy awards show. "No matter how many miserable years I've stuck by you," he'd said, "all it takes is one comment by Sarah, and you toss me aside like garbage. You always choose wrong, Holly. Always wrong."

"Now I am going to make a choice that will give you time to think about your bad choices and how they have resulted in this latest mess," said Betty Jane.

"What choice? What are you going to do?"

"I am going to leave," she said.

This brought me up short. "Oh," I said. Betty Jane was actually going to give me what I had wanted for the last fourteen-plus years. "Well, uh, if that's what you think is best."

"You transparent little worm," said Betty Jane, "I *will* do what I think best. And what I think best is to take them *with me* when I leave. This way you will have plenty of peace and quiet to think about your choices."

"What . . . what do you mean, take them? You can't take them," I pleaded.

"Tut-tut, a bad memory to go with bad choices," said Betty Jane. "You forget that I control the Committee. Me. Not you." She pointed at me. "Not you." She pointed at Sarge. "Not you." She pointed at Ruffles.

"She didn't point at you," I said to the Silent One. "Do something." He shook his head. "You're just going to sit there and pray while my life goes down the drain?" My bitter words bounced off the walls of the Committee's living room. His suffering expression whipped my surging panic into a homicidal rage. "What good are you anyway? You let her go crazy. You won't make her behave? You're useless. Useless. All you do is sit there and pray. You don't help when I need something. I hate you. I hate you. You're useless!" I screamed. He sat quietly on his cushion with sad eyes. I wanted to beat that anguish right off his face. "At least bow your fucking head!" I yelled. Grief pulsed at his temples.

"Holly," cooed Betty Jane, "how many times have I told you never to trust a man who does not speak or wear cologne? It does not matter. He cannot make me do anything. I rule the Committee. I decide."

"But Milton said—"

"Milton. Where is your precious Milton? On vacation." She laughed. "Under a tree in France somewhere. I am the only one who cares, and you turn on me again and again and again."

"Please don't do this. I'll do anything you ask. You can have anything. I'm sorry."

"Holly," screamed Ruffles, "what are you saying?"

"No," I yelled at her. Then to Betty Jane, "I'm sorry. Please don't do this. Please," I begged.

"For one minute," she said, "I considered it, but your fat friend changed my mind."

"Ruffles, do something," I pleaded. She shook her head.

"Too late," said Betty Jane. She snapped her fingers. They were gone.

"*No!*" I screamed.

Oh, God. Oh, God. My breath came fast. I threw myself on Ruffles's pillow. The pain of their departure tore me in half. I couldn't stand it. I wanted to run at the walls. Anything to get the pain away. I got up on my knees and slammed my shoulder against the wall. Ruffles's bag of chips crumpled noisily beneath me like a collision of foil and flesh. I beat at my head with my fists. "No." I didn't want to see that. I hit harder against the wall, screaming, "*No!*" I punched the wall again, screaming "*No*," until all the heat left my body and it started to shake uncontrollably. "No." I hit my forehead against the wall in even-note syncopation. "Come back; please come back."

"Holly." I heard my name from a distance.

"Holly."

I opened my eyes. Blood ran down my forehead.

"Holly, my God, I was about to call 911," cried Sarah.

"Come back," I kept repeating. Sarah's face bounced with my chattering teeth.

She put her arms around me like a straitjacket. "Holly, you're scaring me." Then she took my hand and said, "Come here. You're cold as ice."

Sarah draped a blanket over my shoulders and held on again. "What happened?" she whispered.

The shaking in my body subsided and I said, "They're gone,

Sarah. Betty Jane has taken them. They're gone." I sat on the bed and pulled my thighs close to my chest, trying to stanch the bleeding darkness inside my body.

Sarah sat next to me and put her arm across my shoulders. She brushed back my hair and said, "But she's done that before, Holly. She'll come back. She always does."

Sarah's resigned acceptance sparked enough hope in me to prevent me from saying Ruffles had turned on me, and Betty Jane had never before left with the rest of the Committee. Anguish pulsed like a million tiny heartbeats behind my eyes. Sarah was right. She was always right. Betty Jane would come back. She'd come back with the Committee and everything would be fine. I just had to wait.

I just had to wait.

{ 12 }

I never knew when to stop trying, turn back, or at least go in another direction. I mean, why do something new when the familiar was so familiar you no longer noticed the bruises and you had scars on your scars? So, the morning after the Emmy awards show, when I awoke to the Committee's empty house inside my head, I told myself what everyone does when faced with a hopeless situation and an awareness complete with bold letters and lights flashing, **Abandon all hope, ye who enter here.** I told myself, "This time will be different." Then I twisted myself into the proverbial pretzel of hope and waited.

When the a.m. news shows replayed the video of me clocking myself with an Emmy statuette, calling it a clever comedy, skilled acting, I dug deeper into my conviction that all would be well and maintained the image of Betty Jane and the Committee returning to my open arms. I know Sarah wavered between flying home with me to make sure I held it together, and getting away from me and my missing multiple personalities and back to her male alpha-

bet, Volvo, and sanity. The latter prevailed when I offered her an
out in the form of a weak promise that I'd be fine. How hard
could it be to deplane, grab my bags, and find the car waiting to
deliver me safely to my apartment? Harder than I thought.

I don't remember much of the flight except the effort it took
to focus on trying not to run screaming from anyone who approached, brushed past, jostled, or otherwise invaded the invisible
circle I'd drawn around myself. I always found comfort in flaky
new-age theories, like "Draw a protective circle around you,"
when I was in a crisis. But, just like religion, the theory when
applied to reality generally turned out to be utter crap.

Halfway through the flight home, I wouldn't have been surprised to find an orange BITES sticker next to my seat number, just
like the one my vet posted on Cat Two's file to warn others before approaching.

I arrived home Monday evening to a doorstep empty of the envelope with the work for the following day and a distressing
voice mail. The video of me doing my version of a Saint Vitus'
dance and then knocking myself out on national television had
exploded across every available media outlet. I knew Walter was
going to require an act of contrition that would strain my ability
to project patience for Betty Jane. I told myself I should start re-
penting by arriving at work early Tuesday morning. But the truth
was, I wanted to arrive early because the studio was one of the
few places where I felt a little bit safe, and, more important, I was
banking on work to bring the bolting Betty Jane and the kidnapped Committee back to me and my open arms.

When I reached the recording room at eight forty-five in the
morning, there were only two engineers at the console. "Where's
Mike?" The expected churlishness was unintended this time.

The engineers' faces carried smirks instead of their usual beaten-down bearing, and small beads of sweat broke out on my forehead.

"Uh . . . he's . . ."

"Are we recording today?" I said. "There wasn't anything waiting for me when I got back last night." Neither of them answered me. Inside I felt that creeping feeling that comes when you know you should know what's going on, because it seems clear that everyone else knows. But you haven't the first clue. Instead all you have is the anxiety gnawing at your insides. In the face of this, I did the only thing I could do.

I left the room.

I heard voices in the hallway. I stopped, stood out of sight, and listened.

"Walter, I don't want to agree to this," said Mike.

Shit. He's here? I didn't expect to don the hair shirt so soon.

"I don't give a damn," said Walter. "I've had it. And in Walt's World that means something."

"Let's just put this behind us, Walt, move on," said Mike sternly. Walter opened his mouth to speak. Mike held up his hand. "It's my show."

"You said that in May," said Walter. "I went along with it then. Not now."

"She's been fine for the last several months."

"Did you happen to catch the Emmys?" said Walter.

I turned and walked away from them.

Now what?

I went out to the back alley and lit a cigarette.

"Betty Jane, please," I whispered. I knew Sarah said Betty Jane always returned, but now she'd been gone two hours, eighteen minutes, and thirty-two seconds longer than previous absences.

"Can you please . . ." My voice trailed off. "Please . . ." *I think Sarah was wrong this time.*

What am I going to do?

I started to pace the empty alley.

What am I going to do?

My breath caught.

What am I going to do?

I looked skyward and yelled, "You made your point. You can come back now." My voice cracked with panic.

"Miss Miller?" I turned and came face-to-face with one of the security guards. "You okay?" Great. Another breakdown by Holly Miller in Page Six tomorrow. Only this time, I really was talking to myself.

"I'm fine," I said, "just having a bad day." He nodded and retreated back down the alley. I bit my thumb, hoping the physical pain would stave off the panic and anguish rising like a high tide in the back of my throat.

I slipped in the side door just as Mike turned the corner. "Let's go," he said tersely. *Yeah, right,* I thought.

When I entered the sound booth, none of the cast members even glanced up. Walter stood glowering behind Mike as he told us to pick up where we'd left off Friday, which meant Violet was up, and Betty Jane was still on strike and nowhere near with her picket sign and demands. The floor underneath my feet felt unsteady. *She's not coming back. They're not coming back.*

After my third try at Violet's lines, Mike yelled, "*cut!*" through the talkback. Walter said something to him, glared at me from the other side of the glass; then he left. Mike motioned for me to come out.

When I stood in front of him he said, "Holly, that's it, you're through."

"Sorry. I just need some rest. I'll be fine tomorrow."

In response, Mike handed me an envelope. Inside it I found a notice that said in bold letters, **Termination of Contract**.

I glanced at the engineers. They both turned away, unable to look me in the eye. I scanned the cast in the booth. They had the same expressions you'd find on someone who had finally witnessed the going around, coming around.

I couldn't breathe.

The eyes of all the people in front of me and behind the glass closed in on every inch of the empty expanse I'd become in two short days without the Committee. They kept staring. I didn't move. With each passing second, their pitying gazes felt like the crushing pressure of a deep underwater dive. And right before the last barrier between me and myself shattered into thousands of fragments, I dropped the piece of paper I held in my hand and I turned around and ran.

I ran out of the recording room and out the front door of the studio. I kept running down Twenty-third Street. I didn't know where I was running to; I only knew I needed to run to something. But what, I couldn't at that moment say.

So I kept running.

I reached Fifth Avenue sweating and out of breath. Everything around me seemed unfamiliar and frightening. *Where do I go?* I turned right and picked up my pace again. People parted before me like the Red Sea. New Yorkers instinctively know when to step aside and let crazy pass.

When I reached Ninth Street, I slowed to a jog and turned left. Wheezing like an out-of-tune accordion, I ambled toward Fourth Avenue. Each footfall felt like God had gripped my Achilles' tendons, flipped me upside down, and spanked me against the pavement. Every corner of my body ached. I took two more steps and then stopped at 95 East Ninth Street. I pressed my hands against the walls as I heaved the air in and out of my lungs. Then I pushed down on Milton's buzzer. I heard it sound from the other side of the door. I waited. I pushed it again. I waited. I pushed it again. I waited. I was going for my fourth try when the door opened.

"I need to see Dr. Lawler," I said. I tried to slip past the woman standing in the doorway.

"He's on vacation. Back the middle of September, I believe." She didn't move.

That's right. I had the only shrink in the world who took four-week vacations impeccably timed with Betty Jane's bad behavior.

I dropped down on the steps and started to cry. The woman shut the door behind me.

One of those late-summer torrential downpours, which last from five to fifteen minutes, started when I stood up. People always expect the worst of this kind of rainfall to be short, so they congregate under whatever shelter they can find and wait out its passing in the company of strangers. I walked home instead of waiting, letting the force of the rain soak me all the way through my skin. And even then, what was pouring out of me felt far more powerful than what the sky had to offer. When I reached my building, my shoes were ruined. I didn't care. I pressed all the buttons until someone buzzed me in. I'd decided to break down my door, but then I saw my bag sitting on the table in the entryway. They certainly were fast about returning that to me, I thought bitterly. *At least I can get in.*

I retrieved my keys and opened my front door. As I stripped off my sopping clothes in the foyer, I noticed the message light on my answering machine was blinking. I kicked the sodden mess aside and hit the play button.

"Holly, it's Milton. I've been trying to reach you on your cell phone for the last half hour. My colleague said you were at my office." I pulled my cell phone out of my bag. Three missed calls. "Please call me as soon as—"

The phone rang. I scanned the room. It rang again. There it was over on the desk. I walked over as it rang a third time. I picked it up. "Holly?" It was Milton.

"I think so," I said, relieved. "I'm soaked. Let me call you back in two minutes."

I put on my robe and opened my pack of cigarettes. When I noticed Cat One lurking over by the chair, ready to escape the instant I opened the window, a fresh round of sobs ensued. *I can't do this without Sarge.*

I don't know how long I sat on the floor crying, but it must have been long enough to worry Milton, because the phone next to me started ringing again.

The Emmy video had made it to France yesterday, and Milton said he'd planned to call me on my lunch hour, but then he heard about my collapse on the steps of his office and called immediately. He wanted the story badly enough to encourage me to smoke in my apartment without opening a window. I figured, what the hell, Betty Jane wasn't here to stop me, and the fleeing felines had only themselves to blame for the secondhand smoke they were about to inhale.

Between my rambling and his questions, the whole saga start to finish took an hour and a half and a pack of cigarettes to impart. When I finished, Milton said, "Holly, why don't we set up regular times to check in until I return?"

"Until you return? Aren't you coming home now?" This was a serious crisis. I expected Milton to cut his vacation short and help me get Betty Jane to come back.

"I'll be returning to the office in less than three weeks."

All the anger I'd been holding inside turned into a tornado and Milton became its target. I had never hated anyone more in my life than I did him at that moment. "In less than three weeks," I shrieked. "Thanks for nothing."

"Holly, it is appropriate for you to be angry at me under the circumstances."

"Fucking right it is."

"You are feeling abandoned, and this is a natural reaction."

"I'm not feeling abandoned; I *am* abandoned. First by Ruffles, then by Betty Jane, and now by you."

"I am aware that you feel this way, Holly, which is why I would like to set up regular calls. We have a lot to discuss."

"If you really cared, you'd come home for our regular meetings."

"Holly, I do care. Normally, another doctor takes calls for my patients while I am away, but in your case, I want to speak to you myself, daily, even though I am on vacation."

The mention of other patients stripped away any feeling of uniqueness and reminded me that I paid Milton, end of discussion.

"I pay you to care," I snapped.

"In this case, you don't," said Milton. "I am doing this because I want to."

"You are doing this to make sure I don't go crazy and really ruin your vacation, not because you care." I hated him more than I had a minute ago.

"I will call you each day at six my time, which is noon your time," said Milton.

"You do that," I said, "but don't expect me to answer."

I hung up the phone.

{ 13 }

Five days had passed since my call with Milton. The thought of going outside felt like stepping off a cliff, so it took me that long to muster up the strength to make one trip to the corner store. Once there, I bought enough cigarettes and cat food to lie torpid for several weeks.

I showered only twice in the five days and that was when Peter came over. The first time, all he noticed was the smoky rooms. We had sex and he said he liked being able to smoke in the apartment instead of crawling out on the fire escape. Before he left, he showed me that my windows also opened from the top, so some air could come in without the cats going out. The second time he came over, he commented on how clingy I'd become, we had sex, and then he said he was really busy with the new term. I hadn't seen Peter for a couple of days, and his phone was switched off a lot more than usual. Milton called every day at noon as promised. And I didn't answer, as promised.

It took two more days to realize I really was on life support. All my commercial spots had been pulled, and this meant no more surprise checks would turn up regularly in my mailbox, which meant my rent and therapy would burn up the last of what I had in less than three months. I had two choices: Call Sarah or call Brenda.

Having something like destitution to focus on galvanized me. I called Brenda. I left her at least five messages. Per day. I hated being on the hard-up end of the stick, but I had no choice. When Brenda didn't return my calls, I started to think that Walt's World was galactic. After three days of messages, she left me a voice mail saying I had an audition for a commercial in Midtown, and I breathed a sigh of relief until I realized there was no magic portal to get me from my apartment to there. I'd have to venture out onto the streets of Manhattan, alone.

Somehow I managed to call a car service and it delivered me to the door of the building where the audition was taking place. I arrived to a waiting room full of people chatting merrily and made my way to the harried-looking woman sitting behind a desk.

"May I help you?" she said.

"I'm Holly Miller," I said hesitantly. The Emmy video had received tens of thousands of hits on YouTube after someone posted a link to it on Fark.com with a pithy headline—"When Emmy awards attack . . . and they call it acting." The chatter in the room transformed into hushed tones. I held up my head, feigned indifference, and waited for a response. I needed a job.

"Oh." She nodded her head. "The audition was canceled." Her words echoed off the walls of the now noiseless waiting room.

Canceled, my ass, I thought. I blinked back angry tears and I told myself to maintain dignity, get out of here without making a spectacle. "Okay," I said to the receptionist. "I wasn't told. Thanks."

I turned and walked to the door, hoping my clenched teeth

and fake smile would hold back the bile that had reached my tonsils as the waiting room occupants whispered to one another behind their hands.

A woman stopped me at the elevator. "Do you know where the auditions for the Palmolive commercial are?"

I looked down at her hand on my arm, hoping she would remove it immediately. "No. Sorry," I said. I pulled my arm away and pushed the button for the elevator.

Going down.

Another week, a missing boyfriend, a vacationing shrink, and ten humiliating auditions later, I finally faced the truth—this was not one of Betty Jane's intermissions.

I'd spent almost a thousand dollars on transportation to and from my auditions, because that was the only way to avoid people and get there, and in between I spent the rest of the time chainsmoking and watching the Emmy award show video. All this had done nothing except produce dust bunnies as large as tumbleweeds rolling across the floor of the Committee's living room until they started feeling like boulders pounding inside the walls of my head, reminding me that Betty Jane was gone. Ruffles was gone. They were all gone.

I wrapped my mind around this realization. Then I crushed the thought like a piece of paper in my hand and decided to get revenge.

I walked with purpose all forty blocks to my destination in Midtown. It was almost the middle of September. The city streets remained thick with heat and crowded with people who bumped me on all sides. I didn't care.

I stopped only once, to tip my head sideways toward the skyscrapers enclosing the pale white sky like sandwich bread over a thick slice of cheese. Then my stomach contracted against the wave of dizzying longing. Since Betty Jane had kidnapped Ruffles, my head no longer tilted to the left. My neck ached from the change, and I didn't like the way the world appeared from my new perspective.

I shook it off and walked faster, knowing I should walk slower so I wouldn't be sweat-drenched when I arrived. But I was on a mission and nothing was going to stop me. As I neared Midtown, I noticed the brightly dressed people moved languidly, as if held back by the heat of the day. Barneys loomed large down the street. I had a half block to go.

I arrived at the front entrance, gripped the handle, and opened the door with a flourish. The biting blast of air-conditioning almost knocked me over. My body temperature immediately switched from too hot to too cold. The dried sweat left salty gravel on my skin. I strode in and went straight to the escalator. Once in the shoe department, I picked up the first pair of sandals that caught my eye. I held up one of them to the suited salesman over by the register. He walked over to me.

"I would like to try this in a size seven please."

"Of course. Have a seat and I will be out in a moment."

He returned a few minutes later carrying four boxes. "I brought some other sandals similar to the style you selected, just in case. . . ." He smiled. Just in case I wanted to spend more money, I thought.

I had no funds coming in and no business buying anything. But I still had my emergency credit card. The expiration date on the first card had coincided with the month I shifted my tassel. I had graduated thinking the charge train had reached the credit station and resigned myself to living hand-to-mouth in New York City, figuring I had plenty of company. Then a new card, accompanied by a note from my mother that said, *For emergencies only,* had arrived. I used the card for everything except emergencies. It was never declined. When that card expired, another one appeared in my mailbox, this time with a note from my mother saying she blamed herself for how I turned out; and she apologized to me for being distracted during most of my childhood. The latter comment almost compelled me to write back and tell her she could add the four years I was in college and the few years after it to her timetable. She hadn't returned to New York City since she left me on the NYU dormitory steps my freshman year, and I hadn't been home to California.

I viewed the two postgraduation credit cards as my mother's way of saying, "I am paying attention now." I knew she wasn't, though, because Sarah reviewed the bill and my father paid it.

I removed the lid of the box on the top of the pile and didn't glance at the price. I hadn't spent my father's money in the two and a half years since I'd begun voice-over work. He owed me this one, and if he didn't agree, he could take it out of my inheritance.

"Do you have any of those little stocking things?" I said.

The salesperson reached under the chair next to me and pulled out a box filled with stocking caps, removed two of them, and dropped them in my hand. I untied my running shoes and put my right toe to my left heel and forced off my shoe. I waited for a rank smell to fill the air-conditioned air. Nothing. *Phew.* I repeated the process on the opposite foot. Then I removed my socks, straightened my legs before me, and flexed my feet.

I have a scar in the form of a question mark that starts on the top of my foot and ends right between my big and second toe. I got this when I was six and a half years old on a family picnic. My mother hoped it would fade because I got it at such a young age. Instead of fading, though, the scar grew with my foot, and because of this disfigurement, I was never allowed to wear sandals. The first thing I had intended to do when I arrived in New York was buy a pair of sandals, which was funny, because when I was growing up, shopping was a mother-daughter adventure that never lived up to its promise. Shopping with Betty Jane had managed to transform the memories of shopping with my mother into fond ones. And she also thought scarred feet should not be in plain view, so I never got that pair of sandals I'd promised myself fifteen years ago.

I noticed the salesman watching me. I held up my foot, daring him to recoil in horror at the sight of its wrecked top. He didn't even notice. I put the branded foot in the sandal and admired it. The strap of the sandal cut straight across the scar as if belting a question. I put on the other sandal and walked around.

"I'll take them," I said as I looked down at the shoe mirror that was angled just perfectly for me to appreciate my feet from the side.

"Do you want to try the others?" said the salesman hopefully.

"No, just these today."

"Very well," he said with obvious disappointment. "I'll take them up to the register."

"Actually, can you just drop my running shoes in the box? I want to wear them."

"Of course."

I turned to the front. My scar sat proudly on my foot, making an ugly face. I turned to the opposite side and then the back. A frisson of joy coursed through my body. I was wearing sandals for the first time in twenty-six years, and Betty Jane wasn't there to stop me. I went to the register and pointed to the box on the back counter.

A different salesperson picked up the box, scanned the price, looked up, and said, "Four hundred seventy-nine dollars and eighty-four cents." I felt a small jolt in my midsection. That was a lot of money for skimpy straps sewn to a leather foot bed. Oh, well, like I said, my father owed me.

I exited Barneys thinking about what Peter had said to me last week when I'd told him it hadn't occurred to me to finagle an extra ticket to the Emmy awards ceremony. "After all I've done for you, you're not taking me to L.A," were his exact words. Then he had walked out on me without saying good-bye. I didn't read between the lines of his departure, because these exits were de rigueur. I'd thought he'd be back after a few days and we'd tuck one more ugly incident in the Do Not Discuss file and pick up where we'd left off.

But standing there on Madison Avenue, I suddenly knew that what Peter really wanted was for me to give more of myself. He wanted to stop the come-close, stay-away dance and take our relationship to another level. And, when I realized this, I knew I wanted to meet him halfway. I wanted to put my hand down and beckon him all the way forward. I'd start by apologizing for not taking him to the Emmys and promise to always put him first from now on. Then I'd tell him I was finally ready to give him everything.

Armed with this new awareness, I wanted to find him immediately and tell him. I reached out my hand for a cab. This was too urgent for the subway. When I slid across the bench seat, I said, "Do you take credit cards?"

"Yes."

I asked the cabdriver to drop me at the Fifth Avenue entrance of Washington Square Park. My heart pounded in my chest, but I knew everything would be fine as soon as I found Peter. When I was about fifty feet from the front door of Bobst Library, the front door opened. I skidded to a stop. *It's him.* I opened my mouth to call out his name. Peter stepped back against the door. A smiling blonde appeared. I choked back the words about to spill forth. My blood froze in my veins. All color drained from my surroundings.

I had spent most of my life receiving guidance from the Committee inside my head, and most of the time I didn't want it. But right then I would have given anything to go on autopilot and let one of the Committee members take over. I wanted opinions. I wanted options. I wanted things with Peter to be the way I had imagined them ten minutes ago, before he paused in the doorway of Bobst Library to share a secret with an unfamiliar blonde.

My voice hammered in my lonely head, echoing as if from a distance. *Focus, Holly. Focus.* I shook it off the way a dog shakes off the ocean when it first comes out of the water. It didn't work. The waterlogged thought pounded louder in my head; nobody was in my mind to slap me back to my senses. I stood there feeling confused, like I'd missed the punch line.

Peter ushered the woman ahead of him. I leaned forward to get a better glimpse of her. From where I stood she looked like the perfect woman—tall, thin, pretty, radiant smile. My nose and my ass at that moment grew to ten times their normal size.

Peter said something to her. She smiled. He smiled. Their shiny white teeth snapped around my heart like a bear trap and a new wave of pressure closed in on me.

At that moment, I knew I should turn around and walk away, but I was in the fourth ring of the ninth circle and Virgil was in the library. I knew I should walk away but I didn't. I didn't. Instead I stepped back just out of sight and watched them.

She flirtatiously flipped her blond hair back. Peter put his arm around her waist and they started walking up the street and away from me.

"Walk away," I kept telling myself. Then God turned down his celestial dial, muting car horns, voices in the street, the sound of acceleration from the passing buses until everywhere was silence. People and cars slowed to a stop. All color was subdued to neutral tones. And I walked forward toward Peter and the girl.

I followed them as they strolled along West Fourth Street. The quicksand sidewalk pulled at my feet. Each foot was encased in sludge. Each step was wrenched from the curb. Only Peter's blond hair blazed like a beacon guiding me down the street. In slow motion, I dodged and weaved around pedestrians, always maintaining a safe distance behind Peter and the woman, but close enough to see them lean toward each other every other second to share a secret or a laugh.

The perfect blonde stopped to regard something in a window. I skidded to a halt and waited behind a plant. I thought for sure that the glare from my pearly white feet would give me away. When I looked down now all I felt was remorse. I curled my toes under to try to hide them. This just stretched out the scar more, and then I wanted to take off those sandals and throw them at Peter. But the thought of hurling five-hundred-dollar shoes at Peter struck me as absurd.

When they reached Astor Place, I knew he was taking her to East Village Books on St. Marks. *That bookstore is mine*, I fumed as I crept behind them. Taking that blonde to my bookstore felt like Peter had brought her home and fucked her in my bed.

They stopped. Maybe they weren't going there, I told myself. The sun glared at me through the black lenses of my sunglasses. It blotted out everything but their matching hair. They started strolling again at an accelerated pace. I wondered if he'd seen me. I moved quickly behind them now.

"What should I do?" I asked myself. I wanted to put my hand down and beckon him forward. This had to be a mistake. They're just friends. He can't have seen me. If he had, he'd be thrilled. He'd explain this. *What would I say?* "I'm ready to give you everything"? And if I did, he'd welcome me with open arms, right?

Wrong. What if this isn't a mistake? What if I've lost him too?

My world went dark. I felt like I'd fallen out of a hundred-story building and was descending fast. "Anyone," I whispered, "if you are there, please tell me what to do. Please tell me what to do."

I pushed my belly button back against my spine, hoping to squeeze the helplessness up through my torso and out my mouth. My chest collapsed into my lungs. I hit my toe on a raised piece of the sidewalk and tripped forward, catching myself awkwardly with my left foot. I swayed. The skin on the top of my toe hung back like a box top attached at one side. The blood made my sandal slippery. They crossed Fourth Avenue. I stepped off the curb in pursuit.

I heard a honking horn mimicking the desperate pounding in my heart. I stopped short and jerked my head to the right. The source of the bleating horn inched closer. I smelled burned rubber. I heard the squealing of brakes as they scraped across the asphalt like nails on a chalkboard.

A woman on the sidewalk raised her hands to her mouth. I saw Peter in the distance walking away from me.

I turned back and watched the Yellow Cab move turtlelike in its forward trajectory. I wished it would hurry up and hit me. People yelled on either side of the street. Then the ground gripped me. I saw a phone number written horizontally down the front of the hood. I could read every digit. I slowly lowered my eyelids. The last flash I saw was the sharp teeth of the front grille of the car. I swayed Gumby-like into a C curve to catch the front bumper as it met my knees.

{ 14 }

I stood with my palms flat against the hood of the car as I tried to figure out how I had ended up in the middle of Fourth Street with a bumper kissing my knees. I heaved the air out of my lungs as I stared at the horizontal phone number jailed by my splayed fingers. Then the ground rushed up and met my feet. The noises of the street began to swell a half a beat behind the movement on the street. The returning noise propelled me back to the curb I had just stepped off. I felt the chill of someone walking over my grave. The cabdriver splattered me with a string of profanities. I stared stupidly. All that was missing was the drool. The crowd started moving again.

The cab drove slowly by me. The driver punctuated his rain of expletives with a gesture. I turned and saw Peter and the blonde disappearing up the next block. But not without a backward glance.

I told myself Peter didn't know it was me who'd almost been hit by a car. Had he known, he would have left that woman and rushed to my side.

As my surroundings and the noise synchronized, I turned,

quickened my pace, and ignored the palpable pull from behind as I repeated, "Peter didn't know it was me" until it became fact. After walking half a block, I glanced back to see if Peter had stopped, to see if he was following me. He wasn't. And I started repeating again, "Peter didn't know it was me."

I need to call Sarah, I thought. My shaking hands dug around in my bag until I remembered I didn't have my cell phone with me. Since I'd been fired, the phone didn't ring, the pager didn't beep, and there were no messages. So I'd stopped carrying all mobile modes of communication. There were still phone boxes dotting the city streets. And one happened to be right in front of me.

Ignoring the decades of dirt surely coating the handset, I gingerly picked it up. Holding the handset so it hovered next to my ear, I dialed my sister. She wasn't home. I dropped the phone back in the cradle, pressed my forehead against the handset, and whispered, "Please. Please come back."

Nobody spoke to me; nothing happened. The house I carried around in my head remained a ghost town. Still, I had been whispering this for days. Sometimes yelling it when I was alone. The response was an iron door of silence.

I backed away, stepped off the curb, and then sat down for I don't know how long. I hunched over and cried, unnoticed by the passing pedestrians. The cold concrete crept through my jeans, turning my bones into an arctic loneliness that came only in the deadest of winter. After a while, I noticed the garbage scattered around my feet: a Reese's wrapper, a coffee-stained paper cup, a silver gum paper. I wished one of those street-sweeping trucks would come and brush me away. I finally accepted that wasn't going to happen and I got up and walked home.

The message light on my answering machine was blinking. I hit the play button.

"Holly, it's Milton. I am back in the office and look forward to seeing you today at our regular hour."

He's back.

I'm not going.

He's back.

I'm not going.

For the four hours between Milton's message and our appointment, I alternated between vowing not to show up and relief that he'd returned. On one hand I thought: Let him see what it feels like to open the door and find an empty waiting room. I told myself this would convey my feelings much better than I ever could anyway. Then I remembered I had done this in the early days of seeing him. It hadn't had the effect I'd hoped for. Relief finally won out and I arrived fifteen minutes early for my appointment. I didn't know what I resented more—that I was there, or that Milton didn't look surprised to see me when he opened the door.

"How was the trip?" I said.

"Nice, thank you. Now, catch me up," said Milton. "What have you been doing since we last spoke?"

Milton had checked in every day at noon. I hadn't taken his calls and I hadn't bothered to return them. If Milton really cared, he would have come home the minute he knew I was in trouble.

"Well, just this morning, I was stalking my boyfriend. At least, that's what I thought he was last time I checked. But then I saw him with another woman. He's still coming over to my house a few nights a week. So, I just don't know. I mean, people come, people go. People go to France." I arched my eyebrows. Milton's face remained impassive. *He's not biting.* I sighed. "Oh, and I've been shopping." I lifted up my scarred foot, and we both contemplated it for a moment.

"I've never seen you wear a pair of sandals, Holly," Milton

said. Hooked him with a shoe, I thought. Now we could talk about something really important.

"I haven't worn a pair of sandals since I was six and a half." I put my foot back down. "My mother wouldn't allow it."

"Why not?" said Milton.

"Because, well, it's a long story," I said.

"That is what we are here for," he said. "Life stories, long or short."

"I thought I was catching you up?"

Milton remained silent.

"I don't talk about the past, remember?"

"And look where that has gotten you," said Milton.

"That's low," I said.

"Tell me why your mother never allowed you to wear sandals," said Milton.

I couldn't seem to win anywhere. I sat back with my arms across my chest. "It started with a picnic," I said.

Every summer our extended family gathered together for a picnic. The plan was always to leave early so we'd have a day of fun. That morning the car was loaded up, our shoes were on, and my mother was just getting in the shower. So instead of leaving, we sat rigidly in the kitchen, hostages to her sense of timing. I know I prayed that I wouldn't be the one to break first and show my impatience over waiting.

My father walked in the kitchen and said, "Come on, let's go get doughnuts." Sarah and I looked at each other and I let out a whoop of glee. Doughnuts were the worst kind of contraband in our home. Taking us to eat them was unmitigated disobedience. My father didn't seem to care.

The three of us sat, heady with sedition, in the backseat as my father turned into the parking lot of the doughnut shop. He opened his door and got out of the car. We didn't move. My father laughed when he realized we were too afraid to take that final step over the line. He opened the passenger door and we catapulted into sin and frosted old-fashioneds. After we ate the doughnuts, Sarah inspected each of us for stray crumbs or any other telltale signs. We arrived home just as my mother was putting the finishing touches on her outfit. We were all grateful for my father's impeccable timing.

"Where did you go?" my mother asked my father when she got in the car.

"Kids were restless. I took them for a drive."

My mother looked back over the seat at us and smiled as her eyes scanned each of our faces. "Sarah," she said, "you have something on your face. Lean in."

We held our collective breaths. My mother licked her thumb and brushed off whatever dust particle only she could see with her microscopic vision. Then she turned back to the front and commented on the weather. The sky looked gluttonous with black clouds spilling over the waistline of its too-tight blue trousers. I dozed off in the back of the car while watching the cars flash by.

We arrived late to greetings, hugs, kisses, exclamations of unprecedented growth, and Linda, a friend one of my aunts had brought along, sitting on one of the lawn chairs and clad in a very tiny bikini. The kind my mother wore for sunbathing only in the privacy of our backyard.

My mother and some of the other women commented under their breath about Linda while the men seemed particularly solicitous—did she need a drink, a towel, lotion? I heard the word *divorced*. I had heard my mother say this word before. Usually it resulted in the women being mean and the men nice. Today was no exception. All the men, my father in particular, were very accommodating.

After swimming, the adults prepared food while we kids played freeze tag on the grass. My father volunteered to keep an eye on us. This involved his sitting with his back to us and facing Linda and her lawn chair.

The game was in full swing and Sarah was it. She yelled out, *"Freeze!"* with fierceness. I jumped in the air and landed with a perfect karate-chop pose.

At that moment, my mother walked over to where we were and said to us while looking directly at my father and Linda, "Sarah, go tell your father we need him to help with the barbecue."

"Oh, man," we said without dropping our poses. We expected Sarah to negotiate or put up at least a bit of resistance.

She narrowed her eyes but said nothing. I looked at her. I looked at my mother.

"What!?" my mother snapped at me. I held perfectly still, hoping she would let it go and walk away. "In fact, why don't all you kids come over and help get the food together." She turned and stalked off. Stricken, I let down my arms.

"Thanks a lot, Holly," I heard from several of my cousins and family friends as they passed. I trailed behind them, feeling desolate. I didn't know what I'd done to ruin the game.

Since nobody was being friendly, I made a detour over to my father's table and arrived just in time to hear Sarah say, "Your wife wants you to come take care of the barbecue." She emphasized the word *wife*. Without waiting for him to reply, she took my arm and dragged me away toward the table where all the picnic stuff was laid out.

"Let go," I whispered to her, trying to wrench my arm away.

"No."

"I didn't do anything," I said indignantly.

"She's not mad at you. She's mad at him," Sarah said, pointing her thumb over her shoulder.

"Why?" I asked, confused.

"Because he is probably having an affair with Linda," Sarah said importantly, "or he wants to."

"What's an affair?"

"Never mind," Sarah said, trying to shush me. My aunt approached.

"My dad wants to have an affair with Linda," I said in a matter-of-fact voice.

My aunt's eyes bulged. "Why would you say something like that?" This wasn't the reaction I had expected.

"What did she say?" asked my mother. My aunt turned around. I said again, "Dad wants to have an affair with Linda." Sarah was suddenly very busy pulling out the paper plates.

"*What?*" my mother screamed. Then my father was standing right there and my mother hissed something at him. I couldn't hear it, but I knew it wasn't good.

When she finished, my father came at me with smoldering eyes and a red face. Gripping my elbow, he said through clenched teeth, "You little bitch . . . spreading lies."

What's a bitch? I thought frantically. What did I lie about?

People looked away, pretending not to listen while they readied their picnic stuff. "You're causing a scene," my mother whispered angrily.

"Sarah told—" My father clamped a hand over my mouth and leaned in close to my ear. I could smell the whiskey and cigarettes on his breath. I went limp, as I'd learned to do when he whispered with whiskey breath.

"You keep your mouth shut. If I ever hear you say something like that again, you will wish you'd never been born." He let go. I sat there with saucerlike eyes while invisible hands forced everything I felt down my throat. I didn't cry. I didn't speak. I waited until my parents left and then I got up and walked slowly away.

"Where are you going?" snapped my mother.

"To the bathroom," I whispered. I walked across the lawn and then broke into a run, not stopping until I reached the lake, where I broke the buddy-system rule—never swim alone—and went in knowing I would be in trouble if anyone caught me. When I was waist-deep, I arched my back as I had been taught, and then dropped into the water and floated, waiting for someone to come to get me.

Nobody did. The longer I waited, the more alone I felt. Anxiety and hunger finally compelled me out of the lake. When I was ankle-deep in the water, I thought maybe nobody had come to get me because they had all left. My foot sank in the sand. Something sharp dragged across the top of it. I broke into a run without stopping to look down. As I neared the picnic tables, I saw my father sitting alone with a cigarette pressed between his lips. He struck the match against the book in his cupped hand, and then waved it back and forth in slow motion while craning his head forward. Using one hand as a visor while the other pinched the cigarette between thumb and forefinger, he inhaled. I felt him watching me and I wanted to run to him, leap into his arms, and have him tell me he wasn't mad anymore. Tell me he missed me. Ask me where I'd been.

I ran faster. He turned away. A cloud passed over the sun. The air chilled slightly.

When I reached the picnic area grass I saw my uncle manning the grill. He smiled and waved the barbecue tongs at me. I waved back. He lowered the tongs slowly, paused for a moment, and then dropped them on the ground as he ran toward me while pulling off his new white T-shirt. The look of panic on his face startled me. I stopped. Looked down and saw my right foot covered in bright red blood. Behind me was a wake of bloody grass. The sight of the blood scared me. I felt dizzy and started to cry. My uncle caught me up in his arms and wrapped his T-shirt around my foot. My mother, who had been holding court in the center of the other mothers, was now at my uncle's side.

"You'll ruin your T-shirt doing that," she said in a voice just low enough to keep it out of earshot.

Ignoring the comment about the shirt, my uncle said, "It needs to be looked at, but I don't think it's anything too serious. If someone can take over for me at the barbecue, we'll be back in no time for burned hot dogs." My mother waved over at my father. Over my uncle's shoulder, I watched him toss his cigarette to the ground, get up, and walk toward the car, where we met him.

"Daddy, are you going to go with us?" I whimpered.

"Are you going to keep your mouth shut from now on?" he said with an edge to his voice that speared me.

"Yes," I said.

"Do you promise?" he said, lifting my chin and looking in my eyes.

"I promise. Daddy. Please. I promise."

He got in the car and started the engine. My uncle picked me up and went around to the passenger door.

"Put her in the back," said my father through the open window. "I want to see if she can keep her word. If she can, she can ride up front later."

I sat in the back holding the T-shirt over my foot. At the hospital, my father reached in the car to get me. I flung myself into his arms. As he carried me inside he said, "Holls, I am sorry about earlier. But you've got to watch what you say."

In the waiting room, I sat nestled in my father's lap, watching the blood soak into the T-shirt until it finally started dripping on the floor. I saw through the waiting room window that the clouds had all dissipated and the sun beamed across the face of the sky. My uncle sat mutely beside us. In the exam room, the doctor cleaned the blood off my foot.

"Looks like she got caught by the top of a beer can." Then the doctor opened the wound to check how deep it was. The last thing I remembered before passing out was that the inside of the space between my toes looked like the suction cups on an octopus.

I awoke later in the car. My father held a lit cigarette up to the small opening in the window. The smoke snaked back behind his head and passed across each of us like a cat sniffing and marking and eventually spreading out to settle on the window behind us. The lights from the oncoming traffic outlined my mother's head. My foot throbbed. It was thickly bandaged. I wondered if it was sewn up. But I could tell by the rigid way my mother held her head and the thickness of the smoke in the car that now was not the time to ask.

When I finished the story Milton said, "Do you remember how you felt when you were floating in the lake?" I was perplexed by his attention to this particular detail. I expected him to ask about Linda. Turned out my father did have an affair with her. She was not the first and she certainly was not the last. But Milton and I had long since covered the ground of my father's infidelities and my mother's complicity, and the funny thing was, I did remember exactly how I felt that day.

I closed my eyes and imagined I was floating in that lake. "All I could see was the blank and empty sky. I felt so small floating there, and I was afraid, but not in that primordial-fear kind of way," I said, opening my eyes. "I see that in my cats all the time when I watch them react to something that startles them. They jump a mile high and start moving their legs in the air as if to get a running start when they hit the floor. Where they're going is beyond me. It's not like our apartment is large enough for a reaction like that."

"Yes," said Milton, as he leaned back waiting for me to say more. I sat mute. "So you felt anxious?" Milton presented the word to me as if on a platter in his open hands.

I considered this for a second. "Sort of. But in a way it is like my cats."

"How so?"

"They are simultaneously intrigued and frightened by the possibility that exists beyond the window. Cat Two is satisfied in his minimum-security prison with three hots and a cot."

Milton smiled.

"He has no desire to leave." I raised my eyebrow in a go-figure kind of way. "Cat One always has an eye out for every opportunity of escape."

"Where do you think Cat One would go if he could get out?" said Milton.

"Where he always goes—to the neighbor's roof garden. And then I have to catch him and bring him back. Usually with him demanding a writ of habeas corpus. I think he enrolled in online law courses."

This got another smile from Milton. "Why do you bring him back?" His face went serious again.

"Because it is not safe out there on the roof."

"And?"

"And because I don't want to lose him. I don't want to wake up one day and find him gone. Just like that." I snapped my fingers. "The connection severed as if it was never there. All that is left is the fading memories and feelings."

We sat for a moment. I contemplated the paneling in his office. It was ugly. Kind of that rough, knotty pine with the holes. It belonged in a cabin somewhere in the woods and not in an office in New York City. Turning back to Milton, I said, "That is how I felt that day. I wanted to stay and I wanted to escape."

"But nobody came to get you."

"No. And the quiet closed in on me while I waited."

"Like now?"

"Like now," I whispered. "All my connections severed as if they were never there."

"And this is what is frightening you now?"

"Yes," I said, taking a pillow and pressing it to my stomach. "You can't know the quiet, Milton."

"Tell me about what I can't know then."

"It is filled with questions I can't answer."

"What are the questions?"

"Where do we go? What happens to us? I can't stand not knowing," I said. I heard a siren. I wondered if it was a fire truck or a police car. "That day was the first time I felt that feeling I have described to you ad nauseam," I said, "where my body starts to almost recoil inside and I am pushing to get out of it. I feel like if could just cross that big expanse of nothingness, I would have an understanding. So I push at it. But then it becomes a black hole inside me. I try to ignore it but it is always there," I said, flattening my hands and pressing them into the pillow while my foot did a *rat-a-tat-tat* on the floor. "Looming over me. Wrapped around me." I dropped the pillow and slid to the edge of the couch. I breathed rapidly.

"Stay with this as long as you can," said Milton.

"I'm trying." I jumped up and walked in circles, waving my arms, trying to protect myself from the dread cutting off my air. I thought if I went around fast enough I could get away. But I knew that wasn't true. This feeling was a constant ride-along.

"Breathe, Holly," Milton said, on the edge of his chair now.

"I can't talk about this anymore," I said, facing him. "I can't talk about this."

"Why don't you sit back down, Holly?" Milton gestured to the couch.

"I don't want to talk about this anymore." I sat in the chair with the big pink cushion.

"That's fine."

Milton gave me a moment and then said, "What do you want to talk about then?"

"I don't know."

Milton paused for a second again and then said, "How do you feel about losing your job?"

"Relieved." It rushed out of me, and I realized I did feel oddly relieved. "I feel relieved. I shouldn't feel relieved because I am one royalty check away from welfare." Milton gave me the look that said, *Continue.* "I know I should feel panicked about this right now, but I feel numb. Like the proverbial lamb being led to a slaughter. Why do we say that anyway? It is a sick analogy. I wonder if animals are really numb when being led to the slaughter. I don't think they are. Today I read about a pig on the way to a slaughterhouse that made a run for it at a red light. It took several people to subdue and catch it. I guess it was pretty fat." This last word stuck in my throat.

We were both quiet.

"You are thinking of your own porcine friend taken against her will?"

"Ruffles." As soon as I said her name, grief, the unwelcome visitor, pounded at the door of my chest. Turned out that grief had scheduled the visit days ago and I had conveniently forgotten. Now grief's arrival was an unwanted surprise and I was caught without the Committee's house clean or the laundry done or even the guest bed made. And I couldn't let grief sleep in the Committee's beds.

I didn't answer the door. I sat there willing grief to go away. If I switched off the lights and stereo and crouched on the floor in the Committee's living room, would grief think nobody was home and go away?

The banging on my chest intensified.

I sat there in the uncomfortable pink chair feeling the same way I had at the lake that day.

The banging on my chest intensified.

Go away, I wanted to scream. It didn't. I slid off the chair and crouched on Milton's Oriental rug. My hands covered my ears like protective wear. I remembered how many times I had tried this over the years before I left the family nest. It never worked then and it wasn't working now.

The unwelcome visitor finally broke the Committee's door down and a grief stampede rushed in right over the top of me. Fanning out through the house. Touching the Committee's things. Turning them over. Asking the price with a complete disregard for the history and feelings, for what was at stake. Opening drawers and cupboards, using the bathroom, unpacking, and finally moving in. Then grief, wanting a little fresh air, opened the windows wide and the cold winter of reality blew, with a full-force gale, across me sitting there in Milton's office.

I had lost my Committee.

I had lost my job.

I had lost my boyfriend.

I . . . was . . . lost.

Milton handed me a box of Kleenex. When I was all cried out, I had a hillock of soggy tissues on my lap and we had about ten minutes remaining in the hour. I sat there feeling like a deer that had just gone through the windshield of some errant SUV. But the genie was not going back in the proverbial bottle.

"I have an idea about how to proceed," said Milton.

"Will it bring them back?"

"Do you want them back?" said Milton.

"I do. Oh, God, I do." A fresh round of pain spasms kicked off in my gut.

"We'll start Thursday then." Milton's eyes sparkled.

{ 15 }

Group therapy. Milton's idea was group therapy. I was not thrilled. Not even close. I hated that touchy-feely let's-all-love-each-other kind of crap. Milton knew this and yet he suggested that we try group therapy. And as much as I hated the idea of doing what was sure to be an exercise in exposing new-age bullshit like reflecting back what people said, I obediently sat in an empty waiting room, having arrived several minutes before the appointed time. That I was alone struck me as odd. *Where's the group? They should be here.*

I thumbed through last week's *New Yorker* looking for any of the cartoons I'd missed. By my watch, it was two minutes to the hour. Not even enough for "Shouts & Murmurs." I wondered if Milton had different waiting rooms and doors for groups. He could have a garage-door-opener type of device and push the button so all the doors sprang open at once. Inviting everyone in at the same time eliminated any hint of favoritism. We'd all charge right over the top of him to get to the most comfortable furniture. Or maybe not, since floorboards were more comfortable than Milton's antique furniture. I laughed at the thought.

"Holly." Milton's voice interrupted my amusement. I looked up. He appeared slightly amused himself. Did he know what the source of my mirth was? Then I thought it was funny how people always think they know what is on the other person's mind. And even funnier how it almost never works out to be what you thought they were thinking.

"Yep." I dropped the *New Yorker* back on the end table as I stood. I paused for a moment, nodded, and followed him into his office. It was empty.

"Where is everyone?" I said.

"Have a seat, Holly," said Milton.

I sat on the couch.

"Close your eyes, Holly," said Milton.

I did.

"Do you want to resolve your issues with the Committee through therapy?" said Milton.

I wanted to bolt from the room.

"This is weird." I opened my eyes. "I expected people and a group setting. Not that I want that, mind you. That seems weird too."

"Holly, please just trust me and answer the question," said Milton.

"Okay. I guess so." I closed my eyes again.

"You guess what?" said Milton.

"I guess. I mean, yes, I want to resolve my issues with the Committee in therapy."

They appeared.

My Committee.

The sight of them was dizzying. Goose bumps erupted across my body. I wanted to hug them all. Touch each one of their faces, even the Boy's blurry one. I clapped my hands and laughed. I waved at Betty Jane's sunflower doing what appeared to be a dance of joy before me. I'd have danced too if my feet were steady enough. "They're here, Milton," I cried. "They're back. Oh, they're back."

My smile split wider across my face. Milton nodded impassively. "Betty Jane, the Silent One, Sarge, the Boy, and . . ." I pushed myself forward on the couch. The Committee's therapy room mirrored Milton's. There was nowhere for Ruffles to hide. "And . . . her pillow . . ." I turned to Betty Jane, teeth bared, and said out loud, "Where is *she*?"

"I have no idea what you mean," said Betty Jane inside my head.

"Ruffles is missing," I said to Milton. "Ruffles isn't here. Where is Ruffles?" I said to him and Betty Jane.

"Holly," said Milton, "before we proceed I am going to ask you to do something you might consider unorthodox." That jolted me out of my upset. What could possibly be unorthodox at this point in our work?

"Okay," I said, "what?"

"I would like to ask you to allow all the voices to speak out loud while we are here doing our work. All responses should come from your mouth. It is the only way we can make sure nothing is kept from me."

"Shuffle like a deck of cards, you mean?" The Silent One, the Boy, Sarge, Ruffles, and I used to do this when I was a teenager. Before Betty Jane arrived there was never an issue of control. Ruffles figured out pretty quickly that with her, you couldn't give a fraction of an inch, so we stopped shuffling. "Are you sure it's safe?" I said.

"Perfectly safe," said Milton. Betty Jane's face looked just like it did in the hotel after the Emmys. I blanched. "She cannot harm you, Holly. Remember the rules we agreed upon? The ones that made it possible for you to become a voice-over artist?"

"Vaguely," I said. I thought back to that day in therapy when Milton and Betty Jane negotiated, him for my sanity and her for fame.

"Please trust me."

"Will it help find Ruffles?"

"I'm not sure, Holly, but it will help regardless."

"This is what you meant by group therapy?" I said. Milton nodded.

I alternated between Milton's and Betty Jane's faces. Her caution about my choices felt prescient at that moment. But I didn't know if that was good or bad. If Ruffles were there, I'd choose group therapy, shuffling personalities, and Betty Jane's presence without looking back. But Ruffles wasn't there. I didn't know why but I suspected it had to do with Betty Jane. *Is four better than five? Will I be able to find Ruffles if I agree to do this?* I thought I saw Sarge nod. Maybe I wanted him to. I don't know. All I know is I finally said, "Okay, I'll do that," and then I said to Betty Jane, "Now tell us what you've done with Ruffles."

"You know exactly where she is," said Betty Jane out of my mouth. But instead of being in the Committee's room, I hovered near her like in the old days. I relaxed.

"I don't know where she is," I said.

"Well, that's your loss, then," said Betty Jane.

"Okay," interrupted Milton, "all in good time. Now, here is how we are going to work. We will meet two days a week during your regular sessions, Holly—"

"But what about—"

"Why don't you let him finish," said Betty Jane. Sarge sat forward as if he were going to get up and throttle her. The Boy hid his face in the back cushion.

"Betty Jane, please refrain from interrupting." My eyebrows shot up. I didn't expect this much support. "We will start each session by checking in. A check-in is how we indicate our general mood for the day. It should be fairly short. And since you seem so intent on speaking, why don't we start with you, Betty Jane?"

"Well . . ." She held up my hand and inspected my manicure. I expected that to stop her cold, because I hadn't attended to my nails since she left. "To tell the truth, I am feeling inconvenienced by this whole thing. Coerced is more like it. But I agreed to do it, and a Southern woman always keeps her word." She didn't comment on the state of my nails. In the Committee's therapy room, she was seated on the pink chair that always reminded me of an old-fashioned commode. I heard the flushing sound that always accompanied the sight of that chair. I smiled.

"Sarge?" said Milton.

"Doin' okay," said Sarge. My heart ached at the sound of his voice. I didn't know who I missed more, him or Ruffles.

The Silent One came forth to bow his head, and then he drifted backward. Nobody said a word. Inside my head, Betty Jane arched her eyebrow at me.

"Oh. Me? Well, I feel here. I mean to say, I am here. Okay, we know I am here. I mean, okay. I am okay." I had so many mixed emotions running through me. She rolled her eyes. I looked at the Boy.

"Little Bean. I like to be called Little Bean," he said. I felt a jolt at his new name. I shuddered and pushed it aside. "And I feel lonely," he said softly, "desperately lonely."

Me too, I thought. *Me too.*

I wanted to ask Sarge, Little Bean, as the Boy now liked to be called, and the Silent One if they knew where Ruffles was, but I didn't want Betty Jane to hear. I decided I'd wait until she went to bed to ask and instead sat there and enjoyed their faces until Milton announced that we had five minutes remaining in the hour.

"All right." I said. Then to the Committee, "The apartment is kind of a mess, and, well, I've been smoking indoors. But only because I was afraid to catch the cat without you, Sarge." The lines on his face deepened when I said this. "I know. I'm sorry. The smoke is bad for the Boy, I mean Little Bean . . ." Sarge's eyebrows came together as he closed his eyes. My body went hollow. "Milton?" I said. "They get to come home with me, right?"

Milton shook his head and I felt like I'd been shoved hard. This must be how torture victims felt when they realized the nice gesture of seeing their loved ones was really just coercion to get them to do what was asked of them.

"Then I won't leave," I whispered as I clenched my fists.

"Holly—"

At that moment, everything on the other side of the door to Milton's office seemed black and treacherous. "*No!* I won't leave. I can't. I won't. You can't make me."

Sarge stood up slowly. His eyes were still closed. "Do your duty, soldier," he said softly. My breath caught in my throat. The command was harsh when Sarge said it a second time. I wanted to ignore it, but then I noticed he had a torrent of tears running down his face. He opened his eyes and blinked. "Soldier?"

"HUA," I whispered. He raised a hand in salute. Betty Jane watched the whole exchange with a bored expression.

Somehow I walked out of Milton's office, but I don't remember anything between the Committee disappearing when I closed the door and turning the key in the lock to the door of my apartment.

Milton called me the next day. I answered before the phone could ring a second time. He said he thought it was a good idea for us to speak in between sessions and proposed the daily noon call I'd rejected before. This time I accepted. Then I asked him, "Where is Ruffles; where did she go?"

"Holly, can you please recount again what happened after the Emmy awards?"

I did. When I finished, Milton said, "Holly, is it possible that Ruffles believes that standing up to Betty Jane is what caused her to kidnap the Committee, and because of this she's hiding?"

"That's stupid," I said. "I don't care what she did. I'm not mad. I mean, Milton, come on, no shopping trip can fill the hole a three-hundred-pound friend leaves." My attempt at being flip fell flat.

"I only want her back," I said. "I miss her. I'm not mad."

"Perhaps stating this is enough," said Milton. "I have an idea. I'd like you to go along with me during our session on Tuesday."

Once bitten, twice shy obviously never made an impact on me. I agreed. Then I counted the hours until Tuesday.

On Tuesday, I made my resolution statement and the Committee appeared. No Ruffles. The disappointment rendered me speechless, and when Milton said, "And?" all I could do was shake my head no. Then he said, "Holly, it's time we started talking about the past."

What? Says who? I shot eyeball daggers at Milton. He peered at me over the top of his square lenses. I knew this gesture was meant to remind me that I'd agreed to "go along" with him. Typical that what I agreed to ended up being one of Milton's off-the-menu specials.

A couple of seconds passed; then Betty Jane said, "I agree. Let's talk about the past."

"Oh, really?" I snarled. "Well, if that's how you feel, why don't we start with how you made your way into my life?"

"Go right ahead," she said. "I am sure you'll get the story wrong."

I hated her for being agreeable, and I hated Milton for doing this instead of working on getting Ruffles back.

"Holly?" said Milton.

"Oh, all right," I said. "I have to start with my high school graduation, and Little Bean has to leave the room." Sarge nodded and directed him into the waiting room.

The day after I graduated from high school I walked through the door at ten o'clock in the morning. I had never before stayed out all night. Doing so felt more like a rite of passage than receiving my diploma the day before had.

Sarah and my mother were in the living room drinking coffee. My mother sat on the couch in her bathrobe with unbrushed hair and a face that looked lined and tired. Sarah was next to her holding a coffee cup in one hand and some papers in another.

I opened my mouth to say good morning.

"Dad's gone," said Sarah.

"Gone where?" I said.

During the past several years, my father had spent most of his time traveling. We saw him only on the weekends. After Sarah left for university, I felt as if I were living alone. My mother insisted we eat together when my father was home or if Sarah was visiting. Otherwise, she had dinner in bed with her television set. I am not sure what she did during the day, and she never asked me what I did. I stayed in my part of the house and she stayed in hers. We were strangers sharing space.

"Your father left," said my mother. Holding the dainty saucer in her left hand, she picked up the coffee cup, pinkie extended, with her right. "Moved out." She sipped her coffee. "You drove him away."

"Mom!" snapped Sarah.

"Oh, that's right. She never does anything. Poor Holly. Poor Holly, the lazy, selfish liar, just like her father," snarled my mother.

"You made me what I am," I said. "Go look in the mirror if you want to find the person who's responsible for how I turned out."

"You are going to take me on now, Holly," flared my mother. "Do you think your little blame game will work on me the way it did your father?" I didn't need to answer her. My mother was a heartless woman, and because of this, I knew my so-called "little blame game" would not work with her, because it wasn't a game. It was survival. My father had come this close to breaking me. If it hadn't been for the Boy, he would have.

"Mom." Sarah covered my mother's hand with her own, trying to quiet her. "Maybe you should go get some rest."

"I do not need rest," said my mother. "Get dressed. We are going shopping."

"Shopping?" said Sarah. "Don't you think—"

"What? I have your father's credit cards; we are going to use them." My mother got up. "Be ready in two hours. That is final." She carried her coffee cup into the kitchen.

All told, we spent almost five thousand dollars that day, half of it at the cosmetic counter in Bloomingdale's. My mother had them do a full makeover on me while she and the saleswoman lectured me on the importance of beauty, skin care, lipstick, and so on. I escaped to the bathroom as soon as I could. When I faced the mirror, Ruffles told me I looked like a streetwalker. I unrolled the bathroom tissue and proceeded to wipe everything off.

After my mother went to bed, Sarah and I sat in darkness in my room. "Do you remember Linda?" she said. Of course I remembered Linda. And her tiny bikini. How could I forget her? I slipped my scarred foot out from under the covers and held it up in the air. The curtains were open and the light from the street made my pale foot appear ghostly. "Dad was going to leave us for her. Then the accident—"

Everything went black and I found myself riding in Sarge's Chevy. The Boy sat between us. Ruffles occupied the whole backseat. The rear bumper scraped the pavement, sending up sparks. She usually didn't ride in the car because even the counterbalance of the Hemi engine Sarge had installed was not enough to offset her bulk.

A car careened toward us. Sarge swerved to avoid it. Then he jumped the Chevy off the road. We hit a wire fence. Sarge gunned the motor. The fence stretched until it snapped and we bounced along in a field. After a while Sarge eased up on the gas. Finally he stopped the car and rested his head on the steering wheel. The scene changed back to their living room in my head. The Silent One nodded at Sarge.

"Why do you use that weird voice?" Sarah sounded far away.

"Is it safe?" Sarge asked the Silent One. Safe from what? I wondered. My head nodded. I felt the pillow against my back again.

"Holly, who was that speaking to me?" said Sarah.

"Who spoke to you? What did they say?" I said.

"Holly, what's going on?" said Sarah.

"I can't tell you. I—" Sarge stood. The Silent One held out his arm as if to stop him. "I'm not supposed to tell you," I said. We sat for a moment. The Silent One nodded. "Sarah, if I tell you a secret, do you promise not to tell anyone? Ever?"

"I promise." I told Sarah about the Silent One, the Boy, Sarge, and Ruffles. They couldn't stop me because the Silent One somehow held them at bay. When I finished she said, "I've suspected something like this for a long time."

Even though Sarah was my sister, telling her my secret felt like standing naked in front of a crowd of thousands. Inside my head, everyone but the Silent One waited tensely for the aftershock to hit. After a few minutes, I said, "So finish telling me about Linda."

"You still won't talk about—"

"Tell me about Linda," I said.

"Okay," said Sarah. "Okay. Dad kept seeing her but he wouldn't leave us." She paused. Sarge stood, ready. "You know, all his trips?" continued Sarah.

My shoulders relaxed. Inside my head, everyone let out their breath.

"He broke it off with her after that car wreck. Mom convinced him it was the only way they could make it work. Remember when he stopped drinking?"

"Yeah, that lasted long," I said.

"Well, I'm not denying he was an asshole, Holly. But relationships are complicated. Life is complicated."

I sat back, surprised. Was? Something had definitely changed between Sarah and my father. Me? I didn't believe in people changing.

"He told me even though you and he stopped speaking for the most part when you were fourteen, he still wanted to wait until you finished high school to leave. He wasn't going to be the abandoning father. Mom got the divorce papers this morning. He's moved to Florida with Linda. Transferred to another office."

"How did I not know about Linda?"

"You were always off somewhere." Sarah motioned to my head.

"Now you know where," I said.

"Yeah," she said, "now I know where."

The next day Sarah gave me a copy of the book *Sybil*. But it didn't resonate with me. I didn't remember losing time, and my history seemed intact. But, for the first time, I wondered if there was something wrong with me. I wanted to be normal like everyone else.

Sarah stayed with us for the summer and tried to maintain order while my mother and I went on our respective sprees. My mother did her best to bankrupt my father, while I threw myself into what I thought was normal for an eighteen-year-old—partying.

A few weeks after my father left, I found myself at the first of many summer gatherings. Eddie, the guy I'd had a crush on since I was fourteen, was there without his arm charm, supermodel-wannabe girlfriend. I sat next to him on the couch listening to him as he told the guys in the room that his girlfriend had gone to Europe for the summer. I drank beer after beer while Sarge, Ruffles, and the Silent One watched disapprovingly. Then someone lit a joint and started passing it around. Eddie handed it to me.

"Holly," barked Sarge.

I felt a wall come down between me and those in my head. I inhaled deeply on the joint. After a few passes, Ruffles, Sarge, the Silent One, and the Boy floated above the living room in my head and I floated somewhere between them and Eddie.

I opened my eyes and moved closer to him. My body ached for him. I pushed myself up from the couch and stood there swaying a little. I closed my eyes. Sarge reclined, eyes closed, nodding his head to whatever was coming through on his headphones. Ruffles marveled at the shape and size of each chip she held before she shoveled it into her mouth. The Silent One hovered in the air. His prayer altar had turned into a multicolored flying carpet. I moved my body as if dancing. The living room in my head swayed.

"Check out Holly," Eddie's friend said. I smiled, my eyes still shut.

"Everyone get out," I whispered. None of them moved. I let myself drift backward. "Everyone, out!" I yelled it this time.

The Silent One dropped to the floor. Sarge removed his headphones.

"Out," I yelled again.

The Silent One's face shifted with realization. He nodded to Sarge, who didn't argue. "Take her too," I said, pointing to Ruffles. "And the Boy." They disappeared. The house was empty.

"Guy says if you wanted to be alone, all you had to do is ask," said one of Eddie's friends.

I opened my eyes. Eddie had a bemused look on his face. I heard the door shut. Eddie got up and locked it. Then he walked over and stood in front of me. I couldn't breathe. Eddie kissed me slowly as he pushed me to the couch. I took off my shirt and reached behind my back to unhook my bra.

"Whoa, slow down, Holly."

I froze, my hands still on the clasp of my bra. He pulled my arms down and reached around to unhook my bra himself. I unbuckled his jeans. He laughed and threw up his hands. Within a few minutes our pants were off and he was inside me. I felt like someone had cut me in half. When it was over, I pulled on my clothes and went home.

The rest of the summer I smoked pot, drank too much, and had sex in the backseat of Eddie's car. The house inside my head was filthy. Clothes and dirty dishes were everywhere. My mother was thrilled I had a boyfriend. Every morning over coffee I regaled her with made-up stories about our fabulous dates. I was finally in her club.

A week before I was supposed to leave for NYU, Sarah, my

mother, and I were having morning coffee. I had just finished telling my mother about the expensive restaurant Eddie and I had gone to the night before. I described it right down to the steak tartar. Sarah slammed down her coffee cup. The spoon clanged onto the table. "Holly, you are so full of shit."

I expected Sarge to jump up and defend me. He sat in my head listening to his music.

"Sarah, a lady does not use that kind of language." My mother tut-tutted.

"Holly is not going out on dates. She's stoned all day and parking with Eddie at night. I think he probably *would* take her to a nice restaurant, but all Holly wants to do is have sex."

"What?"

I closed my eyes. The debris and smell of the Committee's room were overwhelming. Sarge's head kept nodding. The Silent One slept on the couch. I didn't see the Boy anywhere. *I hope Ruffles hasn't sat on him.* I giggled.

"She thinks it's funny," said Sarah.

I opened my eyes. Slack jawed, my mother sat frozen across from me. Her smile slid into that mean line I hadn't seen since my father left.

"You are just like your father."

My shoulders tensed. Still no reaction in my head.

"You are forbidden to leave this house."

"But Eddie?" I said.

"You will not see him again. You will pack your stuff and we'll be on that plane for New York next week."

I seemed to be falling through the floor. What did she mean, never see him again?

I climbed out my window late that night and called Eddie from a pay phone. He picked me up, we had sex, and then he told me his girlfriend was due back tomorrow and it was over. He dropped me off in front of my house at four in the morning. My mother found me vomiting up gin in the rosebush.

"How dare you embarrass me like this," whispered my mother as she dragged me into the house.

"I think I am going to be sick again," I said.

"If you throw up anywhere in my home you will regret it for the rest of your life."

That threat and her ability to make good on it gave me some inner strength, and I managed to quell the retching. In my drunken haze, I remember her dragging me into the bathroom and putting me under a cold shower. She alternated between slapping me and screaming at me. I fell asleep on the wet tiles.

"Get up," said my mother. I opened my eyes. Everyone remained asleep in my head. She stood in front of me. The disgust on her face made the bile rise again in my throat. "I said get up. Your sister and I want to speak with you."

"Can I change into something dry?"

"No." She turned and left the bathroom.

I sat down at the kitchen table, shivering. Sarah and my mother sat opposite me.

"You disgust me," said my mother, "wandering around in a daze all the time. What is wrong with you? And drinking like that. How can you expect to get anywhere in life? If you do not get a handle on yourself, you will not be allowed to go to New York."

"Mom, we talked about this," said Sarah.

"No, I have had it with Holly and her nonsense. I put up with your father so that you girls could have both parents. I sacrificed for you, and for what? So that your sister can get drunk and sleep around? So I can receive alimony checks signed by Linda?"

Sarah's eyebrows shot up. "She signs your alimony checks?"

My mother ignored her and focused on me.

"You will never make anything of yourself, Holly. And that is your only hope, because you do not have my looks or grace. Sarah was lucky enough to get them; you were not. You're like Anna. Awkward, with your head in the clouds." Anna was my mother's younger sister. They called her eccentric. I'd always liked her.

"Are you even listening to me? You had better get a foothold on your life," said my mother.

"Who are you to talk about getting a foothold?" said Sarah. "You're the one who buries her head in manners and appearances, enabling everything that went on around here."

My mother opened her mouth to say something but no words came out.

"Holly is going to NYU," said Sarah, "and that's final, Mom."

My mother left the two of us in the kitchen. Sarah told me she went to therapy while she was in college. Nobody ever asked what the extra money was for. She thought our father knew, but they didn't talk about it. "Holly, when you get to New York, find a therapist. You need to get some help."

I went into my room, changed into a dry T-shirt, and got into bed. I curled up around a pillow I held close to my stomach. Then I fell asleep.

I woke up the next day with a wicked hangover, a spotless house inside my head, and a new sheriff in town by the name of Betty Jane.

My mother bought us first-class tickets to New York with my father's American Express card. Sarah came along as mediator. We spent another five thousand dollars on clothes and miscellaneous stuff for my dorm. Before Sarah and my mother left for home, my mother handed me a credit card. "Use it whenever you like," she said. "Your father pays the bill."

"Make sure you put that where we can find it," said Betty Jane inside my head.

"I remember it so differently," said Betty Jane.

"Of course you do," I said. "What is it you remember? All I remember is that life was so much better before you."

"Life was so much better?" snapped Betty Jane. "You were a drug- and booze-addled teenager without structure or guidance. How do you think you finished college?"

"I got into college and finished it because of Ruffles, not you. Where is she?" I demanded.

"'Where is she,'" mimicked Betty Jane.

I started to cry.

"Holly," Milton interrupted, "you called Betty Jane the 'new sheriff.' What did you mean by that?"

"Before her, we were one big, happy family. We got along. We had fun. We laughed. We shared things. We were best friends. She brought rules, and etiquette, and appearances, and Charmin." I kicked my bag. I hadn't yet liberated myself from Betty Jane's toilet paper of choice. "But most of all she brought strife and dissension. We had to sneak around, whisper, tell secrets. Things just changed after she arrived. In a very bad way." I glared at Milton, but it was meant for Betty Jane.

"Oh, how they do forget," said Betty Jane.

"It sounds like Betty Jane's arrival marked the need for someone to be in charge. Someone to help all of you manage life on your own," said Milton. Betty Jane nodded inside my head as my mouth dropped open. How could he say that?

"We were managing fine," I said defensively. Then a fresh rinse of shame over the summer of alcohol, pot, and Eddie drenched me. We hadn't managed fine, but I wasn't about to admit that in front of Betty Jane. I wiped my cheek with the back of my hand. Milton handed me a box of tissues. "The chairwoman of the Committee," I muttered. "She's a cruel leader."

"Most are," said Milton. He sat back and lifted his finger church, and I waited for the ensuing sermon. "The mind is a wonderful thing, Holly," said Milton. "It can create an organized system to manage almost anything." I looked away. "The appearance of the first Committee members marked how your mind coped with trauma. With the door already open, each time you experienced a new trauma, your mind created another Committee member to help manage it."

"There was no trauma before Betty Jane. She brought it, remember? She brought it by arriving, she brought it by leaving, and she brought it by returning without Ruffles. I want her to give Ruffles back to me." Then I said directly to Betty Jane, "Give me back Ruffles."

My head shook.

I closed my eyes tightly so I couldn't see either Milton's office or the Committee's living room. I was afraid this was another one of Betty Jane's tricks. Then my head dropped over to the left.

I heard a tearing sound followed by a loud crunch, and my whole body felt like it would burst. I relaxed my eyes and found Ruffles sitting on her pillow inside my head. I watched her hand dive into the bag of chips next to her.

"What was that about a sheriff and much-needed authority?"

{ 16 }

When I heard Ruffles's voice I didn't think about anything but getting to her. I wanted to put my hands on her, touch her to know she was real, to know she was really here. Without another thought, I dropped into the Committee's therapy room so fast that my feet hit the ground moving; then I dove at her with outstretched arms.

When I was a small child, I used to wait at night for the sound of my father's car. When I heard it in the driveway, I'd run to the front door and leap into his arms as he came through. Even a preoccupied person can't resist the joyous greeting of a small child. Ruffles reacted the same way. She embraced me tightly. I broke into sobs.

Without letting go, she yelled, "Don't even think about it. Sarge, don't let her move one more inch."

I turned. Betty Jane stood stock-still with her hand on the door.

I heard Milton calling my name. "Get out of here," said Ruffles. I resisted. She pushed me. I clung to her. Milton called my name again.

She pushed me harder. "Holly, I can't keep her from taking over for much longer. You have to get out of here."

I didn't move. Milton called my name again.

I wanted to huddle there in the Committee's therapy room, where it felt safe. I wanted to stay with the Committee members I loved. Let Betty Jane have control. Tell her she could deal with the outside world on her own for two weeks. I guarantee she'd be begging me to change places again before twenty-four hours passed. Betty Jane opened her mouth. Even though I hadn't uttered a word, my thoughts were still an open book to all of them.

"Holly," screamed Ruffles, "get out of here!"

I tried to move forward to take control. My desire to stay and Betty Jane's desire to take over became two opposing forces and I was caught in the middle. I panicked. I noticed Ruffles's face was purple with strain and Sarge sweated with effort. *Am I too late?* I tried to move my foot. I couldn't. Betty Jane smiled. No, I thought, oh, no.

I fell to my knees and crawled. The floor felt as if it were covered with shards of broken glass. The tunnel back to control continued to draw in. I kept crawling. "I can make it," I kept repeating to myself.

"Squeeze your toes," said Ruffles. I did and I felt the foam of the couch cushion against my back and butt.

I opened my eyes. Milton stood before me. "Don't ever do that again," he said. His face remained impassive as always, but his tone held a mixture of alarm and anger that I'd never heard before. "If I cannot trust you to stay here, we'll pursue an alternate course of treatment that does not include the Committee." Those words might sound innocuous to you, but trust me, Milton's speech was always layered with meaning, and I knew *alternate course* meant, *Try that again and no more Committee. Ever.*

"But, Ruffles . . ." I said weakly. I closed my eyes.

"Holly, what you just did violates the agreement between Betty Jane and me. You willingly disrupted the balance of power between the two of you. Doing so gives control to Betty Jane. Once given, it is not easy to get back."

Milton knew my life was no picnic lately. I couldn't believe he thought Betty Jane would not let go of control freely given. Besides, the rest of the Committee would help me.

"Holly, you have to trust Milton on this one," said Ruffles. "Not even together could we take Betty Jane on if you hand her control. I'd lose if I tried. We all would." A satisfied smirk danced across Betty Jane's lips. I didn't quite understand, but I knew Ruffles was telling the truth.

I nodded at Milton and he got that I knew I'd barely made it back across a very dangerous line.

Nobody said a word for the remaining ten minutes. I didn't argue when Milton called the hour, and my journey home echoed my earlier journey back to Milton's couch.

My days were reduced down to the two hours a week I had with the Committee and the two or three evenings a week I had with Peter. I still hadn't directly addressed that day with the blonde. Instead I repeated, "Peter didn't know it was me," enough times to view it as a grant of judicial absolution toward Peter. I couldn't afford to lose yet another anchor in my life, even if it was rusted with deception and betrayal. But every action of mine indirectly touched on that day over and over again. Peter's taciturnity meant either he really hadn't seen me, or he was playing our usual game of chicken.

The rest of the time passed unnoticed. Friday through Monday was the hardest. Four weeks, twenty-eight days, or six hundred and seventy-two hours passed before I was able to tolerate seeing the Committee on such a limited basis. Given the difficulty of coping with life outside of Milton's office, Milton and I agreed that for the time being, I should focus all my energy on our work. He even offered to arrange payment so I could stretch my money to cover basic expenses like food and heat without having to take a job or ask my family for help. I agreed because I didn't know what else to do.

Fortunately, Sarge's imprint remained, and I used it to create a routine to keep me sane. Cleaning became one of the best ways to pass the time. After four weeks of this, it occurred to me as I raked the scrub brush back and forth across the kitchen tiles that if I cleaned my apartment any more I'd wear the finish off the furniture and floors. I decided to rebel and have a cigarette off schedule. Smoking seemed to be the only thing I could do without causing any harm.

I sat on the windowsill, so the smoke could float up and out, lit my cigarette, and inhaled. Cat One trotted into the room, sniffed, wrinkled his nose, and turned tail and ran. His claws clicked on the floor in the hallway between the two rooms. Then silence. I imagined Cat One was busy whispering to Cat Two, "Avoid the bedroom and secondhand smoke." I made a halfhearted attempt to blow the smoke out the crack in the window.

A muffled ringing interrupted my smoking. *Where's my cell phone?* I scanned the room and spotted it on the floor by the desk. I dropped the cigarette in the ashtray and retrieved the phone. I didn't recognize the number on the faceplate. I stared at the phone as if doing this would magically tell me who was on the other end.

Answer it. Don't answer it. I hated this indecision. I pressed answer. "Hello?"

"Holly, it's Pam," her voice gushed. *Fuck.* I shouldn't have answered. With all her buoyancy, I always imagined Pam bouncing like a ball through life. On a good day I wanted to hurl Pam the ball against the wall. Anything to mute that cheer. On a good day. Today was not a good day.

"Pam. Hi. How—"

"Listen, I ran into Peter yesterday and he told me you're feeling down."

I felt a knife plunge into my heart. I took the last drag on my cigarette and stubbed it out. "Well—"

"So, I have the most fabulous way to cheer you up!" Pam the ball hit one of her high notes on this sentence. I rolled my eyes and coughed out the inhale. "Sounds like someone has been smoking too much," Pam said in that mother-knows-best tone. I could see her in my mind's eye wagging her index finger at me.

"Pam," I said wearily, "I really don't—"

"Peter said it was the perfect plan." Peter knew that any plan involving Pam was far from perfect. I wondered if his telling Pam to call was meant to provoke me. Before I considered it further, though, Pam bounced on. "So, you know I run an evening theater group for kids between the ages of ten and fourteen?"

Oh, God. I told him no a long time ago. I told him no. Cradling the phone between my ear and my shoulder, I picked up the ashtray and walked it into the kitchen for emptying.

"Holly?"

"Uh-huh." I said it quietly, hoping not to give her an opening.

"Well, we are just starting production on a new play that will run for three nights after the first of the year," Pam enthused. "The auditions are next week." Another high note. *She's in the wrong line of work. I'm sure the Met has an opening for their next opera.*

Relieved, I sucked in the remainder of my pride and said slowly, "The thing is, Pam, I'm not really talking to my contacts over at the studio. So I am not really sure how I can—"

"I don't need your contacts, Holly; I need you!"

Okay, now I'd welcome the humiliating position of explaining why I couldn't toss her my contacts. "Me?"

"You!" It came out like an excited shriek and attacked me through the phone like a jolt of electricity. A pack of grasping, bossy, messy, needy short people skittered across my mind. My hands around Peter's throat trailed right behind. He had told Pam to rope me into doing this. "So?" Pam said.

No way. *No way.* The knife I had felt earlier twisted. God, how I hated Peter at that moment. "Pam. I can't. I mean. I . . . I hate kids. Well, I don't hate them. They scare me. I don't connect with kids. I can't . . ." I raked my hair with my fingers as I scanned the room for my lost pack of cigarettes. "I can't . . . I mean . . ." I saw the cigarettes on the table and grabbed them. "I can't . . . actually . . . work with kids." I lit a cigarette. Inhaled and on the exhale said, "It can't be legal to have someone like me work with kids. I—"

"Come on!" exclaimed Pam. "You'll be a natural. Your show is so popular with kids. How could you not be great with them?"

I wished she would stop interrupting me. I hated to be interrupted. And all her cheer was racing around in my head like a dizzying Hot Wheels car. I steadied myself with a hand on the kitchen counter. "I am not, really. I mean, at the moment—"

"Working with kids will do you good. Get you out of your head."

"What do you mean by that?" I snapped. I didn't know what rankled more—the interruptions or the reference to my head.

"I just meant that . . ." Pam paused here. "Well, Peter said you have been spending a lot of time . . ." Another pause.

"Yes?" I said impatiently.

I waited for her to say, *in a hollow head*. But from my perspective this was better than being out and seeing things like Peter and some string-bean blonde, because if I saw them together again, reality would collide with my perception of the reality of Peter and me.

"Well, kind of feeling sorry for yourself," she finished hesitantly.

"How nice of Peter to think of me," I said.

"Holly, don't take it like that. He was really trying to help."

"Bullshit. He knows how much I can't stand kids. And he certainly knows I'd never agree to help you, because you drive me nuts. What an asshole." The words exploded from my mouth like scattershot out of a hunting rifle. I wanted to grab them and swallow them whole.

"Wow, well, somebody just popped her cork," said Pam. "Anyway, I think it would be perfect, Holly. I really do. We could even get to know each other. Maybe I could change your opinion, at least about kids."

"I . . . uh . . ." My fingers went slack and the burning cigarette they held dropped in the sink. I flipped on the faucet to drown it. "I just can't do it," I said. The noise from the running water washed through my body like a wave of regret. The cigarette became a sodden mess.

"Well, think about it." There was starkness to Pam's voice. It was even and flat. I didn't know what to make of this.

"Okay," I said, "I'll think about it."

"Just don't forget we start auditions next week." *There's that old familiar bounce.*

I held the phone away from my ear. "Now I won't."

Pam laughed.

"Okay, here's one thing you don't know about me," I said. "I never say good-bye."

"Well—"

"Hanging up now." I clicked the end button, cutting off her buoyant reply.

I walked over to the NYU building on Washington Square to surprise Peter after his class. Our table of proverbial "elephants in the room" had expanded to seating for at least twenty, but that didn't stop me from an impromptu act. Why not throw caution to the wind? Look what happened earlier in the day when I smoked off schedule. Besides, Peter had said once that he'd like it if I were more spontaneous. I knew I hadn't imagined it.

When I reached the entrance of the school, I glanced at the watch on the person standing in the doorway. Peter's class should be letting out any moment. I leaned back against the railing in front of the glass entrance and waited. That vantage point offered a view through the window into the lobby. This way if I saw him with someone, I would have time to make a run for it.

Peter's familiar frame and dark blond hair appeared from around the corner. I held my breath and waited to see if anyone followed. *He's alone.* I exhaled. Peter pushed through the first glass door. I stepped in front of the second one, smiled a so-happy-to-see-you smile, and raised my hand in a halfhearted greeting. Peter smiled back but his countenance was questioning.

"Hey," he said, catching my neck in the crook of his arm and pulling me close. He kissed me on the nose and said, "This is a surprise. What are you doing here?" So far, so good.

"I was restless, so I thought I'd meet you. Take a chance that you were free."

He checked his watch. The turn of his wrist further twisted the knife he'd stuck via Pam. We usually didn't meet on weeknights because I had early calls. Peter and I also hadn't talked about the demise of my career. Either he didn't know, or he did and filed it under Do Not Discuss and Wait for Holly to Raise It."

"Sure," said Peter. "Let's go back to your place? I don't want your boss peeved at me 'cause you overslept." His voice sounded sweet, but his eyes were hard and the comment felt baiting. I brushed back my hair and tried to smile.

Peter looked around. I scanned the park myself, looking for blonde hair. He must not have seen her. *Maybe I'm paranoid.* The unseasonably humid October air oozed with tension.

Peter took my hand and we started walking. After about three blocks he said, "You're not saying much."

"No? I guess I don't have much to say." I squeezed his hand.

We were quiet again all the way to my apartment. When we got inside, I poured myself a glass of wine, then walked into the living room where Peter sat on the couch.

"Thanks." He stood up and walked to the fridge.

"I got a call from Pam today," I said to Peter's back.

Holding the refrigerator door open, he turned and said accusingly, "Now I know why you picked me up. You're pissed, aren't you?"

Maintaining eye contact, I tucked my foot underneath me and sipped my wine.

"If you weren't pissed, you'd have said something right when I saw you." He slammed the refrigerator door and savagely twisted the cap off a beer bottle. I stared at him with my mouth in a straight line. "You and your 'we cannot cause a scene' way of thinking held you back until you got me into your apartment.

You are a real piece of work, you know that?" He threw the bottle cap into the sink. It pinged against the porcelain.

"A piece of work?" I said with an even voice. I didn't want the neighbors to hear us. "I can't believe you gave her my number!" Tinges of anger hemmed in my voice.

"What's the problem with that?" Peter waved his hands, spilling beer on the floor.

I put my wineglass on the coffee table and got up for a towel.

"You know I can't stand her," I said, mopping up the mess.

"I was trying to help." Peter sat down in the chair opposite the couch.

I stopped cleaning and sat back on my heels. "Help? Help with what?" I fought to keep my voice low. "Why were you discussing me with Pam?" I shrieked her name, trying to imitate her exuberance. It came out waspish.

"Not discussing—"

"Oh, no, not discussing." I punctuated the last word by throwing the towel onto the coffee table, where it landed with a thud. "You told her something because she thinks her stupid little theater thing is going to cheer me up." My voice was now churlish and rising.

"Try she told me something," Peter said with disgust. "All I said to her is that you have been more off than usual. Kind of lost in your fucking head."

"You . . ." I couldn't say it. I wanted to. I wanted to tell him straight to his face that he was an asshole. I couldn't. If I did, I might have to back it up.

"What?" Peter shot back as if reading my mind. "Say it," he dared me.

Instead, I flashed at him my withering gorgon stare, guaranteed to incinerate. This was a look perfected and passed down like a recipe from each generation of females in my family. It had scorched countless boyfriends, lovers, and husbands. I waited for Peter to spontaneously combust. He didn't.

"I cannot believe you gave her my number!" I yelled, the neighbors forgotten. The cats scratched a Flintstones retreat to the bedroom.

"Oh, come on, what is the big deal?" Peter challenged. "I thought it might be easier for you to talk to a girl."

"*Pam?*" I roared. "It's a violation."

"What?" He sipped his beer. "You are acting crazy. I've never seen you like this."

"It is a violation." I saw spots. My throat was raw. "Taking her to my bookstore. It's a fucking violation. That was mine." I was breathing heavily now.

Peter held his beer midway to his mouth. "What are you talking about?" he said, putting the bottle back down without taking a sip.

"I saw you with her," I whispered. "That blonde." I spit out the last word.

Peter stood up. I recoiled as if he were going to hit me. The backs of my knees caught on the couch. I lost my balance and landed in an unceremonious flop on the cushions.

"That's it." Peter slammed his beer down on the coffee table. "This is bullshit. I can't handle you right now. The semester's in full swing, I'm teaching two classes—"

"Wait!" I cried.

"I need a break," he said.

"A break. Why?" I said.

"I don't have time for this shit."

"Wait," I pleaded. "Can we just reset?"

"No," Peter snapped, "there is no reset."

"What do you mean?" I started to cry. "Don't do this. I'm just stressed."

"Whatever," Peter said coldly.

"I lost my job."

"Pam told me yesterday. After the Emmy awards, right?"

I nodded my head.

"That was six fucking weeks ago, Holly."

"I know, I meant to tell you, I just . . . There wasn't a right moment. A lot's been going on."

"Well, you should have found the right moment instead of turning into such a crazy, lying, needy bitch."

"I was going to tell you, and then I saw you walking out of the library with your other girlfriend."

"What the hell?" The changes in Peter's face told me what I needed to know. They weren't friends, like I'd been telling myself these past four weeks. Peter shook his head. "I need a break. I'll call you."

"When? When I get my job back? You want to know why I didn't tell you I lost my job? Because I always knew you were only staying with me because of it."

"I met you when you were waiting tables."

"And you're telling me if I was still serving eggs and bacon, we'd be together? I don't believe that, because all I know is when I lose my job your first response is to get yourself a new girlfriend without doing me the courtesy of telling me it's over."

"You are a piece of work, Holly." Peter shook his head. "And I don't have a new girlfriend, but you're right—it's over."

"Wait. You said break," I cried. "Please." I stretched out my arms.

"Whatever," said Peter. He grabbed his backpack off the table and knocked my wineglass to the floor, where it shattered, splashing red liquid across the white wall.

"Wait," I yelled, running after him. I slipped on the pool of wine and landed in the broken glass right as I heard the door slam.

{ 17 }

I started the next group therapy session talking about my relationship with Peter. When I saw how much Betty Jane loathed talking about him, I spent four more sessions discussing only my failed relationship, with Ruffles encouraging every word. It was amusing to note that Betty Jane hated talking about Peter when she was the one responsible for the start of relationship in the first place.

Betty Jane had been working the morning Peter came into my diner with three girls and another guy, all of whom had varying shades of flaxen hair and wore nondescript clothing. They were obviously banking on the notion that a greasy breakfast staved off the inevitable hangover brought on from a night of too many cocktails. When I asked if the group wanted coffee, Peter turned and I felt that unexplained jolt of recognition that happens between two people. But I stared because I'd never seen eyes that blue. When I told Betty Jane the group looked like a lot of effort for very little tip, she said, "Not necessarily," and I knew she'd picked up on my instant crush. I expected her to torment me over it, but when he appeared on a Monday morning, alone, she surprised me.

Around midmorning Peter made a motioning gesture when Betty Jane was in control. I sat inside my head holding my breath as she sauntered my body over. Whoever said time moves slowly for those who wait had no idea how slowly. Finally we were in front of him.

"You're pretty funny," said Peter. The words were casual, but his eyes sparkled flirtatiously.

"And you"—Betty Jane pointed my finger at him—"are fresh."

"That sounds like something my mom would say," said Peter.

"Well, your mom must be a very refined woman," said Betty Jane. Peter nodded his head and laughed. While they bantered back and forth, I felt suspended over a million tiny pins.

Toward the end of my shift, Peter beckoned again. This time I was in control. I wore clogs, and still my unsteady gait to his table reached back all the way to the first time I wore a pair of three-inch heels. My face burned cherry red when I stood in front of him.

"Can I bum a smoke?" said Peter.

How does he know I smoke? "Sure," I whispered, "follow me."

I felt his eyes on me as we walked through the kitchen and out to the back alley, and I expected him not to be there when I turned around, because he'd had a close-up of my backside. Peter held the door to the outside open for me. I opened the cigarette box, willing my hands not to shake. "I only have one left." I held it up for him to see. I didn't tell him I had another pack in my bag.

"We can share." He removed the cigarette.

"You have beautiful hands," I said. The kind that should play a piano. Or me, I thought. Peter tapped me on the nose with his forefinger. We laughed and shared the cigarette. When I made a reference to Kierkegaard while bantering with him, he kissed me.

He asked to meet me the following afternoon. I was surprised and thrilled when he took me to Bobst Library. Betty Jane was disgusted and uninterested. But it was too late. Then Peter was more surprised when he found out how much I knew about religion, and he asked me, "Are you a nun?"

"A nun?" I scrunched up my face. This was the last thing I'd ever expect anyone to ask me. I'd made my break with the Church years ago.

"Why are you so interested in Christianity?" Turned out Peter chose to focus on Western religion in graduate school because the concept of religion interested him. The rules didn't.

At the end of our date, Peter said he'd like to see me again. "Why me?" I said. The girls he'd brought into the diner were not less than five-foot-ten and definitely didn't reach triple digits on the scale.

"Why not?" said Peter. I didn't have an answer for him.

Sometimes brains do trump beauty.

Even though I'd worn the tread on Peter and me down to threads, it still felt good to talk about him. So, at the start of the fifth session after Peter declared a relationship vacation, I waited politely for one minute after the check-ins to see if someone else wanted the floor. Nobody said a word, so I spent most of the hour retracing Peter's departure. Occasionally, one of the group members asked a question or made a comment.

When Milton announced we had five minutes remaining, Betty Jane said, "You have only yourself to blame for the predicament you are in. I snagged that man for fun. I never expected to have to endure him for three years. I for one am glad you are rid of him." My mouth dropped in shock. "And," she said, "if I have to hear one more word about that man, I will not return."

"Oh, yes, you will return," said Ruffles to Betty Jane. Before Betty Jane could retort, she said to me, "But, Holly, seriously, come on, enough already about Peter."

"Wow, if I turned around, you'd be able to see the tire tracks you just left on my back," I said to Ruffles.

"Karma sucks," she said. I knew this was residual resentment from the post–Emmy awards argument with Betty Jane, when Ruffles wouldn't let up about who won the award.

Inside my head, Ruffles smiled to indicate she knew I got the message. Even though I marveled at her ability to avoid a battle with Betty Jane, I hoped *she* got the message that I wasn't finding any fair play in this turnabout.

Before I left, Milton said, "Holly, you may want to consider Ruffles's remarks and think about a new topic for the next hour. Perhaps the other significant male in your life?"

"*Et tu*, Milton?" I stalked out, declaring to never return.

On Thursday, just like the hands on a clock, I turned up again at the appointed time. Milton opened the door. I walked into his office, relieved that he wasn't one to remind me that I rarely backed up my threats with action.

Everyone appeared in their usual spots, Betty Jane on the pink commode, the Silent One kneeling on his prayer altar, Sarge and Little Bean on the couch, Ruffles on her pillow. After I settled in, we all waited for someone to begin the check-in. Sarge finally started things off and we zigzagged around until we reached Betty Jane.

She pointed and said with a sniff of distaste, "You smell like cigarettes."

"It's my new perfume," I said.

"You might want to consider exchanging it for something with a more pleasing bouquet."

"I'll make a note to drop by Barneys on my way home."

Betty Jane and I stared like two cats unwilling to be the one who blinks, thereby surrendering dominance to the other. Then Milton said, "Holly, do you remember the first time you smoked?"

Do I remember, I thought. Another pleasant trip down memory lane. But Peter had a fork in him, he was done, and the other option was a silent standoff with Betty Jane. So, I figured, why not?

My father rejected whiskey and hopped on the fast track to godliness when I was fourteen. Enlightenment, Dean Miller-style, happened the day after he crashed his sports car into a creek overflowing from an abundant winter in the mountains. The rescue team found him strapped in, unhurt and babbling, with the water reaching up to his neck. Almost drowning in cold runoff rerouted something in his brain. Up to that point in my life, my father could always be counted on for a steady stream of something different. The something different was usually the latest secretary or assistant at the office. When I heard he'd sobered up and found God, I finally believed that God was a woman.

The phone call came at about nine thirty on a Tuesday night. Ruffles and I were doing homework and making sure Sarah and her boyfriend, watching TV, were not alone. When the phone rang, I looked over to see that Sarah and that guy had disappeared over the back of the couch. It rang again. I knew my mother wouldn't answer it. I picked up the receiver and said, "Hello."

"This is the Palo Alto Police Department; to whom am I speaking?"

"Police," said Sarge. He stood up in a protective stance inside my head.

I held out the phone to the couch. "Uh, Sarah, it's the police on the phone."

My sister's head popped up. "Get Mom," she said. She took the phone from me and started speaking. I went upstairs to rouse my mother.

My mother left the house about five minutes later. Her last words were to tell Sarah to make sure I was in bed by ten.

"Dad's been in an accident," said Sarah.

Having suffered under my father's indifference for the past two years, I found myself ambivalent about his predicament. Sarge remained standing, ready to act. Ruffles paused in eating her chips. I felt her pull me backward and take over.

She opened my mouth and said to Sarah, "Did he die?"

"Your 'I don't care' voice," said Sarah. "No, he didn't die. He's not even hurt."

"Too bad," said Ruffles. She drifted backward and let me have control again.

"More like luckily, or I might not be going to college in a couple of months," said Sarah. "If you're done with your homework, why don't you go to bed?"

The next night I woke up a few hours later to the sound of raised voices and I knew my father had been released from the hospital. Inside my head Sarge wore green fatigues and a helmet, and his face was darkened. Ruffles sat wide-eyed. I noticed the Boy sleeping. The Silent One held his finger to his lips to indicate no talking. I knew it must be bad.

"It is your fault I drink so much. Living with you is like spending every day in hell." The walls and hallway did nothing to muffle my father's angry words.

My mother's response was, as usual, too quiet for me to hear through the walls. I pushed back my covers.

"Do not move from your position," barked Sarge.

I froze.

"Don't even start that shit with me. I am so sick of it," yelled my father.

I pressed my ear against the wall.

"What do you think she said?" whispered Ruffles inside my head.

Sarge made a cutting movement with his hand across his throat and mouthed, *Silence.* We didn't want to wake the Boy.

I heard my parents' bedroom door open. My father pounded down the hallway. I shrank back against my pillows. Another door opened. The hall closet.

"Where are you going?" cried my mother.

Her voice scared me. I had never heard my mother plead like that before.

"I have a trip," was my father's cold reply.

"You don't have a trip." The venom was back in her voice.

More noise. It sounded like things toppling out of the closet.

"You think I don't know?" My mother's voice cracked. "If you like her so much, why don't you just stay with her?" She screamed this.

"Maybe I will," said my father.

"You don't mean that," shrieked my mother.

I sat in the dark, reeling. *Stay with who? And who is this woman on the other side of the wall?*

"I can't stand this anymore."

"But the girls?"

"The girls will be fine."

"Heartless bastard," said Ruffles from her pillow inside my head. The Boy stirred.

"If you leave me," said my mother, "I will divorce you and take you for every penny you have."

"That's the woman we know and love," said Ruffles inside my head.

"You made a promise to me and the girls after—"

"Holly," said Sarge inside my head. The Silent One stood. The Boy sat, frightened, clutching his blanket.

I hovered between my body and the living room inside my head as a sense of foreboding crawled straight up my spine. I knew Sarge wanted to leave, but I also knew he wouldn't go until I was there with him in my head. I fought hard to stay in control.

The shouting from the other side of the wall had stopped. I hovered in black silence for several minutes.

"Holly?" Sarah whispered as she shook me. Even in the dark, I could see my sister's stabbing eyes as they probed deeply into mine. The hallway on the other side of the wall remained silent. Sarah sat back against my pillows, crowding me into the corner.

"Dean, please." My mother was pleading again. "Please don't leave me. I don't know what I was saying. Please don't leave. We can make this work if we try."

My father replied, but for once I couldn't hear what he said.

"Do you think they will get a divorce?"

"Go to sleep, Holly," Sarah said wearily.

The next night my father was home for dinner. My mother declared that he had stopped drinking and we all had to support him. Then she took a sip from the glass of wine sitting in front of her.

The following day, my father came home with a stack of books on spirituality. Within a week, he was doing yoga and talking about Noble Truths, while Ruffles and I remarked about the noble untruth of this latest incarnation of dear old Dean. Six months later, he still had not left town, had not eaten meat, and he was able to touch his toes for the first time in years.

"Who needs booze when the God high is so much better?" Ruffles remarked inside my head midway through his metamorphosis. Even she had to admit that my father's already rakish good looks and smooth charm had gone supernova during his change.

In line with his transformative euphoria, my father tried to do whatever my mother wanted. But it seemed as if every time he cleared a hoop, another one, smaller and higher, appeared. In July, he got a big bonus at work and suggested we go on a trip before Sarah left for college. My mother bought a fancy new car instead.

After Sarah left in August, my father picked me up one day from a friend's house.

"Holly?" said my father.

I looked out the window as he shifted the gears of his sports car and drove too fast. As always, I figured speed was the fifth Noble Truth nobody talked about. Finally I said in a snotty tone, "What?" Downward-facing Dog, lettuce, and green tea aside, I knew the same old rage was still boiling right below the lid Dad held on tight. I didn't trust this new man.

"If I broke my promises to you, Holly, I don't remember. I don't remember a lot of what I did when I was drinking," he said.

Inside my head, Ruffles almost choked on her chips. Then I felt as though a hook wrapped around my waist. I fell backward. Ruffles had never acted like this before. I tried to reorient myself as she turned my tilting head and looked at my father's rigid jawline. "Yeah, well," Ruffles said out of my mouth, "if I heard any promises, broken or otherwise, I don't remember."

I watched my hand pick up the pack of Marlboro Reds that was lying between the two seats. Then it pushed in the lighter, opened the box, and pulled out a cigarette. A pop interrupted the thick silence in the car. My hand raised the lighter to the end of the cigarette and lit it. Smoke blew out of my mouth at my father.

"I don't remember a lot of conversations I have with you," said Ruffles out of my mouth.

The car shot forward as my father savagely shifted gears. "I don't know why I bother. You're a miserable bitch like your mother."

He started traveling again the next week.

"Thoughts, Holly?" said Milton.

"Karma sucks, right?" Then I saw Ruffles's wan face and I immediately regretted my spite.

"Now, how about we have a discussion about 'much-needed authority'?" said Betty Jane. Anyone who didn't see that coming had to be blind.

"You shut up," I said.

"Careful who you choose, Holly," said Betty Jane.

"I'll choose Ruffles any day over you," I snapped. Ruffles looked up with a gleam in her eye. I felt a rush of warmth and protectiveness.

"Let's get back to the memory, shall we?" said Milton.

"What more can I say? My father was a duplicitous jerk who did only what the moment required for the advancement of the most important person in his life—himself. He cheated on his wife. He took all his rage and frustration out on the smallest and weakest person in front of him. That was me, in case you didn't know. And, yes, with the exception of rage and frustration, I pretty much choose men who are like my father. And I'm hanging on to the very incarnation of the man right now. I'm not stupid, you know."

Milton and I sat in silence for five minutes. I know because I followed the second hand on my watch the entire time. We had five more minutes and the hour would be over. I hunkered down to wait Milton out.

He cleared his throat. "Holly, I've been thinking that you might want to add some activities to your daily routine."

"Like what," I said, "the library?"

"What about the theater thing Peter's friend called you about?" said Milton.

"Do you think I've suddenly become Maria von Trapp?" I said. "I'm going to strum a guitar, embrace children, and sing about the hills being alive?"

"Holly," said Little Bean. His voice caught all of us off guard. Since we had started group therapy, Sarge and Little Bean seemed to have taken the Silent One's vow. "You know, you really do have a way with children; you just have to find it." His words reminded me of something I'd heard a long time ago, and I immediately shoved them under the door of the closet in the Committee's living room, where I still never went under any circumstances.

"I'm not looking for it," I said.

{ 18 }

I checked the piece of paper to confirm the address: 52 Water Street; that was what it said on the side of the building. I reached for the door. My hand hanging in the air appeared disembodied. I gripped the handle. It felt warm. I was a bit surprised by this, because it was early November. The smoky blue sky held on, refusing to give way to nighttime. A faint star blinked off in the distance over a rooftop. The first star of the night. At least, it was the first one I saw. Pushing the door open, I glanced back, thinking that I should make a wish. Next time maybe. My wishes never seemed to come true and I was already late.

The place was funky, as advertised. I couldn't tell if the carpet was red or black, or red and black, or just dirty. The lights looked like glowing spiders suspended on their silken webs, ready to bite any prey that strayed underneath. I steered clear of the lamps and made my way over to what I thought must be the entrance. I heard muted laughter. *Here goes nothing.* I clutched the long metal bar with both hands.

There were about twenty rows of faded red velvet seats. I had read that this place was originally a burlesque theater from 1920. The seats certainly looked to be from that era. I saw different faces up on the stage, and in the middle of them the back of a woman who, judging from the medium-length brown hair, had to be Pam.

The woman turned. "Holly." She leaped from the stage and walked toward me. "I was so surprised when you called."

"Well, like I said on the phone, I thought about it and concluded, Why not? Why not?" I hadn't told her the truth on the phone and I'd leave before I spilled it now. Little Bean's words haunted me, but the real motivating factor was that Peter and Pam were best friends. Working with her made me feel as if I were near Peter. He'd become a habit, albeit a bad one, like smoking. I couldn't tell you why I loved to smoke; I could only tell you I couldn't imagine life without cigarettes.

"Why not indeed!" said Pam. *She's making it hard for me to dislike her.* She threw her arms around me and delivered quite an embracing hug from someone who was so short. *Then again, maybe not.*

"I think I just heard a rib crack." I backed away.

"We are just getting started. I was going over the play with the kids. *Cyrano de Bergerac.* Did I tell you?"

I checked the ceiling to see if that last word was lodged up in the rafters. I was going to have to say something to her about the exuberance. See if she would be willing to take it down a notch or twenty.

"Great," I said. "So, I should . . . uh . . ."

"Everyone." Pam rapidly clapped her hands. "This is Holly Miller. She is helping us. And"—she put her hands on her hips—"we are going to help her get here on time."

I started to roll my eyes and then remembered that I was an

adult and these were impressionable kids. One of them stifled a laugh with her hand, elbowed the person next to her, and whispered. Too late.

"Sorry, kids," I said, embarrassed, and then to Pam, "So what should I do?"

"Just sit there in the second row. We're about to start auditions. Did you bring a clipboard and pen? I have an extra one for you."

"I actually did bring those along, as instructed," I said, patting my book bag.

I walked to the second row, sidled past a few chairs, and sat in one that seemed almost sturdy. As my butt met the skinny, stiff springs, I realized I was right—these chairs probably had been here since the twenties.

The auditions started. I had to admit the kids were pretty good. They took this acting stuff very seriously. After the second reading, I started taking my job as casting director, amongst other things to be determined, very seriously, and was making extensive notes about each tryout. Pam whispered to me when the first standout took the stage to read. I agreed with her that this was definitely a candidate for the lead role. Halfway through the auditions, I was whispering to Pam my thoughts about whoever was currently onstage. I started giving direction toward the end.

I had theater practice three nights a week and therapy two days a week. Even though the total number of hours for both was about eight hours, I was more exhausted than when I had a full voice-over schedule or a packed diner. That didn't stop me from having panic attacks about my finances, but Milton was adamant that I continue to focus all my energy on our work. To make do, I returned the forms for the credit card applications that had now replaced the surprise checks in my mailbox and waited for the anxiety tide to go from low to high.

The thought of Thanksgiving one week away transformed my financial panic into free-time panic, because there would be no theater practice Thursday night, and if Milton wouldn't cut France short, he certainly wasn't cutting out turkey. Add to that that Thanksgiving always marked the end of the season for *The Neighborhood*. I hadn't watched the episodes with the new voices. I couldn't for so many reasons. But I heard they were not as good as mine. Either way, I needed to find something to do for six days that made me forget about everything, including the TV show I was no longer on.

I collapsed in the overstuffed chair in my living room and stared at the wall opposite me, hoping it would answer. The wall was a mishmash of pictures, disorganization to the extreme. Worse, there were marks here and there, along with the occasional hole from where I had mistakenly hammered a nail. These marks resembled the scars I carried when I was ten years old and I'd committed the serious offense of using tacks to hang things on my bedroom wall.

On my tenth birthday, I got my first posters. They were pictures of animals with pithy sayings. The Boy loved to read them to me in the afternoon when I did my homework. After a few months, I had dozens of these poetic posters taped all over my room. The posters were taped because my mother never let us use tacks. Tacks left holes in her walls. But those damn posters were always falling off the walls, and finally I decided to buy my own poster tacks with the money she paid me for helping her clean the house. Guilt money, because I stayed home from summer camp one morning when I woke up scared and didn't want to face the sunshine and noisy camp kids.

I thought if I stayed home, my mother would bring me juice like she used to do for Sarah. I thought my mother and I could have a girls' day, and I imagined we'd take our beach blankets, lie on the deck, and enjoy the languid warmth of the sun. I'd read books to her. We'd eat peanut butter and jelly sandwiches. After a while, I'd rub Hawaiian Tropic on the backs of her stubbly legs and we'd laugh when I said her legs felt like Daddy's cheeks late at night. But I stayed home, forgetting that Sarah hadn't done this for a long time and my mother didn't bring anyone juice anymore.

My holiday from summer camp was spent cleaning shutters with an old dishrag because my fingers were small enough to glide along each slat, wiping away the dust that had accumulated in the past forty-eight hours. After the shutters, I pushed the vacuum canister while Mother sucked the shag out of the carpet that hadn't had time to gather dirt since the last pasting she had given it. She gave me a few bucks for my sore fingers and aching back—that and the pleasure of a ride to Lucky Supermarket, where she shopped for dinner.

While my mother pushed her cart up and down the alleys of food, I wandered off to the stationery section, where I located the poster tacks. She noticed me only enough to tell me to use my two dollars if I was going to buy something. And not to slip anything into her cart.

I went to another register and bought the tacks.

When I got home, I went down the dark hallway to my room. My mother's room really. I was just a guest. The decor echoed her personality. It was the same for every room in our house. They were all meat-locker cold, spare. My room was Antarctica, with powder blue walls and white trim around the windows and doors that enclosed the closet when they weren't leaning against the wall, resting after one of my tantrums that resulted in the demise of not too strong hinges. In the family food chain I could feed only on the furniture, the perky little girl's furniture that belonged to someone who vacillated between being a tomboy and a princess. A little girl who played in the mud, wore ripped jeans, and never bathed except when she was thrown, clothes and all, into the steaming water screaming, "Boys don't wash their hair." A little girl who wore frilly dresses and bows in brushed hair pulled into an eye-slanting bun.

My room was filled with my mother's choice of furniture: white little girl's dresser, nightstand, and trundle bed for guests. Furniture with gold trim painted around the edges, perfect like my mother's lipstick. I taped the posters of praying children and Donny Osmond on the walls. She hung the white chiffon curtains that framed the idyllic window offering a view of the woodpile. From the outside all so perfect; from the inside rotten like a bowl of fruit that had been left out for days.

"A grateful girl would love this room," she had said to me once.

Well, not me. I wanted my Hot Wheels tracks snaking about the floor so my cars could drive me away. I wanted my horses grazing freely in their blue shag pastures. I wanted my dented yellow Tonka truck sitting in a prime location, ready to take away the debris that had accumulated in my little city, ready to run over Barbie when she moseyed into my room trying to entice G.I. Joe away from his cowboy adventures in the pillow mountains over in the corner. But my things stayed safely hidden away in my closet sanctuary, peeking out only when the doors came down.

I sat on my bed and ripped the plastic off those tacks. Then I ran my fingers over the cardboard backing, scratching the tips and finally pushing my forefinger down on a tack.

"Ow," I said, sticking my finger in my mouth.

I grabbed the first tack with what little fingernails I had. Then I caught the corner of my Donny Osmond poster and determinedly pushed that tack into the wall. I hoped I made a big hole. I did the same with the other three corners. Donny wasn't falling on my body again.

I reclined on my bed, satisfied. Donny was pierced to the wall. The praying children would no longer slip and turn, their entreaties pointing to hell instead of heaven.

My mother walked in.

I sat up and kicked the cardboard holding the few remaining tacks to the floor. Her eyes followed its descent. Her hands swooped and fingernail fangs caught the cardboard prey. She passed a fleeting glance across each picture on the wall; the red periods of each corner shone like beacons.

"How dare you," she exclaimed.

"I—"

"Who do you think you are?"

She came at me. I recoiled. She slapped me with the cardboard. I covered my face. She caught my wrists, pressing the cardboard that still held tacks against the right one, piercing my skin in her fury. I went limp, retreating into my head. Nobody shifted to take over. I lay there like a rag doll. She let go, tossed the cardboard on the mattress, and left the room.

As an adult, when I hung a picture, I still glanced over my shoulder to see if my mother was there. Then I used really big nails and didn't measure. I usually made quite a mess before hanging a picture just right.

The wall in front of me at that moment certainly was quite a mess. *Maybe I should paint. I wonder how much that will cost. Oh, who cares? Next week that's what I'll do during my free time.*

I was in the middle of a short story in the *New Yorker* when Milton opened the door.

"Just let me get to the break." I held up a finger.

Milton cleared his throat. I closed the magazine and placed it back on the table and stood up.

"You shouldn't have magazines in your waiting room if you don't want people reading them."

I walked into the room, sat down, and closed my eyes. Betty Jane reclined on the couch. Sarge and Little Bean were left to stand.

"Slide over," I said to her. She didn't budge. I wished I'd smoked more before coming in. Betty Jane would probably move if I reeked like a Parisian, but since the session when I had discovered how I started smoking, my stomach had soured before I was halfway through with a cigarette.

Finally, Sarge and Little Bean dropped to the floor. "You don't have to sit on the floor," said Ruffles. "You can share my pillow."

Betty Jane sat up, but they still went over and sat with Ruffles on her pillow. Then she pulled out her nail file, but the scraping had an antsy quality about it.

"Do they know what I think about outside here?" I said to Milton.

"Why? Were you thinking about something significant?" he said.

I wanted to tell him no, but the rest of the memory I'd unearthed while staring at my holey wall came rushing toward me.

"My mother never let things go very easily," I said, "especially not holes in her walls. I'd made a few, so I skipped dinner. I knew I would pay for my civil disobedience, but I hoped to delay punishment as long as I could."

I was lying on my bed, staring at the ceiling and listening to my stomach growl. Dinner was hours ago and my afternoon snack had long been digested. After eleven, headlights from the driveway shone through my window. A car door slammed and the front door followed suit shortly after. I expected the shouting to start any moment. That would come only from my father. My mother's voice always lowered in direct proportion to her anger and my father's rose with his.

I crawled out of bed, inched down the hallway, and stopped short of the entrance. My parents' bedroom was off to the left.

". . . what time . . . and drunk," was all I could hear my mother say.

"Lay off, will you?" demanded my father. "Christ, it's always the same with you."

More muffled words followed; then I heard, "Holly . . . disobedient . . . had it with her."

I ran back to my room, slipped through the slightly ajar doorway, and dove into my bed. I was afraid of the dark. I wanted a light on at night. My parents compromised by leaving the laundry room light on and my door open just enough so a friendly beam of light offered a sliver of hope.

The light disappeared. The darkness closed in on me. My bedroom door slid across the carpet. I smelled whiskey and stale cigarette smoke. I heard my father unbuckling his belt. "Holly," he whispered as he drew back the covers. I turned and scuttled away from him, hitting the wall on the side of my bed opposite my father. He couldn't even wait until morning to deliver the beating my mother had goaded him into giving me.

I shut my eyes and saw Sarge dressed in camouflage creeping along a dark trench. His helmet and face were blackened as usual to help him blend in with the scenery. Back in the foxhole the Boy huddled next to the Silent One, who sat calmly praying.

"Holly," commanded Sarge, motioning me to follow. My eyes rolled back in my head.

"You stay and keep watch," Sarge said fiercely to the Silent One. "I'll get them to safety. Signal when it's time to return."

The Silent One, his face a grave mask, bowed his head.

Sarge held me and the Boy against his body as he moved stealthily toward a dim light in the distance. The darkness propelled us forward. I looked back. I couldn't see the Silent One.

"All clear," said Sarge, putting us down in front of his '57 Chevy. I looked back at a blank wall. "Holly, face forward," ordered Sarge, pointing at the car. He wore jeans and a white T-shirt again. He opened the driver's door and we all got in the front.

The Boy and I rode along quietly. My eyes followed the yellow line on the road as Sarge drove. After about a mile, we pulled into a parking lot. In front of us was a well-lit playground with a large swing set in a sandpit. Everything surrounding it was dim and gray, as if a stage light were concentrated on this one area in the playground.

Sarge parked the car and turned off the engine.

I opened the passenger door.

"Holly, I am afraid," said the Boy.

"Why?" I asked. "This'll be fun."

Sarge sat on a picnic table, his feet on the bench, watching me and the Boy. I waved at him. Then I gripped the swing chains, dropped into the leather seat, and turned to the Boy. "Follow me," I said as I kicked off and started swinging back and forth.

On each ascent I stretched out my legs and then swept them back so I'd go faster and higher. Darkness and light became confused. Finally I pushed the swing up so high I was almost horizontal. Momentum rushed through my body and pressed me forward. Then a bolt of fear shot through my chest. My hands slipped on the chains. I sailed backward. The Boy screamed. I dragged my feet across the ground to slow myself. The Boy sat motionless, clutching his swing chains and crying. When I started moving forward, I dug in my heels, angled my body toward him, and pitched off my seat. In the next motion, I put my arms protectively around the Boy, shielding his back with my body.

"Don't cry," I whispered as I hugged him tighter. "I'm sorry. You're okay. You're okay."

Sarge nodded his head, stood up, and motioned to us.

"Come on."

I led the Boy over to the car. My lower body ached and throbbed against the leather seat. We sat in there for a few minutes.

"Holly," Sarge said, holding my face in both hands, "time to go home now."

I wanted to get out of the car and run as fast as I could. Run past the swings and into the dark night beyond. Sarge patted my head.

When we pulled out of the parking lot, I whispered to Sarge, "Let's keep going. Just drive until we reach the other side of the world. Never come back."

Sarge shook his head sadly and parked in the driveway. I started to feel more solid. I got out of the car, slowly made my way up the walk, and then opened the front door. The Silent One bowed. As I stepped in, my knees gave way under me. I heard the crackling sound of a burning cigarette. I opened my eyes and saw a glowing orange tip over in the corner on my rocking chair. It moved toward me. I smelled stale whiskey and burned tobacco. Then I saw the silhouette of my father moving away.

"Holly, go to sleep now," he whispered as he pulled my bedroom door all the way shut.

I sat on Milton's couch weeping.

"Holly, do you think she knew your father would beat you if she told him about the tacks?" said Milton quietly.

"She knew," said Little Bean. "She always knew."

{ 19 }

By Thanksgiving day the postcard encounters with the Committee had transformed the loneliness I felt into a distant ache, proving that patience does pay dividends, even if they were not the ones I'd waited patiently for. But because it was Thursday, I found myself at loose ends and longing for some sort of company. So I was out walking in sandals despite all the grief they'd caused. For some reason, after my feet tasted freedom, they refused to go back into closed shoes. What was I going to do when it started snowing?

On holidays, Manhattan streets provided an anonymous comfort the usual frenzied pace vitiated and gave unusual sounds a chance to breathe. Or maybe it seemed so on that particular Thursday because all the street sounds were new to me. Maybe that was why the familiar rattle of a Volkswagen Beetle from the sixties, the one that sounded like a bag of rocks and sand shaking, stood out as it approached me from behind. When I heard that sound, my surroundings dimmed and I felt as if I were back in second grade waiting for Uncle Dan to pick me up from school.

My uncle said to me once, "Routine is the momentum that keeps a man going." Our routine started when I entered second grade. It consisted of Uncle Dan transporting me to and from school every day in his powder blue VW Beetle. We called it the School Bug. That School Bug departed our home every morning at precisely seven thirty-five, and it approached the school entrance every day at precisely five minutes past three in the afternoon, which was the exact moment I'd walk through the front door of the building.

He never left me waiting. Not once, and that year those rides were the highlight of my day. In the mornings we'd load up and listen to Bruce Springsteen on the way to school. We usually got through two songs before I exited the car. But the afternoon ride was my favorite, because I got to stand and sing the whole way home.

The following year, when I started third grade, we settled right back in as if only a weekend instead of a whole summer had passed.

Friday, October 2nd was the last day Uncle Dan picked me up from school. The night before, Sarah and I had heard my mother and my uncle arguing. The yelling started after my bedtime. When we heard the raised voices, Sarah turned up her record player. I crawled out of bed, crept up the stairs, and crouched just below the landing, where I could hear but not be seen.

"Sneaking around the house at night imagining things." My mother spoke in a loud tone. I sat up, surprised. She always said a lady never yelled. I ducked back down. My uncle did ghost around the house. We would find him in the oddest places. Usually crouched behind furniture. Sitting at the kitchen table staring at the wall. One morning I woke up in my father's closet and there he was sitting next to me. My eyelids were crusty and I had to pull hard to peel them apart. When I did, the first thing I saw was his arm with the freckles dancing in the curly red hairs. I rubbed the grit out of my eyes and saw the whole of him. Back against the wall. Knees up. His eyes wide open, vacant, staring.

"Elizabeth." My uncle sighed. "I don't deny that I have problems, and I am grateful for all you've done for me. But you, the girls . . . I am concerned for your safety. Holly told me—"

"Holly is a liar," snapped my mother. "She lives in her own little world. You of all people know about that."

"Elizabeth, she showed me the bruises on the backs of her legs." I bit my knee to keep from making any noise. After a visit from my father the night before, I had always tried to sit on the car seat with force to get the first wave of pain out of the way. The act of doing so had a numbing effect, and each sitting down thereafter hurt less and less. By the end of the day I almost didn't notice it. But this worked only if there was a break between the beatings. After I got one, I would make an effort to stay quiet and out of the way, but I didn't manage it that week. Uncle Dan had noticed me grimace as I had tried to gingerly sit on the bench seat of the car. He clenched his teeth and slapped the seat next to me with his hand. I flinched. He apologized and pulled me close. As he hugged me, he checked the backs of my legs. Then he promised that he'd make sure this didn't happen again.

"She misbehaves. She provokes her father. She provokes me. And tell me, is she going to work to put food on the table? Is she going to take care of us? How does she think we will survive? I cannot work. I will not work," snapped my mother.

"I know that life as a single mother, with no education, raising children, having to work, not having money, is a scary thought," he continued. "But isn't the safety of your children, your freedom, your pride, worth more than Dean's money?"

"It is not a question of that. Holly needs to start behaving. Simple as that."

"You know that's not true. My God, Elizabeth, are you so afraid to be poor and on your own that you'd rather hold a man hostage and condone his brutal behavior toward his children? Toward you?"

"How dare you," said my mother.

"I do dare, because I care about what happens to you. To the girls. To Dean. He needs to be free of all of this. You know that. If you had let him leave . . ."

"What are you talking about? You and your crazy notions. You need to be free, not Dean. You need freedom because you cannot cope with what you did." *What's she talking about? What did he do?* My parents always said he was strange because of "The Vietnam." Was "The Vietnam" making my mother angry? I didn't understand.

"I—"

"I think it's time you found a new place to live. You are no longer welcome in this house," my mother said quietly.

I gasped. This was my fault. I should have laughed at the pain when I sat down. I should have been disciplined like Sarah, like my mother, like my father. When my uncle let me slide, I should have refused. But I didn't want to. I had felt safe with him and I wanted that more. But at that moment, hunkered down there on the landing, I wished I had not given in. I wished I had not been the lazy and selfish daughter my mother always said I was. The annoying troublemaker my father always said I was. Had I tried harder, everything would be different. But I didn't, and now, because of this, my uncle had to leave.

"Elizabeth—"

"I would like you to be gone by the weekend." I recognized the finality in her voice. Not even my father could get her to change her mind when she used that tone.

Nobody said a word about him leaving at breakfast the next

morning. That day he strayed from our routine and we drove to school in silence. The Boy wept softly. I wanted to cry too. I wanted to shove the Bruce Springsteen tape into the stereo and turn the volume knob until the music was loud enough to sing away the knot tying in my gut. Instead I rode quietly belted in the backseat.

The School Bug was parked at the curb when I walked out the front door of the school that afternoon. I waved good-bye to my teacher like always. Then I opened the car door and exclaimed, "Where's my seat?"

Uncle Dan smiled and said, "I gave it to a hitchhiker who was tired. He's probably resting on it right now on the side of some highway."

Order restored. I relaxed.

I stepped onto the floorboard, deposited my belongings on the front passenger seat, and then pulled the door shut. Uncle Dan wrapped a bungee cord around my waist and attached it to the handle on the dashboard. Then he started the car and drove slowly out of the parking lot. I extended my arms high over my head until they just peeked out the sunroof. Uncle Dan switched on the music. Bruce Springsteen sang "Born to Run." As we picked up speed on the open road, I closed my eyes, held my arms straight against the force of the wind, and let my hair whip around my face while singing loudly to the open sky the words I didn't understand. My uncle bobbed his head to the music. For those few moments we drove, the lines on his face melted and the weariness disappeared.

We pulled into the driveway. He unhooked me and said, "I wish this old Beetle were a '57 Chevy, but aside from that, another perfect day." My uncle's cloudy eyes belied his smile. We concluded every day with these lines, and I knew this was the last time he'd say them to me. I started to cry. He slid his legs around the stick shift, put his arms around me, and whispered, "It will be okay." Then he held me out before him and said gruffly, "Maintain your routine, soldier, and you'll be okay."

I saluted him and got out of the car.

Early the next morning I woke to the sound of the VW idling in the driveway. The clock numbers glowed from Sarah's nightstand. It was just past four. I heard a door slam. The blackness of the morning rolled over me like the tires rolling down the driveway. I closed my eyes as the sound of the engine faded. When I woke up later I saw a man holding the Boy's hand. He had a scar that started at the corner of his jawline and disappeared down the neck of his white T-shirt. I recognized the military duffel bag over in the corner. The label on it read SARGE.

I rolled over on my side and watched Sarah sleep. I listened to her steady breathing, knowing that tonight I would be in my own room. I closed my eyes again and whispered, "Sarge?" The man nodded his head. I pushed back my covers. It was time to get up. My uncle was right; I was going to be okay.

I stood there on that Thanksgiving-empty Manhattan street watching a different Volkswagen chug past me. It was yellow, not blue like my School Bug. I sighed and turned back toward home.

I called Sarah when I got in. "Hey, it's me," I said.

"You sound sad, sadder than usual." She sighed. "Did something happen? Why aren't you somewhere for Thanksgiving?"

"Where would I be, Sarah?" In past years, I always said I went to friends to avoid going home to California. The truth was after I left home I celebrated the holidays with the Committee. One Thanksgiving Sarge burned the turkey, and every year Betty Jane got drunk. The memory brought on an ache that was so deep tears couldn't find it. I sighed and said, "Pam invited me, but I was afraid Peter would be there." Ironically this year I really had had an invitation.

"Did you break up?" Sarah sounded hopeful.

"Yeah, a while ago," I said. I wanted to tell her exactly five weeks, two days, and twenty-one hours, but that sounded obsessive.

"I can't believe you didn't tell me." She sounded betrayed. I couldn't believe I didn't tell her either. I told Sarah everything. What was happening to me?

"I'm sorry. It's all been so stressful and . . . I don't know . . . I'm so tired of talking about things." This didn't excuse me for shutting her out. "Maybe I'm just angry, Sarah."

"At me?"

"At everyone and everything," I said. We both were quiet for a moment. My foot throbbed. I looked down and noticed dried blood. I must have done that while my feet were in a state of ice cube. "Hey, I heard an old VW bug today when I was out walking."

"Uncle Dan," Sarah said softly.

I swallowed hard. The golf ball lodged itself in the middle of my chest and started to expand. I got up to clean my bloodied foot and sandal while I waited for her to speak.

"What are you doing?" she said.

"Cleaning the blood off my sandal."

"Sandal?" Sarah exclaimed. "When did you buy sandals? Wow. And you wore them? In November?"

"Bought them and bled on them," I said.

"How appropriate," she said with a snort. "Do you remember the day you cut your foot? Just another fun day with the family."

"As I recall, the only fun part about it was the doughnuts."

"I'm impressed you remembered," said Sarah. "Oh, how I

loved pulling one over on her," she continued. "She was so draconian about our diets. Well, okay, you needed it then. But I didn't."

"Right now, I would love to eat. Just eat and eat until every corner of my body is filled."

"Sorry. I am still reeling that you bought sandals. And now you, the ascetic, are talking about eating. Let me get my breath." I didn't tell her I'd bought these sandals two months ago. "What are you doing now?" said Sarah.

"Right now?" I said.

"Yes, right now."

"Right now I am talking to you."

"Before you answered the phone," came her exasperated reply.

"Oh. I was looking for Aslan in the closet."

"Did you find him?"

"What do you think?"

"Shit, Holly." The silence over the phone mixed in with the sound of cars rushing by outside. "Are we always going to talk in circles or talk about it?" Sarah said quietly.

"Okay. I didn't find Aslan in the closet. But I am thinking of taking a walk up to the neighborhood church. It's a better place to find him. But all those crosses, and bleeding feet and hands. I always thought that was kinda creepy—"

"Holly, stop it. Just stop," said Sarah.

"Stop what? I have to go."

"And do what?" she said.

"Nail myself to a cross," I said.

"Christ, Holly."

"Christ is what we started with. He excuses everything. Please forgive me while I—"

"Ground control to Major Tom—"

"Check my Prozac pills and put my helmet on—"

"Come on," said Sarah.

"I really don't want to talk," I said.

"Are you okay? I mean really okay? How's therapy going?"

"Just like this phone call: too much talking about the past. I don't do the past, remember?"

"Seems like you *are* doing the past, Holly."

{ 20 }

The first week in December, I started to wonder if I should wear socks with my sandals. It hadn't snowed yet, but my feet were so numb all the time I was certain I had frostbite. I began carrying socks with me so I could change when I got to the theater at night. I didn't care about blue feet in Milton's office, but I did care what a group of adolescents thought about a supposedly sane adult wearing sandals in thirty-degree weather.

I'd just socked my feet and rubbed them to a nearly numb state when Pam yelled, "Okay," as she clapped rapidly. "Everyone up on the stage." She turned to me. "Including you, Holly."

"What are we doing?"

"I thought tonight it would be nice to spend some time just talking and mingling, since a lot of the kids don't know one another outside our rehearsals."

"Wow, they all seemed like friends to me."

"One or two of them maybe, but for the most part, they come from all over the city. So tonight we have a well-earned break with some sodas and snacks. Talk time. You know, this is the fun part." *Says who?* If she'd warned me, I would have called in sick.

I wandered around the stage muttering hello to the different packs of kids for about ten minutes. Then I saw one of the stand-out girls over in the corner reading a book. I felt her pain. Or maybe she felt mine. Either way, reading seemed better than mumbling, so I walked over to her. "*The Lion, the Witch and the Wardrobe*—that was one of my favorites." I pointed to her book. We'd been rehearsing for almost four weeks and I didn't remember her name. Like I said, I'm bad with kids.

She turned the book over and looked at the cover. "I like it too."

"I hope so; you are reading it, after all." *Oops, too much sarcasm.* She smiled. *Maybe not.*

I sat down next to her. Out of nowhere three kids appeared on the floor in front of us. I wondered how they appeared and disappeared like that. This ability would be handy to have.

"Come on," I said, sliding onto the floor, "let's join them." I patted the ground next to me and the girl reading the book moved to the spot next to me.

"My uncle said that book is about Jesus," one of the boys said, pointing at the book. "He's a priest."

"I heard that," I said with a derisive snort. Then I took the book from the girl and held it in my hands. "Still, in spite of that falsehood, it was my favorite book as a child. I loved all the Chronicles of Narnia." I stuck my hand in the bowl of Ruffles that sat in the middle, grabbed a handful, and popped them into my mouth.

"What are they about?" asked one of the kids.

"These children go into a magical world where they meet Aslan, the great lion."

"Jesus," said the nephew of the priest.

"Whatever. Either way, they have adventures and no parents."

"Really cool adventures," added the girl who was actually reading the book.

"Where Jesus is guiding them."

"Who *is* brainwashing you?" I said. His face paled. *Shit, this is why I should be in the audience yelling cues and not up close and personal with people half my size and more than half my age.* I took another handful of chips and said, "Anyway, I read these books over and over with . . ." My mind went blank. I shoveled another handful of chips into my mouth and, while crunching said, "We just wanted to get to Narnia."

Someone refilled the chip bowl and my hand like a little shovel went right back in. "The funny thing is, when I was six, I didn't know what a wardrobe was. Do any of you?" The girl reading the book raised her hand.

"Of course you know." I laughed and scooped chips.

"What's a wardrobe, then?" one of the kids asked.

"I am getting to that. We didn't know. Right? So, I had this brilliant idea to call Information. 411. My mother used to call 411 when she needed a phone number. Since they were called Information and I needed information, I figured, Why couldn't we call them about a wardrobe?"

"You called 411 to find out what a wardrobe is?" said one of the kids.

"Yes," I said.

"That's dumb."

"Yes, well, so I sneaked into my parents' room." I extended my forearms and made slow walking gestures with my index and middle fingers. I had excelled in the acting classes Mike and Walter had insisted I take. That was how they got my teacher to back up the publicist's story that my Emmy collapse was all part of an act for ratings.

"Picked up the phone"—I picked up an imaginary phone—"and dialed four, then one, then one."

One of the kids made exaggerated pressing motions with her finger in the air. I wagged my finger at her and dialed one number on the invisible phone. She got the idea and dialed the other two.

Holding the imaginary phone, I tried to say in Betty Jane's voice, "Directory Assistance." It came out in my voice. I'd leaped off the high dive, and then noticed there was no water in the pool. Either way, I was going to land. "Hi, I need a wardrobe," I said in the same voice. I waited for someone to say something, but my captive audience waited. I landed fine.

"What?" I exclaimed loudly. If I had to use my own voice, I'd at least embellish with emphasis. "You need the number for wardrobe?" I brought my eyebrows together in confusion. The kids laughed.

"No, *what* is a wardrobe?" I accentuated *what* to show a change in speakers.

"What is a wardrobe?" I held the imaginary handset in front of my eyes, screwed my face up in shock, and then placed it back to my ear. *"Where* are your parents?" I put the highlight on *where* this time.

"My mother is cooking dinner. I'm looking for a wardrobe," I said, making my voice a bit higher but still with a matter-of-fact tone.

"What do you need a wardrobe for?" I said, imitating the operator. I had more kids in the circle now.

"I want to get to Narnia, and Lucy got there through a wardrobe."

"How old are you?" I said it with the previous operator's voice.

"Five." I held up five fingers. "I want to find Aslan." The girl next to me stood up, made her arms into clawed Cs, and opened her mouth in a silent roar.

"*The Lion, the Witch and the Wardrobe.* I know those books." I snapped my fingers. "My granddaughter reads them.

"Can you tell me what a wardrobe is then?" I made a sad face like a mime.

"The wardrobe you are looking for is a tall cabinet, closet, or small room built to hold clothes.

"And that, my friends, is what a wardrobe is—a closet," I said. The kids nodded in unison.

"Anyway, armed with that information, we searched for the entrance to Narnia in each of the closets in our house. At least, the ones that were not off-limits. When that didn't work, we tried it wearing special coats." I helped myself to another handful of chips. "We never made it, though," I whispered. "We never made it to Narnia."

"Lady, you sure like those Ruffles," said one of the kids sitting in our circle.

My hand froze over the bowl of chips.

"Do you want me to get some more?"

"No." I pulled my hand back. The chips turned bitter in my stomach. "No, thanks."

Pam walked over to our little group at that moment and said, "Is Holly entertaining you with her voices?" I looked up at her and I tried to tell her by my bulging eyes not to go there. "Didn't she tell you who she is?" Pam exclaimed. She wasn't watching me at all.

I shook my head. The kids looked at Pam and then looked at me.

"Who is she?" asked the one who offered to bring me more chips.

"She's Holly Miller."

"We know that," said one of the kids with a *duh* kind of voice.

"The voice of Violet and Harriet from *The Neighborhood*." Pam waved her hands about.

"Cool!" was the resounding cry upon hearing the news. This caught the attention of the remaining kids milling around. Next thing, they were all over by us. That instant-appearance thing again.

I sat there on the floor with the girl who was reading *The Lion, the Witch and the Wardrobe* by my side, and an audience of what seemed like an angry mob of pushy short people in front of me.

I could hear them whispering, "She's Violet." The chips boiled in my stomach.

"Holly," shrieked Pam, "do the Violet voice for them." The Argus eyes of those kids shifted over to me, and all the earlier rapport between me and Pam was replaced by my desire to stuff my sweater into her big, fat mouth. I looked around for any quick exit. Didn't stages have a trapdoor or something?

Pam started clapping and saying, "Vi-o-let, Vi-o-let." The kids joined her by the third clap. I felt like I had accidentally wandered into the body of a musician onstage at a sold-out concert and I couldn't sing to save my life. And right now, I needed to be able to sing, as it were.

I peered at their faces. I wanted to snatch those indecent smiles off of them one at a time, starting with Pam. I readied some lines I remembered from my last show, opened my mouth, and the words tumbled out.

One of the kids shook his head. "That's not Violet."

I wanted to crawl under a stage prop and disappear.

———

I didn't sleep when I got home from the theater that night, and I waited for Milton's noon call on Wednesday. When he asked how I was doing I told him I ate Ruffles and I couldn't go back to the theater.

"Holly, it might be time for us to talk again about integration," said Milton.

"What? Do you know what my days are like in between group therapy? And when I'm there I feel like I'm standing outside on the cold streets looking through a glass window into a warm room with no doors. When the hour is up I have to walk away, once more bereft and deprived because I couldn't find a way to get in, and now your solution is to just keep walking?"

"Integration is not walking away," said Milton. "To extend your metaphor, it is more about going into the room and taking it over."

"Yeah, and the Committee disappears. So it sounds more like erasing five-sixths of me. No, thanks."

"Holly, at the moment how much do you know about what the Committee is doing when you are outside of therapy?"

I didn't know what they did when we were not in therapy, which meant they probably didn't know what was happening in my world—or did they? Either way, I didn't like the implication of what Milton was saying, so I remained silent.

Never one to miss the dead-end, do-not-pass signs, Milton told me to consider taking the night off from the theater to re-group. I knew he hoped I'd consider the seed he had planted. I did, and because of this I didn't sleep that night. I had nothing to do the next day while I waited for four o'clock to roll around, so I left the house two hours early and walked in circles around the city. I was still wearing my sandals, and my feet were as blue as my eyes when I reached Milton's office.

For her check-in, Betty Jane decided to comment on my footwear. "You are wearing sandals," she said.

"And this relates to how you feel in what way?" I said. She gave me one of her prissy faces in reply. *Not another standoff. I'm missing this?* "Yes, I am," I said, "even though my mother taught me that it's not appropriate to show scarred feet in public."

"Your mother was right," said Betty Jane.

Before I could retort, Milton said, "Holly, you mentioned yesterday that you ate Ruffles at the theater Tuesday night." *What's he up to? We've never discussed our speaking in between sessions with the Committee.* Judging by the surprise on Ruffles's face, and the vitriol on Betty Jane's, the Committee didn't know what had happened in my life outside of our sessions.

"I don't want to talk about—"

"You ate Ruffles?" said Ruffles. Her surprised look now mingled with triumph. My own irritation at Milton for raising this subject was replaced by curiosity.

"I ate Ruffles," I said.

"Holly, you haven't eaten Ruffles since you were twelve years old," said Ruffles. I was immediately time-transported back to the sixth grade and the first day of school.

"Holly?" said Milton. *He doesn't even bother with the preamble anymore.*

"It started with an essay," I said.

The first assignment of the school year was to write an essay about our summer vacation. The topic was "What I accomplished over the summer." Fresh from my school-clothes-shopping trip with my mother, I knew exactly what to write. The blue-ribbon look on my mother's face in the Macy's dressing room remained vivid in its detail even after three days. When her gaze darted over my shoulder, and then dropped, I knew she'd honed in on my ass, which looked like two misshapen pumpkins stuck to my back-side, and my keg-sized legs attached to it. Over the summer, I had managed to gain twenty pounds in about forty days. I also grew about three inches, but my hope that my mother would focus on this milestone instead of the additional pounds disappeared with her scornful gaze.

In my essay, I drew a parallel between my twenty pounds in forty days and the forty days Jesus languished in the desert starv-ing and hallucinating. His accomplishment was fresh in my mind, as I'd studied it in catechism (the training ground for young Catholics) the year before. I wrote that Jesus was led to the waste-land by the spirit and, once there, tempted by the devil. I was led to the kitchen by insatiable hunger and, once there, tempted by the refrigerator and the surrounding cupboards.

Jesus fasted. I ate. A lot.

According to the nuns, Jesus relied on grace and fortitude instead of human strength to survive. When tempted by the devil, Jesus didn't fight. When tempted by Ruffles, I didn't either. I had no doubt that all that eating required a certain amount of stamina and perseverance, but I felt that ultimately it was grace and forti-tude that helped me endure. I embraced potato chips just like Jesus embraced the cross.

After a summer of snacking, I weighed one hundred and thirty-eight pounds. My upper body remained passably normal. But from the navel down, it appeared as if someone had stuck an air pump in me and forgot to shut off the airflow. Maybe my new look would have gone unnoticed for a few more days, or perhaps for the whole school year, had I not been standing with my back to the mirror in that dressing room. But I barely topped five feet. Between her adult height and heels, my mother had enough lift for a full view. The result of her inspection was a pink plastic hairbrush with stiff bristles across my back and several hair shirts in the form of brightly colored, supersized parachute tracksuits. Sending a twelve-year-old to school dressed like that is the same as nailing her to the cruel cross.

In the end, though, I thought my essay exceptional and my accomplishment well argued. I expected to receive an A. My teacher sent me to the school counselor instead. She read my file while I sat in her office. Then she asked me a couple of questions. When I left I thought everyone was satisfied and I forgot about it.

On Thursday night, Sarah, my mother, and I were all at the dinner table. My father's place sat empty. We ate in silence save for the intermittent scraping of forks on plates and the sound of chewing. Our weekly menu had strayed from the standard tuna surprise, which was no surprise, because we'd eaten it every Thursday from time immemorial. Instead, my mother offered a green salad with bitter dressing.

When we sat down, I said, "Where's Dad?" My mother responded by grabbing a pile of salad with a spoon resembling a forklift and dropping it onto my outstretched plate.

I speared a cherry tomato and popped it into my mouth. I looked wide-eyed over at Sarah. Her fork paused halfway to her mouth as she shook her head. I narrowed my eyebrows in a questioning frown. My mother shot me a look. She'd told me many times that if I continued to frown, I'd have a valley between my eyes before age twenty.

I relaxed my face. The front door slammed. We could always discern the type of mood that would accompany my father into the kitchen by the sound of the door. My mother's attention retreated as she calmly ate her salad. I tried to swallow the masticated tomato. The tidal wave of fear welling in my throat was too great an obstacle to push it over. I held it in my mouth. My father walked into the kitchen, tossed his keys on the counter, went over to the wet bar, and retrieved a bottle of Jameson and a glass. He sat down, opened the bottle, and poured a drink. The salty pulp of the tomato I couldn't swallow made my eyes water. Sarah put her fork down.

My father sipped his whiskey, then removed a cigarette pack from his shirt pocket. He held a cigarette in his teeth as he struck a match. I tried to swallow again but the tomato caught in my throat. I choked and spit it out on my plate.

My father laughed and extinguished the match by waving it in the air. "Well, I see you inherited your mother's gag reflexes."

My mother's eyes smoldered. My parents fixed on each other. My eyes burned. Tears rushed over the bank of my lower eyelids and spilled down my cheeks.

My father dropped his cigarette into the ashtray, held up his palms, and said innocently, "What?"

"Sarah, serve your father dinner, please." My mother pushed the salad bowl in front of Sarah. She filled his plate and handed it to him.

"Yum," he said, "I love salad." He took a mouthful, looked at us, and said, "Eat." My mother calmly forked another bite into her mouth as if she were attending a pleasant family dinner.

We could never gauge my father's mood. A nice voice meant nothing. He might continue joking and make dinner fun, or he could take offense at the blink of an eye and dinner plates would fly. Sarah nodded slightly at me. If we did what he said, we might make it through dinner unscathed.

Somehow I managed to get some salad down my throat. I wished we had a dog that would happily eat anything coming over the side of the table. Would dogs actually eat lettuce and tomatoes, anyway? Then my father started telling jokes. Within moments, I was laughing with him. Sarah stayed cool for a few more minutes before she capitulated and we enjoyed the rest of our meal.

When everyone was done, Sarah and I cleared the plates while my father sat smoking quietly. Usually, he left the kitchen after dinner.

"Holly"—my father inhaled—"your mother said you are making a name for yourself with your essay writing at school?" His voice remained playful. I set the plate I was carrying on the counter.

My mother hadn't said a word. My father seemed to be in a good mood, so I said indignantly, "I thought it was a great essay, but my teacher wouldn't grade it."

Sarah turned on the faucet.

"Elizabeth," my father said in a cloud of smoke, "where is that essay?"

"On the counter," was my mother's dead response.

"Holly"—he pointed at the counter—"could you bring it to me? I want to read it."

Sarah slowly turned the same plate under the water. Anxiety tickled my stomach. My father sat smoking. His gaze didn't leave me as I retrieved the essay and walked over to him.

"Sit down," said my father. I hesitated. "Sit down," he repeated, slapping the table with his hand. I looked over at Sarah. She continued turning that same plate under the water.

My father glanced at the essay, then rolled it up like a baton and stood over me, waving it in my face. "You think this is funny?" he screamed.

I felt dizzy. "I . . . uh . . ."

"Do you?" My father slapped my face with the rolled-up essay. Sarge pulled me back and took control. I sat rigidly inside my head, watching as Sarge received a few more slaps from the paper essay. It looked like a toothpick from so far away.

"You think this is funny?" My father screamed this over and over, hitting my face again and again until the essay was ragged and shredded.

Finally, Sarge balled up my fists and hit at my father's chest. Because it came from my body, the punch probably felt like a gnat stinging an elephant. He didn't react, just kept waving his tattered paper club in my face. Then he turned and disappeared. I sat in the back of my head holding the Boy's hand. We both whimpered. Sarge had my body in a crouch. We waited.

My father returned with a large bag of Ruffles potato chips. He stood over me and yelled, "Here, you fat pig. You want to eat? Then eat." I heard a crash. Sarah must have dropped the plate she was rinsing. My father ripped the bag open with such force that the chips exploded in the air and floated to the ground. He knelt down and forced my lips open with his left hand. His right hand shoveled a big scoop of chips out of the bag and smashed them into my mouth the same violent way couples crush wedding cake in each other's faces on the best day of their lives. He did it again and again. He kept shoveling and forcing the chips down in my mouth until he emptied the bag. Then he scraped the chips off the floor.

When none were left, he bellowed, "Bring me more chips. If my fat daughter wants to eat, then, by God, she'll eat." Nobody moved. "More!" he screamed. Half of a wet dinner plate sailed through the air and collided with the wall. The ceramic shards dropped to the ground like light snowflakes. My father's eyes glowed. "More!" he screamed. The other half of the plate flew and smashed. Still nobody moved. My father dug around the hard-wood for any remaining chips and my next mouthful included small shards of the broken plate.

The Boy let go of my hand and ran forward. He shoved Sarge out of the way and out of my mouth cried, "Daddy, not Holly. Please not Holly."

My mother screamed. My father's eyes darkened with grief and then turned to a murky blue. His hands dropped to his sides. I could feel the knob on the cupboard pressing into the space between my shoulder blades. I tasted the salty grains and blood on my lips with my tongue. I couldn't tell if the saltiness was the chips or my tears. Probably both.

My father stood, picked up the bottle of whiskey and his cigarettes. "You are so disgusting I can't even look at you." As he walked out of the room, he said to the hallway, "No man loves a fat daughter." A bolt of fear mixed with pain cracked my chest so hard I thought it split my sternum.

My mother stood. She didn't look at me. "Sarah, you and your sister clean up this mess and then get ready for bed." Then she left the room.

I closed my eyes and saw the Boy sitting with Sarge in our favorite park. He motioned to me and I sat on the grass beside him. The evening dew seeped through my clothes. The Boy held my hand and leaned his head on my shoulder. I still couldn't see his face, but when I tilted my head and rested it on his, I felt silky hair against my cheek. All thoughts fled my mind. I breathed in and out, letting the rhythm of the act calm me.

After a while, I thought I heard someone saying, "Holly." The voice was faint and distant but closing in on me.

"Holly!" A hand gripped my shoulder. My eyes flew open. Sarah hovered over me. "Holly, you peed on the floor." My tranquillity shattered into fragments.

"Get up." Sarah hooked her hands under my armpits and pulled me. Even though Sarah had four years on me, the strain of lifting my bulk was evident on her face. "Go take a shower. I'll mop this up before they come back."

In the bathroom I dropped to my knees and heaved into the toilet. Jagged bits of chips mixed with blood landed in the bowl.

Sarge, the Boy, and the Silent One hovered with concern. The acrid smell of vomit and stale urine filled the bathroom. I sat back on my heels, not caring that the damp underwear rested on them. I nodded my head and watched the three depart. When I heard the soft click of the closing door inside my head, I pulled down my sodden panties and savagely flung them against the tiled floor with my foot.

At about midnight, I sneaked upstairs and retrieved my essay from the kitchen trash. I hid it along with my other secret treasures in the box in the back of my closet. When I finished covering the box with sweaters, I shoved my neatly paired shoes aside and sat under the hanging clothes.

The next morning, the ache from a buckle pressing into my cheek woke me up. An unfamiliar bulk rested in the left corner of my head. I saw that Sarge and the other two were wearing harnesses with ropes attached to carabiners on the opposite wall. I looked down and noticed that I too was in harness and held by a rope and carabiner.

Sarge told me matter-of-factly, "I have secured everyone until we can reinforce the house. Until then, if you want to meet her, I'll have to belay you."

I nodded. Sarge hooked something to my harness and slowly lowered me down. A woman the size of a baby killer whale sat calmly on a pillow with the proportions of a full-sized bed. She wore a bright purple tracksuit that accentuated her blueberry eyes. She winked and reached behind her and brought forth a bag of Ruffles potato chips. With a chuckle and a certain amount of gusto, she dug her sausage fingers into the bag and brought out a handful of chips.

Sarge somehow righted the house, but my head continued to lean slightly to the left. For the first half of the school year I remained the nerdy fat girl whose polyester legs scratched a snare-drum symphony as I waddled past the snickering classroom. By the end of the school year, I'd lost my summer weight plus twenty more pounds. My mother gushed when she was able to buy me doll-sized clothes. My father took no notice and, beyond the perfunctory good morning and good night, had completely lost interest in me.

If I were inside my head, I'd be standing right in front of the closet of secrets aching to open that door. Not today. Not tomorrow. Not ever, I thought fiercely. And before Milton could say, "Thoughts?" I got up and walked out the door.

{ 21 }

I was out walking again. It seemed to be one of my favorite pastimes lately. I bought a coffee to go and stopped for a rest at Battery Park. I stared out at the Hudson. A ferryboat floated off in the distance. Its lonely horn called to what? Its lost mate? I thought about the conversation my mother and I had had earlier that day. She had called to ask me to come home for Christmas. I still hadn't spent the holidays with my family since I'd moved to New York. My most recent excuse was that I couldn't get away from work. My mother and I had not talked about my job, but when she presented the invitation for Christmas, I knew she knew. Before she hung up, she said, "Be sure to bring your boyfriend. It's about time we met." Another unmentioned episode, but at the time, I was too tired to explain that I had no boyfriend. I told her I'd think about it.

The ferry was docking when I heard a man say my name.

I turned and on the other side of my park bench was none other than Mike Davey, the director whom I could now admit I had had a crush on until he betrayed me and replaced me on *The*

Neighborhood. I smiled at him, but I still tasted his bitter Judas kiss.

"You are the last person I expected to run into here," he said. "What a surprise."

"Yeah, I was out walking, ended up down here. I'm just taking a break."

"May I?" he said.

"Sure."

Mike smiled and sat down next to me. I could feel the heat of his body through my jacket. The iciness I felt thawed. I looked down. "Nice view," he said, looking out at the Statue of Liberty.

I watched the passengers disembark from the ferry that had docked moments ago. "Yeah, the ferries just come and go. I mean, that is what they are supposed to do, right?" I didn't need the Committee to remark on the stupidity of that comment.

"Right," he said warmly. "So, how's it going? Been able to get them talking again?" He pointed at my head.

"What are you talking about?" My heart pounded in my chest.

"Your friends. Holly, I know your secret."

My surroundings blurred. "How?" I forced the word up and out of my throat.

"I'm observant." Then, turning back to the water, he said, "That, and I have a cousin with the same setup, as it were. He's also fully functional."

The award ceremony video flashed in my mind. It worked much better than squeezing my toes to bring my errant spirit back into my body. "Are you sure? I bet there isn't a video, with a million hits, of him knocking himself out at the Emmys," I said sullenly.

"I'm really sorry about the show, Holly. You can't imagine the position I was in." I realized it had never occurred to me that auditioning my replacement might have posed a real dilemma for him. "Forgive me?" said Mike.

I had no reason to, and it was completely out of character for me, but I did forgive him; and, for the first time in my life, I spilled the whole story about the Committee, including their departure after the Emmy awards and group therapy, to someone other than a trained professional or a family member who had to love me no matter what. He was still sitting there when I finished. And, while I spoke, we exchanged eleven flirtatious glances and had two accidental brushes of the hand. Not that I was counting.

"So, you see them twice a week for an hour?" he said.

"Yeah, I'm trying to get back to the way things were. I'm trying to get my life back."

"Have you thought about moving forward instead?"

"You sound like my sister and my shrink." The tone of my voice was like a warning growl.

Mike nodded, and I reveled in the experience of having someone besides family or a paid professional read my thoughts. It was like driving a car for the first time. Odd but thrilling.

"While you're working on that, how are you fixed for money?" said Mike.

"Not well." I had just told him about my Committee and twice-weekly psychoanalytic sessions; how could financial ruin be any more embarrassing? He had to know that all my commercials were canceled and the royalty checks had dried up. Nobody wanted a voice of scandal behind their product.

"Well, I can get you some work if you're up for it."

"Really?" I said, surprised.

"It's not what you're used to, but you can do it, no problem."

"What is it?"

He hesitated, then said, "Doing the recording for a company

phone system." Now I felt like a car stalled in the middle of a busy intersection, and all I wanted to do was get out and leave it there.

"You want me to do phone work? Me? The voice that used to be your star? The voice that people used to request for commercials and movies? You want me to be on some company's phone system?"

"I know it's not glamorous—"

"You bet it's not glamorous," I snapped. "I guess this is all you think I'm good for?"

"Holly." He covered my hand with his. I wrenched it away.

"You have your ratings without the crazy lady with voices in her head. Or, in this case, without the voices. Either way, good to go for phone work."

"Holly, I was just trying to help," said Mike.

Where had I heard that before? "Yeah, well, where's your blonde girlfriend?" I said.

"Huh?" said Mike. I shook my head. "Take the number anyway," he said, pulling out a pen and a business card. He wrote a number on the back and handed it to me.

I looked at it. Looked at him and said, "Thanks. Thanks a lot. I appreciate knowing what you think of my talents."

"Holly," he said, shaking his head.

I stood up.

"I thought you needed—"

"See ya!" I said, turning and stalking off.

"Holly!" he called after me.

This is what happens when you think a perfect stranger can read your thoughts. I kept walking.

DECLINED. I waited for the sirens to start and the A & P grocery security guards to come and escort me away.

The cashier snapped her gum and said, "Declined." The people behind me groaned collectively. Holiday cheer and patience were definitely not in play in the supermarket. They probably wanted to send me to Guantánamo.

"I see that. Hang on," I said, mortified. I didn't know what to do; that was my last credit card. Now my options were either skulk out in shame or try the emergency card. I had been using it a lot too, so the chances were my meager purchases of milk, coffee, cigarettes, and cat food were not going to make it. "Try this." I surrendered the emergency credit card.

I held my breath. The screen read, PROCESSING. We all watched. APPROVED appeared, and the cash drawer sprang open. I signed the charge slip, grabbed my bag, and left vowing never to return. And this was one place where I could make good on that promise.

When I got home, my cats were at the door to greet me. They must have sensed their last meals coming down the street. I didn't have the means to keep them in Fancy Feast much longer. They tripped me as I tried to get into the kitchen. I normally didn't give them canned food at night, but I figured, Why not? At our rate of decline, they might be reduced to catching their dinner by the weekend.

As I scooped the food into their bowls, I thought of the number Mike had given me the other day. Resentment burned a hole in my stomach. I called my bank to check my balance. Negative three hundred sixty-six and change. The gall flipped over into panic.

I picked up the phone and dialed. A woman answered. I told her who I was and said I had gotten her name from Mike Davey.

"I can't believe we're going to have a celebrity do our phone system. You must really owe Mike a favor."

What a laugh. "Yeah. So, when would you like me to do this?"

We made arrangements for the week after the holidays. The pay would be enough to tide me over with a small loan from Sarah. And she said there would be more work if I was interested.

I called Sarah. She said no problem with the loan. I closed the blinds on my windows and sat in my dark apartment.

The phone rang.

"Hello?"

"Is this Holly Miller?"

"That depends," I said.

"This is Bill Rhode," said the voice on the other end of the phone.

"Who?" I said.

"Neil's father."

"Oh." Pam had warned me that I might get a call from a parent. This must be the one. He'd called Pam in a huff about my Jesus disparagement. She thought she'd smoothed it over. And enough time had passed that I had thought she did too. Apparently not. *I wonder if he'd believe me if I said, "Wrong number."*

"Is this Holly Miller?" he said again.

I may as well light a cigarette and listen. "Yes, it is," I said.

"Ms. Miller," said Mr. Rhode. *Who does he think he's talking to, my mother?* "I understand you contradicted my son when he said Aslan was Jesus."

"Contradicted? No, I didn't agree," I said.

"Yes, well, the thing is, my son thinks very highly of you, and I'm thrilled to see him so engaged. That said, faith is important to us. My son and I spoke about your remarks. He told me he thought you dismissed the idea that Jesus is Aslan because you're lost."

Out of the mouth of a child, I thought. "Well, he's certainly right on that front," I said.

"And this is why you direct so much anger at the idea of Aslan as Jesus?" said Mr. Rhode.

Why does he care? "Trust me, God, Jesus, or whatever you want to call him, and I parted ways many years ago and continued in opposite directions. I've long since gotten over my anger."

"Do you really believe that?" he said.

"What? The opposite directions or the anger?" *Come on, Holly.* I sighed. "I'm sorry to be so terse, Mr. Rhode. It's just that I've been having a bad time on and off for most of my life. Right now the bad times are on. And, frankly, God's certainly never done much to help me."

"And you've asked for help?"

"Asked and been ignored enough times to stop believing in God," I said.

"Well, if you are looking for God to solve your problems, then I'd like to suggest a different approach. A paradigm shift expanded to human experiences, if you would." This had to be the weirdest conversation I'd ever had, but his reference to science made it hard for me to dismiss him as I had his son.

"Okay," I said, "continue."

"Rather than viewing God as the solution to anything, try having faith that there is something larger at work on all our behalf. Those who have faith generally find comfort, and it's that comfort that helps them do amazing things. My son's esteem for you makes me think that you must believe in something. Call it whatever you like," said Mr. Rhode.

Even though he reverted back to a more existential argument, I engaged, and we debated the meaning of faith and the idea of a belief in God for twenty minutes.

Finally I said, "I still don't buy most of what you're saying, but you've made your point, and I promise to be more respectful of your son's beliefs."

"Thank you, Ms. Miller."

"Oh, you can call me Holly."

"Thank you, Holly."

"Just don't send me any literature," I said.

He laughed. "My son also said you're funny."

"I used to be," I said.

"Take care of yourself, and thank you for your positive influence on my son."

Mr. Rhode hung up and I sat in the dark thinking about what he had said. Between him and Mike, my fragile new facade was starting to show cracks. Then I thought about Peter and how much I had loved having these kinds of debates with him. And before I could stop myself, I picked up the phone again, dialed star-six-seven to disguise my number to make sure there was no trace of me just in case the call went unanswered, and then punched in the seven digits I'd spent the last seven-plus weeks trying to forget.

He answered. When I heard his voice all I felt was ambivalence.

"It's me," I said.

Silence. The silence transformed my ambivalence into deprivation.

"I miss you," I whispered.

Silence. My breathing quickened.

"I miss you too," said Peter.

I exhaled. "Can I see you?"

"How about tonight?" said Peter. I relaxed. "We can grab a bite after my class."

I called and checked whether the emergency card could cover a bikini wax, manicure/pedicure, and dinner if I had to pay for it.

When I heard the card had no limit, I almost wanted to send the Father a thank-you note. Almost. Instead, I ran down the block to take care of outside business, then home to wash my hair and choose my outfit. I wanted to look careless and casual but also irresistible.

"You look fantastic," said Peter, giving me an awkward hug. *Did he think I was going to look awful? That I had gotten fat? What was Pam saying to him?*

"And I love those jeans on you."

Refocusing on Peter, I said coyly, "I know."

I flirted with Peter all through dinner. It felt as if I were someone else. Later, back in my apartment, Peter poured two glasses of wine while I put on some music. For the first time, I didn't have to wait for the Committee to leave the room.

The bass from the stereo crawled up my legs, making me want to throw off the last vestiges of who I was. I looked at Peter. He smiled. I started dancing, running my palms slowly up my legs, across my hips as I moved closer to him. Then I tipped my head forward and took the ends of my shirt, pulling it slowly over my head. Peter looked puzzled. I threw my shirt on the floor and moved closer, removing one bra strap at a time. Then I reached behind my back, unhooked my bra, and let it drop. Peter leaned back, nodding. I undid the top button on my pants and slid the zipper halfway down. I stood right in front of him and playfully slid my finger back and forth on the top of my panties. I leaned closer and touched his top lip lightly with my tongue. Then his bottom lip. I kissed him softly as I reached down to unbuckle his jeans. I put my right knee down on one side of him and then my left knee on the other side. Straddling him, I brushed my nipples against his mouth, pulling away when he tried to catch them with his lips. Then I kissed him again, pressing harder and harder as I slid one hand into his pants and put the other one in mine. He pulled my hand out and took over. Lifting up, he pushed me back against the couch and pulled off my jeans. When he pushed inside me, I felt numb. He brushed back my hair. With his hands on either side of my face he started to move faster, pushing harder until he came. He shook and then dropped on top of me.

"Did you?" he said. Nice of him to ask now.

"Yeah," I said. He didn't move, and the weight of him on top of me was crushing. It felt good. I put my arms around him and he fell asleep inside me.

When Peter woke up, he kissed me lightly and said, "You're different somehow." The dark room closed in on me. I felt like a flower shrinking back from too much sun.

"In a good way," he said, touching my chin. "Yeah, I like this."

I felt a hardening in my chest. His comment bugged me on so many levels. Maybe he really did like me regardless of my job. But then, he also liked me without my Committee, and I felt like I was nothing without my Committee. But as long as I was nothing, maybe I deserved less than nothing.

"So, what are you doing for Christmas?" I said to the ceiling.

{ 22 }

I wore the wrong outfit to a funeral. I don't remember who died, but I'll never forget my mother's displeasure over my choice of attire. Keeping my mother's displeasure at bay was my excuse for taking Peter with me to California. I kept the part about who called whom vague.

"Whose funeral?" said Milton.

"Oh, who cares," snapped Sarge.

"Yes, let's talk about something else," said Betty Jane.

"Let's talk about the funeral," said Ruffles.

"What did you wear, Holly?" said Milton.

Ever since I'd eaten those damn chips, Ruffles had become very pushy about unearthing the past, and Milton latched onto anything Ruffles supported. Just like that day when I had a good feeling turn bad with Mike, Ruffles's pushing me to peruse the past felt odd and thrilling. I wanted to run, but because she pushed, I continued forward, hoping I didn't end up with the psychological equivalent of taping a phone recording for a business.

"I was six and a half, and I thought the world should be purple," I said.

My father, who left me to dress myself, was to blame for my funeral fashion faux pas that day. I chose everything purple in my wardrobe—socks, underwear, velvet hip huggers with bell-bottoms and a drawstring fly, and a sweater. My choice of shoes were toe-biting black Mary Janes or bright blue clogs with a tiny red heart on the outside edge. You can guess which shoes I picked. It didn't matter, because by the time my father presented me, he'd already dulled the day with his standard whiskey and cigarettes. Not even my mother's wrath penetrated that protective armor.

"Look at her." She swept my outfit with her hand as if to wipe away my clothing blight. My mother always behaved as if I wore purple to spite her, but this time it definitely was the clogs that caused the deepest offense. "My daughter in bohemian clothes, clashing colors, and wooden shoes at a funeral. People will think we can't afford to dress our children properly."

My father was saved by the priest, who interrupted and said, "We're ready for the family now."

Sarah took my hand and said, "Holly, come on."

My mother sat in the front pew next to her sisters and other family members. My aunt motioned to Sarah to come to their pew. Sarah shook her head fiercely and shoved me into the second pew right behind them. She pressed her body into the wooden corner where the side, bench, and back all met. I sat near her with my legs dangling impishly.

Organ music began to play. Everyone stood and turned. My father and uncle walked up the center aisle carrying something. The church filled with plaintive notes and muffled sobs. I smelled frankincense mixed with wax when I climbed up on the pew. My clogs clacked on the wood. I raised my arm and waved hard at my father and uncle. My aunt reached over and tried to pull my arm down. I leaned away from her and kept waving.

"Let her do it," Sarah whispered angrily.

The procession passed slowly by our pew. I waved harder. My father and uncle ignored me. My grandfather walked behind my uncle. Someone was opposite him. On their shoulders was a doll-sized casket. My aunts' husbands walked behind the procession of four. They lifted the small white box up in the air and placed it gently on the gurney set up at the front of the church altar. The music stopped.

"You may be seated," said the priest.

The church filled with the noise of people dropping down heavily. Sarah pulled me down and tucked me back into the corner of the pew. The priest started speaking. People crossed themselves, stood up, sat down, then stood up again.

"Holly?" I rolled my eyes up, straining to see inside my head. Two people—a man and a boy with a blurred face—had been in there for three days now. I called them the Silent One and the Boy because the man had not said a word since he had appeared and the boy seemed to be afraid of everything or crying. Today at least he'd stopped crying.

My dangling legs swung back and forth under the pew. On a forward swing, my clog flew off, hit the back of the pew in front of us, and fell to the floor. Like most old-style European churches, the acoustics were very good. And my clog drop was well-timed with a moment of silent prayer.

I sat frozen like a statue. The offending clog lay on its side, barely concealed by the pew in front of me. My mother whipped her head around, glaring. The heads in front of us lifted and then dropped again. My mother pointed at my shoe and hissed, "Put that back on and sit still."

My mother's standard method of imposing good behavior in

church was to grip a small bit of my upper arm between her sharp red nails and then twist. If I made one peep, she would twist harder. Even at my age, I knew how to mute cries of pain. I shrank back, relieved that she couldn't reach my arm.

When my mother turned again, I slid my body forward and reached for my shoe with a pointed toe. When my foot met the clog, it flipped upright, making a light tap on the marble. I slowly moved back to the bench, keeping my foot flexed so as not to lose my shoe again.

While the priest droned, I tried to follow the story in the stained glass windows on the opposite wall. I concentrated on my favorite—the one where a bloody-headed Jesus dragged a cross anchored over his bent back. The congregation shifted forward to the kneeling position again. I concentrated on Jesus. In my head the Silent One carried the Boy in a piggyback ride. I giggled. Sarah elbowed me.

"Holly, let me out," said the Boy.

The last few days nobody had paid attention to me except to tell me to go play, or sit still on the sofa. Last night when I closed my eyes I felt myself drift backward. I didn't understand what I was doing, but it helped pass the still hour on the sofa, and it was definitely more interesting than watching the whispering people eat crackers and sip wine.

As I slipped forward to my knees I whispered, "Okay." I watched as my arms pulled the offertory envelopes from the box that held the songbooks. The Silent One shook his head sadly. Then I tasted the sharp glue of the envelope seal. My thumbs pulled away and the envelopes drifted, seal up, onto the pew before me. After a while, the pew was littered with envelopes.

"Please be seated," said the priest.

The Boy ceded control back to me.

The priest spoke for a few more minutes. People stood, shook hands, knelt, and then finally filed to the altar for communion. Even though it had been explained to me many times, I still didn't understand why people ate Jesus. I had nightmares about the body of Jesus sliced up into little wafers. What alarmed me most was, What would happen when the body of Jesus ran out? If I used my father as a measure, his body could be sliced into a lot of paper-thin disks that would last our church about a year. A year was not forever. Jesus was going to run out. Then what? I vowed never to eat Jesus. At least he would last a little longer if I abstained.

My mother stood before the priest. She tilted her bowed head up and opened wide to consume Jesus. I felt sick.

"Holly," said the Boy. "Look." He pointed from my head to my mother's dress. The offertory envelopes hung on her butt like too many earrings. I sniggered into my sticky fingers. As my mother made the slow traverse back to her seat, my aunt pulled off one of the envelopes and whispered, "Elizabeth," as she showed it to her.

My mother disappeared behind a column. She reappeared a few seconds later with a small stack of paper in her hand. Her frosty face remained fixed on me until she was seated. For the first time I wished that church services would never end.

Back at my grandparents' house, my mother cornered me in a room away from prying eyes. She held my upper arm in her viselike grip. "The little boy did it," I pleaded with a sob. Every time I said this, my mother yanked harder.

"How dare you blame someone else," she said in her measured voice.

"But he did," I repeated.

"Stop crying; you are making a spectacle," snapped my mother.

Uncle Dan appeared behind her. I noticed his freckled fingers and hammered nails as he gripped her collarbone and said, "Elizabeth?"

She turned. I peeked from behind her.

"Why don't you let me take Holly?" he said gently.

I watched them both through tears dangling on my eyelashes while they held each other's gaze. My mother let go of my arm and walked away without another word. My uncle knelt down in front of me. I closed my eyes and he wiped off my face with his thumbs. Then he picked me up and carried me outside.

When I finished telling the story, Milton said, "Holly, have you ever outright asked the Committee who they are?"

I looked back at him, perplexed. He always chose the oddest things to focus on. "That is what you want to know after what I just told you?" I said.

Milton nodded. "Have you ever asked them?"

I opened my mouth to answer. Closed it. Opened it. Shook my head as if invisible fingers were holding it on either side, nudging it back and forth just a little. I inhaled and said, "No."

We locked eyes for a few seconds. Milton did his thumb-under-the-chin-with-the-forefinger-touching-the-bottom-lip-other-three-fingers-curled-into-the-palm, "I am an analyst peering deeply into your soul" thing. I turned around to see who was behind me. As a joke. Turned back and he still was giving me the "I'm an analyst" look.

"Why would I ask?"

"Why indeed?" Milton paused with thumb and fingers still in place.

"I never thought to do that. I mean, they were there. So why would I ask?" I said.

"It might be helpful to know."

"You mean it would be helpful and I should've asked. Right?"

"I mean what I said. It might be helpful to know. It is up to you if you want to know."

Of course, this did mean that Milton thought I should ask, but sometimes I just wanted him to tell me. All this investigating was exhausting.

"I don't want to know," I said.

"That is not good enough this time, Holly," said Milton.

Ruffles waited expectantly. Betty Jane left the room.

I'm with her. "After Christmas," I said. "I've had enough for one day."

{ 23 }

I checked my watch, three a.m.

"Drink up," I said. "Our flight leaves in two hours." I'd managed to get two tickets at a bargain price by accepting a less-than-ideal departure time on Christmas day.

"Two hours?" said Peter. "I thought you said we were leaving at seven?" The several drinks I'd had that evening didn't do much to dull Peter's sharp tone. He'd wanted to stay in and be romantic because we'd be in the air Christmas morning. It had been my idea to spend Christmas Eve in a bar.

"Oops, I guess I mixed it up."

We paid the check and went out into the bitter December cold. Peter hailed a cab. He told the driver one stop and then we were going to LaGuardia. He didn't speak to me in the car. I didn't care.

Once inside the apartment, I fed the cats, used the bathroom, and then contemplated whether I had packed the right clothes.

"Holly, the meter's running; let's go."

I sighed. "I have the bags; just grab those gifts."

The paper bag holding the gifts tore as I handed it to the cabbie and presents scattered all over First Avenue. Peter sat fuming in the cab as I crawled around retrieving them.

When we arrived at the airport, Peter got out of the cab and headed toward the terminal without saying a word, leaving me to pay for the ride and figure out what to do with the gifts.

"Here's a bag, miss," said the cabbie. I watched Peter disappear through the door. A dull thud pounded at my temples.

"Thanks," I said, "and Merry Christmas." As soon as I said it, I realized he probably didn't celebrate Christmas, but I was too late to be politically correct. I smiled and followed Peter into the airport.

Peter fell asleep as soon as the plane took off, and when the pilot told us we'd reached cruising altitude, I closed my eyes and slept the rest of the way to California.

I flipped down the passenger visor and was checking to see how I looked in the mirror. Peter was driving. We had rented a car because I'd said we'd want to go into the City, as locals referred to San Francisco, to have fun. The real reason was I wanted to make sure I had an escape vehicle if I needed to leave at a moment's notice.

I pulled out my toiletry bag and unzipped it across my lap.

"So who is going to be there again?" said Peter.

"Well, my sister, and her male alphabet—Doug, Elliot, and Francis." I patted my nose with powder, checked it, and then brushed it with one hand as I carefully applied lipstick.

"Sounds like a bad cover band. Who else?"

"My mom." I turned. "Do I look all right?"

Peter made a face at me.

"What?" I said.

"I have never seen you with that much makeup on before."

"My mother . . . Well, it's complicated," I said. Then I pulled out a cotton square and tried to wipe away most of what I had just applied.

"Better?"

"Better," said Peter. "Your mom likes that much makeup?"

"Next exit, right lane. Let's just say it is easier to be what she wants."

"So, who else is going to be there?" He turned right.

"I am not sure if there is anyone else," I said. I flipped the visor shut. My mother would not approve of the makeup or the outfit.

"Left at the next light and then right on Evergreen," I said. I stared out the window at the denuded trees huddled in a row along the avenue. Were they trying to maintain some modesty in their nakedness, or were they just protecting their trunks from the cold? Did trees get cold?

"What about your dad?" Peter said.

"Huh?" I turned toward Peter. I wanted to tell him to stop asking questions. To slow down. Stop the car. Turn around. "Next right and then it's just at the end of the block, 1456 Evergreen."

Peter turned at the corner and I saw the top half of my parents' house beyond the neighbor's hedges. Blue with white trim. We had moved there when I was seven. Even though I'd lived there most of my childhood, I never felt at home.

We pulled into the driveway behind my sister's Volvo.

"My parents are divorced," I said. "My father left when I graduated from high school. Supposedly, he's happily married to the woman he had an affair with throughout most of my childhood." Peter turned off the ignition. His eyes remained fixed on the steering wheel. "Look, here comes my sister." I opened the car door and stepped out. Then I turned back to Peter. "Didn't I tell you?"

"No, you never told me."

Sarah walked through the garage entrance, and then, as if anticipating my next move, she pointed across the lawn. Ah, yes, the front door. That was where my mother would be waiting. I hugged Sarah and walked arm in arm with her over the grass.

There she stood on the front porch in a black Chanel suit with the familiar sunflower pinned to the lapel. I watched her wipe her hands with a dish towel as we approached. I straightened my back and waited for the familiar look of disdain. She'd surely spot everything she hated—velvet pants, sandals, a beret—and she'd intuitively judge the rest of the outfit hiding under my coat.

"Holly," exclaimed my mother. She trotted down the stairs in heels. She was smiling.

"Who's that?" I whispered to Sarah.

"She's making an effort," Sarah hissed under her breath. "Be nice."

My mother threw her arms around me. I felt an unexpected rush of emotion.

I pulled away confused. "Mom. Hi."

I noticed that crinkles surrounded the whole of her eyes, which twinkled with what appeared to be genuine joy. No disgust anywhere, not even lingering amongst the age-old barf in the rosebushes.

My mother reached out her hands to straighten my head. Something she had been doing since I was twelve. She froze. My eyes filled with tears. Her hands hung suspended in the air as if she were about to bless me. Then she placed them on my cheeks and said, "Look, you are wearing your favorite color." Another shock wave rippled across my body. My pants and hat were purple. "I hope those are not the same pants your uncle bought you when you were eight."

"Right. I don't think those would fit."

"If you don't start eating more, they just might." She held me away from her. "Holly, you smell like cigarettes." *I knew she was lurking in there somewhere.*

I sighed. "Who's here?"

"Everyone except Dan."

The sea inside me receded, trying to take me with it. A harbinger of the tsunami to follow, and my inner warning system screamed, *Get the hell out of here.* I stepped back. My mother's hand gripped my upper arm and steadied me.

Peter appeared at my side, putting his arm around my waist as he extended the other. "Hi, I'm Peter." Even though he was my boyfriend, at that moment he felt like a stranger.

My mother let go of me. "Oh, my goodness. How rude we are, Peter. I am sorry. I am Holly's mother. So nice to meet you." She shook his hand.

"Nice to meet you too, Mrs. Miller," said Peter. He looked at both our faces and added, "Now I see where Holly gets her good looks."

"Oh, do stop." She coyly brushed away his comment. "And please call me Elizabeth." As she batted her eyes, I wanted to feel shame and anger. Instead I felt the adult acceptance of parental behavior that you have discovered is ingrained and now mostly harmless.

"Elizabeth," said Peter. His arm slipped from my waist as he held it out to my mother. She accepted it. I thought of how many times I'd seen my parents walk though a doorway in that same manner. And then how many times my mother stalked through the door alone.

"He knows what he's doing," said Sarah. I flashed a hollow smile.

"Uncle Dan is coming?" I hadn't seen him since he left that

morning more than twenty-five years ago. After he left, his name was never mentioned in our house again, and I tucked my memories of him away somewhere safe. A small sob escaped my throat. Saying his name felt like releasing an abscess that had festered for decades. My head dropped.

Sarah placed a hand on my shoulder and whispered, "I know."

"When did they start speaking again?"

"All she told me is that they talked and have put the past behind them," said Sarah.

"Did she get a lobotomy? Or some new medication?"

Sarah laughed. I smiled, inhaled, and turned toward the door.

"He lives in San Mateo now, so we see quite a bit of him. The boys are crazy about him. You know how that goes?"

I nodded in response. I sure did know.

Sarah took my hand. "Come on."

Peter was waiting for me in the foyer.

"Give me a sec," I said.

As Sarah walked off, Peter pretended to hug me but instead whispered harshly in my ear, "Thanks for leaving me standing there."

I stepped back and, without lowering my voice, I responded, "You did okay."

My mother, Sarah, and I were in the kitchen getting the meal ready. As the least-qualified person to be in the kitchen, I stood at the center island supervising their efforts while rolling a baby carrot around on a cutting board as they were putting pots on the stove and pulling pans out of the oven.

"Holly," said my mother, "what are you doing with a guy like Peter?"

"Mom," said Sarah warningly.

She put a steaming platter of potatoes on the counter and said, "Sarah, I may not have the education your father and I provided for you girls, but do not underestimate my ability to see right into the heart of people. Those two are as wrong for each other as your father and I were."

"What do you mean, wrong like you and your former husband?" I said.

"Holly, are you still harboring such resentment toward your father? You need to let that go. Sarah has. I have. It was a different time. We were raised differently. We didn't know as much then as we do now. We did the best we could."

"Well, what a great sentiment. You should have put that in your holiday letter this year. 'We did the best we could!'"

"Holly!" exclaimed Sarah.

"No, Sarah." My mother held up her hand, palm flat, to stop her. "Let her speak. Then I will speak. Holly needs to learn some facts of life."

"I knew I shouldn't have come home. You are never satisfied with anything I do. You are never satisfied with me." I punctuated that last sentence by crushing the carrot with my balled fist.

"You are right. I am not satisfied when my daughter, an intelligent, attractive, interesting woman who has everything going for her, chooses to follow in my footsteps."

"Huh?" I looked up, surprised.

"My God, Holly, do not throw your life away over a man who is so wrong for you just to spite me or your father or your upbringing. You know better. You have choices. As a Catholic girl from Atlanta, I certainly did not have choices."

My parents were both raised Catholic. The Father a poor man from San Francisco, California; Mom a rich woman from Atlanta, Georgia. They met when my father was on a summer road trip across America with his two childhood friends. His last hurrah before buckling down in college. He'd won a full scholarship and had big plans for himself—maybe medicine, maybe law. All I can say is, it must have been some meeting, because my father bailed out on the remainder of his trip and stayed in Atlanta to woo my mother. By the end of the summer, he exceeded his own expectations and his college plans had become husband and father plans. My mother refused to make the financial sacrifices that were required to get my father through school when her father was offering mine a lucrative job in Palo Alto, California, where my mother's sisters had already moved with their husbands. She figured her compromise was getting him back home and wasn't willing to compromise any more. They had a shotgun wedding, then moved within walking distance of one of my aunts. Sarah was born six months later.

"You had choices, Mom. You just made the ones that suited you. Or should I say the ones that spited your parents and your upbringing." As I listened to myself say those last words, I thought, *Hats off, Mom. You made your point.*

She wiped her hands on the towel in front of her and picked up the knife to chop vegetables. I stepped back and leaned on the counter behind me.

Shrieks erupted from the backyard. We all looked out the kitchen window and saw Doug spread-eagled on the lawn with seven-year-old Elliot and five-year-old Francis crawling across his back. Peter stood to the side watching. No doubt he wanted to keep his clothes pristine.

My mother waved the knife in her hand at the window. "Holly, I am not going to stand here and bare myself for you. You can either listen to me or you can wake up twenty years from now and realize time wasted is time you never get back." Peter, thinking my mother was waving at him, nonplussed by the knife in her hand, waved back. She smiled, and I felt a physical jolt, because that was the smile I used when I needed to hide my true feelings. "Holly, have some courage, and for once in your life face reality and take steps."

"Mom." Sarah moved toward my mother as if to physically shut her up. Obviously, this was not unfolding the way Sarah and my mother had planned. Sarah should have known better than to give my mother permission to discuss my life with me and then expect her to obey boundaries.

"You are a fine one to talk to me about facing reality," I said.

"It breaks my heart to see you'd rather blame your father and me for your inability to manage your life," she said. "Would you really rather stay stuck in the past, keeping all of us there with you, instead of letting go, moving on, and finding out who your family has become?"

A dinner plate crashed to the floor. Good thing, because I had no answer for her. Without shifting her gaze from my face, my mother caught the cause of the plate's fall—a little hand filled with chocolates—as it slid back across the counter next to her. I waited for her to scold Francis, who, as the smallest and quietest of the group, had no doubt been dispatched to sneak candy for all of them. She dropped the corner of her mouth, turned, reached for a handful of chocolates, opened his other palm, and filled it. Then she sent him away with a kiss on the head.

Who is this woman? I braced myself with my hands on the counter.

The doorbell rang. Happy for an excuse to escape the kitchen empty-handed, I said, "I'll get it."

"That must be Dan," said my mother.

Walking into the entryway, I felt the same anticipation I used to feel when I left school in the afternoons. I opened the front door half expecting the School Bug to be waiting at the curb. Instead I saw a man I would have recognized anywhere, even though what was left of his red hair had all turned gray, and the lines on his face bore witness to the life he'd led.

"Holly," my uncle said as he embraced me. "Your mom said you were flying out."

"Yeah." I stepped back to let him pass. I checked again for the School Bug and then shut the door.

My uncle smiled. "I sold it a long time ago."

I hugged him tightly. And without either of us uttering a sound, everything unsaid was understood.

"Let me take your coat," I said.

"Thanks."

I opened the closet, pulled out a hanger, and then turned back to him. Time stopped for that moment and I saw a younger version of him sitting next to me in a different closet in a different house. The weariness that hung about him then was barely detectable now.

I shook my head. His eyes squinted.

"I just had this flash of you sitting next to me in my father's closet." My heart skipped and then constricted.

He sighed deeply. "I remember that day." Then he hugged me. "Holly, it's so good to see you."

"You too, Uncle Dan. I've really missed you."

"Sarge," yelled Doug from behind us. I felt like someone had just let all the air out of my lungs. My uncle turned and they high-fived each other. I grabbed his other arm.

He turned back and looked intently at me. "Are you okay, Holly?" The concern in his voice was genuine. I pressed my hands against my temples, trying to force what was coming out to stay in. I took several deeps breaths until my mind went pitch-black. Then I opened my eyes, smiled, and said, "Shall we see what the others are doing?"

After dinner we sat in the living room opening gifts. The rectangular space provided plenty of distance between me and Peter. I staked out the fireplace on one end and Peter sat on the opposite end in front of the tree with the guys.

Elliot was reviewing with Uncle Dan the instructions for the model airplane I had brought for him. Francis stood over by the tree marking a gingerbread man hanging midway as his target. I watched him pull it down and then look around to see if anyone had noticed. He locked eyes with mine as he quickly bit the little brown head clean off. I laughed. Another generation bewitched.

Sarah turned toward me and I nodded over to her son. I didn't have enough fingers to count the number of times Sarah and I had bitten off heads, arms, and legs when we thought nobody was looking. The doughy thickness paired with smart decorations belied the actual teeth-breaking quality of those fat men who caused the branches to slope. Even so, each year we approached them thinking this time they'd taste as good as they looked. They never did.

"Holly." Sarah handed me a big box.

"Wow, Sarah, I didn't think we were going nuts this year."

"We helped wrap them, Aunt Holly," said Francis. Elliot glanced up from his model plane and nodded in agreement.

"One for each, including you," Sarah said.

"Each?" said my mother.

Peter sat down next to me. "What did you get?" he said.

"All those presents." Francis pointed at the box.

"One for each?" said my mother. "Do you know what that means?" She looked askance at Peter.

"No idea," he said.

I slid away from him and placed the box between us.

"It's a sister thing," said Sarah. Doug handed Peter a gift. "Don't worry," said Sarah. "Just like our little gingerbread friends over there, it looks better than it is."

I opened the box and inside were six wrapped presents. I smirked at Sarah. I unwrapped the first one. Ah, a meditation candle. Next the square package. It was a leather cosmetic case. I ran my hand across it, trying to wipe away the bitterness souring my stomach. I reached for the soft package. Hanes Beefy Ts. I couldn't hear it yet, but I knew that the tsunami my body had tried to warn me about earlier was looming on the horizon. I put down the shirts. Three gifts remained. The shape and weight indicated a set of books. My fingers trembled, then chose the other gift. I tore at the wrapping and inside was a rectangular box. I lifted the lid. A hand mirror? How strange. I looked sideways at Sarah. She smiled. Okay, the envelope or the set of books. I slipped my finger under the seal and opened the envelope. Inside was a ragged piece of paper. I pulled it out. The essay I had written for school back in sixth grade. How did Sarah end up with it?

"We can talk about it later," said Sarah. "Open the last one."

I turned it over and wedged my fingers between the wrapping and tape until the gift was free. The Chronicles of Narnia. All seven books. The wave roared at my back.

"Mom read those to me," said Elliot, who had left his plane to watch me open the last of my gifts. "*Prince Caspian* was my favorite." I flashed him a befuddled smile, unsure whether to be grateful or resentful that he had interrupted the vortex building inside me.

"Holly," said Sarah, "you're eating chips."

"As a child, Holly always loved Ruffles," said my mother nostalgically.

That brought me back. "Well, until you put me on a diet," I said. The criticism I used to feel was not there anymore.

"It is always okay to indulge; you just have to moderate," said my mother.

"I know. Just a few." I smiled.

There was one unwrapped box remaining. My uncle picked it up. He turned to my mother and said, "Betty Jane?"

My eyes frantically swept the room for cover. *Was she here? Did she sneak back?* My breathing quickened. I shut my eyes. The Committee's house remained empty, filled with dust instead of Christmas. I opened my eyes again. My uncle looked startled. The scar on his neck pulsed.

"What did you call her?" My question came out ragged, like my breath.

"That's his pet name for me, Holly. Have you forgotten?" said my mother.

"I didn't . . ." The edges of the Ruffles cut at my stomach. I sat back feeling dizzy. Everyone was silent. The Christmas carols on the stereo sounded tinny in the background.

Uncle Dan held out the flat box like a peace offering to my mother.

"Well," she said. She reached for the box. "I have something now that I want to show you girls."

Doug had been around my mother long enough to know they'd been dismissed. "Let's go see if the game is on." He motioned to the men and boys as he left the room.

Sarah and my mother sat on either side of me. My mother opened the box and pulled out a photo album. As far as I knew there was no record of our lives growing up. I didn't remember my parents owning a camera. Sarah and I got Kodak Instamatics for Christmas when I was twelve and she was sixteen, but that was way too late to account for the early years.

My earlier vitriol replaced by surprise, I said, "Mom, where did you get these pictures?" I touched the plastic cover page with photos of my parents' wedding.

"I've always had them stored away in boxes. I finally decided to put them in an album."

As Mom turned the page, Sarah and I both exclaimed at the same time, "Baby Sarah!"

There was my sister, tiny and wrinkled. At her baptism, in her stroller. Crawling, walking. This went on for several pages, the three of us commenting and cooing. My mother lifted the next page and then hesitated. Sarah placed her hand over my mother's and gently turned it. I choked on my laugh. Drew in a sharp breath. My mother grabbed my hand. I closed my eyes tight. I opened them. Squeezed them shut again.

"Aiden," Sarah whispered.

My mother ran a finger across the photo of a smiling boy sitting on a red fire truck. "My Little Bean," she said softly.

The wave crashed down on me. Everything in my body went rigid. Something inside me screamed, *Run for cover*. Something else willed me to stay and look. I beat at it with everything I had. Then the force of that picture dragged me, struggling, forward. I started to cry. Sarah put her arms around me, and then I wept.

My mother patted my hand. My weeping shifted to a low keening.

Sarah rocked me.

"I know it's hard, Holly," whispered my mother.

"You have to forgive yourself, Holly." Sarah stroked my hair and squeezed me tighter.

When there was nothing left. I lifted my head, opened my eyes, and looked at the picture of the smiling boy. I touched the picture lightly and said, "Aiden."

{ 24 }

It was a typical late-August day in the Miller household. My alarm clock went off at five a.m. I crawled out of bed and tiptoed to Sarah's room, quietly opened the door, and crept over to her bed. Sarah had kept her room like a sauna with a space heater running all night. The air was rank with the warm, damp smell of urine.

"Sarah," I said. "Wake up."

Sarah groaned. "What time is it?"

"Early."

At almost eleven, Sarah had long gotten over her shame about wetting the bed since the age of five. She threw back her covers, dragged the blankets and pillows to the floor, and pulled the sheets off the bed.

"Help me," she said as she hoisted up one end of her bed.

Every morning we turned her mattress over; and Sarah always left her heater on regardless of the temperature outside so the flipped side was always dry. I wondered now if it was the adrenaline that made it possible for a six-year-old and a ten-year-old to flip a mattress.

Sarah put on her bathrobe and slippers, then gathered up her sheets and slipped out the glass door. Her room opened onto the back porch and her best friend lived in the house behind us. After hearing about the consequences of being caught with a wet bed, her friend's mother had agreed to let Sarah wash and dry her sheets before my mother woke up. Sarah always slept through the alarm clock and this was how I became complicit in her morning subterfuge.

I went back to bed for another hour and a half of sleep. Aiden's shriek jerked me out of my dreamless state.

Five-year-old Aiden had wet the bed again. I don't know why this surprised me. He wet the bed every night, and every morning my second alarm was the sound of my mother's screams punctuated with a leather belt slapping onto my brother's bare skin. Sarah had never included Aiden in her deal to wash sheets. All I did was tell him to hide his belts instead of leaving them lying around. Maybe he did. Who knows?

Aiden took those beatings every morning. I couldn't stand to hear them. I hated it. So every morning I sandwiched my ears with my pillow to drown out the noise. It never worked.

Once, Aiden called out my name. He knew I helped Sarah. I just pressed my pillow harder against my ears.

When my mother beat Aiden, she'd yell, "How dare you wet the bed! How dare you." As if he did it just to spite her.

I could have stopped it, but I didn't. I could have woken him up too. But I didn't. I could have made Sarah take his sheets. But I didn't.

Aiden used to always say to me, "Holly, we don't have to do what Sarah says. Two against one will win."

I could have used her own bed-wetting as leverage and made

her take his sheets too. The three of us could have managed it. Instead we were two—me and Sarah. We managed fine. Aiden? You can see how he did on his own.

He never asked me for help after that morning when I didn't render it. I think he kept expecting it, though. One thing my parents never managed to beat out of us was hope. And maybe, given the chance, I would have come around.

Aiden was always so good to me. He said to me once, "Don't try too hard to be like Sarah, Holly. She is not a very nice person right now. She will be, though, someday."

At five years old Aiden knew that. And he was right.

I'd like to say that I was afraid of Sarah, but the truth is bigger than that. I wanted her to like me. I wanted her acceptance. Her approval. My brother, Aiden? He looked up to me. He was my buddy, my pal, my confidant. I didn't need his approval.

Sarah didn't like it when Aiden and I played with each other. This broke her viselike grip over both of us. This was a potential alliance of two wimps who could overthrow her tentative reign in the hallways downstairs if enough courage could be mustered. If she lost that power, what then?

I'll never know because, to save myself, I would turn on Aiden like a screw twisting in clay if Sarah commanded it.

Aiden. His name eviscerated me. I had spent most of my life holding him at bay. Sarah tried to get me to talk about him. But I didn't. I wouldn't. When I was a senior in high school, I had to write an essay about my family for some English class. I got an A, but I didn't show anyone. I hid it in a drawer. My mother found it. A family meeting was called to discuss the contents. Sarah came home for the weekend. That was the first and only time I ever slapped her.

Aiden. He dwelled in me like a wound so far beneath the surface that you forget about it until you bump the spot and the pain radiates out and gains in strength like a tropical storm turned hurricane.

Aiden. I saw his smile in my mind's eye. I heard him saying, "Hello," always with the accent on the *lo*.

We were going to try to get to Narnia that day. We had it all planned out. Sarah had permission to go to a friend's for a sleep-over. She wasn't supposed to be home.

It was early afternoon; Aiden and I were in the living room playing with our Hot Wheels while we waited for Sarah to leave. We had a real drag race going, and for that brief period of time we forgot to keep watch on our surroundings.

We were moving freely around the orange tracks, shrieking and laughing with abandon.

"Look at the brats playing with their toys."

We both froze and turned to see Sarah standing in the door-way. The sun from the opposite window shone directly on her face so I couldn't see it when I looked at her.

Something came over me. Maybe it was power I felt because my red racer, gassing up at the pumps, was two laps ahead of Aiden's blue sedan. I don't know.

I turned to Aiden and said, "Don't listen to her. Maybe she'll go away."

Sarah strolled into the room with her hands behind her back. She started to rub the edge of the orange tracks resting on the green shag with the toe of her white go-go boot.

"I was putting away laundry, Aiden." Sarah smiled. "Hanging your clothes up in your closet."

Aiden and I froze. The cars whizzed around for a couple of laps, and then mine went careening off the tracks. Aiden's just ran out of gas and stalled on its way up the loop.

"Don't stop what you are doing on my account," said Sarah. Aiden's car slid backward and flipped off the track.

We all sat there in a quiet standoff.

Breaking the silence, Sarah finally said, "What I have doesn't concern your little drag race anyway."

I stayed still. What did she have? I looked over at Aiden and watched while disbelief crept like insidious ivy up his face. He jumped up in front of her. His head was about as high as her chest. He looked so small and pitiful standing in front of Sarah. He tried to reach behind her but she spun out of his grasp. Her movement was filled with a promise to come back. And she came back.

Ignoring Aiden, Sarah looked directly at me. "Oh, yes," she said, her voice an octave higher, heading toward her planned crescendo, "you might need this." She pulled her hands from behind her back and shook out Aiden's Narnia coat. Our escape coat. Our last hope.

I stared at the coat, then gaped at Sarah. She censured me with flashing eyes. Was I with her or with him?

Her challenge wrapped around me and choked my already wavering self-assurance. Aiden grabbed my arm. I shook him off, picked up my red racer, and moved away from him.

Sarah had done it, sundered the tentative bridge between my brother and me. But that wasn't enough. She wanted more.

"Come on, you little baby," she hissed at Aiden, "don't you want this?" Eyes flashing, power restored.

Aiden whimpered. I sat in the corner. My thumb and forefinger gripped the red car and rolled it back and forth across the carpet.

"Guess," Sarah said, yanking an arm so hard it hung from the coat like a loose limb.

"You." She ripped at the other arm with such force it was completely severed.

Aiden burst like a dam.

"Don't." Her index finger dragged down the inside lining.

"Want." Sarah found fresh material and pulled her finger down again.

"This." She crumpled what was left of the coat and dropped it on the floor.

"Stop it! Stop it!" Aiden screamed, hiding his face in the crooks of both elbows while his hands reached around to cover his ears.

If you took away the scream, hiding his face like this was how Aiden responded every morning when my mother tried to beat the bed-wetting out of him, every time my parents had one of their loud arguments in front of us, and probably the nights when my father smoked cigarettes and drank whiskey in his room because Aiden had yelled, "Daddy, not Holly. Please not Holly," to stop him from delivering the beating my mother demanded I receive for whatever minor transgression I'd committed that day. Sometimes I wondered if getting my father to spank me for any stupid thing was her way of making the punishments equal in our house, because I didn't get the morning bed-wetting beating Sarah and Aiden got.

My mother walked in just as the coat touched the floor. Her stolid gaze swept over us like a cop's flashlight in a dark alley. Her eyes passed me first, Aiden second, and then came to rest on the wrecked coat.

Aiden lay on his side whispering, "Aslan, please, Aslan."

"What is going on here?" my mother said abruptly.

"Nothing," Sarah said. "They are playing. Holly's winning. And, as usual, Aiden is crying." Sarah tilted her head to the right and lazily met my mother's stare. "Oh, and I found another one of those filthy coats." She pointed to the floor.

"I thought I told you to throw those out," my mother barked at Aiden and me as she picked up the coat.

Sarah sauntered past me to the stairs. As she went down, her fingers danced on the green shag carpet lying flat underneath the railing. Before Sarah's head dropped below floor level, she stuck out her tongue.

My mother turned and left the room.

"Do you want to keep playing, Holly?" Aiden asked.

"No," I said, kicking the tracks.

"Okay," he said. "Well, good-bye."

"Good-bye." I didn't look up. He left the room.

About an hour later, I heard Sarah telling my mother she was leaving to go to her friend's. Her friend was just across the street and up the block. Sarah was old enough to cross without an adult. Aiden and I were not.

When she left, Sarah opened the front door enough to squeeze out and then shut it with a soft click. I waited just around the corner so I heard it anyway.

I opened the door in time to see her look to the left, right, and then dart across the street. I threw open the front door and ran right after her. I passed Aiden, who stood in the front yard. "Holly," he called after me.

I didn't look back. I ran into the street without looking left or right.

I heard a horn honk. The beeps came in rapid succession. I stopped. Everything around me slowed. I turned. The black car crawled toward me. I stood glued to the asphalt.

The staccato horn beeps had changed to one long groan. I felt like I had cardboard over my ears, dulling the sound.

I stood there.

The car inched forward. The colors around me faded. All I could see was the black monster creeping closer.

I stood there.

I heard a sound like nails raking across a chalkboard. It mixed with the scream of the honking horn. A bitter smell pricked at the inside of my nose like a thousand little needles. I knew I should move but my feet were stuck.

The car fishtailed toward me. My mouth opened but the scream I wanted to release stayed stuck somewhere in my throat. I turned to see Sarah on the opposite side of the street. Her face was ashen, her eyes as big as plates. She waved her hands and yelled. Her words sounded like static on a radio.

Then something slammed into my back, knocking me into the air. I hit the sidewalk with a thud accompanied by a loud crunching sound.

Sarah screamed, "*No!*"

I was lying on the sidewalk, still on my back.

Sarah screamed, "*No!*" over and over. Her hands covered her ears as if she were trying to block out her own cries.

I sat up.

The front door of our house popped open like a vertical jack-in-the-box top. Uncle Dan shot out and ran toward the street. My mother followed a few seconds behind him.

My uncle's pace slowed to a jog, and then he stopped short of the front bumper of the car. I couldn't see his face. The driver of the car opened his door slowly. Then he stepped around this obstacle and advanced toward my uncle right as my mother hit the ground, sliding on her knees.

I didn't understand. I was on the sidewalk.

I sat there gasping for air. Why were they standing there talking? What was she doing? I wanted to yell, *I'm over here*, but the words wouldn't come out. I waited for them to find me. I became angrier by the second. Uncle Dan and the man whispered to each other at the open car door. I couldn't see my mother.

I pushed myself up off the ground and stood there with my

arms akimbo. They still didn't notice me. I gave up and walked toward the car. In front of it, a pool of thick burgundy liquid spread across the asphalt. My mother crawled around in it, pinching at bits on the ground and holding them up to the sunlight. Guttural sobs heaved from her throat.

My heart beat a dull thud in my chest. I watched my mother open her fist, drop one of the bits in it, and then snap it closed again.

I took three steps forward. A few feet from my mother was a red Converse sneaker lying sideways like it had been kicked off.

I held up my hands, palms flat, trying to block the image before me. I couldn't.

My heart beat faster. I closed my eyes and took two more steps. I touched the warm metal side of the car. The sharp corner over the headlight dug into my palm.

My heartbeat lodged in my throat. I opened my eyes.

His leg was twisted at an odd angle. His sock covered in blood. His head like the hamburger I poked at in the store.

I started to hyperventilate.

I knew where I had to go.

I ran.

I yanked open the front door. She always threw clothes away in the laundry room. I bounced off the wall when I tried to make the turn. Where was it? Where?

I saw it on top of the wastebasket.

I grabbed all the pieces and ran to my father's closet. I pushed back the hanging clothes, then shoved the boxes aside, making a space so I could reach the wall.

I crouched there on my knees and slipped on the dismembered sleeve and then the rest of the coat. I pressed my hands against the wall and begged. I pleaded. I scratched the wall until my fingers were bloody. I importuned until my throat was raw.

Nothing.

I finally curled up in a ball and started banging my head against the wall.

I woke up the next day with a pillow under my head and a blanket covering me. My uncle sat next to me, his back against the wall and his knees bent. He must have heard me stir. He turned to look at me. His face was etched with grief, wearier than I'd ever seen it.

"Aiden?"

My uncle shook his head.

Inside my head I saw an underfed-looking man in a white robe. He comforted the small boy next to him. I couldn't see the face, but I could see the shoes. I blinked my eyes and saw my uncle looking down at me.

I turned toward the wall. It held the bloody marks from my supplications. Anger raged inside me. I knew then that there was no God. If there were, he would have listened to me. He would have saved my brother. At that moment, I turned my back on that wall, those pleas, and the one who would not answer them, and forgot all of it.

Until now.

Holly?" Milton said softly.

      I opened my eyes slowly and concentrated on the white ceiling, breathing and counting as I had learned from the Silent One. I repeated this about five times as the sharp edge of impatience increased around me. I was lying on the couch. My hair was soaked from the tears that spilled over.

    I closed my eyes, pressed my balled hands into the couch cushion, and then pushed myself up.

    "Did you know?" I said to the ceiling.

    "Sarah told me about it years ago, before we started our work together."

    Of course she did. It hadn't occurred to me. "You never said anything, though."

    "I knew you would tell me in your own time."

    I sat there with my eyes closed so tight, spots of light floated behind my lids. Someone had told me once that those spots were angels. I hadn't closed my eyes tight enough to usher in those ethereal specks since the day Aiden died. I listened to the clock tick and wondered if they were happy to find the door open again.

Milton's slacks scraped the chair fabric as he changed positions. *I guess it's time.*

The room inside my head filled my vision. I held my breath. I knew that he would be sitting on the left side of the Committee's couch, as he had been for the last three and a half months.

Still holding my breath, I shifted my gaze to the pink commode on my right. My blood turned to ice water in my veins and froze like a lake across my heart. Betty Jane sat there looking pressed and polished. Her sunflower pin mocked me with its little yellow bonnet.

I nodded my head. The person directly to the right of me tugged at the corner of my eye. I turned and the familiar crew cut came into focus. On his neck was the scar diving from the corner of his jaw into the band of his white T-shirt. A thousand tiny cracks erupted across the glacier that was my heart. I sighed and lifted the corners of my mouth slightly while nodding.

Sarge winked.

I reversed my gaze back toward Betty Jane and then down to the floor where the Silent One knelt on his prayer altar.

"Hello," I said. He bowed his head. A warmth radiated out from my heart, melting the last of the winter in my body. The Silent One bowed his head again.

I inhaled deeply as he had taught me, and for the first time, I felt a calming warmth drop over me. I exhaled and looked down at the pink Oriental rug. I inhaled deeply and looked at the Silent One once more. His face was very serious. His eyes remained fixed on me. I transferred my body weight to my left side, pressed my hands against the couch, and focused on the Committee's therapy room.

I saw a beat-up red Converse sneaker, and on the other foot, a blood-soaked white sock. The sound of screeching brakes and shattering glass rushed at my mind like the Furies from Greek mythology punishing me with their secret stings because I had escaped public justice for my crime. Then a thud that sounded like a piece of fruit splattering on the ground knocked the air from my lungs.

Most people can't help but look when they come across an accident. I couldn't help but run. And at that moment, sitting on Milton's couch, I wanted to do it again. I wanted to get up and run as fast as I could. Crash through the closed door, leaving an outline of my frame and nothing more. But I was anchored to the couch by an overwhelming need to, now, look.

The pain behind my eyes pushed out like the runoff from a particularly fierce storm held back by wooden planks. Then the dam broke. I lifted my head slowly as if it were being pulled from the ceiling by an invisible cord attached to my crown. Through my tears I confronted the face I couldn't look at all those years ago.

One side of his head was caved in and the skin looked like it had been run across by a cheese grater. It was a mixture of blood, pebbles, and shards of glass that caught the light like tiny stars. Aiden's bloody blond curls were caked and matted, making his hair look like a Gorgon helmet of living, venomous red snakes. One eye disappeared behind the mangled mess of his face, and the other dripped with blood.

Staring at him, I heard the echo of Sarah's screams mixed with the tearing sound of my mother's pants as they ripped across the asphalt. The wailing and tearing beat at me like a thousand horrible wings, indicting me as the perpetrator of the hideous crime of fratricide. I wanted Aiden to join their lament. I wanted him to point his finger at me and say, "This is *your* fault." I wanted him to strike out at me with a demand for justice.

Aiden smiled instead.

Aiden's smile was always one of his best features. His teeth were large and perfectly straight. At age five, he had what used to be called the "Pepsodent smile."

I leaned forward, wheezing as I bit my knuckles. Aiden's mouth was gaping and mostly empty. I remembered my mother telling me that after she saw Aiden's crushed head, she crawled through the blood collecting his teeth. She said she was ashamed that this was all she could do while her only son lay dying on the street.

"Right when I pushed you, the car hit me so hard I flew into the air," Aiden told me. "I landed on the hood. My head hit the windshield and shattered it. Then I bounced onto the street."

His words were not meant as an indictment, but each one of them etched into me, leaving scars like the marks I left on the wall at the back of my father's closet.

"And that is where I died," he said quietly.

"Aiden, please forgive me. Please forgive me," was my anguished plea. "Please forgive me." I closed my eyes again. Aiden's mashed face remained.

I remember Sarah telling me I had to forgive myself. But I couldn't. I needed Aiden to forgive me. But how could he?

"Who will forgive me now?" I said to the Committee. All eyes were fixed on me. Nobody said a word.

"Somebody, please forgive me," I cried.

Nobody said a word.

I opened my eyes. My body started shaking as I gulped ragged breaths of air.

Milton pulled his chair over so that he sat directly in front of me. He put his hands over mine and squeezed.

"I remember . . . I remember . . . them . . . trying to tell me . . . what happened." Milton squeezed my hands a little harder. I inhaled deeply and then exhaled, repeating this until the tremors in my body stopped. After a while I said, "When they did, I retreated and let the Silent One have control. He scared my parents with the praying and vacant stares. They finally gave up."

"Holly," said Milton, "I believe you have been in a state of protracted grief for the past twenty-seven years. The Committee has protected you from your grief and kept you mired in it at the same time."

"And the Boy, Little Bean, Aiden, he can't forgive me because he is a part of me?"

Milton nodded. I waited for him to say the next obvious thing. But he didn't. And I was relieved. I hated new-age crap, and Milton was a New York City psychoanalyst—the closest he would ever get to anything touchy-feely was sitting close and taking my hands, as he'd done at that moment.

Milton moved his chair back to its original position. He knew I was safe.

"How did the Committee come here for group therapy?" I said.

"Ah, yes," said Milton. Up went the finger church. But this time it didn't bother me. "When you didn't return my third call from abroad, I called Sarah."

"It's not that I don't trust her, but you guys seem to talk a lot more than I realized," I said.

"Holly, are you aware that before you started seeing me, Sarah wanted to be declared your legal guardian so she could get you"—Milton cleared his throat—"help?"

I sat there gaping. Just when I thought I had my footing, I found out my sister wanted to lock me up.

"She and I discussed it during our initial consultation about you," said Milton.

Betrayal and understanding braided together as I tried to assimilate this new piece of information.

"Ah, you were not aware. And because I anticipated a reaction like the one you are having, I never mentioned it. I suspected that Sarah didn't either, but I never asked her."

"Well, obviously something changed her mind," I said.

"Someone." Milton smiled. "Me." He pointed at his chest. "After meeting with you, I was convinced that you could be helped by rigorous psychoanalytic treatment."

Sarah's sometimes irrational vitriol toward Milton made a lot more sense now. She'd signed on the dotted line for this devil's bargain.

"So, what happened when you called Sarah?" I said.

"She assured me that you were depressed, angry, still without the Committee, but coping all the same. When I heard this, I had an idea."

Here we go. Another one of Milton's brainstorms.

"Since I'd already radically departed from standard treatment methods—"

"I'll say," I said.

"I decided to take a risk and try a new path into your psyche," continued Milton, ignoring the comment. "What did I have to lose?"

A couple of things popped into my mind.

"To pursue this new treatment path, I needed Sarah's help. I convinced her that this new course was the right one, and then we set up regular calls for the last couple of weeks I was in France."

"What did you talk about?" I said.

"Who Sarah thought the Committee members represented for you. As we now see, her guesses were right on target."

"Of course they were," I said.

"Sarah is the keeper of your family history, Holly," said Milton.

I always thought he'd hatched these harebrained recipes out of the sky. Turned out my sister provided the ingredients. I wanted to be angry, but how could I? It had worked.

"How did you know that Betty Jane would come to group therapy?" I said to Milton.

"Even though you were unaware of them, I suspected the Committee wasn't completely gone. I thought instead that Betty Jane, as ruler of the Committee, had forced them to hide with her. Do you recall the deal I made with Betty Jane? The one that enabled you to start working as a voice-over artist? She agreed to resolve conflicts in therapy if I requested it." I nodded my head. "I knew that despite her flaws, Betty Jane was a woman of her word."

Milton shrugged his shoulders and held out his hands, palms up. "I had a hunch that she'd come to group therapy, so I played it."

"But Ruffles didn't come back with her," I said. Then I felt as if all the air were being sucked out of my lungs. I closed my eyes. Ruffles's pillow lay empty over in the corner.

"Ruffles isn't here, Milton. She's not here."

I felt sick. *How did I miss her? I know seeing Aiden was traumatic, but how did I miss her?* Then I noticed Betty Jane's chalky face and I knew that Ruffles's absence wasn't one of her tricks.

"Interesting," said Milton.

"Interesting!" I screamed. "Ruffles *is* missing."

"Holly, yelling is not productive," said Milton. I wondered if strangling him would be. He leaned forward. "Remember the first session, when I made you state that you wanted to resolve the conflicts with the Committee through group?" That's right. He'd made me say the words. "The Committee has been with you the whole time. But because Betty Jane is the ruler, she had the power to decide if they were visible or not. Because she agreed to remain your equal, you had the power to order them back at any time. Inside or outside therapy," said Milton.

It was a new dawn every ten minutes with Milton today. This one didn't include sunshine. "So I could have asked Betty Jane to come back and bring the Committee?"

"It had to be an order, Holly, not a request. You had to exert your power. Remember when you ordered her to bring Ruffles back? She did it."

As I considered the past few months of my life, I wanted to throw something at him. "We waste so much time on examining things, why didn't we examine that moment? Why didn't you tell me I could order her to come back full-time? You had the means to give me back my Committee and you didn't do it."

"No," said Milton, "I did not do it."

"How could you do that to me? I was miserable." And now I was angry.

"Yes," said Milton quietly, "I know you were miserable, but no more so than when you had Betty Jane."

I turned toward the window. Outside it looked like a down pillow had broken over the city as featherlike snowflakes floated from the sky. Milton was sort of right and he was also wrong. But I wasn't going to give him the satisfaction of examining the complexities of his statement at the moment. I needed to find Ruffles.

My eyebrows met in the middle as I concentrated on all of this. I didn't care if I was etching the Grand Canyon between my eyes. "I don't think Betty Jane knows where Ruffles is," I said. "Does it work the same way? Can I order Ruffles back?"

"You can try, but I suspect not," said Milton.

"Ruffles, come back now!" I said. Nothing happened. After the fifth time, I couldn't stand the pained look on all the faces inside my head and sitting across from me.

"How could she abandon me like that? Just leave without saying good-bye?" I whispered.

"Holly, didn't you tell me once you hated it when someone said good-bye because it meant that you would never see them again?"

"So you think I'll see her again? She's hiding like she did when she felt bad about making Betty Jane go crazy and kidnap the Committee?"

"Ruffles is here, Holly," said Milton. "We'll find her in due time." I swear I heard hatching sounds and waited for another one of Milton's barmy plans to surface.

When he didn't elaborate, I said, "So, what happens now?" I didn't know what felt worse, seeing Aiden's mangled face or not feeling Ruffles's bulk in the corner of my head. I felt so dead and exhausted I wanted to sleep for ten years.

"That depends on you."

"The rest of the Committee . . . I can take them back, or leave them here in group therapy?"

"No," said Milton. "Now that the group therapy has exposed the underlying cause, the Committee can no longer stay here. What you do with them next is up to you."

"Is it? If I say I don't want them back, then they just disappear?" I knew this was what I should do. They were in the hallway between wherever they had been and their house that sat inside my head. I was almost free.

"If I let them come back, will Ruffles be with them?" I said.

"I think you know the answer to that, Holly," said Milton.

I felt as if I were in the crush box my vet used when he examined Cat Two. He'd place him in a Plexiglas rectangle and push against him with a panel until he was hemmed in on all sides, trapped like I was now.

The Committee pressed against me like the panel. Even if I

resisted, I'd be pushed to the wall, because saying good-bye brought about the result I feared most—I would never see them again. Saying good-bye meant letting go of Aiden. Like Cat Two, though, even faced with the obvious conclusion, I still searched for a different ending.

"You said the Committee was there to shield me. Protect me. Right?"

Milton nodded his head.

"But Betty Jane didn't let them. She kidnapped them. I was abandoned and alone."

"You were not alone. And you protected yourself with my help and the help of the Committee at our sessions until you were ready to know the truth. When you were ready, you allowed the truth to come forward." I opened my mouth to protest. Milton held up his hand to stop me. "Holly, each member was a part of a complex system. Each had a part to play and they played it. It is time now to let the remaining ones go."

We balanced there on the teeter-totter of silence. It wasn't like I didn't know he was going to say that, but when it finally registered, I felt as if Milton had just let go of a slingshot band and I was the item flung into an airless abyss. A muscle spasm rippled from inside my stomach through my neck like a sonic boom and I coughed out the word, "No."

"*No!*" I said it this time with the fierceness of a mother bear protecting her cubs. "I have to find Ruffles. She might still come back. And I don't want to let go of, well, you know . . ." I didn't want to let go of Sarge, the Silent One, and Aiden. Betty Jane could move along, as far as I was concerned.

"Very well," said Milton. Disappointment skittered across his face.

Then, as if someone had flipped a switch, the expanse of the Committee's house pressed hard at my skull once more. My head didn't move, and even though I felt the weight of having the Committee back in their house, the heaviness that accompanied Ruffles was missing. An aftershock of defeat washed over me and a new torrent of tears started.

"What are you crying for?" snapped Betty Jane. "We have been looking at that bloody mess for years."

Then she stood, arms akimbo, and walked to the middle of the Committee's living room. "Well," she said with the right touch of Southern drama, "I must say, it is good to be back."

She pointed a red fingernail over at the console table and remarked, "The place is dusty and the plants are dead. And someone remove that pillow." She curled her mouth in disdain.

"Shut up," I said. I quickly put my hand to my mouth as if to push back what had just come out, as shock registered on Betty Jane's face. "I want it to stay," I said half apologetically, half defiantly. She rolled her eyes.

"Everyone back where they belong, I presume?" said Milton.

"No, not everyone," I said sadly.

Milton nodded.

"One last question," I said. "The Committee still doesn't know what has been going on in my life outside of these four walls, right?"

"I suspect that they know only what you have talked about in group," Milton said, smiling.

"Well, that's at least an early birthday present."

"Tomorrow, isn't it?" said Milton. I nodded. "Happy birthday."

Yeah, a dead brother, no Ruffles, and the bitch is back. Happy birthday indeed.

When I got home, I saw I had a message on my machine. I sighed. I hung up my coat, fished my pack of Marlboros out of my bag, and went to my bedroom.

Betty Jane sniffed loudly inside my head.

I opened the box. I had one cigarette left.

"This is my last cigarette. I would like to enjoy it in peace. If you talk to me while I'm doing that, I will go out and buy another pack and keep smoking. Understand?"

I could see this was a real dilemma for her. But I knew that in the end she would capitulate, and she did.

I shut the bedroom door so I wouldn't have to hassle with prying Cat One away from the window. I kicked off my shoes, pushed up the glass frame, and then sat down on the sill with my feet on my bed. I shook my last cigarette from the box, brought it to my lips, flicked the lighter, and inhaled.

Who was responsible for Aiden's death? Sarah claimed the right to own the responsibility. I claimed the responsibility and added the guilt Sarah had let go of a long time ago. My mother overruled both of us and claimed the burden for herself. Uncle Dan said maybe nobody was responsible. It was just one of those events set into motion when nobody considered the possible consequences of their actions. In the end, we had to have faith that the world works in ways that we don't understand. That was easy for him to say. My faith bounced off the hood of a car and then shattered on the asphalt twenty-seven years ago.

My mother said that when she saw how badly Aiden's head was injured, she prayed that he would die. When I realized that it was Aiden lying mangled on the street, I prayed that he stay with me. My mother's request was granted. I guess God answers the easy prayers.

My fingertips burned. I was at the filter. I stubbed out what was left of the cigarette and closed the window. May as well see who had called.

I pressed the play button on the answering machine.

"Hi, Holly, it's Rhonda." Mike Davey's assistant. "I wanted to let you know I heard on the QT that last week, when they were coming up with show ideas, your name was mentioned. A lot. Ratings are down. The two people who replaced you aren't cutting it. I think they're going to ask for you back. Hope this is good news for you?"

"Well," said Betty Jane inside my head. She sat at her vanity in a silk robe with a powder puff in her hand.

"Well, what?" I snapped. "You're ready to go back to work?"

"Of course!" She smoothed her hair inside my head.

"Good, because we start first thing Monday," I said.

Betty Jane's face registered confusion.

{ 26 }

The alarm clock sounded. I rolled over and slapped it hard without even opening my eyes. Already half risen from my bed, I pushed myself all the way up and sat there with my head hanging forward and my legs dangling over the side. My eyes remained closed to the outside world. The inside world was as clear as glass. The Committee waited, lined up on the couch, dressed and ready to go.

"Uh," I said, rubbing the sleep from my eyes. "We don't have to leave for an hour."

Sarge jerked a thumb at Betty Jane. Of course. She expected me to sleep beyond the last possible minute and then be running late. I stood up and shuffled off to the shower.

An hour later, I tugged my hat over my ears and said, "Let's go." Sarge and Aiden simultaneously pulled their red plaid duck-hunting hats on their heads and tied the leather strings under their chins. The color of the hats mirrored Aiden's sneakers and his bloody face. I cringed when I thought about the fake-fur earflaps against his injured skin. Aiden smiled inside my head. I knew it was meant to comfort me, but the holes, where his teeth had been, filled me with unspeakable sorrow.

"Focus, Holly," I whispered. The Silent One appeared with his blanket draped across his shoulders, and Betty Jane donned her cashmere coat.

I opened the front door to my building.

"Where's the car?" said Betty Jane inside my head.

"No car," I said.

"We are calling a taxi then?" Betty Jane emphasized *are* like it was a command.

"No," I said in a voice I hoped conveyed steely nonchalance. "We are taking the subway." I accentuated *are* in the same way she did.

She narrowed her eyes and replaced shock with chagrin. "*The subway!*" Betty Jane shouted inside my head as she angrily unbuttoned her coat, yanked it off her shoulders, and threw it on the Committee's couch.

I put my hands over my ears as a reflex, even though it wouldn't abrogate the screaming in between them. *Breathe. Focus. Relax the shoulders. I'm better than the Silent One now. With assistance in the form of the two nicotine patches I applied this morning, that is.*

"I refuse," said Betty Jane inside my head.

"Good for you." I walked down First Avenue.

"You say that now, but you'll be singing a different tune when we arrive and you discover how much you need me," said Betty Jane inside my head. "You are nothing without me," she added with a sharp point in the air.

I continued toward the Second Avenue subway stop. The Committee's house hovered over my head like a cowl.

"I don't need you," I said.

"We'll see about that!" Betty Jane stormed out of the Committee's living room, slamming the door. The pictures on the wall rattled and I felt the corners of the frames poking at the inside of my head. Finally some peace. I straightened my shoulders and quickened my pace.

On the subway, I sat across from a mother and her toddler. The child stood on the orange plastic seat with one hand on his mother's shoulder and the other one on the silver hand bar that ran floor to ceiling. A group of teenage boys opened the door and came through talking loudly. The mother turned her head toward them. The child leaned away from his mother, stuck out his tongue, and licked the silver bar like it was a giant ice-cream cone. Sickened, I moved forward in my seat. At the same time, the mother turned around and cried out in horror as she yanked her child back against her body.

The child, now in his mother's grip, grinned impishly at me as the train drove into the Fourteenth Street station. The doors opened. The mother jumped up, scooped the laughing child off the seat, and made a quick exit out the door. As the train pulled away, I watched her leap the stairs two at a time. The child's legs moved back and forth as if he were swimming sideways.

"On her way to the nearest emergency room for sure," I muttered to myself.

I switched at Forty-second Street and hopped the seven to Times Square. I disembarked there and read the ticker as I made my way over to Fiftieth Street.

The waiting area was shabbier than Al's last studio. When he'd told me he'd downsized the office to save money, I had expected something more compact, not something less luxurious. I didn't think you could do less than the bare-bones decor he used to have. Clearly I was wrong.

I sat in a folding chair while Al's assistant searched for him. I wondered what was taking so long, because the office size definitely didn't require a search party. I glanced at the script to pass the time. *I can do this standing on my head.*

"I can't believe they got a star to do this for them," said the guy manning the counter.

"A dim star. Or shall we say a star that's gone out." I laughed while digging in my bag for my highlighters.

"Oh, right," he said. "What happened anyway?"

It amazed me how people felt entitled to know my business. Besides, anything I told him would land on Page Six the next slow gossip day. I forced my mouth into a friendly smile and said lightly, "I am sure you read about it."

He looked disappointed. "So, you're doing this now?"

"It's a favor for a friend," I said.

Al's assistant returned.

"Did you know that she's the voice of Violet and Harriet from *The Neighborhood*?" he said to her.

"I used to be the voice behind them," I said, reading the script. "They have a couple of other women doing them now." I ran the neon green felt tip across a sentence. Out of the corner of my eye I saw Al's assistant mouthing, *You weren't supposed to say anything.* I smirked. Good old Al. After I had booked the gig Mike had recommended I take, he'd probably covered every inch of the scandal with anyone who'd listen and then said, "But keep it to yourself." I certainly heard plenty of gossip when I was a regular in his studio. Oh, well.

"The show sucks without you," said Al's assistant.

"I've heard. Shall we get started then?" I was tired of this exchange.

The booth in the new place reminded me of a standard office cubicle. It was much smaller and far less hospitable than the last one, and a broom closet compared to the booth we used to record *The Neighborhood*. I'd recently read that the inventor of the cubicle lamented his unwitting contribution to what he called "monolithic insanity." This was a fact only Ruffles would appreciate. The thought brought with it the weight of her absence.

I shook my head, hoping the feeling of sadness would fall off me as I stepped into the booth. When I had booked this gig, the Committee was still absent, at least to me. I planned to rely on my own voice and training as I did the recording. Even though I could probably make a deal with Betty Jane, I decided to stick to my plan and go it alone.

First, I got into character by visualizing myself as a teacher in my late forties. Knowledgeable, honest, someone you trust to give you the right information. Aiden put on a pair of glasses.

"Good idea," I said. "Thanks." Aiden nodded. I was relieved he didn't smile.

I opened the door, stuck my head out. Al's assistant sat next to him at the console. She wore a pair of glasses that would do nicely. "May I borrow your glasses?" I asked.

"Uh . . . sure." She removed her glasses and handed them to me.

"Thanks." I closed the door to the booth.

I put on the glasses, imagined the pacing and inflections a beloved teacher would have. Then I put on the earphones and said, "Ready," into the mic. Betty Jane peeked around the corner from the hallway in the Committee's house. I ignored her and started speaking.

The whole thing took about three hours to do. We paused a few times for bathroom breaks. I used the studio toilet paper. I had to admit, there was no comparison to Charmin. It scraped like sandpaper, but I felt like the impish child on the subway when I wiped. The rest of the day, the memory of the toilet paper periodically visited, and I welcomed it with a smile.

After I read the last line of the script, I removed the headphones and opened the door. I handed the glasses back to Al's assistant and said, "Thanks." Then I said to Al, "Do you think we need a lot of retakes?"

He looked perplexed. "I don't think we need any retakes."

"Oh. Wow. Well. Great." I tried to mask my disappointment.

Working again felt like going back to exercise after taking a long break from it. The sore muscles the next day always felt so good. I knew I was rusty, and I knew my throat would be sore tomorrow, but I felt right for the first time in months, even though I had only recorded answers for an automated phone system.

I removed my coat and bag from the closet and said, "Okay, then, call me if it turns out we need to do any pickups." I put my hand on the front doorknob.

"Holly," called Al from behind me. I turned. The open door rested against my shoulder. "If you ever need to do a demo tape, give me a call and I'll take care of you."

I smiled. "Thanks. I'm not sure how much longer I'm going to be doing this work, though."

"What do you mean?" he said with surprise. "You were great in there. A real professional. Completely different from when you were here before."

Ouch. How bad was I before?

"Well, thanks." I stepped through the door.

"I can't believe those lucky bastards have your voice on their phone system. They should use it for promotion or something."

I smiled and waved at him. As I pulled the door shut, I called out, "It was nice to see you again," and I meant it.

The company phoned me a day later and said they were really pleased with the work. The woman asked me if I was interested in doing a training video for them. When I agreed to do it, Betty Jane collapsed on the couch with an ice pack on her head.

{ 27 }

*C*yrano de Bergerac, opening night. Preteen theater fresh on the heels of the phone system recording drove Betty Jane straight to Vicodin and cocktails. Inside my head, she was passed out on the couch snoring, and I wanted to leave. Betty Jane was the only one who'd spoken to me since the Committee had returned two weeks ago. But I knew the rest of them could hear me, so I asked Sarge to keep Betty Jane away from her "medication" if she came out of her drug-and-alcohol-induced coma. He nodded in assent. I felt relieved and left for the theater.

About twenty minutes before the curtain went up, Pam and I peeked out at the audience. A packed house. Backstage, adrenaline ran high. Five minutes before curtain, I dispensed to my charges pep talks, last-minute advice, reminders, and then I finally said, "Oh, don't listen to me; you'll be fantastic. I know it."

"Thanks, Holly. You've been fantastic too."

My cheeks burned. "Okay." I coughed. "Pam wants us all over here now."

We gathered in the room off to the left of the stage.

"Everyone circle around and grab hands," said Pam, clapping. I took the hands of the two kids I had worked with the most. "Here we go!" shouted Pam as she raised her arms and the arms of the kids on either side of her up toward the ceiling.

Everyone, including me, echoed back, "Here we go!" as we threw our arms up into the air without letting go of one another.

Then Pam cried, "Group hug. Group hug!"

Everyone moved forward until we were a mass of arms and legs.

"Careful with the costumes," I fussed. "Mind your makeup."

"What would we do without Holly!" said Pam, putting her arm around my waist.

"And break a leg!" I said, smiling.

We made it through the show with only a few minor mishaps, the worst being Cyrano's nose falling off during a soliloquy. We corrected the problems on the next night. On the third and final night, I felt a sense of sad finality when the curtain came down, and I shed a couple of tears when the kids went out for their final bow.

We were all backstage, where we had set up for our cast party. Excitement filled the air. I met parents, siblings, grandparents, and friends. All the faces were a blur.

I was hovering at the snack table when Neil Rhode approached with a man in tow. "Holly, this is my dad," said Neil.

"Very nice to meet you in person," I said, "and your son was a pleasure to work with."

"He didn't talk your ears off?" said Mr. Rhode. Then he affectionately ruffled his son's hair and said, "He certainly doesn't shut up at home."

"Dad," groaned Neil.

"And you have been quite an influence on him." He winked at me. I wanted to say Jesus hadn't knocked down my door yet, but I remained silent and respectful of their beliefs. "All he talks about now is becoming a voice-over artist. He watches your show all the time, including reruns when he can find them."

Hearing how much people liked the show left a bittersweet aftertaste in me.

Another parent who'd joined our group said, "Are you an actress?"

"No, I was a voice-over artist," I said.

"Was?" Neil made a face at me. He turned to the parent who asked and said, "She *is* a voice-over artist. This is Holly Miller. Voice of Violet and Harriet on *The Neighborhood*. She won two Emmys." That ought to do the trick. The replay of my last Emmy appearance was no doubt running through their minds now.

"Oh, yeah," said both parents, nodding in unison. *Bingo.*

"I love that show. I hate to say it," but," said Mr. Rhode. "It's not as good as it used to be. But I guess that happens with all shows?" Maybe they hadn't seen the replay? Or maybe they had and didn't care. The latter thought felt odd, as if I had tried on clothes that belonged to someone I didn't know but wanted to.

"It's not as good 'cause Holly's not doing the voices anymore," said Neil. This statement finished washing away the earlier sourness. Until I saw all three making faces at one another to see if anyone had the nerve to ask me what had happened. It was going to be that or the inevitable request. I took what felt like an endless inhale.

"You must get asked this all the time" said Mr. Rhode hesitantly.

Here we go.

"But could you do the voices for us?"

My preference would have been to explain that I had been

fired for my Emmy award performance. I sighed. My hand strayed to the bowl on the snack table.

"She also likes Ruffles," said the kid.

"I couldn't tell by looking at you," said Mr. Rhode.

"Thanks." I brushed the salt off my hands.

They waited expectantly.

I closed my eyes. Sarge, Aiden, and the Silent One sat alert on the couch. Betty Jane was, thankfully, absent. Maybe she'd gone to bed. Aiden motioned for me to try it. Sarge gave me a thumbs-up. The Silent One bowed his head. I opened my eyes and thought about why Ruffles had disappeared after I had remembered Aiden's death. My mind shifted to the mirror Sarah had given me for Christmas. Then my hands dropped and gripped my thighs. I could almost reach halfway around. Normal, same size as always. But I knew.

I smiled and felt a rush known to all actors. That heady feeling you get right before you go onstage for the biggest night of your life and you're exhilarated instead of afraid, because you've spent a lifetime preparing. You know you're going to bring the house down.

I picked up a large Ruffles. Bit into it. Opened my mouth and said, "The Spain in plain stays mainly in the rain." My eyes filled with tears. My audience didn't notice.

Neil yelled out, "Hey, everyone, Holly just did Harriet for us."

The whole backstage quieted down. Blood rushed hot and cold through my veins.

"Do it again," cried one of the other kids.

I closed my eyes once more, took a deep breath, opened my eyes, and then dropped into a monologue that lasted long enough for me to search every nook and cranny of Ruffles's range. I hit the high notes, the low notes, and the in-between notes. I explored newfound territories. It was like coming home to your favorite slippers after walking barefoot in the wilderness for months. When I was finished, I heard a roar of dizzying applause. And I heard the kids muttering, "I told you she could do it."

"Holly, do Violet," someone yelled out.

Betty Jane appeared in the Committee's living room inside my head. Her hair was wild and her eyes blazed. *Oh, God.* Betty Jane was a nasty drunk. I expected Sarge to intervene, but she was too fast, and before he could react, she was on the couch with her hands wrapped around Aiden's throat.

My jaw dropped. "Oh, my God," I whispered.

"Holly?" I felt a hand on my shoulder.

Sarge grabbed Betty Jane by the upper arms and pulled hard. Her back bent into a curve but she wouldn't let go. My hands clutched my own throat.

"Oh, my God," I said.

Sarge pulled harder. Betty Jane released Aiden's throat and Sarge shoved her to the floor, where she struggled.

"Are you okay?" asked Mr. Rhode.

"Oh," I said distractedly. Then, focusing back on the people in the room before me, I said, "Yes, I'm fine. Just no Violet tonight."

The kids groaned in unison.

"Sorry. Next time. I promise." I bit absently into the Ruffles I was holding. Inside my head, the Silent One cleaned Aiden's neck with an alcohol-soaked cotton ball. Betty Jane had disappeared.

At the end of the night, as Pam and I were cleaning up, she turned to me and said, "Holly, what happened with your job?"

I waved my hand in front my face as if trying to shoo away the question. Pam maintained eye contact, waiting for my response.

"You want the truth, I suppose?"

But the truth was a paradox. It was subjective. It was private.

And at that moment, I knew that my private truth didn't need to be on display for the world. My mother was right that some things were better left unsaid. I owed Pam something that resembled the truth, though.

"I lost myself, and now I am neither the whole nor the parts." I paused. Then I held out my hands palms up to indicate that this was all I had to offer.

Pam thought about this for a moment and then she said, "That will be a good thing for you to explain to the kids next year. You need to work on it, of course, but when you get it down, I have no doubt that it will be inspiring and motivating for them."

I looked at her with my eyes narrowed playfully and my mouth curled on one side. "Pam," I said, shaking my head, "I am not planning—"

"Of course you are."

I acquiesced. "Of course I am."

Riding home on the subway, I held my bag close to my body. I told myself this was to make sure my bag did not get stolen. But the subway car was half-full and empty of dangerous-looking characters. The truth was, I did this hoping to fill the hollowness in my gut, because every gain always includes an equal measure of loss.

{ 28 }

It's been three weeks since the Christmas disaster—"

"Ouch!" I poked my eye with the mascara brush in my hand. After the play, Betty Jane had started to time her appearances to startle me.

"I thought you would have dumped that lout by now," said Betty Jane.

"Thanks." I wiped the black glob off the side of my nose. I knew she knew I was thinking I'd rather watch a movie than meet Peter for dinner.

"I never liked him anyway," Betty Jane said inside my head.

What a laugh. Betty Jane's turnabouts rivaled the best politicians'. She liked Peter well enough when he suited her purposes. And she disliked him after I started doing *The Neighborhood* but I wouldn't trade up for someone better.

It was ironic that several months ago I would have given anything for a comment from Betty Jane. Now her remarks only annoyed me. Even though it had been a few weeks since they had returned, the Committee's presence felt odd. I had become so used to having my own mind that it was jolting to hear comments in my head again. Jolting and unwelcome.

"Well, it is none of your business anyway. Can't you go shopping or something?" I replaced the mascara brush in the tube and twisted it closed.

"None of my business? Well!" Betty Jane said indignantly inside my head.

"You had better go away tonight. Or at the very least just be quiet!" I said.

Betty Jane left the Committee's living room in a huff. I was late and couldn't worry about what she might get herself up to later.

I met Peter at Orologio on Tenth and Avenue A. I loved the walls of clocks, and the Italian food was decent for the price. Peter offered to pick me up, but I said I had errands and would just meet him there. He was waiting out front.

"Hi." I kissed his cheek. "Why are you waiting outside?"

"I just got here."

"Oh." I nodded awkwardly. "Shall we go in?"

Before we were even seated, Peter started gossiping about something at the university. All I heard was noise like Charlie Brown and his friends heard when adults talked to them. I nodded and said *wow* a couple of times, and this was enough of a response for Peter.

The waiter took our orders; then Peter said, "You're so quiet tonight. Is there something you're going to cream me for later?"

I laughed. "Nope. Nothing. Honestly."

"After what happened at your mother's, how can I trust you anymore when you say 'honestly'?"

"I think we're even on that front."

The waiter arrived at our table with the bottle of wine. He took in the scene and proceeded to uncork it. He stood there holding the open bottle. I pointed at Peter's glass. "Just pour it," said Peter.

The void between us had grown into a chasm. I didn't know how to cross it anymore. I didn't know that I wanted to. But I didn't realize Peter actually did want to cross it until he said, "I don't know how to fix this, Holly, but can we at least try?"

I sipped my wine. How could we try? As much as I hated to admit it, my mother was right. Just like my parents', our relationship was doomed the day we met because of baggage and projection. With Milton's help, I had discovered why I chose Peter. He liked having a minimum-maintenance relationship that rarely required the FTD-like gestures that were standard for other couples. I figured Peter wouldn't leave a relationship that provided him with regular sex, the freedom to do whatever he wanted without being questioned, and, of course, celebrity parties. The surprise came when he still wanted the relationship after my celebrity, and the fanfare, went by the wayside. Just goes to show that one shouldn't knock the power of mystery. Turned out the quest to find the real me kept Peter a lot more interested than he was when he actually met the real me. He certainly didn't recognize her when she appeared. But I couldn't blame him; I was there too.

"There are too many lies between us, Peter."

We sat silently drinking our wine. The food finally arrived.

Peter savagely forked ravioli and said, "I never lied to you, Holly."

"Oh, no?" I left my food untouched.

"I was protecting you."

I let out a snort. "Thanks for that." Peter continued to eat.

"Dishonesty protects no one," I said. The Silent One bowed inside my head.

"Tell that to yourself." Peter pointed his knife at me. "You never told me you had a brother."

My mouth hardened and my eyes deepened in anger. "I have lied by omission, Peter. But the things I omitted were none of your business."

"You admit that you've lied then?"

"Yes, I've lied. Whereas the things you kept from me were merely because you were protecting yourself from my reaction."

"Do you know how hard it is to be with you, Holly?" said Peter. "You always held me at a distance, and I tried every way to get close to you."

"That blonde at the library was your way of getting close to me?" The people at the tables on either side of us stopped talking.

"She was a friend," said Peter.

I laughed. "A friend? How stupid do you think I am?" Peter glared at me. "I almost got hit by a car that day."

"But you didn't," said Peter.

"But I almost did." At that moment I knew he had seen me. Funny thing was, it didn't matter.

"Do you know how horrible it was to have you leave me there? If you were trying to get close, you have a funny way of showing it." Well, *almost* didn't matter.

"I admit, I made mistakes," said Peter.

"I'll drink to that." I raised my glass.

"Holly, you're making a scene."

"Who cares?"

"Who are you? I don't even know you anymore."

"And you never did. But then, I don't know you either," I said.

"So what do you want to know?" said Peter. "I'm not going to tell you my life is none of your business."

"Nothing," I said. And I realized that I didn't want to know anything. I no longer cared. I had tortured myself long enough over what I didn't know about Peter. I felt like I had dropped a burden I had been carrying for a long time. Maybe this meant I would get a chance at happiness, like my father and Linda, who were happily married, and like my mother, who was a proud single woman.

"Come on, Holly." Now he was trying to cajole me.

For a moment, I contemplated being honest with him. But then I realized that we had no foundation for honesty and it was too late to build one now. Dropping the disguise would just extend the game I'd grown tired of playing. "I think I'm done, Peter."

"You haven't even touched your food."

Our relationship had started with me worrying that he would discover the real me and leave. Why should it end on the same note?

"No, I mean with you. I'm done," I said quietly. I got up and removed my coat and bag from the back of the chair. I stood there for a second and then said, "I wish you all the best."

"Holly—"

"No," I said with finality. "I honestly do wish you all the best. But we're done."

"Who's going to pay for this?"

"You are." I smiled. "Take care of yourself, Peter." I turned and walked out of the restaurant to the cheering from the couch in my head.

My cell phone rang as I put the key in the front door.

"May as well get it over with," said Betty Jane inside my head.

"He's probably calling for your credit card number and breakup sex. It was a nice little performance, but I know you. You'll back down like you always do." She sharpened her nails with an emery board.

I pulled my phone out of my bag. She had not lost her impeccable sense of timing. I pressed the answer button and said, "Hello."

{ 29 }

It was nine in the morning. I stood on First Avenue, wrapped my scarf a little tighter around my neck, and pulled down my hat. The bitter cold ate through my winter coat. Even though the weather forecast called for blue skies, the windchill made thirty degrees feel a lot more like twenty. My breath formed like a ghost in front of me while I walked down the street replaying last night's phone call in my head.

I had recognized the number, but hearing her say my name had still startled me.

"Listen, doll," said Brenda Barry, my former agent, in response to my surprised hello. Then she continued without pausing. "I got a call from the studio. They want you there tomorrow morning, at ten sharp, to run through story concepts."

Brenda hadn't spoken to me since I demanded she stop sending me on those demeaning auditions. She had lectured me and then unapologetically told me that she couldn't afford to make an enemy of Walter Torrent. I knew that meant that he'd told her to humiliate me. And if I wasn't going to suck it up and take it until Walter recovered, she and I were through.

"Wha—"

"Holly," said Brenda, "I don't want to hear any reason why you can't make it."

"Tell her to send our car," Betty Jane exclaimed inside my head. "We must arrive in style." Her palms met under her chin and she covered her mouth coquettishly with the knuckles of her hands.

"How?" I let the word dangle there as I tried to find the rest of the question. I'd heard that Walter said he didn't care if God himself wanted me back, I would never do voice-overs for *The Neighborhood* again. *Who trumped God?*

"Never mind how. You be there tomorrow. I'll call a car service."

"No, thanks." I was still dazed. "I can get myself there."

"You!" sputtered Betty Jane inside my head. "How dare you rob me of my entrance." This unbridled anger was becoming commonplace for her.

"Gotta run. Good luck." Brenda hung up.

In a cold, flat voice, Betty Jane said, "You can rot in hell, Holly Miller. My voice will never come out of your mouth again."

"Is that a promise?" I retorted. Even though the haughty words sounded good, the tiny flame of hope flickered and faded. Betty Jane's was the voice Walter loved. If she didn't speak, the session would be a déjà vu of my last day on set.

When I woke up the next morning, I asked myself, *Why go?* And the answer was because even though my career had been taken down by a wrecking ball named Betty Jane, I was still a professional. They had booked me, so I'd show up. On time. I checked my watch. Plenty of cushion to get down to Chelsea Piers. *Ready?*

Inside my head, Betty Jane opened an eye and then quickly shut it, but she didn't budge from her bed. Sarge and Aiden were dressed as usual in their matching navy peacoats, and the Silent One was wrapped and up for walking meditation.

When we reached the street, I felt a rush of longing for the old days with Ruffles narrating. Today's course was perfect. With her guidance, I could have done a gold medal run to the subway station. Without her, I did only a silver, but I made it to the station without incident.

When the F train pulled in, the Committee's living room switched to a subway train inside my head. Betty Jane continued her pretend slumber, so her canopy bed was in the middle of the Committee's subway car—pink satin right in between the poles. I noted with satisfaction that the garbage strewn in my car was mirrored in theirs. It brushed right up against Betty Jane's white dust ruffle. When we boarded the M23, the scene in my head switched to a bus. Betty Jane's bed dipped in the middle to fit in the aisle. The canopy pressed upward like a steeple and crushed against the ceiling. I ruminated on the strange world I lived in as the bus ferried us down to the Chelsea Piers.

The same guard who used to cover for me when I would sneak out to smoke greeted me with a wave of his hand. "Will we be seein' you around here again?" he asked.

"Hopefully," I said brightly.

"Good luck then."

"Thanks." I smiled and waved as I continued on.

In the lobby the receptionist said, "Hello," and handed me the story line. I scanned it. Betty Jane's eyes sprang open. I felt a tap on my shoulder. I looked up and saw Mike.

"Hey," I said shyly.

"Hey," he said. His hand was still resting on my shoulder. "How are you feeling?"

I held his gaze for a moment, and then looked down and said, "Honestly, I'm a little scared. I can't do Violet today." Inside my head, Betty Jane threw back the covers and swung her legs over the side of the bed. Then she stood up and stalked out of the room with the bed disappearing in her wake.

"Can you do Harriet?" said Mike.

"If they want her," I answered in Ruffles's voice. From the lines they'd given me, it looked like they were considering expanding Harriet into a larger part. I was afraid to ask him, though.

"That one sounds perfect." Mike squeezed my shoulder and then took his hand away. The heat from it lingered for a few more seconds and I wondered if it was bad to date your boss. "I am not going to lie to you, Holly. If ratings weren't dipping, and fans weren't writing in, you wouldn't be here."

"I understand," I said, biting the inside of my mouth.

"I'll push the Harriet story line first. Just steer clear of Walt's World until things get back on track."

My stomach plummeted to my feet.

"To torment like always," said Mike.

I laughed and relaxed.

"Good luck, and see you in there." He gave me a little tap with his fist on my upper arm. Aiden used to do that when I had to go confess some misdeed to my mother. I felt my shoulders relax.

"Thanks," I said with a small smile.

About ten minutes later the receptionist said, "Holly, they're ready for you now."

I entered the room. The same one I had done my first reading in. That day seemed so long ago, and that girl was gone. I looked around to see who was there, greeted the casting director, the director, and Walter. Mike walked in. I said hello to him and then stood there waiting for what was next.

Mike looked at the script and said, "Why don't we start with Harriet?"

Walter nodded his head and grunted, "Fine."

He's not bitter. Then the words *diva, entitled,* and *I made you* rang fresh in my head. I inhaled deeply and launched into the lines they had given me earlier. I moved around the room, punctuating my monologue with hand movements where appropriate. Walter sat there nodding. Once or twice he asked me to change the pace or tweak a tone.

"Bravo," said Mike.

"I've been working on this voice in my spare time," I said. "I've expanded the range quite a bit."

"Let's hear it," said Mike.

I did the same monologue I had done for the parents and kids at the play the week before. When I closed in on the finish, Walter was leaning all the way forward on his chair. I put my palms on the table and slid forward, saying my last lines almost inches from his face.

Walter clapped and said, "Fantastic!" Then to Mike he said, "This fits right in with the idea to push out this character a bit more."

Funny, Walter had always preferred the Violet character. *I have him. Cue the band.*

"Okay, let's switch now to Violet."

My feat became a false note. Mike shook his head slightly.

Betty Jane appeared in the Committee's living room and said sweetly, "I'll do the voice." I adjusted my breathing to match Betty Jane's breathy Southern drawl. "Oh, no, sugar," Betty Jane gushed, "you need to let me have control. It's the only way."

I had been doing Ruffles's voice without shifting, so I ignored her and read the first line.

My knees drooped. All blood rushed from my head. I heard slacks slide across leather as Walter and Mike shifted in their chairs. *I can't go through this again.*

"Sugar, we can be on top once more," Betty Jane said sweetly. "But . . ." she said sharply. *Here we go.* Whoever said Southern belles are sweet never encountered this sour pie. "I have some requirements." Betty Jane pulled her mirror out of the drawer and started to inspect her pores.

I watched Walter as I listened to her. His impatient body language screamed, *I told you so.*

"All I am asking for is our original agreement with some teensy-weensy adjustments. If you just say yes, we can work out the finer points later. Without Milton," she added hastily.

Everyone waited. All eyes were on me. I remembered the scene last July, when Betty Jane refused and I stood there stupidly, just like I stood there now. The only difference was that then I had the protective glass of the booth between me and them.

I opened my mouth. Closed it. Picked up my glass and sipped some water. Betty Jane also sipped something.

"Holly, honey, it's just li'l ol' me. I'm on your side. I just want us to be back where we belong again." Betty Jane smiled and fluttered her eyelashes.

I closed my eyes again. Opened them. Looked at the lines. "I—"

"Walter, let's table this," said Mike. "We have a lunch meeting in Tribeca and about ten minutes to get there." I swear I saw Mike wink at me. I said a silent thanks.

Walter checked his watch. I held my breath. Betty Jane fluffed her hair. Being late was Walter Torment's middle name. My knees shook. I put out my hand and tried to steady myself on the table. It slipped on the sheets of paper. They skidded off the side and floated to the floor.

Betty Jane said, "Darlin', all you have to do is nod your head. Then everything will go back to the way it was."

I squatted down and collected the scattered script. As I picked up the pieces of paper, I thought about how much I loved my job. The work was creative. It turned my eccentricities into something that people actually liked. I missed the fan mail. The calls from my agent saying so-and-so company said they wanted Violet from *The Neighborhood* to do the voice-over for their commercial. It was tedious work for sure, and the scheduling made everything hectic. But I missed every single minute of it. Then I thought about my two Emmys and wanted another one. I wanted ten more. I wanted people cheering for me when I rebounded from scandal and adversity. The award show still rankled, but I could change it all right now by ceding control to Betty Jane.

I straightened the script. Walter's Prada shoes reminded me that the enmity between us was mutual. But Walter was not wrong when he'd said he had made me. Of all the diners in all the world, he had had to walk into mine. This made me smile.

"Okay, Holly," said Walter from the other side of the tabletop. I almost knocked my head on the table when I stood up.

"Just say you agree and I will put that pathetic performance you just did to shame," Betty Jane said with a snap of her fingers. Brightly colored lights appeared and began flashing around her. Sarge, Aiden, and the Silent One shook their heads. Betty Jane's lights glowed more brightly, making their bodies appear as silhouettes.

Yes, I missed this work. I hadn't known how much until I'd

walked back in here and breathed life into their new story line. I wanted to come back.

"Holly!" barked Walter. I froze. "We'll get on the horn with Brenda and work things out. I am in L.A. until next week. Production starts in March, and, given your history, I'm going to monitor things closely for the next few months just to make sure we're good. When I get back, I want to hear what you've come up with for Violet."

I exhaled quietly. Betty Jane snapped her fingers and the lights disappeared. I had a brief glimpse of mottled anger on her face before the mask convened it. She sat down indifferently and picked up her nail file.

"Thanks so much, Walter, for giving us this chance again."

Aiden buried his head in his hands. Sarge looked angrier than I had ever seen him. The Silent One sat stone faced.

I decided to walk home from Chelsea Piers, and for once my chosen mode of transportation suited Betty Jane. As soon as we reached Twenty-third Street, she transformed the Committee's living room inside my head into a mirror avenue, but with roped-off sidewalks, cheering crowds, and no traffic. Then a garishly decorated parade float appeared under her feet and began to roll down the avenue. Betty Jane's attire transformed into a blue satin gown. The jeweled sunflower she wore at the Emmys was pinned to the fur wrap covering her shoulders and it matched the jeweled tiara she wore on her head. She cradled dozens of long-stemmed red roses in her left arm while she did her practiced wave with the right. The couch holding the others sat behind her like discarded refuse.

The walk home took about two hours. Betty Jane floated along the whole way, waving at the cheering crowds on her avenue, occasionally blowing a kiss. Snow started to fall when we reached Fifth Avenue. I watched the flakes drift to the ground and I thought about how these fragments become whole as soon as someone forms them into a snowball. By the time I arrived at the front door of my building I knew I was willing to do anything to have my life back again.

{ 30 }

I sat in Milton's waiting room tapping my foot on the floor. I had given up on the *New Yorker* two minutes ago. I couldn't focus on the comics today. Sarge, Aiden, and the Silent One sat in their mirror waiting room inside my head without touching their magazines either. I knew they were as nervous as me if *Car and Driver* and *Catholic Weekly* sat on the table. Betty Jane flipped casually through *Vanity Fair*. No doubt shopping for a whole new back-to-work wardrobe. Milton finally opened the door.

I rushed in and flopped onto the couch. The Committee scrambled for spots in their matching therapy room inside my head.

"I got called back for my show. I went to the studio yesterday. They wanted to do story lines for Violet and Harriet. I did Harriet; then Walter wanted Violet, but Mike saved me with a lunch meeting, so that is on hold until next week, when I have to come back in and read those lines. My agent called and my new contract is ready." It all tumbled out in one breath. "I'm back."

"You've been busy since we last saw each other," Milton said, considering me. I hadn't told him about doing Ruffles's voice at the theater a couple of weeks ago. I wasn't prepared for the aftermath.

"Not by choice, believe me."

"And now? Now that you can do Harriet"—Milton gave me a knowing look, but I didn't know what he knew—"what will you do about Violet?"

"Betty Jane said we can reimplement the old agreement and go back to the way things were."

"Ah," said Milton.

All Committee members sat very alert.

"She has a few modifications, though."

"I said without him," snapped Betty Jane inside my head.

"And what are those?" said Milton.

"I didn't ask." I shook my head.

"Why not? Don't you think it's a good idea to find out what you're agreeing to before you agree to it?"

"I realized that if I have to go back to the way things were to keep that job, I'd rather wait tables."

"*What?*" Betty Jane screamed inside my head. The other three applauded.

"I decided I'm going to call my agent and tell her I can't do Violet."

Milton's face remained impassive, but the almost imperceptible glitter in his eyes belied something else as he waited for me to continue.

"You stupid, worthless worm," said Betty Jane inside my head. "I made you, and now you would rather go back to waiting tables. How dare you." She spit that last sentence out like it was rotten food.

"Responses?" said Milton.

"She is telling me I am a worthless worm. How dare I? The usual." I sighed.

"How do you feel about that?"

"It's a bit scary, risking my job." Inside my head Betty Jane looked up with renewed hope in her eyes. "I guess I have to see how good my agent is. If she wants her cut, she'll work it out for Harriet." Betty Jane kicked a pillow across the Committee's living room inside my head. "And if she can't work it out, I can always do training videos and phone work."

"Oh, agony," cried Betty Jane as she paced the Committee's living room, digging at her perfectly coiffured hair with her red nails.

I tapped my head and said, "She's not happy."

"I should think not," said Milton.

"Maybe even trade-show announcements," I said. Betty Jane exploded inside my head. "She's upending furniture. At least the pieces she can lift." I rolled my eyes upward.

"Holly, think about what you are doing!" shouted Betty Jane inside my head. She stumbled across the room with her arms outstretched. If I didn't know better, I'd swear that she had been drinking again. I pitied her at that moment.

"I don't care if I ever do voice acting again."

"You don't mean that!" cried Betty Jane. The motion picture of my career as a voice-over artist played behind her. I was unmoved.

"I am not willing to sell my soul a second time," I said.

The "this is your career" movie stopped abruptly.

Sarge and Aiden grabbed Betty Jane by the wrists and dragged her toward the door inside my head. Her hair was in disarray. Her shirttail untucked. Nail polish chipped. She dug her spiked heels into the hardwood floor. Sarge and Aiden tugged her arms and continued forward. Her right heel snapped and then the left heel snapped. Betty Jane struggled. She scratched and spit at them. They dragged her to the door. The Silent One stood and opened it. A waterfall as big as the Niagara flowed outside.

Sarge and Aiden swung Betty Jane back and yelled, "One."

Betty Jane screamed.

Back again. "Two."

Betty Jane howled.

Back again, and then on the final big swing Sarge and Aiden cried, "*Three!*" And they let go.

Betty Jane hurtled out the door.

She managed to hook her fingers around the doorjamb and then she gripped it like a barnacle on the hull of a ship. The tips of her fingers whitened around her chipped nails as she clutched at the wood. The water rushed right up to the doorway. The strong current loosened Betty Jane's hold. One hand slipped off.

She cried out inside my head, "Holly, please."

My resolve weakened.

Betty Jane dug her remaining hand all the way into the wall. The other hand came around and reattached itself. Her head appeared in the doorway. Two mascara-marked trails extended from the eyes to the jawline.

"No!" I said.

Betty Jane cried out again inside my head, *"Please!"*

Compassion and pity welled up.

She smiled. It was that old evil, crafty smile.

"No!" I said again with conviction.

The smile vanished and, for the first time, Betty Jane looked stricken.

I wanted to be free of her.

"I want to be free." I closed my eyes. "I want to be free."

I was in the Committee's room. The Silent One bowed his head. I motioned to Sarge and Aiden for help. The Silent One stopped them with his hand. Betty Jane had pulled herself half-way back into the house. I strode with purpose across the room, passing the heels of her shoes still lodged in the wood. I reached the front door. Betty Jane and I stared at each other the same way we did in group therapy. Betty Jane's face was fierce with deter-mination, her makeup smeared.

I pried one hand loose from the doorjamb. Her arm flew back. She looked down at her body. I pried the other hand loose. Then I kicked her with my foot. And just as I had imagined so many times during group therapy when Betty Jane sat on the pink commode, I heard a loud flushing sound and Betty Jane swirled away. The echoes of her scream lasted quite a while after she disappeared.

I turned to Sarge, Aiden, and the Silent One. I smiled. I hugged them. I wanted to dance. We were free now. Then the scene in my head transformed to the driveway, and sitting there was Sarge's sparkling-clean '57 Chevy. "Wait a minute!" I said, alarmed.

"Holly, it's time for me to go," said Sarge.

Tears filled my eyes. I told myself I didn't mean for him to go too, but deep down in that place I ignored, I knew his departure was inevitable if I made the choice I had just made. Still, I said to him, "You don't have to leave."

"But I do, Holly," he said gently. Betty Jane was right: I always chose wrong.

Sarge lifted my chin with his finger and said, "You made the right choice, soldier. This is the right choice. HUA?"

"HUA," I said through my tears.

He got in his car. Turned the key. Gunned the motor. Put the car in reverse and backed out of the driveway. He idled in the street for a moment. Then he shifted the car into drive. Flipped on the stereo. Winked at me. Waved. Hit the gas. The powerful engine roared and the car shot forward. The song "Badlands" by Bruce Springsteen mingled with the motor. I stood until Sarge and his car completely disappeared.

Aiden. My stomach lurched. I felt his hand slip into mine. I turned. Aiden's face was completely healed. He smiled. All his teeth were back in place.

"Not yet!" I cried.

"Holly, it is time. You don't need me anymore."

"I do need you. You can't leave me. Oh, Aiden. You can't leave."

"You don't need me anymore, Holly," said Aiden. "You have Sarah. You've had her since the day I died." I did have Sarah. At that moment, I felt overwhelmed at how much of my burden my sister had carried all these years. How much I never knew.

He led me back into the house. We sat on the couch. Aiden leaned against me; I pressed my cheek lightly on his head. I wept. Aiden's hand became lighter and lighter until I was holding nothing. Aiden was gone. I could still feel the softness of his hair on my cheek. I clutched at the blanket he always carried, buried my face in it, and sobbed.

After a while I felt a hand on my back. The Silent One. I looked up. He bowed his head.

"Holly," the Silent One's voice sounded like all the notes on a musical scale. I had heard it only once, but I never forgot the melodious sound.

When the Silent One said my name, I knew I'd reached the second-to-last page in this chapter of my life. I used it as a respite, just like I did when I was reading a book I didn't want to finish. I needed to come to terms with this ending because it meant acceptance that I had no power and no control over many things in life.

"Holly," he said again. The sound of his voice made me realize that it was time to read the last page and close the book.

"Yes," I said quietly.

"Do you know who I am?"

"You can't be who I think you are because I stopped believing in you the day Aiden died."

"Do you know who I am?" repeated the Silent One.

I remembered Mr. Rhode telling me that God is whatever we need him to be. It is just a matter of faith. Then I reflected on the day in the closet when I had tried to get to Narnia. I had pleaded for Aiden to stay with me. And at that moment I knew that I had gotten an answer to my prayer. It just took me twenty-seven years to see it. "If you were answering prayers," I said to the Silent One, "why didn't I get to Narnia?"

"How do you know you didn't?" He winked.

Am I there? Nah. Narnia was too big to carry around in my head. Besides, I felt ready to live in the real world.

The Silent One nodded. Then he picked something up off the floor and handed it to me. I opened my palm and received the gift. As I closed my fingers around it, the Committee's room disappeared.

"Thank you," I whispered. This time I knew they were truly gone.

I opened my eyes. Milton sat there contemplating me.

"They're gone," I said. "The Committee, the house, all of it." Milton nodded his head.

"I made Betty Jane leave." I wiped my eyes.

"How do you think you were able to banish Betty Jane?"

"I am Ruffles," I said.

Milton smiled and said, "Yes, you are, and then some."

"Hang on there. Ruffles minus about three hundred pounds," I said. Milton laughed, and I appreciated his giving me a way to cover the awkward moment. "How?"

"Psychic weight," said Milton. "You buffered Ruffles with so much fat that you couldn't see who or what was hidden underneath the surface."

The only thing people got wrong when they said I walked around with my head in the clouds was the clouds part. My head was in the Committee's house, sitting on a large pillow in the left corner of the room.

"At the theater, they asked me to do Harriet and it all came together," I said. "I did her voice."

"Your voice was always a close match to Ruffles's," said Milton. "Her weight reflected confidence, which you did not have until you integrated her into your core self. Once you did that, her voice became your voice."

"But she did the integration by not returning after I'd unearthed the memory of Aiden's death."

"Yes, somehow having your history intact enabled you and her to integrate without your being aware of doing so," said Milton.

"Has my voice changed?" I said. I hadn't noticed, but my lack of awareness didn't surprise me anymore.

"It has, yes," said Milton. "A couple of weeks ago I noticed the difference, and then I knew you had integrated her."

"I'm sorry I didn't tell you," I said. Milton shook his head and I was grateful for the pass he'd given me on this rather large detail. But after what I'd been through, I had earned it.

"So, I guess I am not going to get my job back now that Betty Jane is gone," I said. And at that moment, I felt the full weight of their departure. They were all gone.

"Good-bye," I whispered.

A heavy sorrow spread throughout my body. I felt small. Fragile. Alone.

"Holly." Milton leaned forward. "Remember, we always keep the best parts of the ones we love."

{ 31 }

Who was the Committee and how did I end up with it? This was what Milton and I would spend our time on now. I thought after I let them go, I would graduate, or something, from analysis. But instead of handing me a diploma, Milton told me the real work would now begin. After what I'd just gone through, I admit to a feeling of unease over what the "real work" journey looked like. Especially since I still had an aversion to introspection. But fear didn't stop me from taking the first step and on Tuesday afternoon I sat, alone, in Milton's waiting room. Waiting, because that was what one did in a place like this.

I reached over for the *New Yorker*. My hand paused in surprise. *Car and Driver*? As I thumbed through the stack, I noticed that Milton had added most of the Committee's magazine selections. He still drew the line at the unrealistic women's magazines. I guess because he had patients—me included—who obsessed about ass size.

The doorknob turned. I felt a jolt of anticipation. Milton peered through that doorway. "Holly," he said softly.

I nodded my head. Checked my nicotine patch—I was down to one—then stood and followed him.

"So here we are," he said as I took a seat on the pink commode.

"Here we are."

"Any thoughts since our last session?"

I had let go of my Committee and he asked me a question analogous to, "Did you enjoy your breakfast cereal?" Then I realized there really was no right question to convey what had happened. "You took an awful risk giving Betty Jane more power." Arching my eyebrows I added, "What if it hadn't worked?"

"Well, worst case, your life would be ruled by a vacuous, entitled self who floated through life without responsibility or conscience," said Milton. "You would be employed and hoarding Charmin." He smiled.

I laughed. "But it could have backfired."

"I agree. It could have," said Milton. "We were not making progress. The voice acting gave me an opportunity to understand Betty Jane's power. I knew that you were stronger than she, and the other Committee members were benevolent. You had chosen people who represented different aspects of comfort and security." Before I could say it, Milton held up his hand. "Even Betty Jane. At any rate, once you recognized that you ultimately had control, I knew you would be able to integrate them. In time," he added.

"In time? Funny how you are so nonchalant about time. It was hell."

"Remember I told you when we began our work that it would get far worse before it got better?" said Milton.

"Yeah. But I had no idea what I was agreeing to. Had I known, I don't know that I would have done it. But"—I nodded my head—"being on the other side of it, I am glad I did."

"Holly," said Milton, "you should commend yourself on your effort to take on the hardest task any human being can face."

"What is that?" I said.

"Most people form a fragmented life in an effort to escape boredom. They pursue things that are elusive, emptily self-serving and escapist possibilities instead of self-knowledge. The Committee was that for you."

This must be the start of the real work.

"The fragmented life is a despairing means of avoiding commitment and responsibility. In order to raise oneself beyond the merely aesthetic life, a life of drifting in imagination, possibility, and sensation, one needs to make a commitment," said Milton.

"What have I committed to?"

"You have to ask?" He sat back.

"I guess not," I said. My gaze drifted to the window.

"Then the answer is . . ."

I turned back, looked Milton straight in the eye, and said, "Myself. I have committed to myself."

"And that, Holly"—Milton maintained the eye contact—"is quite an achievement."

We shared an embarrassed silence.

"And how do you feel now?" he asked.

"I am scared," I said, "but I also feel excited. Kind of like Bambi starting out with wobbly legs hoping to become strong enough to run. Sappy, I know. Especially from me, but that is how I feel."

Milton considered this. "It's an apt analogy."

We talked for the remainder of the hour. Ironically, I didn't feel an urgency about the time. For once, it felt as if there was enough. And I knew that from now on, there would always be enough.

When I left Milton's building, I decided to walk. I wanted to appreciate these last moments. Imprint them in my mind. I wasn't ready to share them with the noise and jostling of the subway, and I didn't take cabs or use a car service anymore on principle.

I ambled along slowly until my wobbling legs felt strong.

EPILOGUE

At the end of February, my phone rang right as I turned the corner of First Avenue. Peter. I hadn't programmed his number into my new cell phone, but I still recognized it. I reflected on how the thought of not speaking to him for more than two months had been unbearable to me a year ago. The phone rang for the third time. After one more ring it would go to voice mail.

I pressed answer. "Hello."

"Hey, it's me." I waited for the familiar lurch, like someone had dropped a cannonball in my gut.

"I know," I said. I felt nothing. Time and distance really do work if given the chance, I thought. I tucked away this insight for the next time I found myself facing a possibility I couldn't or didn't want to accept.

"How are you?" Peter's voice was tentative. I finally understood that in his own way, Peter had loved the image I projected to him. But that image required a monumental effort to maintain.

How could he really know me when I had only recently met myself? I wish there were a way to truly see and know yourself as another does. But there isn't.

"Pam gave me your number," said Peter.

Pam and I had talked about Peter after we split up. She had told me I should take comfort in the fact that Peter genuinely loved the woman I had made him think I was.

"I wondered." Even though she had given him my number, my friendship with Pam was one of the good things to come out of my failed relationship with Peter. Who would have thought?

"So, I am defending my dissertation next week," Peter said awkwardly.

"Good luck with that," I said. I meant it. Peter had languished as a student when we were together. Our separation appeared to have had a positive outcome for him too.

"I'd like to see you, Holly. How about tonight?" I listened to his breathing. I used to love to do that at night while he slept. I told myself it was because I loved him, but really I was trying to find the clue to what gave him such peace. Now I would never know.

"Tonight's not good," I said. "I'll call you."

We both knew I wouldn't call. I probably should have just told him the truth. But I had learned that a lady lets a man down easily.

When I arrived at my front door, I saw two large envelopes and one brown paper–wrapped parcel. I picked them up in a stack. I recognized the envelope on the top, so I transferred it to the bottom of the pile. The next one was from my mother. I had told Sarah what had happened in Milton's office and left it to her to fill in my mother. Facts were Sarah's job. I didn't know if my mother and I would ever talk about the years after Aiden had died. But for my part, I preferred to move on and see what the future held. The only depth in our relationship was the ugly scars from the past. No point in building a bridge over those. Still, I hoped that somehow we'd finally find a common ground in the vast expanse of superficiality.

I tore at the envelope with my teeth as I turned the key in the dead bolt. The contents inside made me laugh. Sarah must have been thorough in her telling, and even with her faults, my mother's gesture showed me that she understood—or that she at least had a sense of humor.

I dropped both envelopes on the side table and looked at the parcel. The handwriting on the paper was Sarah's. Sort of heavy, I thought. I tossed my keys on the table, lifted the strap of my bag over my head, and dropped it on the floor.

I went into the living room. I removed the brown paper from the package Sarah had sent. Underneath it, I found a box neatly taped shut. Smiling, I thought about how Sarah was so meticulous about the littlest details. I pushed my finger in between the box flaps and slid it around all four sides. With the box bottom on my lap, I wiggled the top off. The contents inside were wrapped in pink tissue paper secured with a little gold sticker. I parted the paper. On top was something in bubble wrap. I caught my breath. Then I carefully lifted out the item underneath.

I held it against my chest and closed my eyes as I buried my face in the satin lining. Distant laughter from a time long past echoed in my head. Peace gently knocked on the door of my heart. After a moment I opened my eyes and picked up the note that had fallen onto my lap.

Dear Holly,
You left this in Dad's closet the day after Aiden died. I repaired
it and then kept it hidden all these years. But now, I think it's

only fitting that you have Aiden's Narnia coat. I know that's
what he would want. May it help you find your own way.
    Love,
    Sarah

Now the three of us really were together.

Holding the coat close to my body, I picked up the bubble-wrapped object. Inside the wrapping was a framed photograph of me and Aiden wearing our Narnia coats. We were holding hands. Our faces bore smiles of promise. The promise of innocence, adventure, and escape. I hugged the coat close to me, hoping for a lingering scent of my long-dead brother. I was sure I could smell him. But I also knew that memory is a powerful thing.

As I sat there, grief finally packed its bags and left through the back door.

My phone rang just as I was getting into bed. Ten o'clock. I smiled. I knew it was Mike. Tomorrow was the big day—my first day back on *The Neighborhood.* It was a strange feeling to be able to count on someone other than my family or analyst without fear of what it would cost.

After I was rehired, Mike started calling me a couple of nights a week under the guise of monitoring the situation for Walter. He always called right at ten o'clock. We'd now shared twelve phone calls, or fourteen hours and twenty-two minutes of conversations about everything except work. Not that I was counting.

Before we hung up, Mike suggested we meet for dinner Friday night to discuss the week's progress.

"It sounds like you're asking me out on a date," I said.

"If you're lucky," said Mike.

I laughed. "See you tomorrow."

"Tomorrow." The phone went dead. I still hated good-bye, and somehow Mike had just intuited this. I never told him.

Before I turned off the light, I put the photograph of me and Aiden on my nightstand. It was the last thing I looked at before I went to work the next morning. I took public transportation.

"Holly, we're ready for you."

I smiled and said, "Great. I'm on my way."

I walked into the room. The others were already in the sound booth in front of their mics.

"Hi, Holly." Everyone waved, including the people behind the glass.

"Hi," I said.

I went to open the door.

Oh.

I stopped, held up my index finger, and said, "One sec."

I reached into my pocket. I pulled out my mother's sunflower and pinned it to my jacket. Then I opened the door.

Shana Mahaffey lives in San Francisco in part of an Edwardian compound that she shares with an informal cooperative of family, friends, and five cats. She's a survivor of catechism and cat-scratch fever, and is a member of the Sanchez Grotto Annex (http://www.sanchezannex.com/), a writers' community. She welcomes all visitors to her Web site, www.shanamahaffey.com, and is happy to meet with book groups in person or in cyberspace (phone/ webcam/the works).

shana mahaffey

This Conversation Guide is intended to enrich the
individual reading experience, as well as encourage us
to explore these topics together—because books,
and life, are meant for sharing.

A CONVERSATION
WITH SHANA MAHAFFEY

Q. Where did you get the idea for your novel Sounds Like Crazy?

A. I've always been fascinated by how the mind works, in particular by our ability to find creative ways to survive when faced with loss, guilt, fear, anguish; and by our inability to forgive ourselves and others. Pondering these ideas led me to discover the flawed narrator of the novel—Holly Miller—whose childhood was so painful, she fractured her mind into five additional personalities, allowing them to become an inexorable part of her.

Q. Are the voices in Holly's head—the Committee—representative of real-life events you've had, or did you feel that they made the best story?

A. Many of Holly's life experiences are based in part on my own experiences or those of people close to me. I chose the aspects from these experiences that best fit Holly and her journey, and then developed them until they were what I needed to make Holly the person you meet at the start of *Sounds Like Crazy* and the person she becomes by the end.

Q. Do you have multiple personality disorder?

A. Ha! No. Although if you ask one or two of my ex-boyfriends, they might give you a different answer. In all seriousness, I believe everyone has aspects to his or her personality that dominate in times of crisis or heightened awareness. For example, I am very squeamish about blood. The thought of something as simple as getting a blood test causes me to become light-headed, sometimes to the point of fainting. However, one day I came home and found my cat's nose torn and bleeding. I didn't for one minute think about passing out. Instead I grabbed something to stanch the flow and got him to the vet. When it was all over, I had my reaction, complete with nearly fainting in the vet's office. Does this mean I have multiple personalities? You tell me.

Q. What type of research did you do to understand multiple personality disorder?

A. I read quite a few books on the subject and I did a lot of research online. According to the psychiatric community, multiple personality disorder (MPD) is no longer a diagnosis. Rather, the condition is called dissociative identity disorder (DID). The deeper the trauma, the more the person dissociates. Whatever acronym you want to apply to the condition, the most poignant information I found was in the blogs and comments written by people who are truly suffering from a fractured psyche. This helped me understand how someone like Holly would cope under the circumstances, and it helped me feel compassion for her and for anyone suffering from DID.

Q. How did you come up with Milton's treatment approach to Holly?

A. My own demons drove me into treatment when I was twenty. Mine were nothing like what Holly has to cope with in terms of DID or MPD, but they were enough to help me fail all my courses at university. When this happened, I was given a choice: See a therapist or go home. I had the same reaction Betty Jane does—I thought it would be easier to deal with a quack than leave school. I was referred to a man very much like Milton. At the end of our first hour he told me I had one month to clean up my act and follow his prescribed program. We'd regroup after thirty days and he—not I—would decide if we would continue treatment. Maybe it was the survivor in me who recognized the real deal, because I did an about-face and never looked back. We worked together two days a week for six years, with phone calls between sessions. The work we did changed my life. It was no picnic and I hated him much of the time. That said, looking back on what that process did for me, I feel nothing but gratitude for the time and effort of my "Milton." I know that I would not be the relatively healthy, happy person I am today without him.

Q. Keeping track of all the characters in Holly's head, and the nuances of each personality, seems really tough. How did you tackle that job?

A. I'd love to say that the story unfolded for me the way it ultimately ends up in the novel. But the truth is that to differentiate each character, I had to write each story separately and then find a way to weave them all into the book. All I can say is thank God for Paul McCarthy, Kevan Lyon, my early readers, and finally Ellen Edwards, because there was a lot of reviewing and a lot of moving stuff around before the story got its footing.

Q. Does reading other books while writing hurt or help your creative process?

A. A bit of both. I am such a chameleon that if I read any commercial fiction while I am writing, I immediately feel a different voice creeping into my own writing. This is heartbreaking for someone who is as avid a reader as I am. Thankfully, I can read nonfiction, which is great, because I needed to do research for *Sounds Like Crazy*. The other assistance comes from my old standbys—a few beloved books I've probably read more than a hundred times since childhood—The Chronicles of Narnia (all seven), the Amber series (five books by Roger Zelazny), the Belgariad and Mallorean series (ten books by David Eddings). I know these books so well I can recite lines from them. Suffice to say, they are so familiar the writing does not influence my own; as a result, like old friends, they are always available when I need to escape to another world without impacting my own writing.

Q. How much did the process of writing affect the ending? What I mean is, did you get into the characters in unexpected ways, to the point that you often found yourself changing how the story would end? Or did you start with a fixed ending and work backward?

A. I had a fixed idea of different personality types I wanted to explore. The idea was flexible enough, though, to allow each character to unfold for me over time. So, I guess the best answer, is I started with a template, but as my writing evolved, each character told me who she/he was.

Q. *Did you develop "alternate endings" like the ones we're now familiar with on DVDs?*

A. I tried to end *Sounds Like Crazy* in a way that is open to the reader's interpretation. I know how it ends for me, but when I talked to early readers, I realized that only a few of them read the ending as I thought I wrote it.

Q. *Are you considering using Holly's character in future novels?*

A. One of my favorite authors, Robertson Davies, writes trilogies in which characters cross over into other books in the collection, sometimes as a significant character and other times as a mere mention. I have always enjoyed this style of writing because it provides me, the reader, with different perspectives on a character. And when it is a favorite character, I am thrilled to meet him or her again. All to say, you might meet Holly, Peter, one of the Committee members, Walter, Pam, and/or one of the kids again in a future novel. You just might.

Q. *How did you decide to make Holly a voice-over artist?*

A. I was in a writing workshop several years ago and we were discussing my book. At this point, I had Holly, the Committee, and the backstory for how the Committee came to be. We were struggling to pinpoint exactly what was missing when the woman running the writing group exclaimed, "She needs a job. Holly needs a job." We stopped discussing the book itself and turned to the very important task of finding the perfect job for Holly. After a few moments, the person sitting next to me said, "Voice-over artist." When I considered a voice-over artist with voices in her head, I knew Holly had found her job.

Q. *Have you had experience doing voice-overs?*

A. When I settled on the idea, I had zero experience with voice-overs. I went to the bookstore, bought a bunch of books, and started reading. After I got a sense of what a voice-over artist does, I went online to find voice-over artists. Turns out, I had one—David Henry Sterry—in my writing community. I bought him breakfast and he gave me the inside scoop. I also e-mailed several working voice-over artists. Mark Evanier was kind enough to respond to and answer my questions. Another friend in my writing community, David Gleeson, is a Grammy-winning music producer. He gave me a complete tour of his recording studio and showed me firsthand how the work is done. Besides figuring out how doing voice-overs works from a practical standpoint, I learned that doing voice-overs is a pretty cool gig to have. If I wasn't writing and if I had the voice for it, I would love to be a voice-over artist.

Q. *Who is your favorite character in the book?*

A. Taking the scenic route to the answer, I'll share one of my fondest childhood memories. When I was a child we used to go to my maternal grandparents' house on Corbett Drive in Burlingame,

California, for weekends and throughout the summer. My mother is one of four children; I am one of eighteen grandchildren. Suffice to say, with such a large crowd of cousins, we had a lot of fun.

My grandparents had a small pool in their backyard. To play anywhere other than by the stairs on the shallow end, you had to first show that you could swim the length of the pool. I desperately wanted to join the older kids in the deep end, but I was only five years old and terrified of drowning. My father, grandfather, and four uncles had a long discussion with me to find out what was preventing me from trying. When I told them, we struck a deal: They would position themselves around the pool edges, ready to rescue me at the first sign of danger. I agreed and went to the deep end to prepare myself for my swim. I remember marking where each one of them was. Then I inhaled, dove, and started doing the crawl to the other side. The thing is, I'd never learned the proper breathing technique of turning your head to the side for air. Halfway through my swim, I ran out of air and lifted my head. Next thing, I heard splashing and screaming—"I got her, I got her"—and I had about ten pairs of hands holding me high up in the air. Man, was I angry, because I'd almost made it. But I never forgot how secure I felt, and looking back as an adult, I feel an even deeper appreciation for all of those men who wanted me to feel safe. Of course, my swimming lessons resumed in earnest after that. I got to swim in the deep end of the pool, and I had the perfect template for the character of Sarge.

Q. Who is your least favorite character?

A. Peter. I think most people have had at least one relationship that is all wrong for them. I have had more than one. The guy or the girl who made you feel light-headed when you met him or her. The one who made you ignore your gut instinct to leave because you could always find another reason to stay. The thing is, Peter is my least favorite character not because of who he is but because of how hard it was to write him and to write the relationship Holly has with him. He is kind of the Judas character in *Sounds Like Crazy* because he is necessary to help Holly grow as a person. I know from my own experience that having a relationship like Holly's with Peter, and then having the courage to finally leave it, is what helped me grow the most as a person.

Q. *What is your writing process?*

A. I find a theme or an idea I want to explore and I ponder it, sometimes for months. After I have a solid understanding of the theme, I figure out how I want to explore it through storytelling. Once I know this, I go back to pondering until I have a beginning, and then I continue until I know where I will end up. For my writing process to work, I have to know how the story is going to end before I can start it. Once I have the beginning and end, I can invite the characters to come forward and show me how they want to get to the end. The characters are free to take whatever path they choose, but they are never free to change the end.

Q. *What do you hope to do in the future?*

A. I hope to keep writing novels until the day I fall over dead.

QUESTIONS
FOR DISCUSSION

1. Do you think Holly is a likable character and do you sympathize with her condition?

2. Why is Betty Jane in control of the Committee?

3. Siblings often play pivotal roles in our lives. Is Holly's sister, Sarah, helping or hindering her in her quest to live a normal life?

4. Holly frequently finds herself in difficult predicaments. Is she a victim or does she have a hand in creating the problems she faces?

5. Why is Holly's relationship with her mother so significant?

6. Do you agree with Milton's approach to treating Holly? Why and/or why not?

7. Why is forgiveness such an important element of the story?

8. Holly and Peter have a dysfunctional relationship, yet they

stay together for several years. What keeps them together? Have you ever remained in a dysfunctional relationship, or have you observed someone close to you while he or she remained in one?

9. Who is your favorite character and why?

10. Some of the characters in *Sounds Like Crazy* are not very likable. Who is your least favorite character and why?

11. Many people have a token or memento that represents something important to them. The sunflower pin is such a token in the novel. Are there others? Do you have a token or memento that is important to you?

12. *Sounds Like Crazy* is a novel about healing. Discuss the healing process that Holly and some of the other characters undergo. Have there been events in your life that initiated a healing process?